SUSAN A JENNINGS

Anna's Legacy

The Sackville Hotel Trilogy – Book Two

SaRaKa InPrint

First edition published by Tellwell with SaRaKa InPrint 2016

Revised 2nd edition Published by SaRaKa InPrint 2021

Cover Design SAJ Designs

PLEASE NOTE... The author writes in CANADIAN STYLE ENGLISH with CANADIAN SPELLING. The reader will notice slight differences compared to both British and American spelling.

Second edition

ISBN: 978-1-989553-17-6

This book was professionally typeset on Reedsy.
Find out more at reedsy.com

Dedicated
With much love
to
My wonderful mother,
The late Betty (Elizabeth) Jennings 1920-2021
Whose greatest gift to me was her unwavering strength.

Mother and Daughter relationships are special.
As a daughter to Betty and mother to my daughter,
Rosemary, it is impossible to describe because
there is no other love like the depth of love
between mother and daughter.

Contents

Author's Notes

⁓⦵⦵⦵⁓

Anna's Legacy: Book II *of The Sackville Hotel Trilogy* opens a new chapter in Anna's life. Anna and Bill in this series and Alex in Book I are loosely based upon real people. While the first book in the trilogy, *The Blue Pendant*, was inspired by real events in their lives, *Anna's Legacy* takes that foundation in an entirely fictional direction and none of the stories presented in this book are founded in any way upon real events.

Anna's Legacy continues Anna's journey and although the story could be a standalone, it is written as a sequel with minimal explanations of the events preceding the start of this novel. Therefore, it is recommended that the books be read in order.

I had fun writing *Anna's Legacy* and I sincerely hope you enjoy reading it as much as I enjoyed writing it. Whether it's a review, an email or a comment, I always appreciate hearing from my readers. Without readers, I would not be an author. I love chatting about my characters, those that you like and engage with and those that you loathe—like Mr. Pickles, who seems to be the most hated character in *The Blue Pendant and there is more to come in Anna's Legacy.*

What people are saying!

The Sackville Hotel Trilogy - The Blue Pendant - Anna's Legacy - Sarah's Choice.

A selection of comments from readers like you.

A brilliant read, From Sally in the U.K.

"… I was totally engaged with both the story and characters from the very first page right through to the end and can't wait for a sequel. A must for anyone who enjoys historical novels. Highly recommend this book.

A gripping read… Amazon Kindle Customer

The story is gripping from the beginning to the end, to the point that I read the book in an afternoon - I am now looking forward to reading the sequel.

Unbelievable book… I love it! ….Evelyn B an Amazon Customer

Amazing book!!! Heartwarming and heartbreaking all at the same time. Loved the characters, the history was spot on and it took over my life until I read the last page. Is there going to be a sequel?….I hope so!

Better than Downton Abbey!… Angela from Canada

From the moment I opened The Blue Pendent I knew I was in for a ride. The characters are so well developed, I could see the story unfolding like a movie in my head. What a brilliant story - not only of the lives of the people, but of history, society and the events of the day. I loved it from start to finish. What a journey! This story is right up there with some of the best historical novels - a wonderful glimpse of the courage and determination - and love - that carried these families through some of the greatest social transformations in modern history. I can only hope that Ms. Jennings is writing a sequel.

It's an absolute winner! …Audrey from Canada

Susan Jennings debut novel, The Blue Pendant, is a book that will plant your feet firmly in the elegant English Bexhill-on-Sea Hotel, witnessing the lives of the staff hierarchy and some of the patrons. Anna, the protagonist, has a fascinating life—one that crosses the Atlantic and never missing an interesting, and sometimes unpredictable, beat. The prose is crisp, one becomes very familiar with the characters, and the clear, changing scenes waste no valuable time. I generally read either old or contemporary books, however, I'm so happy I didn't miss the Blue Pendant.

Steady read

Reviewed in the United Kingdom on July 4, 2021Anna's Legacy - Easy and very readable. I live in Hastings someone the Sackville well, it's glorious apartments now. Liked the characters portrayed. Just about to start the third one

Anna's Legacy

Reviewed in the United Kingdom on June 1, 2021

Another chapter in the life and times of Anna and the Sackville story, joy and sadness I really enjoyed it.

Sarah's Choice

Reviewed in the United Kingdom on June 17, 2021

A lovely series of books following the fortunes of the Sackville Hotel and the family who developed and ran it. Wonderful story of a family through different countries but always returning to the Sackville Hotel

Very interesting people, written in a way that make you really care about their lives.

A lovely saga

Reviewed in the United Kingdom on November 20, 2021I thoroughly enjoyed trilogy with its ups and downs. It had me gripped.

I was a little disappointed that whoever proof-read these books missed so many errors, including the use of American terms for English items. (Sorry but I am but if a grammar freak!)

*A note regarding style.** The author writes in Canadian style English with Canadian spelling. The reader may find some differences in both English and American spelling.

The New Sackville Hotel – April 1948

꧁ꕥ꧂

As the Southampton skyline drew closer, Anna's throat tightened and her knuckles turned white on the ship's railing. She smiled at Bill as she felt his warm arm encircle her shoulders. *He knows me so well,* she thought, and immediately relaxed. He lightly kissed her cheek, smiled and gently brushed a greying curl from her forehead.

"Nervous?"

"A little. We have a big challenge in front of us."

Bill sighed. "Did you ever imagine the day would come when we would sail into Southampton together?"

"No, did you?" She leaned her head against his shoulder. "The last three years have been a roller coaster ride and there were times when I thought we would never get together, let alone sail into Southampton after a trip to India."

"Starting a new life in our fifties is a little bizarre." Bill shook his head, "But I feel younger and more together than I did twenty years ago. I'm not sure how to describe it; ecstatic, elated or just plain happy. Working with you to put The Sackville Hotel back on the map, I couldn't ask for anything more."

"Wisdom and life experience finally pay off," she said with a laugh. "I think I could have managed with a few less life experiences…" The public address system blared, drowning out Anna's words as a garbled voice told the passengers to gather their belongings and wait for debarkation instructions.

Shivering slightly, Anna pulled her wool jacket tightly around her shoulders. The cool April air was a contrast to the hot Indian climate. Despite the long sea journey, it seemed that her body wanted to hold on to the heat. She had enjoyed the voyage, thankful for only a couple of bouts of seasickness. As wonderful as it was to be with Bill, it had been a disappointing trip for them both. India was not the country she had imagined through Uncle Bertie's stories and Rudyard Kipling's books. Independence had caused hatred, riots and rivalry. The violence was sad, frightening and deeply disturbing. Even more disturbing, Anna thought she recognized one of her fellow passengers as an orator who had fired up the already volatile crowd in Calcutta. His eyes had momentarily caught Anna's from his soapbox as the police rescued them and whisked them to safety, and now on the ship he stared at her whenever their paths crossed, but he never spoke. It was an intrusive stare that made Anna feel uncomfortable. Bill thought she was being paranoid. To appease him, she reluctantly agreed, but could not shake an inner instinct of potential danger.

Anna switched her thoughts to the hotel and their new home, and the familiar butterflies fluttered in her stomach. She wondered how the renovations were progressing. More to the point, she wondered how many problems had arisen.

She looped her finger into the black velvet ribbon at her neck and twisted the blue crystal pendant, thinking of Uncle Bertie all those years ago when she had first arrived at Bexhill train station. Another chapter of her life was beginning, at the same hotel. Thirty-five years ago, she had been alone with Uncle Bertie's globe-trotting inspiration, his gift of a blue pendant and words of wisdom. "Follow your dreams and don't let anyone take them away," had comforted and inspired her many times. She had followed her dreams: three months ago, she and Bill were married and together they now owned The Sackville Hotel.

The public address system boomed a polite goodbye to the passengers and suggesting they make their way from the lounge to the gangway.

Anna straightened her floral cotton dress and patted the full skirt on her broadening hips and thickening waist. The small-waisted skirts of today's fashions would have suited her well in her younger years; she had always been proud of her tiny waist. She sighed and buttoned up her jacket, pulled on her cream-coloured gloves and pushed some wispy, greying golden brown curls under the small blue hat that sat on the crown of her head. Although Anna liked to look nice, she had never been particularly fashion conscious, but three months of brushing shoulders with the elite had rubbed off a little.

Bill leaned towards her, his aqua eyes a little faded with age but still tender and admiring. He buttoned his blazer; even the ever-casual Bill had dressed the part during their trip.

Walking down the gangway, Bill whispered in Anna's ear, "Remember what happened the last time you walked down a ship's gangway here?"

Anna giggled. "Yes, some handsome man stood at the bottom and asked me to marry him. I was a little embarrassed."

"You were embarrassed! Can you imagine how I felt, down on one knee and trying to propose in front of thousands of people." Bill winked his special wink and smiled. "When you walked onto the gangway, all those people disappeared. I only saw one person, *you*. However, when the crowd roared, I did question my choice of venue." They both laughed.

Passports in hand, they passed through the formalities without incident and made their way to the train depot. James Lytton, who was both a friend and the general manager of The Sackville Hotel, greeted them at the Bexhill station.

Bill and James loaded the luggage into the trunk of the two-tone green Hillman Minx, Bill's pride and joy. "She looks good, James," Bill said, standing back and admiring the shining car.

"I gave it a good clean and polish especially for your return," James replied, getting into the passenger seat and letting Bill drive.

Anna sat in the back, thinking of her first arrival in Bexhill. Remembering her toe pinching in her new boots as she and Carter walked from the train station to the parked horse-drawn buggy, the horse clomping along the promenade and her big, totally inappropriate, blue hat flying off in the wind. A gentle smile crossed her face as Bill pulled the car under the portico. *The front entrance,* she thought, remembering how insulted she had been on that first day as Carter drove the buggy to the service entrance. He had called her "hoity-toity" and said, "We's staff, and staff enter by the service entrance. It's more than me job's worth if Mr. Pickles catches us at the front." Anna spoke the words aloud. Bill gave her a questioning look.

"In my misguided youth, I thought it beneath me to enter by the service door and that's what Carter said to me the first day I arrived at the Sackville. I never dreamed that one day I would not only enter by the front door but own the hotel."

"I remember a feisty, innocent young lady making a grand entrance in a big blue hat. I fell in love with you that very first day."

"I think I did too, but I was too stubborn to see it."

Anna looked at the spring garden and entrance. "It certainly looks different from when we left three months ago." A new doorman, dressed in the burgundy-trimmed dark green of the hotel livery, opened the car door for Anna. Doffing his cap, he bowed slightly and said, "Welcome home, Mrs. Blaine. I'm Albert, the new daytime doorman."

Anna looked at him quizzically. "I am surprised to see you, Albert—we're not due to open for another month and a half."

"Mr. Lytton asked me to come in to welcome you and Mr. Blaine, and to show off our new uniforms, which arrived yesterday."

"Thank you, Albert. You look magnificent in the Sackville colours."

Bill took Anna's arm and they stepped purposefully up the stairs to the massive glass and oak front doors. She could hardly contain her excitement as she stepped into the opulent, refurbished lobby. Her feet sank into the thick new green carpet. The cleaned and repaired chandelier sparkled like new. The sun streaming in through the long windows caught every prism and scattered rainbows on the walls, and the polished mahogany reception counter, a feature Anna had insisted must stay, shone like glass. The cubbyholes behind the counter looked strangely naked in their emptiness. Anna pulled a face at the only piece of furniture, a tattered chair.

"I had hoped that the upholsterer would have finished recovering the lobby sofas and chairs but he assured me they will be here tomorrow. I held off the delivery of the new tables and lamps thinking you might want to see them first."

"Yes, I would. And there's no rush. We still have six weeks. It all looks wonderful so far. You must have worked hard. How much help did you have?"

"The contractors we hired before you left did most of the heavy work. I kept Amy Peterson on full time as head housekeeper and she has been a great help. I've interviewed some minor kitchen and dining room staff and I asked Albert to start work early to help with moving furniture. But I thought you and Bill would like to be part of interviewing the main staff. I have advertised in the newspaper.

"Excellent. Where's Amy?"

"She is in the staff dining room interviewing maids. Shall I call her?"

"No, I'll talk to her later. We'd like to go to our rooms." Anna turned to Bill, who had wandered over to the dining room. "Bill, can you get the bags please?"

Bill turned and smiled at Anna. "We have staff to do that, Anna. Albert has already taken the luggage up to our suite."

"It will take me awhile to get used to being waited on."

"There was a time when 'Papa's little girl' expected to be waited on." Anna and Bill laughed at their private joke.

James jumped in front of them and opened the ornate brass lift gates. "I want to show you your new home. The renovations went well; I hope you like them. But we can always change things if it doesn't suit you."

Walking along to Suite 305, Anna had a sense of déjà vu. They had chosen this suite as their private apartment not only for nostalgic reasons—it having been Lady Thornton's suite in the early days—but because it was tucked away from the paying guests. It had two bedrooms and the layout allowed them to install a small kitchenette. The plate on the door had been changed from Suite 305 to a wooden plaque that read simply PRIVATE in gold lettering. James opened the door and gave Anna and Bill each a set of keys.

Anna took a sharp breath upon seeing the same chandelier hang in the entrance and she half expected to hear Lady Thornton's voice calling her to begin typing her correspondence. Gingerly, she stepped into the lounge: the sofa and chairs were new, picked out by Anna and Bill before they left for India, but the little roll-top desk still sat in the corner by the window, and the dining room table, chairs, and sideboard were all the original too, freshly-polished and reminding Anna of many luncheons with Lady Thornton. The French doors were open to a small, impracticable balcony and the soft lace curtains fluttered in the breeze that carried the scent of the sea and the sound of waves gently rolling onto the beach. Bill sidled up to Anna. She breathed in the quietness and leaned against him.

James cleared his throat. "Well, I have things to do, so I'll leave you to unpack."

In unison Anna and Bill called goodbye to James and stepped closer to the French doors. Bill wrapped his arms around her as she nestled into his warmth. "Happy to be home?"

"Yes, it feels good. I think it will take a little getting used too. Some things are so familiar it feels as though time has stood still, and yet I feel we are in uncharted territory." Anna stared at the few people walking along the Promenade, dodging April showers. No spinning parasols or long swooshing skirts accompanied by stiff gentlemen as when she had first glimpsed the Promenade. Fashion had changed: the skirts were short, the men more casual and there was a sense of freedom, even laughter. The waves rolled onto the empty beach, there being nothing to disturb them. She had a sense of the calm before a storm, but whether it was a physical storm brewing somewhere over the Atlantic, an emotional calm, or just a rest before a mountain of work waiting to be done, she couldn't tell. Anna turned to look at Bill. "Are *you* happy?"

"I couldn't be happier. I have a wife I adore and a hotel kitchen full of culinary possibilities." Bill grinned, teasing. "I'm not sure which comes first, my wife or the kitchen..." He hesitated before adding affectionately, "Dearest Anna, you will always come first."

Anna smiled, feeling safe next to Bill. Loving him now was so different from young love. There was no anxiety, no sense of urgency, just comfort, contentment and knowing they were there for each other.

The renovations were ninety percent complete. All the guest areas had been painted and decorated with new carpets and wall coverings. A dance floor had been installed, with a platform for a trio or quartet for dinner dances. The lounge area furnishings had arrived. Comfortable chairs and sofas had been reupholstered in soft, restful pastel shades. Anna was pleased that she had resisted the bright, fashionable post-war colours. The wooden side tables blended well with small, warmly-glowing lamps in conversation groupings.

The lobby had been reconfigured, eliminating the massive general manager's office, which allowed for a new lounge area next to the concierge's desk for guests waiting for reception services or transportation. Two new offices were built next to the telephone exchange and located to the side of the reception desk, one for Anna and one for James. Both offices were bright with windows looking across the Promenade to the sea, a contrast to the old dark original office and dispelling the vile Mr. Pickles' aura. Anna wondered how such things could linger for so many years. *Perhaps it is me that can't let it go.*

Standing at the reception desk, Anna brushed her hand across the polished counter and the new registration book. She grinned at James, her fingers tracing the script of gold letters with the new name: The New Sackville Hotel.

"I remember doing this the first day I met you. I had never felt such soft leather or seen real gold leaf before—symbols of a prestigious hotel. I think perhaps you and I are the only people who truly understand the meaning."

"Yes, you are right. We are guardians in a way. We helped it grow in its heyday; your work kept it going through the first war and I kept it going through the second. We almost lost it but, like the phoenix, it has risen from the ashes." James' eyes glistened with moisture. The hotel was James' life and meant as much to him as it did to Anna.

Averting his stare, she said, "The guest areas have come together nicely, James. How are we doing with the staff quarters?"

"Most of the staff live out, so I suggest we close off half of the staff quarters. I have assigned Mrs. Banks' old sitting room to Amy as her head housekeeper's office. I have already supplied her with a desk and filing cabinets. Bill can use one of Mr. Pickles' rooms as his office and the other for any storage that needs to be under lock and key. The staff dining room stays as it is, but it could use a coat of paint. Actually the whole of downstairs could use a coat of paint, but it can wait. The laundry could do with updating, but I wondered what you thought about sending the bed linens out. I did get some quotes and I think it is cost effective."

"I like that idea. It will reduce our capital investment, but we'll still need a couple of new washing machines for the guests' laundry. What have you done with the kitchen area?"

"The contractors are behind with the kitchen construction. Bill is down there now, and not very happy. Other than the kitchen, the workers have finished. A few items are on order, and with the post-war shortages I am keeping my fingers crossed. If Bill doesn't get the kitchen equipment we've ordered, we could be in trouble."

"Did we stay on budget?" Anna asked

"It's hard to say." James dropped his gaze, hesitating. "There are some outstanding bills and the kitchen equipment has not been bought yet."

"I'd like to look at the accounts."

James walked Anna into her new office, and invited her to sit at her new desk. She was delighted to have a window. Clouds moved slowly across the sky, allowing the sun to pop out for a second or two. Anna took in a deep breath as she saw a million stars dancing on the sea. The corners of her mouth began to curl, until her Cheshire cat grin spread from ear to ear.

"Thank you James, this is lovely and so very different from…" Anna looked up not sure what to say.

"I wanted you to have a bright office with a view of the sea and far from memories of the oppressive old Pickles' office."

"You did well." Anna's grin slowly turned downwards. "James, I never told Bill what Mr. Pickles did to me. I think he suspected, but I could never tell him the whole truth and Alex went to his grave not knowing anything."

"Your secret is safe with me." He looked at her with sympathy in his eyes, cleared his throat, smiled and asked, "How does it feel to be back?"

"It's a strange feeling. I'm excited, for the most part. All the new things make it feel like a new place, but every now and then a chill touches my spine as though ghosts from the past are hovering around me, then it quickly passes. It can't be Pickles; he's still alive. Or is he?"

A tap on the door startled Anna, interrupting their conversation. "Can I come in?"

"Of course, Bill. Come and look at my beautiful view. Your timing is perfect as James and I were about to go over the accounts and discuss what is finished and what still needs to be done."

"I was coming to talk to you about the kitchen. It's not going well. I'm in danger of losing my temper with the workmen—such a lazy bunch."

James raised his eyebrows. "It must be bad. I have never seen you lose your temper. It's usually me who loses mine." Anna nodded in agreement and all three laughed.

"I suggest we deal with the kitchen first," Anna said. "Gentlemen, take a seat and let's get started."

James went to collect the paperwork from his office and Bill took advantage of his absence to give Anna a peck on her cheek. "Happy?"

Anna's head nodded up and down. "And you?"

Bill moved to the chairs in front of Anna's desk. "I keep wanting to pinch myself, even in the chaotic kitchen, when I think is this really all mine."

James returned and sat in the vacant chair, placing a pile of folders and papers on Anna's desk. "Everything is here." He pulled a thick folder from the bottom of the pile. "This is the file for the kitchen renovations."

Bill opened the file and the longer he stared at the papers the deeper his frown. "The kitchen is over budget and weeks behind. James, what happened?"

Anna reached over to read the financial statement. Fear gripped her inside; these numbers were more than they could afford and the kitchen was not even functional yet, with only five weeks before opening. She glanced at James, waiting for him to answer Bill's question.

"The reason we are behind is, as you deduced Bill, the workmen are lazy and slow. I already fired one company for padding the bills and charging for work not done, which is one reason why we are over budget. I have been searching for a more reliable company. Since the war there is so much building going on that these companies can pick and choose, and if we complain or don't pay their prices, they quit and move on to the next job."

Anna thought for a minute. "How far along are they? Has all the heavy reconstruction been done in the kitchen? I'm assuming all the guest areas are complete."

James spoke next. "We are waiting for furniture and linens for the guest rooms. The lounges and dining room are more or less finished. Downstairs is a different story. The staff room and hallways need painting and the kitchen is a mess. But the kitchen extension and the reconstruction is complete. Most of the stuff left is carpentry—shelving and the like—painting and electrical."

"Are we signed into a contract?" Anna was trying not to show her concern. There was no more money and without a finished kitchen, the hotel could not operate.

James' round jovial face broke into a grin. "They wouldn't give me a contract. A gentleman's agreement is what he said; all that means is if a better job comes along they can move on. Funny, I wasn't happy about it at the time. I never thought it might work in our favour."

"Instead of hiring a big company, let's hire a carpenter and a painter to do the finishing. What do you think?" Bill glanced first at James and then Anna. "The electrical is a different matter."

"I have been thinking of hiring a full time handyman with carpentry skills. My rationale was that it would be more cost effective to have someone on staff."

"Good, go ahead James," Anna said. "But there's still the electrical issue."

"I might be able to help with that too. An old army buddy of mine is an electrician and he owes me a favour. I'll talk to him."

Anna turned her attention to Bill. "Bill, what do you want to do about the current workers?"

"Get rid of them now."

Lost Money

⚜

Angry words filtered into the lobby; the labourers were not happy that they were being fired. Anna had never heard Bill shout or use profanity, but he matched the outrage of the lazy workmen and sent them packing. Anna wondered if they were doing the right thing. Only five weeks before opening and they had a non-functioning kitchen and a fully booked hotel and dining room.

James' military friend, Ben, agreed to finish the electrical work in the kitchen but another week had gone by and no suitable handyman had been found.

Amy placed a tray of tea on the little round table in her office. Anna poured for them both; after three hours of interviewing maids, the tea was welcome. She looked around the familiar room, remembering another time and her own orientation with Mrs. Banks in this room.

"This takes me back," Anna said.

"Yes, I remember. I was in awe of your blue suit and that big 'at, I mean hat, and I wondered why a lady like you was working at the hotel."

"I'm afraid I was rather a spoiled young girl and I had many lessons to learn."

"I'm so pleased you decided to buy the 'otel, hotel. I'm excited about the opening and having some grand guests again."

Anna smiled at Amy's attempt to correct her dropped h's. She liked Amy. She always had, and now as an experienced hotel housekeeper, she was a big asset to Anna.

"Amy, how many maids have you hired so far?"

"Two chamber maids who will live in and take turns doing morning teas. I will be training them a week before the opening. I told them they could move into the staff quarters the end of next week. Bill wants to hire the kitchen maids. I have another two who will come in daily and I'd like to hire a senior maid and possibly a couple of charwomen; they would be cheaper than maids. Who's hiring the dining room staff?"

"James has hired a maître d' and I think the two of them will hire the waiters. I'll go and talk to Bill about the kitchen staff. Can you manage here?"

The passageway to the kitchen was ominously quiet Anna thought as she turned the corner into a bare dusty room that looked nothing like a hotel kitchen except for the old Aga cooker on the back wall. Bill had insisted it stay, although he had ordered a new set of modern gas cookers. He was talking to Ben, the electrician, but the lack of activity worried Anna.

"Hello Ben, how's the electrical going?" Anna said, glancing at Bill.

"I expect to be finished by the end of the week."

Bill slapped Ben on the shoulder. "I am pleased with the progress. Ben's doing a great job. But Anna, I'm concerned about the shelving and painting. Any news on a carpenter?" Anna shook her head.

"Ben, would you be interested in something more permanent?"

"Thank you Mrs. Blaine, but I have enough to keep me busy. But I do know someone who might be interested. I feel sorry for the lad and this might be just what he's looking for."

"I need someone who can paint walls, build shelves, mend furniture, change light bulbs—that kind of thing—and is reliable. Why do you feel sorry for him?"

"Woody lives two doors down from me and the wife. My eldest went to school with him and the kids teased him something rotten because he's a bit slow. He's always whittling or carving with pieces of wood, hence the name Woody; I've no idea what his real name is. He's older than my lad, maybe twenty-five. He lives, or lived, with his grandfather, a carpenter, where he learned his trade. They did odd jobs for some of my customers. He's a good worker. His grandfather died about a month ago and poor kid doesn't know what to do. My wife has been feeding him. We have no idea what happened to his parents; never seen them. Doris, that's my wife, says the landlord is throwing him out. He's…" Ben pointed to his head, "but his work is good and he's clean and very polite. Needs direction, that's all. And I would think somewhere to live."

"I would like to meet him. He has the skills we're looking for and he could live here in the staff quarters. A lot will depend on how much direction he needs. Bill can help him with the work in here but how will he cope as a full time handyman? Can you bring him in to talk to us tomorrow?"

"I'll bring him with me in the morning, he can help me and you'll get a good idea of what he can do."

"Good. We'll leave you to get on," Anna said as she and Bill walked up to the lobby and into Anna's office.

Bill closed the office door and gathered Anna in his arms, brushing the frown on her forehead. "Why so worried? It's coming together nicely." Anna kissed him and pulled away to sit behind her desk, gazing at the sea. "We have three weeks to get the kitchen finished. I am worried. What if this young fellow doesn't work out? If he's slow, that's not a good thing."

Bill sat in front of Anna's desk, watching her. "It is going to be fine. Everything will get done in time. I think this fellow Woody will work out all right."

"Bill, I want to go over the accounts. I am worried about the finances. We are running out of money."

"All the major renovations are done and paid for. Aren't they?"

"Mostly, but we had to dip into the operating budget to pay for the overruns. I know enough about accounting to know we have no safety net, no contingency, and that's dangerous in a new business." Anna cleared her throat, something she did when nervous.

"You really are worried. What do you want me to do?"

"Nothing. James and I will determine where we can cut back and if necessary we'll talk to the bank manager." Anna took a deep breath and sighed. "Something I would rather not do. The best thing you can do is get that kitchen up and running."

"I can pick up a paint brush and I'll twist Ben's arm and see if he'll give us a couple of extra days. If the new guy works out, we could have the kitchen ready in record time, ahead of schedule." Bill paused, "And I just had an idea. What do you think about opening the restaurant for paying guests a week before the grand opening? Even if it was only local people from Bexhill and Eastbourne, it would bring in revenue and train the staff."

"I like that idea, but will we be ready?" A sceptical frown creased Anna's forehead.

"It'll mean working a lot of hours but I'm convinced it can be done."

"Okay, talk to James, but make sure we can make enough profit over the staff wages. What about food and menus?"

"The menus are all done. Remember we worked on them on the ship and I already have the suppliers set up." Bill leaned over the desk and squeezed Anna's hand. "Stop worrying, it will be all right. Now, I have work to do in the kitchen." Bill walked to the door, turned, smiled and gave Anna his affectionate wink.

Anna had been up for hours working in the office. She watched the sun rise over the sea, heard the gulls squealing as they wheeled through the morning sky. Dark clouds sat on the horizon and she wondered if a storm was brewing over the English Channel. She felt those dark clouds on the edge of her own horizon—the opening of The New Sackville Hotel. She glanced down at the ledger on her desk, red ink jumped at her and her stomach clenched in panic. "I don't understand this," she said aloud. "There was more than enough money in the bank when we left for India. Even with overruns we should not be in the red." Deep in thought, the clouds approaching across the sea prompted a dark thought. *Had someone been stealing and fiddling with the books?* The only person who handled the books was James. "No!" she said aloud, "No, James wouldn't do that, would he?"

"Talking to yourself?" Bill walked into the office carrying a tray of coffee and toast. "Hey, what's wrong? You look as if disaster has struck." Bill put the tray down and leaned over the desk, touching her cheek. "Are you going to tell me about it?"

Anna sipped her coffee and idly nibbled the corner of a slice of toast. "There was enough money in the accounts to cover expenses and renovations before we left. I can't account for all the money and it looks as though someone is stealing and altering the books, but there's nothing obvious."

Bill stared at the approaching cloudbank and then at Anna, immediately understanding what she was saying. "James?"

"No one else has the authority to touch the books or the money."

Bill shook his head, his eyes full of anguish. "I can't believe it. There must be an explanation. Did you go back to the beginning? I mean when we first opened the account at the bank?"

"No. Can we go over it together this morning?"

Anna and Bill pored over the ledger, losing track of time. There was a knock on the door and in walked James.

"Good morning…" James stopped glancing at the ledger and reading the troubled look on both faces. "Is something wrong?" Silence permeated the office.

Anna cleared her throat. "There's something wrong in the accounting and I asked Bill to help figure it out. Have you noticed anything unusual? I mean while we were away."

"No, except I was surprised we had gone through the contingency so fast but that was after you returned from India." James paused, his eyes flitting from Anna to Bill to the ledger. "You don't think…no, you trust me, right?"

"Of course we do, James. But we need to find out if there has been a mistake in the accounting. By my calculations there are several thousand pounds not accounted for." Anna watched the colour drain from James's face.

"Please, believe me. I balanced the books based on the bank statements you gave me before you left. You yourself went through the ledger with me only two weeks ago. I know by the time we paid those workers off it put us in the red. Look, if there's an error, it's an honest mistake; allow me to work on it and find it."

"Definitely there is a mistake, but so far we haven't found it." Anna frowned, seeing pain deep in his eyes. Was it the pain of a falsely accused man, or guilt? She wanted to think it was the former, that there was a logical explanation for this discrepancy. "The reason I have asked Bill to look at the ledger is because he has fresh eyes. You and I can easily miss something. I would like you to do the dining staff interviews this morning. Bill and I will join you when we're finished, and if we have not found the problem by this afternoon we'll all work on it."

"All…right," James said slowly, frowning and glancing over his shoulder as he pulled the door closed.

"Well that was awkward," Bill whispered.

"I'm convinced there is an honest mistake, as James put it. I would trust James with my life."

"Me too."

It took two hours but suddenly Bill grabbed the ledger and pointed to one of the first entries. "It's not there."

"What's not there?"

"The last transfer from Chicago. The first transfer went ahead no problem, I moved the money from my account to the hotel account. But there should have been a second transfer of about £5,000. I instructed the bank to move it to the hotel account and close my foreign account while we were away. I never thought to check it. The money was never in the hotel account so James wouldn't know it was missing. However, it does not explain the fact that the money appears to have disappeared. The bank has some explaining to do."

Anna stood up from the desk and moved to the window, stretching her back, aching from tension and hours of bending over the ledger. She held her hand out to Bill and said, "Blue sky; those dark storm clouds have moved on. I am grateful, and sorry I doubted James." Bill squeezed her hand. "I'll give James the good news and I'll head to the bank now. Can you meet Ben and the handyman in the kitchen?"

It was music to Anna's ears as she approached the kitchen: the rhythmic swoosh-swoosh of a saw blade and the tap-tap of the hammer. She waited and watched in the doorway; Ben and Woody, engrossed in their work, didn't see her. Woody was a tall wiry young man with an aquiline nose, high cheekbones and a grin that filled his face. The wood he was sawing dropped to the floor and made Anna jump. Woody picked the wood up and brushed his hand over it as though apologizing for having dropped it. He slid it on to the wall brackets and carefully adjusted it. She knew immediately that this young man was right for the job.

"Sorry to intrude Ben, I came to meet Woody."

"Woody," Ben called over the hammering. "Mrs. Blaine would like to talk to you." Woody took his hand off the unfinished shelf and turned to face Anna. She noticed his body stiffen and his grin disappeared.

She tried to smile encouragingly and stretched out her arm. "I'm pleased to meet you Woody." He hesitated but took her hand and shook it lightly but firmly.

"I'm Woody,"

Sensing how nervous the boy was, Anna decided to interview him here in the kitchen. "I'm Mrs. Blaine. This is my hotel. I own it with my husband, Mr. Blaine; you'll meet him later." Anna waited for a response but Woody just nodded his head. "Woody, I was watching you work and I noticed how much you enjoy your work. Ben tells me your grandfather taught you the trade."

"Yes, my grandfather is dead. I used to work with him."

"You must miss him very much."

Woody shuffled his feet and brushed his hand across his face. "I do…I got no one else. But Mr. Ben and Mrs. Doris have been kind to me."

"I'm sorry for your loss, Woody." Anna touched him affectionately on the

18

shoulder.

"I don't need to ask if you can build shelves, I've seen it for myself. Did your grandfather teach you all kinds of carpentry?"

"Yes miss, I can build shelves, make cabinets. He showed me 'ow to build coffins too."

"I don't think we need that skill." Anna smiled at his refreshing innocence. "How about painting? Can you paint walls?"

"Yes miss, I like painting. I like to do things neat." He went to the door and pointed at the edges. "This is not a good job."

"What about maintenance?"

Woody frowned and shook his head. "I don't know miss."

Anna realized he didn't understand the word maintenance. "I meant, changing light bulbs, mending broken chairs, sweeping floors and keeping things neat."

He nodded his head up and down enthusiastically. "Woody good at mending and always keeps things neat."

"Good. Woody, would you like to work here all the time?" He nodded again and Anna saw a glimmer of a grin. "You can live here too if you would like that. We have staff quarters on the top floor. You could have your own room." Woody's face exploded into a Cheshire cat grin that even Anna couldn't match.

"Mr. Ben, is it okay if I work here and live in this big house?"

"Yes, Woody."

"That's settled then. I'll have Mrs. Peterson make up your room and you can move in when you're ready. Perhaps Ben and his son can give you a hand." Ben nodded yes. "Come to my office after lunch and I'll do the paperwork and show you your room and give you a tour of the hotel."

Thanks to Woody and Ben working long hours, with some help from Bill, the kitchen was finished ahead of schedule as Bill had predicted; the equipment installed and the cupboards bursting with food. Bill opened the restaurant early to train the staff and bring in a few desperately needed extra pounds.

19

The issue of Bill's money had not been resolved; it appeared the bank had lost it. So close to the opening, Bill had no time to argue with the bank. They would have to manage.

Training maids without hotel guests was a challenge but Anna and Amy drilled them with theoretical scenarios and by mid May they were ready to put their learning into practice. Anna invited her family and friends to be their guests for five days prior to the official opening day for the purpose of training the staff.

Satisfied that the hotel would be ready for guests, Anna sat at her desk watching the seagulls wheel their patterns of freedom through the clouds, while trying to shrug off an anxiety that tightened the pit of her stomach. Two things were worrying her, not the least of which was the bank issue. The bank manager insisted they had not lost any of Bill's money and rather than helping them he was showing signs of nervousness about the climbing overdraft. Anna understood his uneasiness. It would only take one major unexpected expense and a drop in projected income to make them insolvent. £5,000 had to be found or they would not be able to meet the payroll, and worse they would have to cancel the opening. Just thinking about it set Anna's heart on edge and sent her stomach into turmoil. As hard as she tried to force positive thoughts into her head, the enormity of the situation overwhelmed her. Her hand slid to her neck, feeling the soft pile of the velvet ribbon and the coolness of the blue crystal pendant. Uncle Bertie's words came back to her, "Follow your dreams and don't let anyone destroy them."

"Uncle Bertie, give me a sign. Show me what to do."

A knock on her office door startled her and the pendant dropped onto the desk. She stared in horror at the frayed ribbon, her heart sinking. The knock came again but louder this time. Taking a ragged breath, she called, "Come in."

Ralph Smyth, the maître d', walked in. "Mrs. Blaine, when will the new table linens be arriving?"

"I'm surprised they are not here. I will look into it and let you know, Mr. Smyth. Other than table linen, is the dining room ready?"

"Yes. Training is going well and most tables are booked for the pre-opening and we're fully booked for the opening and all of that week."

"Thank you, Mr. Smyth." Adding under her breath as he left the office, "And you, Mr. Smyth, are my other worry."

James had hired him. His credentials were perfect, perhaps too perfect: his experience and references from both The Savoy and The Dorchester in London were impeccable. She didn't trust him, but had no idea why. She wondered why a man educated at Rugby, one of Britain's finest private schools, was content to wait tables. He said he was born in London; his mother was a society lady and his father a banker but they had both been killed in the London blitz. She didn't believe him. He certainly had the mannerisms, dress and posh accent of a private school graduate. His colouring was dark: black hair, brown eyes, and although his skin was white, he looked tanned—it was April. There were occasions when his accent had a lilting element to it, which he corrected quickly. *Imagination or fact?* Anna thought, but there was something about him that disturbed her.

Gazing at the blue pendant lying on the desk, a tear dropped softly onto the crystal. She wiped it with her finger and felt a warm arm on her back.

"I didn't hear you come in."

"Why the tears?" Bill gently slid a wet curl, behind her ear.

"Uncle Bertie's pendant broke. Is that a sign? A sign that we'll be bankrupt before we even open."

"No, of course not. The money will be found. Anna, look at me." Bill gently placed his fingers under her chin, "I promise everything will be fine. You did the projected sales, there will be more than enough money coming in as soon as we open. The bank will wait until then." Bill picked up the broken ribbon. "The ribbon is old and can be replaced, the pendant is as beautiful as ever."

"I think you're right." Anna threaded her arm in Bill's. "What would I do without you."

"I know I'm right. You are not alone. Those days are over. Like it or not, you have me."

"Bill, what do you think of Mr. Smyth? There is something disturbing about him."

"Like what?"

"I don't know, but there is something about Mr. Smyth that is niggling me."

"He seems okay to me. He's very well qualified and knows what he's doing. He was working in London until he came here. He's not as good a maître d' as Alex, but Alex was exceptional."

The Grand Opening

Anna joined Amy on the first floor, giving the guest rooms one last inspection. They stepped back together, admiring the finishing touches of cushions, lamps and ornaments that gave the rooms that personal touch. Closing the door, Anna smiled at Amy and said, "We're ready, and from the sound of it, just in time." Voices floated up through the open staircase. She ran to the curve of the stairs and looked over the railing, stopping to take in the view of her family: daughter Isabelle, with husband, Sandy, and her precious granddaughter, Sarah.

Instinctively, Sarah looked up to the landing. "Nana!" Anna ran down the stairs and scooped Sarah in her arms. She hugged Isabelle. Sarah, having wiggled out of her arms, was exploring the lobby.

"Let me look at you. You must be tired. How long was the drive from Edinburgh? Your rooms are ready; I have given you a suite near our apartment. Are you hungry, or perhaps you'd like a drink or a tour of the hotel? Did Albert get your bags?"

"Mum stop, you're rambling," Isabelle said placing her hand on Anna's shoulder.

"I'm sorry. I am just excited to see you. What would you like first?"

"I would like to unpack and have a nice long hot bath. I think Sarah wants to explore," Isabelle flipped her arm, adding, "and Sandy can do whatever he likes."

Anna took the keys from cubbyhole 303, and gave one to Isabelle and one to Sandy. Glancing from one to the other, Anna felt the tension. Isabelle, pursed her lip, turned and entered the lift. Sandy stared at his feet. "I think I'd like a beer, I'm dry after the journey." He looked at Anna. "Is the bar open?"

"Yes, follow me." Anna led the way. "Is everything all right, Sandy?"

"Of course. We are both very tired."

A little voice came from behind. "I'm not tired."

Sandy laughed. "I bet you're not. You slept in the car. Daddy had to drive."

Albert followed them into the bar. "Sorry to interrupt, Mrs. Blaine, but Lord and Lady Thornton, and Mrs. Castillo have arrived. Mr. Lytton is checking them in."

"Thank you, Albert. I'll be right there."

Anna patted Sandy on the shoulder and said, "Enjoy your drink," as she walked towards the reception counter.

"Darcy, Belle, Julia, how lovely to see you."

Darcy kissed Anna on the cheeks. "I hope you don't mind that we are earlier than expected. We took a detour to visit Felix in Rugby but he's cramming for final exams. He's been accepted at Oxford but needs good marks. Visiting parents were too distracting, or so he said."

"No, I'm delighted." Anna hugged Belle. "You look lovely as always. How is Felix?"

"He's doing well." Belle turned to Darcy, who nodded as he signed the guest register.

"Julia, it is wonderful to see you." Anna was not sure whether to hug or shake hands. "It is good to have you with us."

Anna did not know Julia well, but their chance acquaintance on a train journey in Canada many years ago had sparked a friendship. Anna felt the warmth of Julia's embrace and instinctively sensed the friendship rekindle.

"Where's Bill?" Darcy asked.

"He's in the kitchen, of course. Thoroughly enjoying being the Executive Chef of his own hotel. Why don't you go down and see him? The bellboy will show the ladies to their rooms. I'll meet you all later for cocktails. Sandy, my son-in-law, is already in the lounge bar if anyone would rather have a drink first." More guests were arriving and Anna excused herself.

The hotel was a buzzing beehive and Anna's excitement was buzzing along with it. She felt like doing cartwheels through the lobby and laughed, thinking, *Not exactly appropriate for the proprietor of The New Sackville Hotel.* She really wanted to stand at the reception desk with Mr. Lytton and register the guests as they came in, but that would not be fair to Miss Jenkins, the front desk clerk. She decided to mingle in the lobby and greet guests as they arrived.

A taxi pulled up under the portico and a lone woman stepped out. Anna was shocked to see the woman was her sister, Lou. She hardly recognized her; she was so thin and limped slightly as she climbed the steps to the massive front door. Albert opened the door for her. Her face drawn and empty, she didn't see Anna at first.

"Lou, how are you? Where's Robert?" Anna had a million questions, but Lou's eyes, told her to stay quiet.

"Anna, I'm so glad to be here. Robert couldn't come." Lou looked away. "Please don't ask."

Anna put her arms around her. "Thanks for coming. I'm..." Anna felt Lou wince and gasp. "Lou what's wrong? Are you hurt?"

"Silly me, I tripped on the stairs with my suitcase." Anna took a closer look under Lou's hat, pulled awkwardly to one side. Heavy makeup poorly disguised a purple eye. Anna wanted to cry, seeing her sister in such pain.

"Let's get you settled in your room. I'll have Amy send someone up to run you a hot bath."

Lou smiled, wiping her wet cheeks with her gloved hand. "Thanks, I'll be fine. You are busy. But a bath sounds good; the train journey seemed really long. Has Charlie arrived from Canada? I'm looking forward to meeting our sister-in-law and niece."

"Of course you haven't met Beth; she is lovely. You will like her and Charlotte is a sweet pre-teen: shy and quiet. Their ship docks in Southampton tomorrow. I'm looking forward to seeing Charlie, I miss him."

"Me too, he always knows what to say and do." Lou sighed. "You, dear sister, were always closer to our brother than me and I was jealous," she teased.

Anna was about to add something when Sarah came bounding up. "Great-Aunt Lou, would you like to explore with me."

Anna replied, "Aunt Lou is tired, perhaps later. Sarah, can you see if you can find Mrs. Peterson?"

Sarah ran off and Anna escorted Lou to the reception desk.

In a matter of a few hours, the hotel had come to life with guests—mostly family and hand-picked friends to allow the staff to practice all they had learned. The paying guests would fill the remaining rooms on the day of opening. Anna wanted to ease the staff into daily routines without overwhelming them, and it seemed to be working.

Anna decided on a simple black dress for dinner. It wasn't new, she'd had it altered; post-war rations limited the amount of new clothing, particularly evening wear. The hourglass-style fitting suited Anna's figure; a little rounder than in her youth but still flattering. A string of pearls contrasted the black fabric. She glanced at the blue pendant and the frayed black ribbon and couldn't help wondering if it was an omen or just coincidence; the ribbon was old and couldn't last forever. She reminded herself of the excitement and activity in the hotel and challenged her thoughts, saying aloud, "Does that look like something is going to go wrong?" Satisfied, she headed for the lounge bar to join her guests for cocktails.

After drinks, Anna proudly led the group to the Emily Carr Dining Room. She adored the paintings of Emily Carr, a Canadian artist she had encountered on the same train trip to Vancouver where she had met Julia. Her collection of art had been stored at Lou's farm after she sold the King's Head Inn. She had deliberately designed the Emily Carr Dining Room to replicate the King's Head dining room.

A large round table big enough to accommodate all the special guests was reserved for the family. Bill was not able to join them, preferring to supervise the kitchen. Anna placed Julia at her side and Lou next to Isabelle. Isabelle looked stunning: her tall slim figure—inherited from her father—suited the slinky, emerald green gown that enhanced her hazel eyes, matching her no-nonsense personality. Anna wondered if her choice of seating arrangement was appropriate as Lou, a farmer's wife, was anything but fashionable. But Lou seemed to be comfortable with Isabelle. And where was Lou, anyway?

"Has anyone seen Lou?" Anna asked.

"Oh Mum, I forgot to tell you. Aunt Lou said she wasn't feeling up to dinner. She offered to watch Sarah and she ordered meals to be sent up to our room." Isabelle gave Anna a knowing look.

"Are you sure she's all right?"

"Yes, she's fine. Just a little sore from her fall." Isabelle raised her eyebrows, and closed the subject.

Anna nodded very slightly and turned her attention to Julia. "Julia, how do you like living in England? Are you planning to stay or return to Chicago?"

"It is wonderful to feel free and welcome at Hillcrest Estates." She looked down at her hands, avoiding Anna's gaze but, too late, Anna had already seen the pain and sadness. "Darcy and Belle are perfect hosts and it is a beautiful estate. I would like to stay, but I think it more likely that I will split my time between England and Chicago. I would also like to travel in Europe."

Placing her hand on Julia's arm, Anna said, "A great deal of comfort can be found in traveling and I know you love to explore." Julia nodded and smiled. Anna wondered if she was remembering the train speeding through the Canadian Prairies. Anna would have liked to spend more time talking to Julia, but she had a table full of guests to entertain.

"Sandy, have you travelled outside of Britain?" Julia asked.

"I'm afraid not. At least not for pleasure—a couple of short trips at the end of the war. I'm quite envious when I hear Anna and Bill talk about India. I would like to go to Europe, but Isabelle has no interest and the war has spoiled a lot of Europe."

"It will rebuild in time. I made several trips to Italy before the war and it is a beautiful country," Julia replied.

Anna moved her gaze to Lord Thornton. "Darcy, how is the estate?"

"It is doing well, thanks to Belle. The Inland Revenue almost closed us but Belle came up with some fabulous ideas that have saved us."

"Life must be so different for you, Belle. Do you miss America?" Anna asked.

"No, I don't." Belle replied. "I was born in Alabama, one of America's southern states. Life in the south is quieter than the fast pace of Chicago. I find the British way of life similar in style to my childhood. I enjoy the estate and working with Darcy. A lady of leisure I will never be. We are opening the gardens and a tea room for the public this summer."

"Some days, I would like to be a lady of leisure and be waited on hand and foot." Isabelle's face tightened. "I get tired of running after Sandy and Sarah, it's thankless..." She stopped, glancing at Sandy, who was deep in conversation with Julia and hadn't heard Isabelle's comment. "Sorry," Isabelle said, letting her lips part but arresting a smile. "I think I'm bored. I miss working in retail."

"I didn't know you worked in retail." Belle's face lit up with excitement. "You'll have to give me some tips. I'm thinking of adding a gift shop at the estate."

Isabelle replied distractedly as she watched Sandy laugh with Julia. "Of course. I would be delighted." Taking a deep breath, she interrupted, "Sandy, did you hear that?"

Sandy turned and gave Isabelle a blank look. "I'm sorry, I didn't hear what you said."

"That's obvious." Isabelle retorted.

Mr. Smyth approached the table, bowed and asked, "Mrs. Blaine, was the soup to your liking?"

"Excellent!" Darcy replied for Anna. "More wine please?"

Mr. Smyth clicked his fingers and glared a reprimand at the wine waiter. He was not pleased to see empty wine glasses. Anna's face showed relief, even though one tension had been replaced by another. Isabelle was obviously upset with Sandy, and Anna wondered what was going on.

After dinner, Sandy and Darcy excused themselves and went to the bar for port and cigars. Isabelle said goodnight and retired. Anna ordered coffee and liqueurs to be served in the lounge for Belle and Julia; they had a lot to talk about. Julia had suffered greatly under the violent hands of her deceased husband, Luigi. His death had left her a very wealthy woman, able to do whatever she wished, and she now volunteered her time and money to the woman's program at Chicago University. Anna surmised that it was Julia's way of paying back for Luigi's gangland activities.

Not being used to late nights, Anna had trouble waking up the following morning and Bill pecked her cheek as he was leaving. "I'll see you at ten and we'll discuss the menus and the bank."

Anna leaned into him, feeling his warmth. "The bank has made a mistake."

"I agree, but I have to go. See you later."

Anna made herself a coffee in the new kitchenette. Sipping from a china cup, she flipped through her clothes and decided on a slim-fitting burgundy skirt with matching jacket. She wasn't sure she could get used to the short, waist-length jacket, but it was modern and the colour suited her. She felt younger in it. It seemed she was more aware of her age and style these days, perhaps influenced by Belle and Julia. Both were a few years younger than Anna, with more money and fashion sense, making Anna want to look her best.

The atmosphere hit her as she descended the circular stairs into the lobby—the hotel was alive. Her desk had the day's list of guests on it and the calendar had been updated; it was feeling like a hotel, and she forgot about the challenges until Bill joined her at ten o'clock.

He placed a pile of papers and menus on the corner of Anna's desk. She glanced at them and said, "I'd like to talk about the bank first. Don't you think there's something strange, even mysterious, about the way they are denying the money ever reached the them?" He nodded in agreement and they discussed their options. To Anna there did not seem to be a satisfactory solution. No matter how they looked at it, the bank had the upper hand.

"It will be fine, I promise." He leaned across the desk, taking Anna's hands in his. She smiled, wanting to believe him. "We'll talk about the menus another time. I have to go." He opened the office door and almost tripped over Charlie.

The crisis temporarily forgotten, Anna screamed, "Charlie! When did you arrive? Where are Beth and Charlotte?"

Charlie stretched out his arms, embracing Anna. She clung to him, feeling tears run down her cheeks. "Sis, it is good to be here." He dabbed her tears frowning. "Is everything all right?" Anna nodded, suddenly concerned that Beth and Charlotte were nowhere to be seen. "Beth and Charlotte?"

"We arrived about an hour ago. Miss Jenkins said you were in a meeting and not to be disturbed. Albert showed us to our room. Beth and Charlotte are really tired and are resting. They'll be down for lunch. I couldn't wait to see you. The hotel is magnificent. Sis, I am so proud of you."

GRAND OPENING - THE NEW SACKVILLE HOTEL. Anna read the banner stretched across the portico with goose bumps popping up all over and butterflies in her stomach. Bill was at her side, just as excited and squeezing her hand. He gave her a wink. "I'm stuck for words. Is this really happening? A year ago I thought I was losing you and I couldn't see beyond my own fear."

"Despair is what I felt last year. Not anymore. That stubborn 'papa's little girl' finally grew up," Anna said, giggling. "I have guests to attend to, and you have a kitchen to supervise."

Satisfied that everything was ready, Anna went to the suite to change. She bumped into Bill as he was leaving. "Wow! I'd almost forgotten how handsome you are in a suit and tie. Are you ready?"

"I think so. I need to make sure the appetizers are ready for the champagne. I'll see you in the lobby."

Sitting on her dressing table was a small box with a blue ribbon wrapped around it and a note on top that read simply: "I love you." Anna opened the box and there, attached to a new silver chain, was Uncle Bertie's blue pendant. On the brink of tears, her throat tightened with love for Bill and memories of Uncle Bertie. She fastened the pendant around her neck and chose a blue and gold sleeveless, full skirted dress, a small blue hat, mostly to keep her wayward hair smooth and to allow her natural curls to fall from beneath it. Finally, she thought, fashionable hairstyles that suited curly hair.

The lobby was full to overflowing and guests lined the curved staircase four abreast. The dignitaries included the mayor, complete with the gold chain of office that seemed to weigh the poor fellow down, and Mr. Kendrick, looking very frail sitting in a wheelchair. Anna and Bill joined them in front of a red ribbon stretched across the open front doors. The mayor made a waffling speech about tourism in Bexhill. Anna introduced Mr. Kendrick and wished him a happy ninetieth birthday. Mr. Kendrick spoke of his ownership and the history of the hotel, and how he met the young Anna Neale; his pride and confidence in Anna Blaine, with husband Bill, was unmistakeable. The ribbon was cut, the champagne bottles popped and cheers roared, toasting Anna and Bill and The New Sackville Hotel.

Bill winked at Anna as he excused himself to check the luncheon. Anna knew how hard it was for him to leave this important meal to the sous-chef, but she had insisted he join her and their guests in the dining room.

Satisfied that the meal was under control, Bill stood by the new brass gong, and with great pomp and ceremony the gong boomed, announcing luncheon. The guests meandered into the Emily Carr Dining Room, escorted by Mr. Smyth and his senior waiters. Anna gave an approving smile as Mr. Smyth escorted Lord and Lady Rhodes to their table. He had even charmed Lady Rhodes into a smile, which was no easy feat. Bill joined Anna and they led their personal guests to the extended family table. Busy talking, Anna bumped into a weedy little man with sharp features. As she apologized, she realized she had almost knocked Mr. Nitty to the ground. Stifling a giggle, she apologized to his frosty face, wondering if such features were a prerequisite for bank managers. Mr. Nitty could have been a clone of any bank official she had ever dealt with. He introduced his wife, a round woman with a snooty face, wearing an expensive, ill-fitting mauve dress, more suitable for a twenty-year-old than a woman in her fifties.

"An excellent reception, Mrs. Blaine," Mr. Nitty smirked at Anna. "Perhaps more than I expected under the circumstances."

"Why would that be Mr. Nitty?" Bill asked. Moving closer to Anna, he lifted his eyebrows feigning puzzlement.

"Oh, Mr. Blaine." Seeing Bill, Mr. Nitty's smirk changed to a cordial smile. "I know how the ladies like to spend money. It is sometimes difficult to say no but we have to be firm. It is not rational of us to expect our wives to understand."

Bill's cheeks turned pink; Anna tugged at his sleeve and whispered, "Not now."

Anna felt Bill hold his breath for a second before slowly breathing out and saying, "We are delighted that you and Mrs. Nitty were able to come and see what a fine hotel this is, and as you can see we are not short of guests. In fact, we are fully booked for quite some time." Anna beckoned to Mr. Smyth to show the Nittys to their table. "A pleasure meeting you, Mrs. Nitty. Enjoy your luncheon."

Anna glanced at Bill, trying to stop the sinking feeling in the pit of her stomach. Her intuition was rarely wrong, and right now she sensed that Mr. Nitty was her enemy.

Bill pecked her cheek. "Don't let his placating attitude bother you. You've dealt with bank managers before. He knows The New Sackville is one of his biggest accounts. This is a small town and a woman running a business is difficult for him to comprehend."

"You're right. But he has a way of undermining my confidence. A little girl being reprimanded by her father leaps into my head. Mr. and Mrs. Nitty are not the most charming people."

"Like you said to me, now is not the time." Bill linked his arm into Anna's. "May I escort my beautiful wife and co-owner of this magnificent hotel to our table?"

Anna smiled and bowed slightly. "With pleasure."

First Season of Success

⁓⊱⊰⁓

"Follow your dreams." Uncle Bertie's voice rang in her head as her fingers fondled the blue pendant.

"I did follow my dreams and you would be proud of me. There were times I thought I had lost everything, but you kept me going."

"Talking to yourself?" Isabelle smiled at Anna and sat next to her in the lobby.

"I didn't realize I had spoken aloud. This pendant means so much to me. It will be yours one day. I know you think your mum is crazy but I believe this pendant and Great Uncle Bertie were the key to this hotel's success."

"Mum, that's nice. It's the hotel I want to talk about. I think you know how bored I am in Scotland. I would like to work here, promoting the hotel. I was good in retail."

"I know you did well at Drapers. They were sorry to see you go, but isn't promoting a hotel different to retail? And I remember how you hated the King's Head Inn. Why is this different?"

"Mum, this is a superior hotel, not a pub with guest rooms. I'm sorry, that didn't come out right."

Anna smiled at her daughter and her grandiose attitude, a trait that Anna had had in her own youth. "Would you want to move from Scotland? What about Sarah's school and Sandy's job, and where would you live?"

"I know there are things to work out. I really want to know if you could create a job for me. I can put this hotel on the map. Would you think about it?"

"It is an interesting idea. I'd have to discuss it with Bill, and we would want to know more about your plans."

"I already have some ideas. We leave the day after tomorrow. Can I meet with you today? If you agree, I would like to start in September in time for the school year."

"My goodness, it sounds as though you have made your mind up. Isabelle, please understand this has to be a business arrangement. We need to think carefully." Anna looked at her daughter. They had had many differences in the past. Was working together a good idea? Isabelle had a talent for promoting and the hotel needed a good marketing program. "I'll see if Bill can meet us at four this afternoon, before he gets busy with dinner. I would like James to join us too. Do you want to bring Sandy along?"

"No!"

"Why not? This will affect Sandy and his job." Anna didn't like Isabelle's emphatic no.

"I will ask him, but I doubt he'll be interested." Isabelle brushed an imaginary hair from her skirt. "I wonder where Sarah is."

Anna watched Isabelle walk to the lift. She had seen the lie in her eyes and surmised that Sandy knew nothing of her plans. She understood her daughter: Isabelle had inherited her father's art of charm and manipulation.

The meeting took place at four that afternoon and as Anna had expected, Sandy did not attend. He had taken Sarah to the beach. She wondered if his absence was a result of Isabelle's manipulation or if he genuinely was not interested. Bill and James were impressed with Isabelle's plan, as was Anna. The amount of detail in the document indicated she had been working on this for some time. It had not escaped Anna that Isabelle had avoided any kind of eye contact with her all through the meeting, concentrating her efforts and charm on Bill and James. She had to admit that from what she could see it was a good, solid plan. It was what she couldn't see that worried her.

Bill usually went up to the suite for a rest before starting the dinner rush. Today, Anna decided to join him.

"What do you think?" she asked.

"I think it will put The New Sackville on the map."

"Maybe. What about the expense? Isabelle didn't mention salary, and she doesn't come cheap. And the kind of advertising and touring she's talking about is expensive."

"I suggest we offer her a salary we can afford and she takes it or leaves it. As long as we have control over how much money she spends, I don't see the problem."

"You're probably right. Part of me thinks it would work, but part of me," she hesitated, "is leery. I'm afraid Isabelle has a hidden agenda."

"I know you think she is her father's daughter. Anna, its time you trusted her. I believe she wants to help us and I think she can."

"What about our finances? The bank is happy right now, but there will be a lull in revenue in the next month, until high season. Then we will have two or possibly three good months before winter sets in. Without that money from Chicago we have no financial buffer."

"I say we take the risk and James agrees. We have three months before September. By then we'll have the money from revenue and Chicago."

"I'm not good with risking money. But if, and *only* if, we have sound revenue through the summer, I'll go along with you for now. I'm prepared to offer her twelve months from September. If it doesn't work, Isabelle has to understand we'll discontinue."

"That sounds fair. Shall I tell her now?"

"No, let's do the numbers first. We can do it by letter. Tell her it looks positive."

Normally cautious Bill had been influenced by Isabelle. Anna wasn't ready; she needed time to put things into perspective. *Isabelle won't be pleased,* she thought, but stalling her would make her think and give her time to sort out the issues with Sandy. Anna thought a marketing program was a good idea. Perhaps not one as grand or as expensive as Isabelle had suggested, but if modified it could work well. However, working with her daughter would be a challenge.

It was a tearful goodbye to the Wexford's as they began their long drive back to Edinburgh. Cousins Sarah and Charlotte hugged goodbye, not knowing when they might see each other again. Isabelle said nothing about coming back, making it obvious to Anna that Sandy had no idea of her plans and was content to return to his job.

The hotel was getting quieter by the day; the only guests left were Charlie, Beth and Charlotte, the Thorntons and Julia. Anna enjoyed this little group and was glad of the breather before paying guests arrived for the summer.

Bill had finally received a letter from the Bank of Chicago to say that the money had been transferred to Barclay's Bank on March 20th as Bill had expected, so the transfer should have been completed while he and Anna were in India. They apologized for the delay, stating that clearance from the U.S. authorities had taken longer than normal, quoting dates and transaction numbers for both the transfer and the receipt of transfer from Barclay's Bank signed by W. J. Barnes. Concerned about the contents of the letter and consequent meeting with Mr. Nitty, Bill asked Charlie for his advice and support. Charlie's secret military missions and more recently his civilian job with the Royal Canadian Mounted Police gave him insight and interviewing skills that Bill did not have.

Mr. Nitty was pleased to receive Bill and Charlie in his office, offering refreshments and pleasantries deserving of a high-profile account.

"Mrs. Blaine is not joining us?" he asked. "I hope she is well."

"My wife is well thank you. I invited my brother-in-law to join me as he has experience in international affairs."

Mr. Nitty seemed to miss the point of Charlie's presence and nodded his head cordially. "Ah, gentlemen, it is a pleasure. Money matters are far too complicated for the ladies."

The hackles on the back of Bill's neck stood straight up as he listened to Nitty's attitude towards Anna. He wisely held his tongue, distracting his rage by pulling the Chicago letter from his inside pocket. "We are here to discuss *this!*" Bill unfolded the letter and slapped it with the palm of his hand on the desk.

"What's this?" Mr. Nitty squinted at Bill and his face reddened with anger as he picked up the letter and began to read. Bill eyed Charlie as beads of sweat formed on Nitty's bald head and the colour drained from his face. Now the colour of parchment, Bill was afraid the banker might pass out. The silence buzzed in Bill's ears and he took a breath to speak but Charlie prodded his thigh to quieten him. They waited. Mr. Nitty gasped for breath, coughed and opened his mouth to speak, closing it again without a sound. Bill glanced at Charlie again, Charlie motioned his head, no, and they stayed silent.

Mr. Nitty fumbled in his pocket and retrieved a key that unlocked his desk drawer. Bill felt Charlie stiffen, his eyes on high alert until he saw the silver flask appear. Mr. Nitty's sweaty fingers slipped as he unscrewed the stopper and throwing his head back he swallowed a copious amount of liquid from the flask and quietly replaced it in the desk drawer.

"Mr. Barnes was my assistant manager until he resigned two months ago and moved away from Bexhill." Mr. Nitty cleared his throat. "He was asked to resign because of some irregularities in his accounting, but we could not prove any theft or fraud—just incomplete entries. I had no idea he had received the Chicago transfer or how he managed to conceal it from the bank. I will of course investigate."

"Did you report this to the police?" Charlie asked politely.

"No, there was nothing to report at the time." Mr. Nitty shuffled in his seat and was looking quite unwell.

Charlie ignored the discomfort and nodded towards the phone. "Call the police now."

"Mr. Neale, I appreciate your concern." Mr. Nitty hooked his finger in his collar and pulled it away from his neck. "It is not necessary to call the local police. I can handle this internally. I will make sure Mr. Blaine's money is recovered."

Bill stood up; not believing the little man's obstinacy. "If you won't report this crime, I am walking to the police station with this letter and I will accuse you of fraud. Do you have any idea of the trouble you have caused the hotel? Telling my wife you would close us down!" Bill could feel his anger escalate at the thought of Anna's anguish over the missing money. He caught a fleeting look from Charlie, the meaning clear—to sit down and shut up.

"Yes, well…I regret that, but head office had become nervous about your account." Suddenly Bill understood. The bank's reputation and Mr. Nitty's livelihood were at stake. He was terrified. Bill wondered if his fear had something to do with Barnes? *Could he have been involved? No, he's not capable. He's covering up for his own incompetence and poor management.* Bill was jolted from his thoughts.

"Call the dam police station!" Charlie repeated.

The receiver trembled in Nitty's hand, his facial expression had turned from fear to resignation. His secretary's voice could be heard, "Yes, Mr. Nitty?"

"Connect me to the police station, I wish to report a crime."

Barclay Bank reimbursed the money within days of the police report. At which point Anna and Bill moved their accounts to the Westminster Bank in Eastbourne. Mr. Nitty was fired and W. J. Barnes was never found, but at last Anna and Bill could breathe easy.

During the summer of 1948, The New Sackville blossomed into a thriving hotel, building a reputation for excellent service and exquisite cuisine. The hand-picked staff took pride in their work. Anna had taken a liking to Woody; he was perhaps the most willing and hard-working member of the staff. Contrary to her initial thoughts that he would need a lot of supervision, it turned out that he needed the least direction of the staff. He settled in well to the staff quarters and Amy took him under her wing.

This was more than she could say for Mr. Smyth. He was an excellent maître d'hôtel, and the running of the Emily Carr Dining Room was always perfect and the guests had high praise for him, but Anna didn't like his harsh attitude towards his staff. James was constantly smoothing issues with waiters threatening to leave. Fortunately, Mr. Smyth did respect and get along with James, much more so than he did with Anna. Mr. Smyth's ego was too large to recognize that he was teetering on the edge of self-destruction.

It was rare that either Anna or Bill ate in their suite, even though a small kitchen had been installed. Anna either snacked at her desk or, like today, after having been up for hours she went into the dining room for a late breakfast. Mr. Smyth usually left his head waiter to deal with the breakfast shift. Sitting at the family table, she ordered poached eggs with toast and coffee. She noticed Woody behind one of the waiter's service stations, which was strange as dining room maintenance was usually performed outside of meal times. She immediately sensed something was wrong and went to talk to him.

"Woody, is something wrong?" Woody shuffled his feet and avoided looking at Anna, something she had not seen him do since the day she interviewed him.

"Mr. Smyth made me come in and repair this cutlery drawer. I'm not supposed to be here when guests are here. But he gets angry if I don't do as he says." Woody froze, his fear palpable. Anna turned to see Mr. Smyth approaching.

Without acknowledging Anna, Mr. Smyth leaned in towards Woody and spoke directly into his ear, "What the hell are you doing here? You are not to be in the dining room during mealtimes."

"Repairing the drawer. You told me to come." Woody glanced at Anna.

"No I didn't," he whispered, "you imbecile."

Anna stared directly at him. "Mr. Smyth, my office now! And Woody, find something else to do. Come back and finish this later."

Anna followed Mr. Smyth to her office, stopping to ask the waiter to bring her some coffee and toast, seeing as she was not going to get her breakfast. She couldn't believe what she had just witnessed. She stared at him as he stood in front of her desk. "Sit down, Mr. Smyth."

"I'd rather stand," he said, defiance written across his cold face.

"I asked you to take a seat." Anna watched him hesitate, purse his lips and take a breath, readying to say something.

Anna raised her voice. "Sit!"

He reluctantly sat on the edge of the chair, his posture defiant. *What was wrong with this man?*

"I am appalled at what I just witnessed. You instructed…" Anna raised her hand as Smyth attempted to interrupt. "I will ask the questions. You deliberately misled Woody and then reprimanded him, calling him names. What is your explanation?"

"Woody disobeyed my instructions. I don't think his simple mind can understand instructions." Smyth folded his arms, the action meant to challenge, but he changed his mind and rested his hands on his lap.

"I have been watching you closely and, frankly, Mr. Smyth, I don't like what I see. Woody was not lying. You misled him. I won't accuse you of lying, but there was, at best, a misunderstanding. Chef Bill and Mr. Lytton think highly of you as a maître d'hôtel and I have had several positive comments from guests who remember you from The Savoy. However, I am aware that Mr. Lytton has had to speak to you regarding your harsh attitude towards your staff. Never forget that respect is earned, whether it is your staff or superiors."

"I am harsh, as you say, with the staff because they need the discipline. Being a good waiter takes much learning and practice. I learned from the best hotels in London and I want The New Sackville Hotel to reach London hotel standards."

I can't argue with that, she thought as she acknowledged to herself how he had succeeded in neutralizing the situation.

"I too recognize your experience, but as qualified as you may be, Mr. Smyth, please remember that nobody is indispensable." Anna waited for him to retaliate but silence followed. His demeanour now subservient, he cleared his throat and simply said, "I'm sorry, Mrs. Blaine. It won't happen again."

Anna was momentarily stuck for words by the sudden change—her thoughts trying to figure out this complex man who seemed to challenger her more than anyone else. *A Jekyll and Hyde? A bit dramatic,* she thought. *Was she the only person to see it?*

"Take this meeting as a warning, Mr. Smyth. I expect you to be more considerate with your staff and, in future, if you require Woody's services in the dining room, please make your request through Mr. Lytton. That will be all. Return to your duties."

Anna sat at her desk, nibbling toast and sipping cold coffee. She was tired of dealing with hide-and-seek agendas. Business was not a game. Thankfully the bank had come clean and Smyth's apparent change of heart was encouraging.

Next she had to deal with her daughter. Isabelle was due to start work in two weeks but Anna had been kept in the dark about her plans. She worried about where they were going to live and if Sarah's school had been found. She even questioned the need for Isabelle's grand marketing plan. The hotel had experienced close to eighty percent occupancy so far and August, the busiest time of the year, was booked to capacity and the Emily Carr Dining Room rarely had an unoccupied table. However, a one-year trial period had been agreed upon and Anna was a woman of her word.

Isabelle had been vague about the exact date they would arrive and Anna was surprised when a large trunk appeared in Isabelle's name, but not Isabelle.

Anna telephoned. Sandy answered, "Hello."

"Sandy, I wondered when you were coming. A large trunk arrived earlier today."

"Isabelle sent the trunk separately. She and Sarah left last night on the sleeper train and plan to stay in London for a couple of days. She said she would call you from London."

There was silence on the line. "Sandy, are you still there?"

"Um...yes. Mother, I won't be coming for a while."

"Is everything all right between the two of you?"

Another silence. "I can't get away...it's the job." Sandy's voice trembled.

"I know something is wrong."

"No, everything is fine. This is a terrible line and I can hardly hear you. I'll have to hang up." The line crackled and then went dead. The receiver hovered above the cradle for a few seconds before she hung up. Anxiety sank into the pit of her stomach. A knock on the door irritated her, she didn't want to be interrupted—she needed to think.

"I hope I'm not interrupting."

Anna's mood immediately lightened, hearing the southern drawl she would recognize anywhere. "Julia, how wonderful to see you. What are you doing here? Staying, I hope. Look at you, I don't know how you keep looking so young." Julia's porcelain-like face never aged, and her light blond hair hid most of the grey. Anna admired her tiny, slim figure that hadn't changed for years.

"I decided to give Darcy and Belle a break. Felix arrived home unexpectedly and not in very good humour. His studies are not going well. Too much procrastination, I suspect. Mum and Dad needed to have a heart-to-heart talk with the boy so I called the hotel yesterday and almost had to beg for a room. But here I am."

"I'm sorry to hear about Felix. He's too bright and clever for his own good, and young at seventeen to be heading to Oxford. Children don't grow out of their problems as they grow up, they seem to get bigger problems. I am not sure what Isabelle is up to but she is arriving here in a day or two without Sandy. Did I tell you she is joining the staff as marketing manager?"

"Yes, it's a great idea. Perhaps Sandy has to wait for a transfer or something."

Anna nodded, hoping that was a reasonable explanation. "I am very happy to see you; I need a distraction. Let's go into the lounge and have a drink."

"Mrs. Blaine," Miss Jenkins called as they walked out of the office. "We are fully booked and have no vacant rooms. Mrs. Wexford just called saying she was arriving tomorrow. I'm sorry but I don't have a reservation for her and nothing until after the weekend."

Anna sighed, annoyed at Isabelle's assumptions. She thought for a moment. "What room is Mrs. Castillo in?"

Miss Jenkins hesitated, opening the guest register. "Room 207. It's a double room. It was the last room we had."

"Perfect," Anna said.

"Julia, would you be my guest and stay with Bill and I in our suite? We have a guest bedroom and it's quite comfortable."

"I would be delighted."

"Miss Jenkins, give Mrs. Castillo's room to my daughter and granddaughter and have a maid make up my spare bedroom and ask the bellboy to move Mrs. Castillo's belongings after breakfast tomorrow."

A brief pang of guilt entered Anna's mind for not offering her spare room to Isabelle. Secretly excited at the thought of having Julia as a guest in their suite, she justified her decision based on the comfort for one versus two people.

Isabelle and Sarah arrived the following afternoon. The reception desk took the brunt of Isabelle's anger. Expecting a suite, she was not pleased to be given a double room. Sarah was in tears, looking for Nana.

Anna and Julia were finishing lunch when they heard the commotion. Excusing herself, Anna went into the lobby. A tearful Sarah ran towards her and Anna ordered Isabelle to join them for lunch.

"Mother, it's about time. I came to run the hotel. They don't have a suite for me! If they treat me like this, how do they treat guests? I deserve better."

"Stop right there, Isabelle. First of all, this hotel belongs to me, and your job is to promote it. Your disrespectful behaviour at the reception desk will never happen again. We are fully booked. This is a good thing. You should be pleased." Anna took a breath, annoyed but sadly aware that the room issue was not the source of Isabelle's anger.

"Why are you so upset?" Anna asked, "It isn't the hotel." She reached over and touched Isabelle's hand and saw her eyes filling with tears. "What is wrong? Did something happen in London?"

"No, it's Sandy." Isabelle glanced at Sarah, then at Anna.

"We can have this conversation later." Anna squeezed Sarah, who was standing at her side. "Sarah, tell me about your trip to London? Did you go to the Tower and see the Crown Jewels?" Anna wanted to distract and protect Sarah from her parents.

Family Affair

I sabelle stayed out of Anna's way. Sarah danced around the hotel, enjoying the attention from the guests and staff alike. Sarah, with her mother's short curly red hair, and beguiling hazel eyes—a true Shirley Temple—won the hearts of most guests. Even at eight years old she had learned the art of conversation and when she should and should not intrude.

Anna had assumed that Isabelle and Sandy would want to live in their own house off the premises. There was no need for Isabelle to live in, but Isabelle had other ideas, albeit she suggested it was only temporary until Sandy got his transfer, sold the house and joined them. Anna knew that was unlikely, but played along with the charade. The hotel could not afford to fill one of the best suites during the high season, but agreed that Isabelle and Sarah would occupy a suite until the spring, or until Sandy joined them. Anna suggested converting the half of the staff quarters that they no longer needed on the fourth floor into an apartment for the family. Isabelle was appalled at such a suggestion.

Sarah started school, September rolled into October and then November, and still no plans for Sandy to move from Edinburgh, nor even to visit. Isabelle said she was too busy for visits anyway.

In September, the hotel was at half capacity with late holiday-makers, which was good for the season. By October, Isabelle had put a program together for companies to hold executive conferences at the hotel, and based on the restaurant's reputation for fine dining, she developed getaway weekend packages. Early November was dismal; even the restaurant was slow. Unconcerned, Isabelle looked forward to December, having enticed several large companies to host their Christmas parties at The New Sackville.

Anna sat in her favourite spot in her office, gazing at the sea. The usual greyness of November was temporarily broken by yellow sunrays pushing through the grey clouds, patches of yellow reflecting on the waves. A symbol of bright things to come, she thought. She was surprised that she and Isabelle had been able to work together and thrilled with the hotel's progress.

The shrill ring of the telephone made her jump and Isabelle came running into the office. "That's for me!" Anna pushed the telephone towards her. Picking up the receiver she said, "Hello, Isabelle Wexford speaking." The one-sided conversation continued with Isabelle repeating, "Yes, of course."

Replacing the receiver, she looked at Anna and started to giggle and jump up and down. "I just booked a society wedding, two hundred guests, for mid December—Tuesday the 14th. That is only weeks away."

Anna saw a rare glimpse of her excited little girl in Isabelle and she felt just as excited. A society wedding would do wonders for The New Sackville's reputation. "This is marvelous news, but I can't help wondering why they are booking so late and why not in London?" Anna raised an eyebrow. "Perhaps the wedding is…shall we say rushed for a reason."

"Maybe, but does it matter? Mr. Howard, who I am assuming is the spokesperson for the family, just said that the wedding had been planned for the spring in London but because of business circumstances it had been moved forward. He and the bride's mother will be traveling from London tomorrow to see the accommodations."

Anna smiled. "We had better get to work. The bride is not coming?"

"I don't know. He just said that he would be accompanying her ladyship, the duchess.

A shiny chauffeur-driven Bentley pulled under the portico at 11:30 the next morning. Anna and Isabelle stepped out to greet the duchess; an imposing woman of about the same height and age as Anna. Her youthful complexion belied short grey hair that curled neatly against her head. Her bright red lipstick popped out from the short black veil of her hat. A fur stole, possibly mink, Anna thought, sat elegantly on the shoulders of a fitting black suit with pencil-slim skirt. Mr. Howard, who appeared to be the chauffeur as well as secretary, introduced the Duchess of Norbury and then disappeared. Anna introduced Isabelle and James before escorting the party to the lounge for coffee.

The Duchess made no secret of looking around the lobby and lounge. "Mrs. Blaine, I commend you on your taste in décor. I admit to being skeptical when Lady Thornton suggested a hotel in Bexhill. But this is as good as the Knightsbridge Hotel in London. They were booked up for the Christmas season and couldn't change the date."

"Thank you, Your Grace. I hadn't realized it was Lady Thornton's recommendation that brought you here. I must write and thank her. We are old friends. They were here for the grand opening in May."

"You are acquainted with the Thornton's *personally*?" the duchess's voice rose in surprise.

"Yes, my husband has known Lord Darcy Thornton for many years. His mother was a regular summer guest here after Lord Thornton died on the Titanic."

"Oh, really." The duchess appeared uncomfortable; in fact, Anna thought she saw a flicker of fear. "I don't have much time. Shall we discuss the wedding?" She continued hurriedly, "We had planned my daughter's wedding for the spring but owing to an unexpected government posting overseas, my son-in-law to be will be leaving the country in January and wishes his bride to accompany him." The duchess took a sip of coffee. "His stay in India will be six to twelve months and my daughter does not want to wait until his return to get married. Personally, with the current troubles in India, I think she would be wise to wait but she has it in her head that it will be a glamorous posting. The young today are so impatient."

Anna interjected, "My husband and I have just returned from three months in India. It is a beautiful country but most of the glamour has gone. I fear your daughter will be disappointed."

The duchess frowned, betraying the worry of a parent. She moved her head to one side and said, "Is it really as bad as the press reports?"

"In some areas, yes, it is. We stumbled on a few places where there were riots. We were traveling independently and did not realize the dangers, which in retrospect was foolish. There is no love lost between Indians and the British, but the violence seemed to mostly be between Muslims and Hindus and there is a terrible anger directed towards half castes. Being on a government posting, I think the government will brief your son-in-law and daughter on the dangers and will undoubtedly be vigilant about their safety. Unfortunately, this will limit their movements and ability to travel to see the country, but it will keep them safe." The duchess sighed but did not reply.

"My daughter, Mrs. Wexford, will show you around the hotel. My husband, who is the executive chef and Mr. Lytton, the general manager, will join us in the Emily Carr Dining Room for luncheon."

"How lovely; the hotel really is a family affair."

"Your Ladyship, shall we begin?" Isabelle asked. Having been quiet and in awe of the duchess, she had finally found her voice after glancing at Anna for support. Anna's discreet nod and smile was acknowledged. Anna felt her chest puff out with pride for her daughter, knowing her experience with society women during her years in retail would be useful with the duchess.

Anna watched the two women approach the lift and wondered if everything was all right. She asked herself why the duke had not been mentioned and the references to the bride and her preferences had been minimal. An overbearing mother perhaps, but the duchess didn't strike Anna as being that kind of person. And why had the bride not attended the meeting?

Final wedding details were decided during lunch. The wedding was not going to be as elaborate as Isabelle would have liked—the guest list had been cut from two to one hundred—but it was a duke's daughter's wedding. Isabelle was in her element. Other than direct wedding decisions, Anna found the duchess to be vague about the family and guest list, and she could not shake the feeling that she was missing something.

In spite of Anna's misgivings, both she and Isabelle were aware that the wedding would be a real boost to the hotel's finances and reputation—an added bonus to the Christmas week and New Year bookings. Isabelle's plans for extra perks, such as gifts to each guest, concerned Anna. Isabelle explained that the cost of all the perks was built into the price. Still not convinced, Anna was concerned that the price would be too high and people wouldn't book. She soon discovered that rather than being a deterrent, the high price was appealing and the bookings came rolling in. Isabelle was right, the rich will pay for things that they want and Christmas away from home seemed to be what they wanted.

Anna was delighted that Isabelle and the hotel were doing so well but also relieved to have a break before the wedding and Christmas rush. She and Bill had hardly seen each other in the last while and she had sadly neglected her guest, Julia. She walked down to the kitchen to find Bill.

"Anna, what can I do for you?"

"I came to chat. I've hardly seen you lately. Why are you so busy? The hotel hardly has any guests."

Bill put down the menu he was studying and guided Anna to his office, wrapped his arms around her and kissed her. "I don't do that often enough." She relaxed in his arms, leaning against his shoulder, remembering the first time she had run into his arms thirty something years ago and she still felt the same warmth, love and security. "I agree with you. But why are you so busy in the kitchen?"

"Anna, we have a wedding to prepare for and the duchess has requested quite a wedding breakfast menu. That's a lot of extra work on top of Christmas preparations. I want this Christmas to be like the Christmases we used to celebrate here in the hotel before the Great War. Do you remember all the things Chef Louis prepared? I kept all the recipes."

"Oh yes, I do remember. The Christmas tree in the lobby and the carol singers."

"That is your department, or is it Isabelle's? I have enough with the food. Anna, I would love to stay but I should get back to the kitchen. I'll try and finish early tonight."

Disappointed but understanding, Anna went up to the suite. Julia was in her bedroom packing. Anna had forgotten that Julia was returning to Hillcrest Estate for Christmas.

Julia looked up. "Packing is always a little sad. I shall miss you. My stay here has given me time to think. I have decided to return to Chicago after Christmas. I have been avoiding settling Luigi's estate. The memories of his bullying are hard to go back to. I have decided to sell the house and everything in it. I want to start a new life and I am going back to Alabama to find a new home. Most of my family is long gone but I have cousins I was close to before I married Luigi. I will try and rekindle some of the friendships that Luigi had forced me to abandon. Once I'm settled, I will travel again. Perhaps you will join me on some of my travels."

"I would like that very much. The hotel should be running well in a year or two. I'm hoping Isabelle will be able to take over. I feel guilty for having been such a bad hostess. But if the quiet time helped you, I don't feel too bad."

"It has and I have enjoyed the solitude."

"I have some time on my hands today. Can I exonerate my appalling behavior and take you into Eastbourne to do some Christmas shopping? I hope you don't mind traveling in James' MG sports car. James needs Bill's Hillman to pick up some guests from the station."

Anna loved driving with the MG's top down and the wind blasting through her hair, but the November weather was too cool. Today she would enjoy the invigorating coastal road with Julia. Laughing and talking with Julia, Anna realized how serious she had become. They toured the shops, enjoying the Christmas hustle, and finished at The Grand Hotel for afternoon tea.

"The last time I was in this hotel was in 1915, asking Bill to be Alex's best man. Bill was the head chef at the time. It was that day that I realized how much I loved Bill. Strange, because I also thought I had lost him forever and stubbornly married Alex."

"I always knew Bill was running away and I suspected he loved someone very deeply," Julia replied. "After Belle returned to England, Bill was my only friend, certainly the only person I could trust. He was very kind to me in Chicago."

"And you risked your life for him by helping him escape his marriage." Julia went quiet, her face dark with memories.

"Speaking of marriage, the Duchess of Norbury has booked the hotel for her daughter's wedding in December. It is a rushed affair brought forward from the original spring date. She said Belle recommended The New Sackville. I wondered if you had met her at any of the society social events?"

"No, the name isn't familiar. Why do you ask?"

"There is something odd about the whole thing. Nothing I can put my finger on. It's probably nothing. Isabelle thinks it's fine, but then she is all wrapped up with the status of a royal wedding." Anna laughed. "I don't think it's very royal, I suspect there's not much more than a title." Anna stopped talking, taking a breath. "I think that's it. Is it a genuine title? I've wondered about that. Perhaps I'm sensing that there is no money or no title, or neither."

"Talk to Belle. She will know whether they are genuine or not. And what about contacting the London hotel and asking why they cancelled?"

Anna nodded as they stood in the Grand Hotel's entrance waiting for the valet to bring the car to the front. The silent journey back to Bexhill conveyed the depth of their thoughts and physical tiredness.

That evening, everyone gathered in the dining room at eight to dine with Julia. Bill's undying gratitude to Julia allowed him to abandon the kitchen to dine with the family. He sat next to Anna and they held hands under the table like a pair of school kids. The staff was happy to be busy; the previous week had been the quietest since opening. Mr. Smyth watched his waiters like a hawk. Anna noticed he was quick to reprimand, making the waiters nervous. The less experienced were already jittery, knowing they were serving the esteemed hotel owners. Part of her liked the attention but the other part flinched at the notoriety. Anna didn't condone Mr. Smyth's attitude, but she had to admit that all the wait staff were exceedingly polite without being intrusive, and sharp, snappy and immaculate in their black tails, white shirts and white gloves. All the attributes essential for silver service dining room staff. Anna knew that Bill's goal was to get a Michelin star rating if and when it was reinstated in England.

"It is not often that I sit on this side of that door." Bill gestured towards the service door. "And although I do say it myself, that was an excellent dinner. Only six months since we opened and our reputation is already spreading. Not many hotels can boast a royal wedding."

"I have travelled in America and Europe and The New Sackville is superior to most hotels I have stayed at and it is close to the Dorchester or Savoy in London." Julia took a sip of wine.

"Our maître d' brings his expertise from both of those hotels." Isabelle smiled, touching Mr. Smyth's arm. "I don't think it will be long before the dining room will reach such a high standard. Don't you agree, Mr. Smyth?"

"I do my best, madam." Anna almost missed the fleeting eye contact as he filled Isabelle's wine glass.

Both gestures were far too familiar. Was Mr. Smyth flirting with her daughter or was Isabelle doing the flirting? She glanced towards Mr. Smyth, who glanced back, a tiny smirk on the corner of his mouth or had she imagined it? Bill sensed her uneasiness and frowned. "Anna is something wrong? It's not the dessert is it?"

"No, the ice cream was cold on my tongue." Bill looked puzzled at her untouched plate. "I haven't tried the apple strudel yet. I bet this recipe is from Kenwood Bakery."

"You owned a bakery?" Julia and James said in unison.

"Many years ago Alex and I owned a bakery in Toronto. Our baker's family originated in Austria and his pastries were beyond excellent."

"During that time I worked at the Royal York Hotel in Toronto. Nick originally gave me the recipes for the Royal York, but the pastry chef didn't use them. I kept them and I am so glad I did. The bread you had with the soup was one of Nick's recipes too"

Anna's gaze followed Mr. Smyth as he moved from table to table, stopping to speak to Lady Rhodes, a regular guest in the early days of the old Sackville and now in her eighties. Anna remembered a disagreeable lady with many double chins that concertinaed into her neck, and the chins had multiplied over the years. Mr. Smyth said something to her and Anna saw her lips relax and break into a smile. *He certainly has a way with women,* she thought forcing, her attention back to the current conversation.

"Isabelle, do you remember the bakery?"

"Mum, I was pretty young, but I remember Henry. I called him my special friend. He made me a fairy castle cake for my fifth birthday and I remember Papa buying me a red tricycle but I never understood why you were mad with Papa"

"I can't say I recall, it was a long time ago." Anna did recall. She and Alex had planned to choose the tricycle together; that was why she had been mad at him. It seemed trivial now.

The dinner over, James and Bill went to the lounge bar for brandy. Julia, Isabelle and Anna decided to have coffee in the lounge. Walking out of the dining room, Anna realized that Isabelle was missing. Anna turned to see her talking to Mr. Smyth; she detected the familiarity again. Julia followed her gaze. "You look worried. What is it?"

"Is it my imagination or is there something too familiar between my daughter and Mr. Smyth?"

"I hadn't noticed. I think she is thanking him."

Julia caught the morning train to London and Anna busied herself with the grand wedding plans. Having received the impressive guest list in the morning post, she called a meeting with Amy to assign the suites and rooms.

Glancing at the list, Amy said, "Mrs. Blaine, we don't have enough suites, we are short by at least one. I will have to ask Mrs. Wexford to move for a couple of nights."

Isabelle will not be pleased, Anna thought. "I'll ask Isabelle to move. What room can you give her? Remember it must have a room for Sarah. Can you find two nice adjoining rooms? We are going to need Suite 303 for Christmas too."

"Who needs adjoining rooms?" Isabelle asked, closing the office door.

"You do. I'm sorry Isabelle but we need your suite for the wedding guests and all the suites are booked for Christmas."

"I'm not moving, Mother. Give the adjoining rooms to the guests."

"We agreed that you would move if necessary. The time has come. I expected you and Sandy to want your own house off the premises." Anna waited for a response but Isabelle's face tightened with resolve. "If you would rather live here, take up my offer of a fourth floor flat. Isabelle, you need to understand that guest rooms, and especially the suites, are revenue." Still no response. Anna was getting tired of her princess games and decided to appeal to her sense of grandeur. "Would you consider a penthouse?"

"Penthouse? I like that idea. Do you think it's possible?"

Amy stood up. "I'll leave you to it. I have to check on the maids. If you will excuse me, I'll be back later."

"Thanks Amy, give us an hour?"

Anna waited until Amy had closed the door. "I'll have an architect take a look and see how expensive it might be. We can talk to Sandy when he comes. When is Sandy joining you?"

"I don't know when Sandy is coming. We're splitting up."

"What!"

"You heard me. Separating. Sarah and I will make our home here."

The tension vibrated the silence.

"Now you know."

"Why?"

"Who knows why? These things happen."

"But Sandy has always been a good husband, a good father and he adores you or is there a side to him I'm not seeing?"

"That's the problem. He's too nice and, frankly, plain boring."

"What about Sarah? Shouldn't you try and work it out for Sarah's sake?"

"Nothing has been worked out yet but you had better get used to the idea of divorce. I don't want to discuss it any further." Isabelle walked towards the office door, turned and looked at Anna. "I'm sorry, Mother. I know I have disappointed you." There was genuine regret in Isabelle's hazel eyes. Anna wondered whom the regret was for: Sandy and Sarah, or herself.

The office walls seemed to close in, her thoughts focused on this tragedy. She liked Sandy, there was nothing about him not to like; he was a good man and had always been there for Isabelle, even in tough times. What had gone wrong? And Sarah—did Isabelle have no consideration for her daughter who adored her father? Was she jealous? The last thought provoked a deep sense of guilt. Isabelle had always loved her father more than she did Anna. She remembered how she had hated the idea of motherhood, but the day Isabelle was born it all changed and she understood the depth of a mother's love. A little part of her had always believed that the reason she found motherhood difficult was some kind of punishment. Was history repeating?

Maybe I have an opportunity to set things right. Isabelle always gets her own way. I will not let Sarah suffer due to her mother's selfishness, much of which, I must admit is my fault. Isabelle is not going to dictate how I run this hotel. It's time to take control.

Anna marched into the Emily Carr dining room, glancing at the pictures on the wall reminded her of Emily Carr's strength, her struggle to be an independent woman and her success as a talented artist. Isabelle was talking to Mr. Smyth, more than talking, there was an intimate laugh between them and as Anna approached, stifled grins.

"Isabelle, I need to speak with you."

"I'm busy, can't it wait?" Anna bubbled with anger at Isabelle's defiant face. Whatever was going on here she needed to nip it in the bud.

"No it can't wait. What is so important that you have to interfere with Mr. Smyth's work?"

"We were discussing the menu for the wedding." Isabelle's red hair was quivering with temper.

"The menus are discussed with Mr. Blaine not the maître d'." Anna led the way to her office.

Words exploded from Isabelle's mouth, "How could you speak to me like that in front of the staff."

"Perhaps because of your inappropriate behaviour with the staff and disrespect for me."

"I don't know what you mean." Isabelle looked away and blushed slightly. "What is it you want?"

"Respect," Anna stated "Isabelle, whether you are my daughter or not, I am your boss at the hotel and you will abide my decisions." Isabelle's mouth opened. Anna put her hand up. "Let me finish. It is your job to promote this hotel and you are doing a wonderful job. Word of mouth is the most powerful form of advertising, which I am sure you are aware of. It is important that those guests who have requested suites for the wedding and Christmas are accommodated. Isabelle, you will vacate your suite. Sarah can stay in our spare room and I will have Amy move you to an adequate room near my apartment."

"You are just angry because I'm leaving Sandy. Nice, Mother! I can't say I expected any support from you."

"I am concerned, not angry, about your situation. I'm upset that you have no consideration for Sarah. However, we can discuss that later. Right now, the hotel is the subject of my concern. I am asking you to do your job and consider the guests first."

"If you don't want me here, I can leave you know."

"It may have escaped your attention that the hotel was doing well before you came here. I expect that with your expertise it will do even better. But if you choose to leave I'm sure we will manage. Leaving seems to be your answer to everything." As the words came out of her mouth she thought of Alex. Leaving was something he had done without thought, because he was impulsive. Isabelle was like her father in many ways, but it was not impulsiveness that drove Isabelle, it was entitlement.

Communication remained tense between them, but Isabelle took the room and Sarah was moved to Anna's spare room.

The Tainted Duchess

Anna woke and cuddled up to Bill. "Time to get up," she said, yawning.

"Waking up to your sweet voice makes my day." Bill rolled over and hugged her. She pushed him away laughing, "Sweet voice, indeed. You sound like a love sick teenager." Anna swung her legs to the floor.

"Just because I'm older doesn't mean I can't love you." He grabbed her arm playfully pulling her back into bed. She felt the pleasure of his warm breath on her neck as he whispered, "I'll always love you."

The truth was Anna felt like a teenager when Bill gently caressed her and whispered his love. She couldn't help herself as she succumbed to his soothing voice moving closer to feel his warm skin against hers. The day's plans disappeared.

Out of breath and content they rolled on to their backs and stared at the ceiling. Bill broke the silence. "Being a love sick teenager isn't bad for a couple of oldies."

Anna punched him good-humouredly in the arm. "Who are you calling oldies? We may not be teenagers but we're not old, we're still newlyweds."

"Does eleven months married, count as newlyweds? Anyway, I always feel young when I'm with you." Bill smiled and Anna chuckled, leaning over to kiss Bill's cheek.

"Enough of this fooling around, I've got work to do. Today is the day the Duchess of Norbury arrives with the bride. I know I should be happy about this royal wedding but the duchess has some rough edges. I called Belle Thornton and asked her to check it out for me. Belle doesn't know the family but does remember meeting the duchess on one occasion and is investigating."

"You worry too much. I'm sure she is fine and the revenue she and her entourage, and guests, are bringing to the hotel is a welcome boost for November."

Anna sighed. "That's just it. They have not paid a penny yet towards the wedding or the guest rooms. The duchess says the duke will settle the accounts but I have yet to meet him."

Bill frowned. "Yes, that is odd. Is he coming today?"

"No, just the bride and the duchess. The duke is arriving the morning of the wedding. He has duties at Buckingham Palace and can't get away any sooner."

"Well that sounds impressive," Bill said as he began dressing.

Studying the wardrobe, Anna picked out a navy suit, with pleated skirt and neat fitting jacket, and held up a cream-coloured blouse, nodding her approval of the outfit.

Taking a deep breath to fasten the skirt she said, "I don't mind getting older but I do mind my expanding waist and bulging tummy," she said, patting her midsection.

Bill came up behind her and put his arms around her waist. "I love every bit of you and I think you look fabulous," he whispered, in her ear. "Now, I must go and check that the staff have started work. I'll see you in your office with coffee and toast in about half an hour."

Pulling her shoulders up to her ears, she felt the warmth of his lingering breath and brushed her hair, trying to tame it into waves and loose curls. The stylish curls were easy but smoothing her hair into waves was a problem and required bobby pins to keep it in place. She gave the mirror one last glance, touching the corner of her eye, "Crow's feet," she said, giving a sigh.

"What are crow's feet, Nana?" Sarah stood behind her, rubbing her eyes.

"Good morning, sweetheart. Well, they are little lines we get around our eyes and they get thicker as we get older. Are you ready to get up?" Sarah nodded, just as there was a tap on the door and Isabelle came in to get Sarah ready for school. They exchanged cursory good mornings. Anna went to her office.

As usual, Anna sat at her desk watching the sky lighten as the dawn slowly rose from the east, casting peach coloured hues on the calm sea. She loved the quiet and solitude of this time of day, giving her time to gather her thoughts. She didn't like the tension with her daughter. She worried about Isabelle and Sandy and the thought of a divorce in the family. It would bring heartbreak and a certain amount of ridicule, and no matter what they did or said, it would impact the hotel's reputation. The "what-will-people-think" attitude did not bother her as much as the effect on Sarah and Sandy, and she was not convinced that Isabelle really wanted a divorce. Her daughter was certainly willful at the best of times, but something else was going on. Anna sensed she had a secret. Had something happened in Scotland? And what was the smiling and giggling about between Isabelle and Mr. Smyth? There was no doubt in Anna's mind that Smyth had a hidden agenda.

She unlocked the cabinet and her fingers flipped through the alphabet to the S's. Smyth, Ralph M. She opened the file that contained three sheets of paper. She read through his application, adequate but minimal and no personal information. She read the two references and again the information was stark, as though it had been written to answer basic questions and nothing more. Any kind of reference from The Savoy or The Dorchester was indeed a good reference, so why was she questioning the content? James had made notes at the bottom of both letters after telephoning Mr. Smyth's superiors. Again the notes were very specific about his work, with "highly recommended" at the bottom. Although personal information in employee files was not expected, some indication of the person could usually be found, their marital status, family or where they were born, but there was nothing here, it was as though the employee existed on paper, but Mr. Smyth the person did not.

"Penny for your thoughts?" Bill asked placing a tray on Anna's desk.

"Mr. Smyth bothers me. Did I tell you I caught him flirting with Isabelle, and Isabelle seemed to be enjoying the attention?

"Isabelle always enjoys attention. I agree with you about Mr. Smyth."

Anna handed Bill the file. "Give me your opinion?"

"His references are impeccable but there isn't much here."

"That's what bothers me. If you look at the other personnel files, there are snippets of personal information."

"Perhaps he's a private kind of person. James is happy with his credentials and I have no complaints about his work."

"He can be rather harsh with the waiters…" Bill's forehead creased into his baldness. "Waiters need to be disciplined. Anna, you are too soft with the staff."

"I know. Anyway, I am keeping an eye on Mr. Smyth and I'd like you to do the same." Anna poured the coffee and they sipped in comfortable silence.

The Duchess of Norbury and two young women arrived by taxi from the train station. Albert sent the bellboy to inform Anna.

"Welcome to The New Sackville Hotel, milady. I trust your journey was comfortable," Anna said, noticing she was wearing the same outfit, including the mink stole on her shoulders, that she wore the day they met.

"Trains are always grimy but the duke could not spare the chauffeur. He will join us tomorrow. Allow me to introduce my daughter, Lady Philippa, and her bridesmaid, Miss Rose Wilson."

Anna stretched her arm and shook Lady Philippa's hand, turning to Miss Rose Wilson who hesitated, only touching the tip of Anna's fingers.

"The girls will stay in the suite with me tonight, but when the duke arrives I would like them to have a room close to our suite. And Mr. Howard will need a room close to my suite too."

Confused by Mr. Howard's title and role, Anna had expected the chauffeur to stay in the servant's quarters but today he was acting as the duchess' assistant and was currently speaking with James at the reception desk. Anna approached the desk and turned the leather bound hotel register towards the duchess for her signature.

"Mr. Lytton, I will show the duchess to Suite 303 and would you check with Mrs. Peterson for the room number for Mr. Howard and the room for the bride and bridesmaid for tomorrow. The duchess has requested rooms close to her suite." James smiled, raising an eyebrow with a nod, that told Anna he understood the room arrangements needed to be changed.

"Milady, I have arranged rooms for your servants in the staff quarters but I need to inform the housekeeper how many rooms to prepare."

The Duchess's face turned red, she coughed and fidgeted with her hands, her gaze resting on Miss Wilson. "I decided we could manage without my maid for one night. The duke's valet will arrive with the duke so he will need a room tomorrow." Anna thought, *A duchess without a lady's maid?*

"I'll show you to your rooms. Your luggage will be sent up." Anna turned, surprised at how little there was. She expected a duchess to travel with mountains of bags and trunks. "I would be honoured if you and your daughter and Miss Wilson would join us for dinner tonight. My husband and daughter would like to go over the final wedding arrangements.

Over dinner, it was noted that the final arrangements had been pared down yet again. Only fifty confirmed wedding guests. Anna saw Isabelle's disappointment and hoped Bill had enough time to reduce the food orders from the suppliers.

The duke arrived with little fanfare and no chauffeur or valet. He had driven himself, explaining the chauffeur had been called away on a family emergency and his valet had fallen ill at the last minute. The duke himself did not look well. He was a thin man, with deep wrinkles to his pallid face, and he looked much older than the duchess.

The groom, Mr. Gerald Burton, and his family arrived shortly after the duke. His family, although not titled, were extremely wealthy; the owners of Burton Breweries, an old, established and thriving brewery. Perhaps not the match the duchess would have liked, but marrying a title these days did not mean wealth; both world wars had taken a terrible toll on the aristocracy.

That night, after Sarah had been tucked up in bed, Anna, Isabelle, Bill and

James met in the apartment to go over the last minute arrangements.

James looked serious. "The duke has not paid for anything yet. The Burtons paid when they arrived and some of the guests paid for their rooms, but several of the duchess's guests have informed reception to add their expenses to the duke's tab."

"I had an argument with the florist today," Isabelle added, "They insisted that the hotel pay the bill as the duchess had told them to put it on our account. I had no choice."

A loud bang made everyone jump followed by loud angry voices from the suite next door. "What was that?" Anna said. A male voice boomed and a female voice screamed, the words inaudible but there was no doubt it was the duke and duchess. "I think we should knock on the door. James?"

James opened the door and stepped over to Suite 303, the voices were now loud and understandable. "I can't believe you would make all these lavish arrangements."

"But it is our daughter's wedding."

"Tell me how are we going to…" James knocked on the door.

"Sorry to disturb you sir, but is everything all right?"

"Of course! What is the meaning of this intrusion?"

"My apologies, sir." James felt the wind in his face as the door slammed. The voices lowered to an intense whisper as he returned to Suite 305, almost knocking Anna over in the doorway.

"James, I want you to meet with the duke in the morning before the wedding and insist on a payment. Make up an invoice to cover the rooms and expenses so far and double check with him about paying for his guests. If he's not paying, then ask him to inform his guests they are responsible for their hotel bills. And make up bills for every guest."

James arrived before eight the next morning to prepare the guest accounts. Miss Jenkins knocked on his office door.

"Mr. Lytton, the duke is asking for his bill."

James looked with surprised. "That is good news, Miss Jenkins. I am working on his account now. Please show the duke into my office and order coffee and pastries." Miss Jenkins frowned and hesitated it was unusual for guests to settle accounts in the office. "Now please!"

"Good morning, Your Grace. Please take a seat. I am working on your account but there are some rather delicate financial matters that I thought would be better discussed in the privacy of my office."

The duke's face turned a bright pink. "And what matters would they be?" He fidgeted in his chair and sniffed. The tension in his face relaxed slightly as the maid entered with a tray of coffee.

James stared at the duke, sensing his deep discomfort. "Coffee, sir? Perhaps you would like something a little stronger with your coffee?" The duke's eyes widened making no attempt to hide his eagerness. "Yes, Mr. Lytton that would be pleasant. I have a trying day ahead of me." James went to his cabinet and took out a bottle of brandy and two glasses. The duke downed the brandy in one gulp. James left this glass untouched.

"Sir, the matter I wish to discuss with you is regarding some of your guests. Miss Jenkins tells me that several guests have requested that their hotel bills be added to your account. I would like to confirm that this has your approval."

"What!" The duke's ears went purple and James expected steam to be emitted at any moment. With a quick glance at James, he picked up the brandy bottle and helped himself to a full glass. "I have enough trouble paying my own bills." He stopped to swallow a gulp of brandy. "My wife and her damned friends, always trying to impress." He gulped more brandy and breathlessly said, "The only bill I will be paying is mine." He emptied the glass and calmed down. "My apologies, Mr. Lytton. My wife is extravagant and overly generous with an insatiable need to impress her friends. A duke's title does not mean wealth and the estate has suffered badly during the war. Are you married?" James shook his head. "You're a lucky man."

James had a sinking feeling the duke was not able to pay his bill, which was several hundred pounds. "Here is a list of the guests I spoke of. I will make up their accounts but I would be obliged if you could mention to them that you will not be paying for their accommodation."

The duke was fidgeting again. "I can't do that. Just hand them their bill and explain there was a mistake. Preferably after the wedding."

"As you wish, sir." James decided to pass the task to Anna. She had a way of calming irate guests.

"And this is your account so far. The hotel would be obliged if you could settle this bill and I will make up a final bill after the wedding and before you leave."

The duke said nothing, but counted out a pile of one, and five pound, notes, handing the bundle to James. "Thank you, Mr. Lytton," the duke said, picking up his glass and draining the last drop of brandy before leaving the office.

Cash in hand, James knocked on Anna's office door and joined Anna and Bill for coffee. "Money from the duke. It was quite an interview. I felt sorry for him. As we had already deduced, the duke has financial problems and an extravagant wife." James pointed to the wad of money. "I will leave this in the safe. The duke refused to pay for the duchess' guests. Anna, can you talk to these guests? They will not be happy."

"At least part of the bill is paid and I'll think of something to tell the disappointed guests. We have a big day today."

"Even if the Duke and Duchess of Norbury are not as they seem, some of their guests are high society. I would like to see them returning to The New Sackville. So let's do a good job. Has anyone seen Isabelle?"

Anna found Isabelle in the dining room with Amy and Mr. Smyth, arranging and decorating tables. The dining room looked surprisingly festive with white garlands, flowers and silver bows, Anna wondered how they had managed; decorative things were a luxury during the post-war shortages.

"Amy, the decorations look beautiful. How did you manage?"

"I had to be creative, but it is amazing what you can do with a little and the maids all helped."

Anna turned to Isabelle. "Can you spare me a minute, in my office?"

Isabelle shrugged. "I suppose so."

Anna wanted to break the ice between them. "I am tired of this feud

64

between us. Today is a special day, the first society wedding at The New Sackville and for the most part because of you. If it is to be a success, we need to work together."

Isabelle shrugged again.

"Please Isabelle, we may have our differences but in the end our goal is the same—to see the hotel successful."

"You're right, Mother. But can you treat me with some respect?" Anna almost retaliated with "I will when you earn respect," but she held her tongue.

"Of course I will. I appreciate and respect your talent as the hotel's marketing expert." Anna felt the coolness subside and hugged Isabelle, the hug was not returned but she sensed some warmth, and that would do for now.

"Mum, could you check with Bill as to what time he's serving the appetizers, I asked Ralph...crum...Mr. Smyth to check the cellar for wine and champagne."

"I'm on my way down to the staff room to meet Bill now, we have some extra staff arriving." Anna held her breath. Isabelle's reference to Mr. Smyth's first name had taken her off guard, confirming her growing suspicion. *Now is not the time,* she thought. Smiling at Isabelle, she left the office.

A Royal or Pauper's Wedding

Mr. Smyth closed the cellar door and nodded to Anna as she took the last step on the stairs into the passageway leading to the kitchen. A voice from the staff room shouted, "Ravi! It is most fortunate to see you at this magnificent hotel. You work here?" Anna stopped, turned and watched Mr. Smyth halt at the staff room door. "Balaji, quiet…" Tense, agitated whispers ensued.

"Why the frown?" Bill's voice prompted Anna to look up, lowering her voice and steering Bill into the kitchen. "Mr. Smyth again. It appears one of the temporary staff knows him."

"Anna, my love, he's worked in many hotels. It doesn't surprise me that he would know other waiters or hotel staff. Stop worrying, we have work to do."

"You're right." She surreptitiously squeezed Bill's hand, making sure the kitchen staff didn't notice. "Let's go hire some waiters."

Four temporary waiters were hired, including Balaji, to work under Mr. Smyth for the wedding. Neither man showed signs of knowing each other and this time it was Bill's turn to be suspicious. He frowned, remembering Anna's comment as he watched the two men treat each other as strangers.

The hotel looked magnificent. Flowers had been arranged in massive vases in the lobby: laurel leaves, holly with red berries and champagne-coloured roses, more greenery than flowers, masking the post-war shortages, exquisitely arranged and accented with cream satin bows. A red carpet ran from the portico into the lobby.

Cheers and applause rang through the lobby as a chauffeured Bentley returned from St. Andrew's Church and pulled under the portico. The bride appeared in a tea length strapless white satin dress, the only adornment a small bow at her waist. Her blonde hair was swooped up into curls on top of her head and a comb secured a veil that covered her bare shoulders. She held a single champagne rose. The simplicity was stunning.

The groom, in black tails and grey top hat took her free hand and together they climbed the steps.

Isabelle and Anna stood at the back of the lobby. Anna sighed. Looking towards Isabelle she said, "I wonder how much love there is? Neither has smiled or even glanced at each other." Isabelle raised her eyebrows and nodded in agreement, nudging Anna as the only bridesmaid, Rose Wilson, appeared behind the bride in a pretty, short-sleeved pale turquoise dress. Elegance would not describe her gait as she wobbled off her stiletto heels. Only Albert's quick action stopped her landing on the floor. "That was close," Anna whispered to Isabelle. "And the duchess is positively shimmering in pastel pink silk, and that hat?" Isabelle muffled a chuckle, exchanging knowing glances with her mother. The duchess's slim pencil skirt forced her to shuffle like a not so elegant Geisha girl. A wide saucer-shaped hat decorated with delicate pink flowers looked better suited to a teacup than perched on the duchess's head. Anna grinned.

The groom's family may not have been titled, but their appearance was tasteful and appropriate. Mrs. Burton wore a fashionable Chanel dress in rich navy with a small matching hat, enhanced by a short veil and ostrich feathers set neatly on the side. Mr. Burton bowed politely. Neither made any comment, Anna had the feeling they were not convinced this was a good marriage, but having a son married to a duke's daughter would no doubt be good for business.

Anna leaned towards Isabelle. "One would expect the elegance of a duchess to outshine a mere commoner. But I see a tramp contrasted by Mrs. Burton's elegance. I think there is more to the Duke and Duchess of

Norbury than meets the eye."

"I agree, Mother. Did you ever hear from Belle Thornton?"

"No, which tells me she doesn't know them and is investigating."

Anna returned to her office, leaving the wedding in the capable hands of Isabelle. She needed to work on the Christmas bookings; several of the wedding guests had asked if there were vacancies. The spin-off from the wedding that Anna had hoped would happen.

James knocked on her office door. "I have the accounts ready. Shall we go over them together? I'll start with what is outstanding on the duke's account."

"How much did he pay yesterday?"

"Two hundred pounds, which included meals, suite and bedroom. It did not include the wedding breakfast, flowers or miscellaneous items. I expect the bill to be another two hundred pounds or more."

Miss Jenkins put her head around the office door and handed Anna the afternoon post.

Anna shuffled through the envelopes. "Ah, a letter from Belle. Maybe this will tell us more about the duke and duchess."

A sense of melancholy came over Anna as she brushed her fingers over the Thornton's coat of arms on the envelope. It brought back fond memories of typing old Lady Thornton's correspondence in her youth. The old woman had had faith that Anna would find her dream, and she had been right.

She read aloud: *"Dearest Anna, I barely remember the Duke and Duchess of Norbury. I met them once at a house party but know little about them. I asked my friend Lady Cardish, who moves in royal circles, if she was acquainted with the Norburys. I thought that would be a good start as you mentioned the duke having business at the palace."*

Anna looked up at James. "I have to pinch myself when I hear Belle talk about royal circles. She is such a wonderful friend to me and treats me no differently than she treats royalty." Anna laughed, "Except I don't expect her to curtsey."

"You have many friends, Anna, due your own kindness and knowing who you are."

"James, you'll make me blush, and I wasn't always this nice." James laughed and nodded in agreement.

Anna continued to read. *"The Duke of Norbury, or Reggie as his friends call him, was a known playboy in his youth and a great disappointment to his parents. His father constantly bailed him out of gambling debts and other unsavoury occupations to avoid scandal. It is said that his mother died of shame as her only son cavorted with badly behaved royals. His father died young too. Reggie inherited the dukedom when he was only thirty and surprised everyone by taking his responsibilities seriously until he secretly married, Maud Little, a Drury Lane actress. She is quite the talented actress, who practices her talent daily to appear the perfect duchess. Society was shocked further when Lady Philippa was born six months later."*

Anna stopped reading and chuckled. "Well that explains why I wasn't sure about the duchess. She certainly is a good actress." Anna continued, *"The family felt the full effects of society's disapproval. The duchess thought throwing lavish parties and spending hundreds of pounds on extravagant outfits would win her approval in society. Instead of approval, the duchess in particular became a laughing stock. The duke faired a little better within his own circles, but I would assume that the changing times and extravagant wife have depleted his resources.*

Lady Cardish's parents were close friends of the old duke and were privy to the heartbreak of Reggie's parents, this is not gossip. While writing this letter I received a telephone call from Lady Cardish. What I am about to write is in the strictest confidence: The Norbury estate is expected to go up for auction in the New Year. Lady Philippa's wedding was brought forward before the Duke of Norbury's estate collapsed completely. It is thought that the Burton's have no idea of their daughter-in-law's family ruin."

James raised his hand to stop Anna reading. "That explains the rushed wedding. The Burton's think their son is marrying royalty and have no idea about the scandal that is about to break."

"Um," Anna said as she scanned the remainder of the letter. "The Burton's wanted the prestige and an invitation into the royal inner circle, as do many of the nouveau riche. It doesn't sound as though this duke can do that. I don't like the sound of this." She looked at James and read, *"In answer to your*

question, the Duke and Duchess of Norbury are genuine. The above explains
their behaviour.

*The duke is as poor as a church mouse. Be very careful about how much they
spend on this wedding. It is unlikely that he can pay his bill. I would also caution
you not to be taken in with titled guests. Wedding invitations were sent to several
hundred people; the majority declined. Most of the guests with the exception of
the Burton's guests are from Reggie's circle of friends, who may be titled and
appear affluent but their bank accounts are barren. The lesser known titles sponge
off unsuspecting friends and acquaintances. The duchess is not an unsuspecting
victim. She bribes their acquaintance, and the duke pays the bills to appease his
wife. The problem is that it would appear the duke has no funds."*

Anna closed her eyes. Resting her elbows on her desk, she put her chin
on her clasped fists. Her throat constricted into a ball as the seriousness of
the situation sank in; several hundred pounds could go unpaid.

"We need payment. This wedding was supposed to give the hotel a
financial boost not plunge us into ruin. However, I am concerned about the
hotel's reputation. Dissatisfied guests with wagging tongues, for whatever
reason, can do as much harm."

"Anna, I don't think it will ruin us but it will make a nasty hole in the
financial statement, which Mr. Nitty will question."

"I have no intention of allowing these privileged toffs to take advantage
of us. We have to be creative." Anna sighed, took a breath, and laughed a
sneaky laugh. "That's it! Reputation. Their reputations are the key. James,
make the invoices for all of the guests and have the bellboy deliver them
by hand in a public place immediately after the wedding. I think these
hangers-on have money; they just prefer to spend other people's if they can.
Leave the rest to me."

"And the duke's bill for the wedding? I haven't added it all up yet but with
the dinner and wine, the flowers and extras it will be in excess of £300, a
considerable sum." James handed her a list.

Anna pointed to the subtotal. "Make an interim invoice today, for this
amount £245. The balance, we'll bill him when we have a final total. Insist
he pay it tonight. Make sure if there is an argument, it is at the reception

desk, not in the office. Call me; I'll be waiting in the office. Don't worry, I'll sort, *His Grace*, out."

James raised his eyebrows. "Rather you than me."

Anna smiled, not feeling as confident as she appeared. But she was determined that the hotel was not going to suffer at the hands of some small minded, dishonest, entitled royals.

The bride and groom set off on their honeymoon with cheers from well-wishers and family. The official festivities over, Anna watched the guests gather in conversation groups in the lobby, lounge and bar. The duke and duchess had settled in the lobby lounge, across from the reception counter, with Mr. and Mrs. Burton. Anna's satisfied grin filled her face. "Couldn't be better," she said under her breath.

She decided to save the Duke's envelope until last, and sent the bellboy to deliver the bills to the parasite guests first. One by one, they approached James at the reception desk, whispering that there was a mistake; His Grace would be paying the bill. James politely informed them that His Grace had advised the hotel that guests were responsible for their own accommodations.

It wasn't long before the duke and the Burtons realized there was a problem. The duke excused himself and approached James, who was keeping busy sorting papers. Anna listened and watched the complaining guests try to push envelopes into the duke's hand. The duke politely returned the envelopes, and making no attempt to quieten his voice, he said, "Gentlemen, it has been my pleasure to entertain, wine and dine you at my daughter's wedding. I thank you all for sharing in this wonderful day." He leaned in towards the gentlemen, nodding at other guests as they passed and said, "Gentlemen, rest assured you assumed incorrectly that I would pay your bills. If you have embarrassed yourselves with insufficient funds I suggest you take it up with the hotel management."

Anna held her breath and glanced at James, who stood motionless. The silence was charged with anger emanating from four red-faced, huffing gentlemen. She let out a long breath as one of the group stepped forward, wrote a cheque and handed it to James; others followed. The duke walked towards his wife and sat down, resuming his conversation with the Burtons.

James picked up the last envelope and approached the duke. "Your Grace, the invoice to date."

The duke frowned, obviously displeased. "This is most irregular, Mr. Lytton. I prefer to discuss this later and in private."

Anna was taking a risk. She had breached protocol by delivering the bills and asking for payment in public. Any financial transactions would normally be discreet at the reception desk and any dispute would be settled in private. The duke had embarrassed his guests into paying. He must be aware she was doing the same to him. Secretly, she had relished the duke finally getting the spongers to pay up. For all his faults, the duke was the victim of circumstances.

"Your Grace, forgive me." Anna pushed in front of Mr. Lytton and took the envelope from his hand. Acknowledging the Burtons and the duchess she said, "Please excuse us. Your Grace, if you would follow me into the privacy of my office." Anna had decided to change tactics.

The duke was angry; Mr. Lytton had embarrassed him in front of the Burtons. Embarrassing him further by demanding payment in the lobby would not be forgiven either by the duke or observing hotel guests, undoubtedly putting the hotel's reputation in jeopardy. James stood with his mouth wide open as a thunderous duke followed Anna. She sat at her desk and realized Belle Thornton's letter was in plain view. About to slide it out of sight, she instead decided to leave it out, with the Thornton coat of arms prominently displayed.

"Please accept my apologies for Mr. Lytton's behaviour." She hated blaming James for her idea but she had no alternative. She took the invoice and glanced at it. "I need to check this. Please excuse me for a moment." Anna left her office, deliberately closing the door. She had seen the duke glance at Belle's letter and was sure he would read it while she was out of the room.

James glared at her. "What are you doing?"

"I'm sorry, I know I changed plans on you. I'll explain later."

Anna opened her office door and took one look at the duke's pallor and poured two glasses of brandy.

"Thank you, Mrs. Blaine. He pointed to the letter. You are acquainted with Lord and Lady Thornton?"

"Yes, I knew Lord Thornton's mother well. My husband became close to Lord Darcy Thornton and his wife when he lived in Chicago."

He swallowed the brandy in one gulp. "And Lady Cardish?"

"I have never met her." Anna felt sorry for the duke. He had the look of a naughty boy having been found guilty of a mischievous crime, his crime being the bankruptcy of his estate. She felt his despair, she saw his eyes moisten and realized he was a caring man with poor judgment that people, including his wife took advantage of.

"You know?" he said.

Anna nodded.

"Do the Burtons?"

"No, you can rely on my discretion. I won't insult you with lies, Your Grace. Your wife was spending a great deal of money and billing it to the hotel…" Anna hesitated, wondering how to word her next comment. "And I just wasn't sure who you were."

The duke smiled briefly. "A duchess traveling without a lady's maid, who was actually acting as the bridesmaid and a duke without a chauffeur or valet."

"Something like that, although I didn't realize the bridesmaid was Her Grace's lady's maid. Please understand that I have a business to run. This is our fledgling year and I can't afford for bills to go unpaid."

"Perhaps if I ran my estate as a business, things would be different." The duke pulled a chequebook from his pocket. "The hotel did a wonderful job for Philippa's wedding. The staff has been kind and efficient, especially Mr. Smyth."

Anna bristled at this remark. "Mr. Smyth, what exactly did he do?"

"As you are aware my wife lacks the finer subtleties of a society upbringing and at times can be demanding. Mr. Smyth lavished her with attention and he made her laugh as he steered her away from disaster several times. It may surprise you, but I love my wife and it is nice to see her treated with respect. And for my daughter it was important to me that she had the wedding of her dreams and to be married to a man who will care for her. The next few months will be difficult for her as the estate is sold."

"What will happen to you and your wife?"

"We still have the London townhouse. Our social life will be over. Maud will be devastated." He ripped the cheque out and handed it to Anna. She hesitated. "Mrs. Blaine, I promise you the cheque will be honoured by the bank."

"Thank you. I'm glad we had this conversation. I can't imagine what it's like to know your life will disappear under the auctioneer's gavel. You have my deepest sympathy and I, most sincerely, hope you are able to find a new path."

"You have been very kind, Mrs. Blaine. Thank you. Now I must get back to my guests. We will be leaving early in the morning." Holding the door open, his face pleaded with Anna.

She smiled. "My lips are sealed."

Isabelle Vulnerable

I t was unusual for Anna to close her eyes again when the alarm clock woke her at five. In fact, it was unusual for her not to be awake before the alarm. She felt Bill cuddle up with a contented sigh. She turned, smiled and kissed each closed eye. "Time to get up. You're as tired as me."

"Um, I could stay here all morning." He wrapped his arms around her. "I love you more each day. How many days are there in thirty-five years?"

"It's far too early for arithmetic and there were some pretty big gaps in those thirty-five years." They laughed and Anna soaked in his warmth. Her desire was as fresh and intense as it had been all those years ago. She slid her leg over his, pressing her lips between his neck and shoulder. "But I know what you mean."

Bill gently brushed a single curl from her eyes. She stared, feeling herself plunge into his aqua eyes; his caressing hands took her breath away.

Anna sat up. "No, Bill stop, this morning sex is becoming a habit." She laughed. "It's a pity we're so darn tired at night. Listen, I think I hear Sarah and the kitchen will send out a search party if you don't show your face soon."

Bill laughed. "Not quite. My new sous-chef, Dave, is young but quite competent." Bill jumped out of bed and began dressing. "I am pleased with his performance and cooking skills. He did well over the wedding rush."

"Does that mean you will take some time off now and again?" Anna said, pulling on a bottle green skirt.

"How's your day today?" Bill asked.

"We have the meeting this morning. The wedding was our first big event and I want to talk to everyone about what went well and where we need to make changes. One of my goals is to have the staff take pride and participate in the overall success of the hotel. I'm meeting Isabelle afterwards to review the Christmas bookings. James and I need to go over the accounts in detail. I want to make sure we made a profit from the wedding." Anna stood in front of the mirror and smoothed her skirt.

"Why the big sigh?"

"Oh, I'm losing my figure. I can't say I like this getting old."

"You look perfect to me. Hey, I used to have hair on my head, and now this." Bill pointed to his paunch. "If I keep this up I'll look like Chef Louis."

"As long as you don't develop Chef Louis' temper, I'm fine with a few extra pounds." She patted his belly playfully, making him laugh.

"Can you do everything this morning? I'd like to take the afternoon off."

"Maybe. James can wait until tomorrow, which might be better anyway, after he's been to the bank."

"Meet me in the dining room and we'll have lunch together. I have to go, it's nearly six o'clock. I'll see you at ten. Your office?" Anna nodded as Bill opened the door almost bumping into Isabelle.

"Good morning Mum, Bill." Turning to Anna she added, "Bill's late this morning."

"We both slept in." Anna felt her cheeks flush slightly. She coughed. "I'm tired from the tenseness of the last few days. And here comes another sleepyhead." Sarah walked down the hall in baby-doll pyjamas, rubbing her sleepy eyes. Anna bent down and kissed her.

"Time to get ready for school. Hurry up and get dressed."

Amy Peterson was the first to arrive for the meeting. Anna had a fondness for Amy and enjoyed the opportunity of being alone with her. Amy's tiny frame made Anna think of the early days at the Sackville. She remembered a laundry maid surrounded by steam puffing from a hot iron. Now she stood before Anna in a trim black skirt, neat white blouse and high-heeled shoes. The only hint of her work was a bunch of keys dangling from her waist. Life had not been kind to Amy, from her orphaned childhood to Mr. Pickle's rape and violence, but she was a survivor and amongst all this she had married, had two children and worked her way up to the position of the Sackville's head housekeeper. Now in her late forties, she was a strong woman and an excellent housekeeper. Other than stature, there was nothing tiny about Amy.

"How did you manage our first big event?"

"No problems that I am aware of. The maids worked well and I didn't receive any complaints from guests."

"No doubt due to your management and training. Housekeeping runs smoothly because of you. I am grateful."

"I had to step in on behalf of a couple of the younger maids who received unwanted advances from male guests." Amy shook her head. "I quickly put them in their place."

Anna smiled. "I bet you did!"

"I was a little afraid they may twist it and complain to you."

"Never let the guests intimidate you. I would like to know of any incident involving inappropriate behaviour of either the guests or the staff. If anyone complains, I'll let you know, but please know that I trust your judgment. We both know the maids need protecting."

"I can handle it."

"I know you can. We have both been victims of sexual violence and I don't want any of my staff to suffer, and that includes silly maids who are flattered by the attention from these devious men. So, please keep me informed."

"Of course."

James interrupted as he brought in some extra chairs and took a seat. A waiter followed with a tray of tea, coffee and biscuits. Amy sat down next to James. Anna gathered some papers from her desk and greeted Bill. Peering around the door into the lobby she said, "Where are Isabelle and Ralph Smyth? Miss Jenkins, please tell Mrs. Wexford and Mr. Smyth we are waiting for them. And bring your steno pad and take a seat. I'd like you to takes notes." Anna took her seat. Bill poured coffee and they waited.

A loud peal of laughter came from the lobby and Isabelle swung into the office, her red skirt flounced as she entered. Her hand adjusted a matching red kerchief at her neck, she pressed her fingers to her lips and gave a shrug, wiping the grin off her face. "Oops, sorry we're late." A smug-looking Ralph Smyth closed the office door behind him and pulled the chair out for Isabelle and took the seat next to her.

An awkward silence fell over the office as eyes tried to avert from Isabelle and Ralph Smyth. Anna glared at them both, cleared her throat and began talking.

"I called this meeting for two reasons. First of all, I want to thank you all and secondly to allow each department to understand the challenges and responsibilities of the other areas of managing the hotel.

"Lady Philippa's wedding was our first major event and a success, thanks to everyone. Please make sure you thank all your staff for a job well done. I will go around the table and ask each of you to say a few words. Point out the things that went well and where we need to improve, and if there was an opportunity for one department to help another. I am also open to new ideas and to how we can improve the service to our guests. Miss Jenkins will take notes, which will be typed and circulated after the meeting."

An hour later Anna called the meeting to a close, pleased with the enthusiasm and fresh ideas. Her goal of getting the staff involved was a success and everyone left the meeting inspired.

Returning to her desk, Anna motioned to Isabelle to sit down. She had not liked the display of familiarity between Isabelle and Mr. Smyth, especially in front of the staff.

Isabelle sat down and glared at her mother. "If you are going to comment on Ralph and I being late for the meeting, don't."

"Really! I thought our meeting was to discuss Christmas bookings and activities. But now that you mention it…" Anna paused. "It was an awkward moment. Flirting among the staff is discouraged; you and Ralph Smyth giggling like school children did not set a good example. Isabelle, what were you thinking? And that dress is more suitable for the Palais de Dance than work."

"I'll dress how I like." Isabelle looked somewhat contrite. Anna thought the outfit was for shock and nothing more. But she couldn't help wondering why the change in dress and behaviour. She wondered if it was Ralph Smyth's influence?

"I don't trust Ralph Smyth. There is something sneaky about him. And I don't like how familiar you are with him."

"It is none of your business, Mother."

"In this hotel it definitely is my business. You may be my daughter but you are also an employee. If you want any chance of becoming a business partner in this hotel you will need to behave in a businesslike manner. Isabelle, it is hard enough for women in business these days; we have to compete with men and be better than men and that includes earning respect from male employees. How can you expect Ralph Smyth to respect your authority if you flirt with him? One day you could be his boss. Attitudes take a long time to change."

"Oh, you may have a point, I'll be more careful." Isabelle thought for a moment. "But, Mother, I have to say, I do think you are being dramatic. Ralph and I are just friends."

"Being friends is still too much. It's important you keep your distance from employees. Speaking of friends, has Ralph mentioned his friend Balaji, one of the new waiters."

"Balaji is a good waiter, but I don't think they are friends beyond work. Mother, your imagination is running away with you. Ralph makes me laugh; there is nothing more."

"Maybe that is so, but too much familiarity can be misinterpreted by staff and guests. Just remember you are a married woman."

"Sandy and I…well let's just say things are not good and I'm not the only one having fun."

"Sandy always seems so stable. Is something going on in Scotland?"

Isabelle shrugged. "Sandy is a pretty boring person but he gets along well with my friend Judy." Isabelle rolled her eyes. "A little too well." Anna saw a brief shadow of sadness and Isabelle's eyes moistened.

"When Sandy arrives for Christmas, you need to spend some time together, have some romantic dinners. Take Sarah to Eastbourne, be a family again." Anna thought about how she and her friend Sophie had struggled with the Bill and Alex relationships. "I have more experience than you may think. I can help. We should talk about what is going on in your life."

"I can manage my own life, thank you Mother."

Anna felt the hurt of the familiar barrier, but afraid for Isabelle she continued. "Long distance relationships are difficult. Why don't you sell the house in Edinburgh? Sandy could look for a job near here; engineers are always in demand. If not Bexhill, maybe Eastbourne?" Anna hesitated. When Isabelle remained silent, she took the opportunity and continued. "The offer is still open to convert the fourth flour into a family apartment or Sandy might prefer a house in Bexhill."

"Stop! Mother, stop." Isabelle brushed her hand across her cheek. Anna frowned to see her daughter's eyes full of tears.

Isabelle lowered her voice, "Just stay out of my life. Things happened in Scotland and I don't want to talk about it. As you said earlier, I'm here to discuss the hotel's Christmas bookings. Let's get on with it."

The meeting transitioned to business, although Anna had difficulty concentrating. The hotel was close to capacity for Christmas and New Year's. As Anna had hoped, several of the wedding guests had booked for the holiday season. Isabelle had a vast line-up of activities planned, including a local choir to sing carols around the tree every evening.

Content that Isabelle had everything under control, Anna met Bill in the dining room.

It was unusual to see Bill in the dining room dressed in a suit. He smiled as Anna approached the table. "I thought the meeting went well this morning." Bill put his head to one side. "But you don't look happy. Is everything all right?"

"Yes and no. I am pleased with the meeting this morning. Isabelle has some fabulous activities planned for Christmas and we are ninety percent booked for Christmas week and about seventy percent for the week before and after."

"Then why so glum?"

"Isabelle. We had an argument. I can't talk here."

"Ah! About Mr. Smyth, no doubt. I agree that was rather awkward. Enjoy your lunch and we'll talk about it this afternoon. I fancied a walk along the Promenade. If it's not too cold."

It was a crisp sunny day; the sky bright blue and the sea calm. Even the wind was little more than a breeze, quite unusual for December. Bill and Anna walked hand in hand, silently enjoying the fresh air and solitude.

Bill spoke first. "What is going on with Isabelle and Ralph Smyth?"

"She tells me they're friends. I don't know whether to believe her or not."

"I don't trust Smyth. I sense he is taking advantage of her. Why is she so vulnerable at the moment?"

Anna related her conversation with Isabelle adding, "I made it clear to her that behaviour like today will not be tolerated. I think she understood. But I'm worried. Something happened in Scotland between her and Sandy but she wouldn't say what."

"Sandy arrives in a few days. I expect they will sort things out."

"Honestly Bill, I'm not sure." She shook her head and guided Bill to a bench. "The sun feels warm, too good to be true for this time of the year. Sometimes I feel that way about the hotel. I'm waiting for disaster to hit."

"We are doing well. A good Christmas season is just days away. We'll make enough profit to see us through until Easter. I think we are past the worst. The Emily Carr Restaurant is doing well, even in the slow times there are enough bookings from outside the hotel to make a profit. Isabelle has several corporations booked for March. She is doing a great job of selling. It was a good decision to bring her on board."

"You're right. The economy is picking up. I would like to see rationing stopped. How does that affect the dining room?"

"Not much. I'm used to working around it. The King's Head was far worse."

"I can't stop thinking about Ralph Smyth. I told you about his friend Balaji. Isabelle says they don't know each other, but I know what I heard."

"I agree. But he's a very good maître d'. And didn't you say Lord Norbury had high praise for him. I can't fault his work. I'll had James look into his background, and Balaji's, and see if there is connection that would explain the strange behaviour. Now, will you stop worrying and enjoy the afternoon?" Bill pulled her close and she laid her head on his shoulder and listened to the tinkling pebbles as the waves receded from the beach. She thought about the contrast of how the seas had always been grey and stormy when she and Alex walked along by the beach and with Bill it was calm.

"It'll be five years since Alex and I made a toast to the New Year. Time flies." Anna said.

"I still miss him." Bill stood up and they walked towards the pavilion. "I wonder if Alex is why Isabelle is vulnerable at the moment. Perhaps it's the time of year. She took Alex's death really hard."

"Maybe. But Alex didn't die until March."

"True, but it was a dramatic Christmas season, between Alex's illness and Robbie being shot down. It was a Christmas I will never forget." A sudden gust of wind whipped the waves and blew clouds over the sun. Anna shivered as they reached the closed pavilion. "Remember having tea here?"

"Yes, a hot cup of tea sounds good. It's getting cold.

Christmas 1948

The day before Christmas Eve, Sarah waited at the main door all day for her father to arrive. She sat in Albert's chair, watching him carry suitcases and brightly wrapped boxes to the brass luggage trolley. The bellboys were smiling and obliging in their neat green uniforms and round hats with red trim, all of them young, anticipating generous tips as they escorted guests to their rooms. Sarah played a game, trying to guess what was in the boxes. She liked talking to Albert, but today he was busy and by lunchtime she was getting bored.

The Christmas tree was spectacular, full of twinkling fairy lights, silver icicles and brightly coloured baubles. Isabelle appeared with an arm full of parcels. "Sarah, help Mummy put the presents around the tree."

Sarah's eyes lit up. "Are any for me?"

"No, these are for the guests. Arrange them nicely. I'll go and get some more from my office."

Sarah shook the parcels as she placed them carefully under the tree. She wondered where her presents were and if Santa Claus had read her letter. She had asked him for a set of paints and a colouring book, and a puppet—a real puppet with strings to make its arms move and legs walk.

"Sarah! What are you doing? I told you to arrange them nicely under the tree." Sarah looked at her mother and then at the colourful boxes. "I did."

"It's a mess Sarah." Isabelle clicked her tongue as she moved the parcels around and rearranged everything.

"Let me help." Sarah knelt down pushing a box under the tree.

"I'll do it." Isabelle gave an exasperated sigh. "You go and play." Sarah's eyes filled with tears and she ran towards Albert, tripping and knocking the tree. Albert caught Sarah before she fell; the tree wobbled and several baubles fell to the floor.

"Now look what you've done," Isabelle yelled.

Sarah burst into tears. Anna came from her office, just as a glass bauble crashed to the floor breaking and scattering shards of fine glass in the carpet. The tree gave one last wobble and thankfully stayed upright. An audible sigh of relief spread throughout the lobby. Albert had told Sarah to sit in his chair out of the way.

Anna scanned the scene. "Isabelle, what is going on?"

"Sarah was fooling around and almost knocked the tree over."

Sarah looked embarrassed. "Nana, I'm sorry. I didn't mean to."

"It's okay, sweetheart, accidents happen. We can fix this." Anna was getting tired of Isabelle's short temper and the way she treated Sarah. "Isabelle, it is not the end of the world." Anna wanted to add and don't yell at your daughter, she doesn't deserve that. But she would wait until they were in her office. "I'll have Amy send a maid to clean up. Albert, make sure the guests stay away from the broken baubles. She glanced over to the reception counter; both James and Miss Jenkins were busy. Isabelle, go and help at reception. I'll find Woody to make the tree more stable."

"I have work to do." Isabelle pursed her lips.

"Do as I ask please." Anna leaned towards her and whispered, "I know you are under stress but don't take it out on Sarah or the staff. Talking to the guests will take your mind off Sandy's impending arrival."

Isabelle moved to the reception counter and Anna went to find Woody.

Albert instructed a bellboy to guard the tree while he greeted the arriving guests. Sarah had stopped crying and joined Woody, who was securing the tree. She liked working with him; he was fun and made her laugh. The tree secured, he picked her up and sat her on his shoulder so she could attach the new baubles to the higher branches. Perched on Woody's shoulders she suddenly shouted, "Daddy!" Woody lifted her down and she ran to greet Sandy as he climbed the portico steps.

The family ate dinner together that evening. Anna had insisted, knowing everyone would be busy on Christmas Eve. Even Bill stole some time from the kitchen to welcome Sandy. Anna was both relieved and surprised that Sandy and Isabelle were getting along. Balaji, who had joined the permanent staff, served the family. Anna was pleased that Mr. Smyth was doing his job as maître d' and leaving Balaji to serve tables.

Christmas Eve was magical. The choir sang around the tree all day while guests and staff hummed various carols. Anna arranged for the guests to be transported to St. Andrews Church for midnight mass, and upon their return Bill served hot toddies, cocoa and brandy with sausage rolls and slices of pork pie, with mince pies and Christmas cake for sweet. Each guest received a present from under the tree. It was three in the morning before Anna and Bill crawled up to their suite.

"We have four hours of sleep before the family arrives for our Christmas morning." Anna yawned.

Bill caught the yawn saying, "I have arranged for Dave to do breakfast, so I don't have to be in the kitchen until nine. Our breakfast will arrive here at eight."

Bill headed for the bedroom and Anna added a few presents under the tree.

Anna awoke to an excited Sarah jumping by the bedside. "Happy Christmas, Nana, Grandpa. Look what I found in my stocking." Sarah held up a box of paints and a sketch book. Mummy and Daddy are getting dressed. Can you get up now?"

Anna looked at the time, seven, and was pleased that she had managed to sleep past her usual 5 AM. "Did you look under the tree?"

"I did and I can't wait to open my presents. *Please* get up, Nana."

Bill and Anna dressed quickly, just as Sandy and Isabelle came in, followed by Balaji wheeling a steaming trolley full of breakfast. Sarah was allowed to read the labels on the parcels and hand them out. Santa had been very generous. The last present to be opened was Sarah's Santa present. She pulled the ribbon and ripped the paper, and opened the oblong box. "My puppet! Thank you Santa." Sandy helped her undo the strings and hold the criss-cross bars. She wiggled them to make the arms and legs of the little girl move. The puppet's name was Heidi. Heidi had blonde pigtails and was dressed in a straw hat and a white dress covered in daisies. "She even has boots," Sarah squealed, picking up the puppet's feet.

"What a lovely Christmas morning," Anna said, satisfied that her family was together. Sandy and Isabelle's coolness was hard to ignore, although tempered somewhat by their daughter's pleasure. She felt the smooth lapis in the blue pendant. She didn't wear it often these days, but at times when she missed loved ones—Uncle Bertie, Papa and Mother, and Alex—it seemed to bring them all together.

Bill finished his coffee. "Time to get to work. Happy Christmas everyone, I doubt I'll be finished until late tonight. Anna, a word please?" Bill guided Anna to the bedroom and handed her a blue velvet box. "Happy Anniversary, our first of many." Anna opened the box, an eternity ring circled in tiny diamonds twinkled. Bill placed it on her finger. For our eternity, my lovely Anna."

"It's beautiful. Thank you." She wrapped her arms around him and they kissed. Bill gently moved them apart. "I have to go. See you later." Anna walked him to the door and kissed his cheek.

Isabelle stood behind them and smiled as Anna showed her the ring. "An anniversary present."

"Oh Mum, I'm sorry. In the holiday fuss I had forgotten and now I must go. I planned a treasure hunt for the children this morning." Isabelle kissed Anna. "Happy Anniversary Mum. Sarah, do you want to come?"

"No, I want to stay with Daddy."

"Sarah, I expected you to join in with the guests. You can play with Daddy another time."

"No I can't. You'll send him away," Sarah pouted. Silence followed, Isabelle breathed in as though to speak but scowled instead.

Sandy broke the tenseness. "What time is the treasure hunt? I'll bring her and we can all join in."

"It's for children. It doesn't include you."

Sandy gave Isabelle a "stop-this-now" look. "That's fine, tell me what time and I'll bring Sarah down to join in."

"The children assemble in the lobby at eleven-thirty." Isabelle left without saying goodbye.

Relieved the argument had not escalated, Anna saw Sandy's sadness. She wanted to say something but decided it was better not to interfere. "Sandy, I have to check on the guests. I gave Miss Jenkins time off to be with her family. I'm afraid a hotel Christmas is work for us."

"Don't worry, Mother. We'll have fun. I have a lot of catching up to do with my little girl who is not so little these days. You are growing up far too quickly." Sarah nodded enthusiastically.

The festive atmosphere fueled Anna's ego. The New Sackville was a success. Those leaving after Christmas made tentative bookings for next year; others extended their bookings to the New Year's Celebrations, which promised to be a sell-out. Bill had prepared a six-course meal, with a buffet at midnight. Dancing until the wee hours, streamers and balloons, and of course champagne.

Darcy and Belle Thornton with their son, Felix, were their guests for New Year's, a difficult time of year for Anna and she appreciated the comfort of friends. The closer it came to New Year's Eve, the more Anna thought about Alex. It wasn't like the King's Head Inn, where everyone knew him and toasted him with fond memories. The only staff members, who remembered him were James and Amy. Amy would be with her family but James was close to Alex and would be at the hotel. Anna had a plan.

The New Year's Eve party was a sell-out; extra tables had been brought in and every seat was occupied in the Emily Carr Dining Room. The dance floor so full that dance steps were small and intimate. Anna had invited her personal guests to be near the bandstand at midnight. She ordered trays of the best Scotch whiskey and champagne to be brought in to the room at five minutes to midnight. Anna stepped onto the stage and spoke to the bandleader. The music stopped and she stepped forward, one hand on the blue pendant around her neck and the other held a glass of whiskey.

"Ladies and Gentlemen, thank you for coming to The New Sackville to celebrate the ringing in of a new year, 1949. Tonight is a special night for me. Many years ago, before the First World War, I worked at the Sackville, where I met both of my husbands. I married Alex Walker and we moved on and bought a pub, the King's Head Inn in Rugby. Alex became ill and died. The New Year's Eve before he died, he asked me to grieve for a short while and then marry his best friend, Bill." Anna beckoned to Bill to join her on the stage, "And then get on with my life and be happy. His only request was that every New Year's Eve we toast his memory with a good Scotch whiskey. He was a Scotsman and loved a good party. All the patrons at the King's Head knew him well and every year we toasted his memory. Here at the Sackville, there are few who would remember him. You are all acquainted with his daughter, Isabelle," Anna beckoned to Isabelle and Sandy, "and her husband Sandy. Mr. James Lytton, our general manager, was a good friend to Alex. At the stroke of midnight, I invite you to join me in a toast to Alex. He would be so proud to see you all here tonight. Please help yourselves to either whiskey or champagne. We have two minutes to go." Anna nodded to the band to play as they counted down the seconds. A roar of "HAPPY NEW YEAR" filled the room, trumpets blew, squeakers squealed and streamers floated in the air, wrapping around anything they landed on. Anna waited for a lull and raised her glass. "To Alex." Anna kissed Isabelle and wiped a tear.

Isabelle smiled and said, "Dad would have liked that." Bill kissed Anna and guided her to the dance floor and whispered in her ear, "Well done. I was wondering how we would toast Alex this year. He would have loved this party. This dance is for him."

"He would have liked being back at the Sackville. I wish he was our maître d'." Anna felt Bill pull her closer. She rested her head on his shoulder, and whispered, "Speaking of maître d', I just saw Isabelle and Ralph Smyth sneak out of the room holding hands. Where is Sandy?"

"He's at the table talking with Julia."

The mood broken, Anna pulled back from Bill. "I think we have a problem."

"I agree." Bill led Anna to the table.

"Where is everyone?" Anna said, studying Sandy and wondering if he had seen Isabelle go out with Ralph.

"Belle and Darcy are on the dance floor and Isabelle went to the powder room. Julia was telling me about life in the American South. It's so different from here."

"It certainly is. You should ask Bill about his life in Chicago." Bill nudged Anna and shook his head.

"Not really a part of my life I'm not proud of." Bill glanced at Julia. "I need to check on the buffet. I'll be back in a minute."

Isabelle in the Eye of the Storm

⁓᧞⳽᪥⳾᧞⁓

The buffet table had a forsaken after-the-party look about it, the savoury section littered with empty serving dishes, chocolate and strawberry mousse spilled in ugly globs on to the white cloth of the sweets table. The silver coffee urn was cold and empty. Balaji was alone, trying to clear away used plates; Bill grabbed him by the sleeve. "What is the meaning of this? Where is Mr. Smyth?"

"I think he went to get more chocolate cake and fruit salad." Balaji shuffled his feet. "He'll be back any minute."

"This table is a disgrace. Clean it up and send a waiter for more coffee and I'll find Mr. Smyth." Balaji hesitated. "Do it, now!"

It wasn't like Bill to lose his temper with staff, but he was angry and embarrassed. His feet bounced as he marched out of the Emily Carr dining room through the baize door to the kitchen. As he passed the staff room he saw Isabelle and Ralph in what looked like an embrace. Anger burst from Bill. "What the hell are you two doing?"

Isabelle leapt backwards knocking the Welsh dresser. "We needed extra napkins. The spare ones are kept in this cupboard."

Red faced and ready to explode, Bill took a deep breath, not sure whether to reprimand Isabelle and send her back to Sandy or tear strips off Ralph Smyth for the messy buffet table.

"Mr. Smyth, the buffet table needs your attention, it's dirty and empty.

Balaji is alone and he needs help to clean the table. Where are the waiters?"

"I sent the temporary waiters home. I thought we could manage. I'm sorry, Chef."

"That was a mistake Mr. Smyth. Pay attention to your work." Bill's eyes flipped to Isabelle and filled with hurt and anger. Smyth quickly stopped a passing waiter and lead him into the kitchen.

"Isabelle." Bill frowned and shook his head. "What are you thinking? You are a married woman with a child. Your husband is upstairs waiting for you. Smyth is an employee. Need I say more?"

"Uncle Bill," the endearing term took Bill by surprise and he calmed down as he realized how vulnerable Isabelle was at the moment. "Ralph is a nice man. He makes me feel good. Sandy and I are having problems."

"You won't solve them by embracing another man. Go back upstairs and join the table. Here, take a tray of cheese and tell them you were helping me. Tomorrow you and Sandy have to talk this through." Bill's stare challenged Isabelle. "Promise me!"

The grandfather clock chimed the half hour, Anna looked up, three-thirty. She yawned as she and Bill walked through the baize door into the lobby. She smiled at Henry sitting bolt upright in his doorman's chair. The polished brass buttons on his green greatcoat reflecting the prisms of light from the chandelier, his white-gloved hands placed neatly on his thighs. The only indication he was sleeping was his gentle rhythmic snore and his head slightly bent to the right, pushing his peaked cap over his eyes. She whispered, "Good night, Henry."

The lift gate clanged in the now silent hotel. Bill pulled the lever for the third floor and placed his hand around Anna's waist. Yawning, she leaned on him as they walked to their suite. Suddenly angry words sputtered from Isabelle and Sandy's room.

Sandy's voice said, "I saw you! Hand in hand as you walked out of the room. Don't deny it. You didn't go to the powder room, you went for a snog, with Mr. Smyth—love-crazed teenagers. I see how he looks at you."

Isabelle's voice screamed back, "Are you any better? What's going on with you and Judy?"

"Nothing is going on. She's just a friend, and your friend too."

"You expect me to believe that when I get letters from Judy saying what a wonderful time she had at the theatre with you. Oh, and how was dinner?"

"Isabelle, stop being silly. I told you I took her out for her birthday."

Anna and Bill stopped outside their door. Bill pointed to Isabelle's door, which was ajar, allowing the argument to spill into the hallway. Shocked and embarrassed, Anna stood rooted to the spot, torn between pulling the door closed and letting Isabelle and Sandy know they had heard the row or leaving it open for all to hear.

"Sandy, it's over. I want a divorce."

"What! No, Isabelle. We can work this out. What about Sarah?"

"Sarah will stay with me. The solicitors can arrange visiting privileges or whatever they do. I'm going to bed." Isabelle's voice grew louder, "You can sleep on that couch." The door slammed shut. The voices now muted, Anna and Bill closed their door.

"I am afraid for them. Isabelle, Sandy and Sarah. I don't understand. Is she having an affair with Ralph Smyth? Sandy is a good man. It doesn't make any sense."

"I wasn't going to tell you but obviously, based on what we just heard, Sandy saw Smyth and Isabelle walk out of the dining room tonight…" Bill hesitated, "I caught Isabelle and Smyth embracing in the staff room tonight. I sent him back to work and had a talk with Isabelle."

"What shall we do? A divorce in the family. And Sarah, what about Sarah?"

"Darling, there is nothing we can do. It's Isabelle's, life not ours. I am too tired to talk about it." Bill rolled over and fell asleep. Anna lay on her back, trying to process the evening's events. She thought of Alex and wondered what he would do; remembering how Alex had indulged his daughter, she decided Alex's solution would probably make it worse. She couldn't help thinking that Smyth had manipulated this whole thing—but why? Perhaps she should fire him, but on what grounds? Cavorting with the bosses' daughter, a willing partner. No, she thought that would not work, she'd lose Isabelle altogether.

The hotel felt like the morning after the night before. Usually bustling with guests and staff by seven or eight in the morning, it was already nine and those few that were about crept quietly. Anna was having trouble concentrating and went into the dining room for coffee. There were only three tables occupied. She sat down and rubbed her eyes, swollen from lack of sleep. Balaji approached her table and poured coffee. "Good Morning, Mrs. Blaine. How are you this morning?" Anna looked at him and wondered how he could be so cheerful. "I'm well, but tired. How are you? You had a busy night last night."

"Thank you for asking. Balaji grateful to work at the Sackville, no sleep good for me."

Anna smiled at Balaji's English with Indian cadence. "What happened at the midnight buffet? Mr. Blaine was quite upset."

"I apologize. Guests very hungry. Mr. Smyth had trouble."

Balaji turned to leave.

"What kind of trouble?"

"It's good, now resolved. Mr. Blaine put it right." Balaji moved away quickly. Anna watched him. He was a good waiter and she liked him. He treated the guests well, but she suspected he knew more about his friend Ralph Smyth than was apparent.

"Good morning, Anna. You look how I feel this morning."

"Mostly lack of sleep. Come join me, Belle. Where is Darcy?"

"A little too much brandy last night. We had room service bring breakfast and he went back to sleep. Felix has gone off to explore Bexhill, at Sarah's request. She is showing him the sights. I thought I'd join you for coffee. I have to say, this hotel is the only place in England that knows how to serve coffee." They both laughed. "Bill's influence from his Chicago days, no doubt."

"A wonderful party last night. I'm so glad we came. Why the frown? You should be elated that the whole hotel is buzzing with how marvelous everything is at The New Sackville Hotel. Not many hotels can brag about such success in the first year. What's troubling you?"

"My daughter is having marital problems. Honestly, I don't know what to do. She has always been willful and spoiled, but right now her behaviour is bad even for Isabelle." Anna lowered her voice, "There's a problem with Mr. Smyth, the maître d'."

"I thought there might be. I saw the subtle glances last night."

"Sandy saw…" Anna stopped as Smyth poured Belle's coffee. "Mr. Smyth, we've changed our minds. Lady Thornton and I will have coffee in my office, and send some shortbread and Christmas cake."

"As you wish, Mrs. Blaine."

"Belle, we'll chat in my office."

Mr. Smyth clicked his fingers to a waiter and shot a venomous stare towards Anna's back as she left the restaurant. Anna, momentarily lost her balance, Belle caught her elbow.

"Anna what is it?"

"Not sure. My goodness, I really must be tired."

The waiter placed a tray on the coffee table. Anna poured, offering Belle a sweet treat.

"Shortbread. Does Bill make it here?"

Anna nodded, munching on fruitcake. "I love this office. I often sit here watching the people on the Promenade and the waves roll up and down the beach. It's clear today, but storms start brewing right there on the horizon." Anna pointed out to sea. "I watch the stormy darkness approach as it consumes the sun and blue sky."

"Is that how you are feeling now? The darkness of your daughter's indiscretions in the centre of the brightness of the hotel's success."

"Spot on. I am at a loss. Last night I overheard her ask Sandy for a divorce. Never an easy child, Isabelle and I have had our difficulties. But an affair with an employee?"

A tap on the door and Bill's head appeared. "Am I intruding, or is there a spare cup of coffee in that pot?"

"Come in. I was telling Belle about Isabelle."

Bill sighed. "What do we do? Anna is convinced there is something mysterious about Smyth. I don't see anything mysterious. However, he was distracted last night and I have no doubt that Isabelle was the distraction. He wasn't watching the waiters and the buffet table was a mess. I wish I knew more about him."

Belle and Anna said in unison, "Darcy!"

Heads turned as the office door opened. "Did I hear my name?"

"Darcy, perfect timing," Bill pulled another chair up to the coffee table.

"We want you to get to know Mr. Smyth."

"Me? Why?"

"Remember sitting on the bench near the service entrance, talking to me when I was a mere under-chef? I spilled out all my worries and you told me how good I was and to look for work where I would be appreciated. Gosh, that must have been in 1915. I sat on the bench thinking, "Why am I talking to this toff?""

Anna looked surprised. "That was the year I married Alex and when you moved to The Grand Hotel. I didn't know it was you, Darcy, who encouraged Bill to leave The Sackville. But I do remember Bill telling me how you kept popping up in strange places."

"Darcy, you were easy to talk to. I'm not sure how easy Smyth will be. He keeps to himself. Not just private—he's secretive."

"I've had an idea," Anna said. "We might not be able to reach Smyth but Balaji is very friendly."

"How will that help?" Belle asked.

"Balaji and Ralph Smyth knew each other before they came here. I heard Balaji greet him as Ravi. It could have been Ralphie, a familiar term one would expect between friends. But since then, they've pretended they didn't know each other before."

"What do you want to know?" Darcy took a bite of shortbread. "Oh, this is good."

Anna answered, "I want to know where he came from, what is his connection to Balaji and why is he trying to woo my daughter."

"I'll see what I can do. If you will excuse me, I need to find my son."

95

Everyone except Belle and Anna left the office. Sitting side by side, Belle patted Anna on the arm. "Don't look so worried. Darcy will get you answers."

"I know. I worry about Isabelle. Do mothers ever stop worrying?"

"No. I worry about Felix all the time. He's bright and clever but prefers to fool around rather than study. He's already had an extra year at school and I'm not sure if he'll make it to Oxford this year. Darcy will be disappointed."

"We both need a break. The sales start in Eastbourne tomorrow. I'll ask Isabelle if she wants to join us. Now I had better get back to work."

"Good idea," Belle replied, leaving Anna's office.

Shopping had always been one of Isabelle's favourite pastimes so it was no surprise to Anna that she agreed to come to Eastbourne. She drove Bill's Hillman Minx and Belle sat in the front, giving her the opportunity to chat. Anna sat quietly in the back.

"Isabelle, I am impressed by your marketing skills. Some of the Christmas activities were amazing. Watching the children run around the hotel on a treasure hunt on Christmas morning made me think that some children's programs might bring more families to Hillcrest. I could do with your help."

"I would be happy to help. What is it you want to do?"

"I opened a small gift shop at Hillcrest, but I'm not sure what to sell. It didn't do too well. I have an inventory of cheap souvenirs that no one wants."

"Your visitors don't want cheap, they want high quality souvenirs that reflect Hillcrest Hall's culture. How much money do you want to make?"

"We have to find ways to bring in substantial revenue. The expense and upkeep of the house and estate are far beyond what the tenants and farming income generates. We opened the house up to the public last year and both Darcy and I are overwhelmed by the public response. Darcy can't understand why anyone would want to view the way he lives. Being an American and fascinated by the British gentry before I met Darcy, I understand completely."

"If you were a visitor to Hillcrest, what would you like as a memento?"

"I'd never thought of looking at it that way. I would like a china cup and saucer. If I was a wealthy American, I would probably buy the whole tea service, but it would have to be the same pattern I had seen in the house."

"You answered your own question."

"Isabelle, would you come down to Hillcrest and suggest what I should be selling in the store and help me design some children's programs?"

"I'd love that. I could bring Sarah down at Easter." The car slowed to a crawl and Isabelle pulled into a spot by The Grand Hotel.

Anna Threatens Mr. Smyth

～⚬❧⚬～

While the women were exploring Eastbourne, Darcy went to work. The dining room was empty, the day after New Year's Day most guests had eaten early and were on their way home. Woody was repairing a hinge to a door on Balaji's service station. He looked up. "Breakfast over, sir."

"I know I was looking for Mr. Smyth or Balaji. Do you know where they are?"

"No sir, Woody mending door."

A voice bellowed from behind Darcy. "Woody, I've told you before not to talk to guests." Ralph Smyth gave a loud sigh. "I don't know why you work here."

"Sorry, Mr. Smyth." Woody put his head down, turned the screwdriver one more turn and scurried out of the dining room.

Darcy frowned. "I'm afraid I am the culprit. I was asking Woody where you were."

"He's a simpleton. I don't know why Mrs. Blaine puts up with him. How can I help you, Lord Thornton?"

"Mrs. Blaine is a kind employer." Darcy examined the new hinge. "Woody does a good job. Calling him a simpleton is a bit harsh, don't you think? I wouldn't let Mrs. Blaine catch you saying such things."

Smyth repeated, "How can I help you, sir?"

Suddenly Darcy realized he hadn't thought of what to say and criticizing him was perhaps not the way to start. "I like to thank the staff personally and I am curious about the work you do. You run the dining room well, Mr. Smyth. Where did you get your training?"

"I worked in London for a time." Darcy waited for him to continue. "At the Dorchester and the Savoy."

"I'm impressed. The New Sackville is a good hotel but it's not the Savoy or the Dorchester. What made you want to work as a waiter? You have a cultured voice. I would guess you were educated at a good private school. Not too many Rugby or Harrow old boys finish up waiting tables."

"Rugby actually. I enjoy the work and I have personal matters to attend to and The New Sackville suits my needs."

"My son is in his final year at Rugby. Your friend, Balaji did he go to Rugby?"

"Balaji is not my friend, he's a waiter here. Please excuse me, Lord Thornton, but I have work to do. Why all the questions?"

"Just being friendly. You are a strange man, Smyth. I would say you are harbouring a secret."

"Sir?" Smyth frowned.

"By the way it isn't a good idea to flirt with the bosses' daughter."

Smyth face glowed red. Darcy couldn't tell if it was guilt, anger or embarrassment. Before he could comment, Darcy said, "Good day, Mr. Smyth."

Darcy walked up to the reception desk. "Miss Jenkins, do you have a copy of today's *Telegraph*?" Darcy took the newspaper and tucked it under his arm. "Miss Jenkins, would you ask Balaji to bring a pot of coffee and some of that delicious shortbread to my suite."

"I'll have it sent up right away, sir."

"I particularly want Balaji to bring it to me."

Miss Jenkins frowned. "Of course. I'll see if I can find him."

Darcy nodded to other guests as he climbed the stairs, preferring some exercise to taking the lift. He felt the greyness of winter and turned on the lamp by the sofa. Glancing at the sea—also grey, reflecting the clouds—he wondered if a storm was brewing in the English Channel.

A voice from beyond the door called, "Room Service," and Balaji carried a tray to the coffee table in front of Darcy.

"Shall I pour, sir?"

"Yes, please. Balaji, how long have you worked at the Sackville?"

"Since Mr. Blaine hired me for the big wedding in early December. I was temporary staff but honoured to stay for the Christmas season and hoping to stay permanently."

"You're a good waiter. I am sure you will have that opportunity. I'll put a good word in for you with Mr. Blaine."

"Thank you, sir." Balaji gave Darcy a big smile. "I am most grateful."

"I was talking to Mr. Smyth earlier this morning. I understand you knew each other before you came here."

Balaji stopped pouring. "Is that what Ravi, I mean Mr. Smyth, said?"

"You look confused. You either know him or not."

"We worked at the Dorchester together when Ra…Mr. Smyth was only a waiter."

"You must know him well if you are on first name basis. I thought his first name was Ralph but you called him Ravi, that's an Indian name."

"I don't know, sir." Balaji continued pouring coffee.

Darcy laughed. "I remember Mr. Blaine giving me that same look many years ago when he was the under-chef at this hotel. I was visiting my mother, Lady Thornton and needed to talk to someone. Bill was sitting on the bench in the courtyard and I joined him. I'm not much for the stuffy British class system. I like to get to know people."

"You are complimentary, sir. But I grew up in service in India." Balaji frowned. "Mr. Blaine used to be sous-chef and now owns the hotel?"

"Yes, he worked hard like Mr. Smyth who went from waiter to maître d'. Does he come from India too?"

Balaji looked over his shoulder as if expecting someone was following him. "Ravi swore me to secrecy and I don't know why. Our mother's worked on the same estate, for a British family and we went to school together. My father worked at the tea plantation, but I never met Ravi's father. When his mother died of fever he changed and became angry. It was unusual, but the family took care of him. If they hadn't, he would have been a beggar on the street. I heard my mother say she thought Sahib might be his father. Ravi was anything but grateful—he hated them. The family sent him to England to go to school, but we kept in touch. Ravi helped me pay for my passage from India and found me a job at the Dorchester. He has been kind to me and a good friend, but I didn't see him again until here. I came here to work at the wedding. I've said too much. I must go. Mr. Smyth will be looking for me."

"Thank you, Balaji. You have been very helpful."

Balaji gave Darcy a worried look. "If Mr. Smyth finds out I talked to you, he will fire me."

"I won't say a word, and if he attempts to fire you, go and see Mr. Blaine or Mr. Lytton. You will not be fired."

Darcy drank his coffee and relished in the luxury of Bill's melt-in-your-mouth shortbread, mulling over his conversation with Balaji. Mr. Ralph Smyth certainly had a secret but Darcy wondered if it was big enough to warrant such strange behaviour or was there more. By the time he had read the paper, it was close to lunchtime. He and Bill had arranged to spend the afternoon together after the lunch rush and before the ladies returned from shopping.

Bill enjoyed getting out of his own kitchen and eating food he hadn't cooked. They walked to the old familiar Fisherman's Nook that had taken on a more sophisticated look since Nosey had passed away. His legacy lived on in the excellent ale and steaming mussels.

"I managed a conversation with both Mr. Smyth and Balaji today," Darcy said opening the pub door to a thick haze of smoke.

"That was fast. What did you find out?"

"Your Mr. Smyth certainly has a past we didn't know about. It seems he grew up in India." Darcy continued to relate Balaji's story.

Bill rubbed his forehead. "Interesting, but why so secretive? He must have his reasons for not wanting us to know his past. What do you think?"

"Mr. Smyth was born and raised in early childhood by an Indian mother who worked on an estate, father unknown. But with his white skin, his father might well be English. Balaji implied hanky-panky on the estate, which would explain his public school education after the death of his mother.

"Things are pretty rough in India. Anna and I were shocked at what we experienced during our honeymoon. If Smyth was known to be a half-caste, he would have been ostracized. That's what he's hiding. I bet his English father sent him here to keep him out of danger."

"It sounds plausible, Bill, but we are guessing. And what bearing does it have on his employment at the Sackville?"

"You're right. Smyth's attitude indicates more than just hiding a past. It's almost vengeful" Bill frowned. "Against who though? His friend Balaji, who knows more than he's telling? I don't see animosity there. The only place I see it is with Anna. He doesn't like taking orders from a woman, and he knows Anna does not approve of his flirting with Isabelle."

"Maybe we need a private investigator."

Darcy raised an eyebrow. "Kind of sleazy, don't you think?"

"My experience with Paddy O'Reilly in Chicago was not sleazy at all. PIs have a way of uncovering the deepest of secrets. But I'm not sure it would work here." Bill looked at his watch. "We'd better get back ourselves. Dave will need a break before we start dinner."

Attacking Anna

~~~~~~~~~~~~~~~

I sabelle stopped the car under the portico. Albert opened the rear door for Anna and the front door for Belle. Isabelle had already opened the boot and was handing parcels to the bellboy.

Eyeing the parcels being piled onto the cart, Albert smiled and said, "Ladies, how was your trip to Eastbourne?"

"A great deal of fun, and expensive," Anna replied, turning to Belle and Isabelle she added, "I have some work to do, so I'll see you two at dinner. Be a dear, Isabelle and put my shopping in the suite for me." Isabelle nodded as she joined Belle in the lift.

"Will you join me in my suite for a cocktail? I'd like to talk about Hillcrest."

"I'll drop mother's parcels off and be right there. Pour me a dry martini, I'm parched."

Belle unlocked the door to her suite, leaving it ajar for Isabelle. She poured herself a sherry and mixed a martini for Isabelle while she contemplated how she was going to approach the subject of Ralph Smyth. Just as concerned as Anna, Belle wanted to warn Isabelle of the dangers. Knowing Isabelle's fiery relationship with her mother, she had decided she should intervene. She placed the glass on the side table just as Isabelle walked into the sitting room.

"Which shall we tackle first, the gift shop or children's activities?" Isabelle said taking a sip from her glass. "Cheers!"

"Cheers." Belle smiled. Ignoring the question, she said nothing.

"Is something wrong?"

"Isabelle, I admire your talent for merchandizing and I do want your help at the estate, but there is something else I would like to discuss."

"Oh and what is that?"

"I'm going to be blunt. Mr. Smyth."

Isabelle's face turned to thunder, her cheeks red and her jaw dimpled with tension. Her pursed lips barely moved as she responded, "My mother has put you up to this. Ralph and I are friends, nothing more."

"For you that may be true, but Ralph…he has other motives."

"Like what?"

"He is not a nice man. Believe me, I have met my share of disreputable men and Ralph is definitely one of them. I don't know what his motives are, but rest assured his friendship with you is to serve his own purpose."

"What is it with you and mother? He's a friend. He makes me laugh."

"He's the kind of man who will hurt you. Putting his affections aside, Isabelle, you are married with a daughter."

"I don't see what that has to do with it."

"It has everything to do with it. Don't think your little fling goes unnoticed. Both guests and staff are well aware that something is going on between you two. Whether it is true or not, it's what people perceive that is the reality. Flirting with staff is frowned upon in any work place. How can your staff have respect for you and your authority when they see you blatantly break the rules?"

Isabelle calmed down, the tension left her face and she became quite pale. "I see what you mean."

"One day this hotel could be yours. At the very least, Bill and your mother will bring you in as a partner. What happens then? How will your friendship with Ralph be perceived by other employees and how much respect for your position will you get from Ralph? This isn't about you and your mother, it is about you and your position in the hotel."

"Mum said the same thing. I hate it when she interferes in my life and, anyway, this is about Sandy."

Belle stared at Isabelle, her forehead creased questioningly. "Sandy? I don't understand?"

"I think he's cheating on me with my friend Judy. I wanted to get my own back."

"I find it hard to believe that Sandy would do anything like that."

"So does everybody else, but it's true."

"Are you flirting with Ralph to punish Sandy, or is it to upset your mother?"

Isabelle fidgeted in her chair. Picking up her glass, she focused intently on her drink before taking several sips. "I know there is something going on. I can tell by Judy's letters. She tells me about how kind he was to remember her birthday and how she enjoyed the theatre."

"And what does Sandy say?"

"Not much. He said he took her to dinner for her birthday and he happened to have a spare ticket to the theatre."

Belle frowned. "That doesn't sound like an affair to me. But to be honest Isabelle, unless you patch things up it may well become an affair."

"See, I told you he's having an affair." Isabelle picked up her drink and finished it one gulp. "I'm going to change for dinner."

Belle stood up and grabbed her arm. "Please consider what you are doing and think carefully before making rash decisions. Flirting with Ralph Smyth is folly and will hurt a lot of people and no one more than you."

Isabelle shrugged, releasing her arm. "Enough Belle! I see your point. I intend to keep my distance from Ralph from now on. I want to own this hotel one day. Sandy is a different story. I want a divorce."

"Please try and work things out. What about Sarah and your reputation?"

"Sarah, I worry about. I don't care about my reputation. Divorce isn't the scandal it used to be."

"If you want ownership in this hotel, you do indeed need to worry about your reputation."

One foot out of the door, Isabelle turned and looked at Belle. "Do you really think being divorced would affect my work?"

"Perhaps. But I think living in the hotel with your husband and daughter as a family would be beneficial. Take up your mother's offer to build an apartment on the fourth floor. If Sandy is with you, he's not taking your friend Judy out, he's taking you out to the theatre or dinner. All I ask is you think this through and talk about it to someone. I'm a good listener."

"Belle, I would like to talk to with you. But promise you won't judge me and can we keep it between the two of us?"

"I promise I won't tell your mother and in exchange I do want some advice on generating revenue for the estate."

"I'm looking forward to a visit to Hillcrest, Belle. Thanks." Isabelle closed the door. Belle sighed, not entirely convinced that Isabelle would do the right thing, but she hoped her drive to succeed in the hotel business might help her come to the right decision.

It was a rare evening when Bill joined the family for dinner, but with a competent sous-chef and the hotel quiet after the Christmas rush, Bill and Anna arrived in the Emily Carr dining room first. Balaji greeted them and pulled the chair out for Anna. As she sat down, she saw Isabelle whispering intently to Mr. Smyth. Isabelle had her back to her but Anna could clearly see Mr. Smyth's face and he was angry. More than angry, he was controlling his rage. Anna shivered. She had seen that look before and it scared her. She jumped and gasped as she felt a tap on her shoulder.

"Anna, what is wrong?" Belle touched her arm frowning.

"Oh, sorry. I was miles away." She looked at Belle and directed her eyes to Isabelle and Mr. Smyth.

Belle whispered, "I think I know what that is about. We had a talk and Mr. Smyth is history."

Anna raised an eyebrow. "That is good news. Here she comes, we'll talk later." Bill arrived, giving Anna a quizzical look. She shook her head slightly, not wanting Bill to ask questions. He nodded an understanding, smiled and stood up to greet Isabelle. "You look wonderful. Is that a new dress? Green brings out those sparkling eyes."

"Thank you. Yes, I bought it this afternoon." She twirled around the full skirt flaring out in soft waves, showing a frilled white petticoat.

Anna saw the cute little girl she remembered playing with Alex. "You always had an eye for pretty things. You used to twirl like that for your father when you were little. The dress suits you well."

Isabelle blushed and sat next to Bill, glancing towards Mr. Smyth, which did not escape Anna, causing her to shiver again as she felt his stare on her.

"Where's Darcy?" Bill asked.

"Right here," Darcy said.

Bill laughed. "How do you do that, Darcy? I've never known anyone pop up like you do."

"Ha, ha! I don't know," Darcy said, sitting next to Belle. "I apologize for being late. I was on the telephone with my estate manager. A bit of a problem with one of my tenants." He took Belle's hand in his. "I'm sorry dear, but it looks as though we'll have to leave tomorrow."

"Oh no. Can't you stay, Belle?" Isabelle pleaded.

"I am tempted, but I have a lot to do before Easter when we plan to open to the public. The gift shop is quite the challenge. Isabelle I'm counting on you to be our guest and help me organize the gift shop."

"I can't come until Sarah's school holidays at Easter. Will that be too late?"

"No, I'll make do with what I've got until you arrive at Hillcrest."

"Ah, mulligatawny soup. This is new to the menu, so your comments please," Bill said as Mr. Smyth placed a steaming bowl in front of Belle.

"It smells wonderful," Belle replied.

Mr. Smyth served Isabelle next and leaned towards her, a little too closely. Isabelle stiffened and glanced up to see if her mother was watching but she seemed deep in conversation. Mr. Smyth moved to the service station and took another steaming bowl of soup. Glaring at Isabelle as he approached, he didn't see Anna reach for her wine glass until it was too late, and when he pulled back, the hot soup poured into Anna's lap.

Bill jumped up, helping Anna to her feet and holding the hot soup-soaked dress away from her skin.

"Oh Mrs. Blaine, I am so sorry. "

Bill interrupted, "What the hell were you doing?" Bill's face was almost purple and his hand trembled.

Anna took a deep breath to ease her stinging legs. "It's all right, Bill. I'll go and change."

"I'll come with you. Isabelle can you go down to the kitchen and get the first aid kit and bring it to our suite?"

"Is Mum going to be all right?"

"Yes honey, I just need the kit." Bill turned back to Mr. Smyth. "Get this mess cleaned up." Mr. Smyth beckoned to an assistant waiter. Bill put his hand up. "No. Mr. Smyth, you will clean up the mess. Balaji, please show our guests to another table. You will be serving us tonight. Mr. Smyth, after you have cleaned this up you are relieved of your duties."

"But, sir!"

"You heard what I said. I'll speak with you later." Mr. Smyth's face darkened with humiliation and anger.

Bill helped Anna to their suite and she undressed, exposing bright red patches on her thighs.

"Stay where you are. I need to treat those burns."

Anna gave an unconvincing laugh. "Since when did you become a doctor?"

"Burns are something I deal with every day in the kitchen. Now lie back on the pillows and try to relax."

Bill disappeared and came back with cold wet towels and laid them across Anna's legs. She winced. "I'm sorry but I need to cool off the burns. It may stop them blistering. They don't look too bad, but they will be sore for a while."

"I need to get changed, our guests are waiting."

Isabelle arrived with a large white tin box and handed it to Bill.

"Mum, are you all right? Ralph...I mean Mr. Smyth, was staring at me and not paying attention."

"What's wrong with him?"

Isabelle looked sheepishly at her feet. "I think it might be something I said."

Bill gently removed the towels and patted Anna's legs with a dry towel.

"Isabelle, what did you say to him?"

"I told him our friendship was inappropriate and starting immediately he was to address me as Mrs. Wexford at all times. He laughed and said 'You've been talking to your mother.' I walked away and joined you at the dinner table. I could see he was angry."

"Angry enough to hurt me?" Anna took a sharp breath as Bill placed gauze over the burns.

"There that will stop your dress rubbing. Are you sure you want to go to dinner?" Bill kissed her forehead. "Darcy and Belle will understand."

"I'm fine. It feels much better. Bill, go and join our guests, they will be worried and hungry. Go ahead and start the soup." Anna smiled. "I think I'll pass on soup tonight. Isabelle will help me dress and we'll be down shortly."

Bill glanced from Anna to Isabelle. "If you're sure?"

"Yes, now go!"

The suite door closed and Isabelle looked at Anna. "Mum, I can't tell you how sorry I am. I'm not making excuses but I can't believe he would do this deliberately; he was always kind to me, although I often found him to be driven by something and I had the feeling that it had something to do with you, but he would never talk about it."

"Deliberate or not, he wasn't paying attention. He should have seen me pick up my wine glass. However, he blames me for your change of heart. What changed your mind?"

"I had a long talk with Belle and she confirmed your theory about damaging my reputation in the hotel."

"Well, I'm pleased you came to your senses. Now, let's change the subject and enjoy the evening. Pass me the blue dress with the scoop neckline and pleated skirt. The material is soft and won't be heavy on my legs."

Mr. Smyth

✦

After dinner, Belle and Darcy went to pack, Isabelle took Anna up to the suite and Bill went to the staff quarters to find Mr. Smyth. Even before Bill knocked on the door he sensed the room was empty, but knocked again to be sure. "Mr. Smyth!" He opened the unlocked door and glanced around the room. He remembered the space. This had been Alex's accommodation and nothing much had changed. The iron bedsteads had gone, replaced with a divan bed and a warm eiderdown had replaced the heavy horsehair blankets. A black maître d's suit was lying on the bed. *He must have changed,* Bill thought. Anna had added a comfortable armchair and side table in all the staff rooms. The washstand with the mirror over it still stood on the only straight wall, but a portable record player now sat where the jug and washbasin had been. Several records lay next to it and Bill bent his head to read the labels: *Some Enchanted Evening* by Perry Como, *Nature Boy* by Frank Sinatra.

He likes the crooners, Bill thought and began whistling *Some Enchanted Evening* and then stopped as he recalled Isabelle humming that same song. Not unusual he thought until he spotted her red kerchief hanging on the back of the washstand. Isabelle had been in this room. He stooped, around the dormer window, remembering how Alex had not been able to stand straight due to the sloping roof ceilings. The same desk sat in front of the window. Several airmail letters addressed to Mr. Smyth were scattered on the desk. Bill turned one over to see the return address: Calcutta, India. He picked up a photo of a beautiful Indian woman smiling with gentle kind eyes, draped in a sari, and a family resemblance to Mr. Smyth. "She must be his mother," Bill said aloud, placing the frame back on the desk. His eye caught some thin writing paper with the words *Dear Father, I hope you are keeping well or as well as can be expected. In my last letter I said I hoped to visit you again in the summer. It looks as though that might be sooner. I made a big mistake this evening and I think my position here will be terminated. It is not what we had planned. I'm sorry…* A large ink spot obliterated the next words and there was no more writing.

Hearing movement in the corridor, Bill left the room and quietly closed the door. Woody's door was open and Bill tapped lightly. "Woody, have you seen Mr. Smyth this evening?"

Woody came to the door and opened it wide. He looked nervous, and stared down at his slippered, shuffling feet. "Mr. Blaine, is something wrong?"

"No, no, Woody, everything is fine." Aware of Woody's nervous disposition Bill hurriedly tried to calm him. "Mr. Smyth is not in his room and I wondered if you had seen him."

Woody nodded. "Mr. Smyth very upset. He yelled at Woody on the stairs."

"Do you remember what time that was?"

Woody smiled. "Woody knows exactly what time." Woody was such a gentle soul Bill thought, and numbers were his friends. Of course, he would know what time he saw Mr. Smyth. Woody added, "It was eight-fifty-seven, Woody always in his room by nine."

"Thank you, Woody, you're a good man." Woody smiled, blushed slightly and closed his door.

Bill ran down the four flights of service stairs to the staff room, which was empty. He could hear activity in the kitchen, meals for late diners still being prepared. Balaji came out of the kitchen carrying a platter of sweets.

"Balaji have you seen Mr. Smyth?"

"Mr. Smyth was very upset by the incident in the dining room. He's very remorseful."

"Balaji, you are a good friend but what happened should never have happened. You're a waiter. You know that."

"Yes, Chef. I saw him leaving by the back door about nine. He said if anyone asked, he was in his room."

"Well, he's not in his room."

"I'm sorry, Chef. I don't know where he went."

"When you see him, tell him I was looking for him and I'll meet him in my office at eight in the morning."

"Chef, I might not see him but I can leave a note in his room."

"Thank you, I would appreciate that, Balaji."

Bill climbed the service stairs and went into the bar, where he found Darcy.

"I thought you were packing?"

"I usually leave that to my valet, but as Harris didn't come with us this time, I let Belle do it."

"You still have a valet?"

"Not really. Since Gordon passed on, our new butler, Harris, acts as valet if I need one. But his butler duties require him to stay on the estate." Darcy sighed. "Can I buy you a drink?"

"Yes, I'll have a brandy."

"How is Anna? I am assuming you have fired Smyth."

"She's sore but I'm hoping the burns won't blister. And no I haven't fired him yet. I can't find him. Balaji said he went out. He left his room unlocked and I took a look inside. The photo of his mother confirms Balaji's story, and there were airmail letters from India on his desk, so he has connections or friends in India. There was a half-written letter to his father. I thought Balaji said he didn't know his father."

"Interesting. Well, if he left personal things I would imagine he intends to come back."

"He's an experienced waiter. I didn't see what happened. Did you see anything?"

"No I was listening to you. I'm used to being waited on and I don't pay attention to servers."

"What time are you planning on leaving tomorrow?"

"Around nine or ten, after breakfast."

"I'll see you at breakfast. Good night."

Anna woke to a commotion outside. She looked at the clock, ten minutes to five. "Bill, are you awake? What is that noise?"

"It sounds like a fight." Bill jumped out of bed and peered through the heavy curtains. "A bunch of youths scrapping. Drunk probably. They're moving away." The noise stopped. "Time to get up. How are you feeling this morning?"

Anna stretched. "Ouch! A bit sore, but not as bad as I expected."

Bill rolled the covers down from her legs and gently removed the gauze. "Most of the redness has gone. Is this where it hurts?"

"Ouch, yes."

"There is a blister there. I'll get the burn ointment." Bill reached for the first aid kit. "This might sting a bit. I'm putting a light dressing on to stop it rubbing."

Walking down the hall towards the lift, Bill began to chuckle. "I'm sorry to laugh but you look as though you lost your horse." His expression changed to worry. "Is it that sore? Perhaps you should stay home today."

Anna laughed, enjoying Bill's warmth. "No, it just catches a bit between my thighs. I'll stay in the office today. I won't be walking around much." They both laughed.

Henry, the night porter greeted them as they exited the lift. "Good morning, Mrs. Blaine, Chef. There was a bit of a scuffle outside earlier. It woke..." he cleared his throat, "they ran off as soon as I opened the door."

"We heard them," Anna replied, smiling at Henry's slip of the tongue. He was usually snoozing when she came down in the morning.

Anna pulled the curtains open in her office. It was still dark, the moon hidden in clouds. The sun would not be up for another hour or so, if at all. The sea was neither stormy nor still, and the iridescent white caps rolled over slowly and then bounced onto the beach. Anna sensed urgency. She moved to the chair behind her desk and a sharp pain shot down her thigh reminding her of Mr. Smyth. She gasped aloud, not sure if it was the pain or fear that aroused a terrible dread inside her. It was irrational, but she couldn't shake it.

"Penny for them?" Bill said, placing the usual tray on the corner of Anna's desk.

"I was thinking about Ralph Smyth. There is something about him…. Do you think he deliberately spilled that soup?"

"Honestly, I'm not sure. I asked Darcy but he didn't see it happen either. I went to his room last night to talk to him but he wasn't there. Woody said he saw him on the stairs and he had gone out. After yelling at Woody. Poor guy, Smyth really has it in for him."

"I'm surprised he went out. He had to have known you would be looking for him."

"He expects to be fired. There was a half-written letter saying as much on his desk, addressed to his father. And, I was disappointed to find Isabelle's red kerchief on the back of the washstand."

"Let's hope that is over now. I thought he didn't know his father? Not that it is any of our business. What are we going to do?" Anna asked.

"I've left a message for him to meet me in my office at eight this morning. Whether or not last nights' incident was an accident, Smyth has to go."

"I agree. Suggest he resign. If my daughter had not encouraged his advances, things might have been different."

"You may be right. The hotel will be quiet until June, giving us plenty of time to hire a new maître d'. Balaji can take over in the meantime. Do you want to be there and we'll do this together?"

"No, I'll let you do it. Be careful if he gets angry. In fact, I suggest you have someone close by in case he gets violent."

Bill frowned. "Anna, I think you are being paranoid." He bent and kissed her on the cheek. "Did I ever tell you how much I love you?"

"Yes, many times, and I love you for it. Now run along, I have work to do." She smiled, watching him pour her another coffee before taking the tray out and closing her office door. Bill always made her feel warm inside and she glanced out to sea, seeing a weak sun lift from the horizon, dark clouds gathering around it. A storm was coming; thick, sleet-filled rain began sliding down the window. Anna shuddered and pulled her jacket tight around her middle.

More Mr. Smyth

⚜

Bill stepped off the stairs into the service area, heading for the kitchen. The smell of bacon invaded his nostrils and he closed his eyes, relishing the aroma—he loved crispy fried bacon. When he opened his eyes he saw a sheepish, dishevelled Ralph Smyth standing outside his office door.

"Mr. Smyth, you are early." Bill looked at his watch. "It's only six-forty-five."

"Early, sir? I don't understand."

"I left a message for you to meet me at eight." Bill opened his office door. "Wait in here. I'll be with you in a minute." *He certainly appears remorseful this morning,* Bill thought as he handed his tray to Daisy, the dishwasher who stared at Smyth.

"Take a gander at that, Chef. 'Es bin up all night from looks of 'm." Daisy chuckled and scurried into the dish room. Bill had difficulty keeping his expression serious. Mr. Smyth in distress was a sight to be seen.

Migrating towards the aroma of bacon, he walked into the kitchen and called to Dave: "We have about a dozen guests in the hotel for the next few days, only do one roast of beef for tonight and cut back on the lunch menu. I'll leave that to you, Dave. I have an interview in my office. Please don't disturb me unless it's urgent."

"Yes, Chef."

Bill poured himself another coffee and stole a rasher of crispy bacon, savouring the crunch and salty flavour. "That's good bacon," he said to the prep cook, taking a second piece.

He rubbed his greasy fingers on his white coat as he entered his office. Mr. Smyth was drinking coffee, his hand shook and the cup rattled as he placed it on the saucer. "Mr. Smyth, you don't look well. A night on the town?"

"Yes, sir. I was upset after my mistake in the dining room. It has never happened before and it will never happen again, sir."

"No it won't, Mr. Smyth. In case I missed something, please tell me what happened?"

"I know I shouldn't have gone out but the incident had upset me so much I went to the pub and…"

Bill interrupted, barely able to control his voice. "I'm not talking about your drunken orgy. I don't care that you were upset and needed to drown your sorrows. I care that you poured hot soup on my wife."

"Yes, Chef. I'm sorry Chef." Bill backed off, the smell of sour alcohol made the bacon churn in his stomach. "I'm not sure what happened. I admit I was distracted and I didn't see Mrs. Blaine reach for her glass. When I pulled back, the soup spilled."

"And what was your distraction? As an experienced waiter, you know how aware you have to be at the table."

"I do know and I can't believe what happened. I am extremely sorry. How is Mrs. Blaine?" Bill thought he actually sounded remorseful.

"She is recovering."

"I know it's not an excuse, but my father has been taken ill. I received a letter yesterday morning and I am worried about him."

Surprised by Smyth's reason, but remembering the letter on his desk, it did sound plausible.

"Mr. Smyth, I am going to be blunt. It has not escaped me that you do not show Mrs. Blaine the respect expected from an employee and flirting with the owner's daughter is yet another breach of hotel protocol. The soup incident may have been an accident, but accident or not it should not have happened. If one of your waiters had had *this accident* what would you do?"

"He'd be dismissed." Smyth answered quietly.

"Give me one good reason why I should not fire you now?"

Smyth drew in a sharp breath, it was his turn for humiliation and Bill thought he saw moisture in his eyes. But was it an act or was he genuinely sorry? Sorry for whom?

Smyth stared at his feet and fiddled with the buttons on his jacket. "Sir, I have the utmost respect for Mrs. Blaine and I apologize if I have shown otherwise. I am not myself. My father had a heart attack and almost died and he is still very ill. Mrs. Wexford has been kind and I'm sorry if it has been interpreted as flirting." Smyth took his eyes off his shoes and stared at Bill. "Mrs. Wexford gave me no indication that I was being inappropriate." Bill couldn't argue the last statement but wondered why Isabelle had not mentioned his father's illness.

"Mrs. Blaine and I have discussed your behaviour, the incident in the dining room and your duties as a maître d'. We both agree that for the most part you are an excellent maître d' and the guests like you. However, under the circumstances we would like you to hand in your resignation."

Bill sat back in his chair and waited. The silence was so great that Bill imagined he could hear Smyth's mind turning over options.

"Chef, I don't want to leave the Sackville." Bill got another blast of stale alcohol and grimaced at the sourness as Smyth became agitated. "I'm truly sorry for what happened to Mrs. Blaine. Worrying about my father, I have taken my focus off the job. It won't happen again. Please give me another chance." Smyth's voice went up an octave and Bill wanted to smile with sweet revenge at this egotistical man pleading for his job.

"Balaji will take over your duties today. Go and clean up and sleep off the alcohol. If you are truly sorry, I want you to show it by apologizing to Mrs. Blaine. Meet us in her office at two this afternoon."

"Does that mean I keep my job?"

"No, it means I want you to apologize to Mrs. Blaine. Now get out of my office. Tell Balaji you are ill or something and ask him to take over until further notice."

"Yes, Chef." Smyth jumped up, almost running out of the office. Closing the door tightly, he leaned against it and whispered, "That was close." He moved down the passageway muttering, "I need to play my cards carefully if I'm to keep my job. I dread to think what the old man will say if I can't carry out his wishes, and if I'm not here I can't get Isabelle back. I know she's only pleasing her mother. Damn, why did I have to look at Isabelle at the very moment *she* reached for her glass?"

Bill rubbed his eyes and leaned back in his chair, wondering how successful he had been. Answering his own question he thought: not very. "In spite of everything, I suspect Ralph Smyth is going to be around for a while yet." Mentally weighing up what the consequences might be, he checked in on Dave in the kitchen. Seeing that everything was under control, he went up Anna's office.

Pleased to see Bill, Anna smiled and said, "So how did it go with Mr. Smyth?"

"I'm not sure. I asked for his resignation but I'm not sure we're going to get it. He gave me a sob story of his father being seriously ill and he asked for another chance. I let him assume not, but asked him to apologize to you and told him to meet us here at two this afternoon." Bill continued with the details.

"Mr. Smyth has a vulnerable side to him. Do you believe his story?"

"Anna, I don't know, he seemed genuine. Let's see what he has to say this afternoon. Time for breakfast, I am starving. The smell of bacon has been wafting by me all morning."

Balaji escorted them to the table where Belle and Darcy were waiting. "Good morning everyone." Anna sat and asked Balaji to find Mrs. Wexford. Sarah, dressed in her navy-blue school uniform came bounding into the dining room, followed by a subdued Isabelle dressed in a smart dark business suit and white blouse. "Breakfast is not my best meal, but I wanted to say goodbye. Belle, it's only a few weeks before Sarah and I will be at Hillcrest."

"Auntie Belle, I can't wait for Easter. Will you have rations for chocolate Easter eggs?"

"I'll see what I can do. Perhaps Mummy and I can find enough." Belle added, "I'll be so glad when this rationing business is over. As long as cook hasn't indulged in sugar while we've been away we should have plenty of coupons. Don't worry Sarah, you will have lots of sweets."

"Come, Sarah, or you'll be late for school." Isabelle took Sarah's hand. "I have some errands to run in town, so if I'm not back by the time you leave, have a safe trip and we'll see you at Easter. I'll see you later, Mum."

Anna smiled, her head bent with approval. "Isabelle, you look very smart today. I like that jacket. Bill and I have planned a meeting at two this afternoon. Can you come earlier? I need to bring you up to date before the meeting." Isabelle nodded.

At one-thirty Isabelle knocked and without waiting flung Anna's office door open. Bill was already there, in deep conversation with Anna. They both looked up. "Isabelle, what is it?"

"Sorry if I'm interrupting but I have some very exciting news. I just took a booking for Valentine's Day

"That's nice, but right now we are were discussing Mr. Smyth. Your mother has already told you that I met with him this morning and his excuse was he was distracted because his father is seriously ill. Do we give him a second chance or do we insist he resign? Did he mention his father's illness to you?"

"His father?" Isabelle's voice was sharp. She hesitated and added, "He might have said something, I don't remember. He didn't talk about his family, except he mentioned his mother had died when he was a kid."

Anna knew her daughter well and was convinced that Smyth's father's illness was a surprise to her. Anna kept her focus on Isabelle. "If we decide he can stay, can you maintain the employer-employee relationship with him? Bill told him we are aware of his flirtatious behaviour. He denied it, saying you had been kind to him and you were friends."

"I've been telling you all along we were friends. I am aware that even friendship is inappropriate and I have told him so. To answer your question, yes, I can maintain an employer, employee relationship. As far as I'm concerned, he can stay."

Anna stared thoughtfully at Isabelle but said nothing. Her thoughts were ambivalent. She wanted to believe Isabelle but something niggled her.

Isabelle ignored her mother's stare and paced the room. On the verge of laughing, she said, "In fact, we need Mr. Smyth. That Valentine's booking that I was telling you about is for Lord and Lady Cardish, friends of Belle and Darcy. It will be a big event. Belle has already told us that Lady Cardish moves in royal circles. We need a maître d' who knows what they're doing and, despite his short comings, the guests like him a lot. And for the record, I'm prepared to give Mr. Smyth the benefit of the doubt that the soup incident was a genuine accident."

Anna raised an eyebrow at Isabelle's change of heart. She looked to Bill to respond. "Well that forces the issue. There isn't time to hire and train a new maître d'. I was leaning towards giving Smyth a second chance. What do you think, Anna?"

"I hate to admit it but, under the circumstances, we need Smyth, but he doesn't need to know that. I suggest we offer him a month on probation, which covers Valentine's Day. He will report directly to James. I'd like an impartial opinion on his performance. He stays away from you, Isabelle. Is everyone in agreement?"

"Agreed." Bill and Isabelle answered in unison just as the office door opened and James and Ralph Smyth entered.

Bill did the talking, offering Smyth what they had discussed. Anna watched carefully. James accepted the added responsibility and Smyth seemed relieved to have another chance. Isabelle didn't attempt to look at him.

Anna asked, "Mr. Smyth, I understand your father is ill. Does he live close by?"

Smyth hesitated. "No, he lives in Devon."

"Would you like some time off to visit your father?"

"No, thank you. He is being taken care of at the moment." The corners of his mouth lifted, a fleeting secret smile that only Anna noticed.

Valentine Party

Anna was delighted at the prospect of a busy hotel in February, the quietest month of the year after November. She felt the old euphoria that she had experienced in her younger days during the Great War, when Mr. Pickles had had no choice but to put her in charge of the front desk. Mr. Smyth had settled, tending to his duties with even more diligence than before. James reported that his attitude towards staff had softened somewhat and he even had a good word for Woody. And most importantly, he avoided Isabelle. Anna wondered if she had judged him too harshly. Isabelle practically ignored him. Busy answering to Lady Cardish's requests, she remained focused on the Valentine's Party.

The morning before Lord and Lady Cardish were due to arrive, Anna and Bill walked through the lobby at their usual five-thirty. Henry was pacing by the front entrance instead of snoozing in his chair. His expression was troubled and he was rubbing his hands with agitation.

"Henry, is something wrong?"

"Mrs. Blaine, I'm worried. Twice during the night, the front bell rang. Thinking it was a guest late from an evening out, I opened the door and there was no one there. The second time was about five minutes ago and I saw two youths running away and a third one brandished something towards me—he appeared to be threatening me. He said something I couldn't hear and ran away."

"Should we call the police?" Anna looked at Bill.

"Henry, do you think they were serious or pranksters?" Bill asked.

"They looked like kids, pranksters, but they gave me a scare."

"If it happens again, don't open the door unless you are certain it is a guest, and call the police if it isn't. It sounds like kids not expecting anyone to answer."

Anna frowned as she walked to her office. "What is wrong with the youth of today? Out all night getting up to silly pranks. Where are their parents?"

"I don't know but I don't think they'll be back. Henry probably scared them away. I'm off, no time for coffee this morning; a big couple of days ahead."

"Good mornin'," a breathless voice called from the lobby.

"Good morning, Amy. Thanks for coming in early this morning." Anna frowned. "Have you been running? I said early but you didn't have to rush. I know you have a family to get ready in the morning."

"Oh no, Mrs. Blaine, everyone gets themselves up now. There were a gang of youths 'anging, I mean hanging, around the corner. They made me nervous so I ran a bit."

Hearing Amy's comment, Bill halted, his brow knitted with concern. "Must be the same kids that Henry told us about. Did they threaten you?"

"No, my past catches up with me sometimes and I overreact. They gave a whistle." Amy laughed, "Quite a compliment really, I don't get many whistles at my age."

"As long as you are all right." Amy nodded to Bill as he headed to the service door. Anna called after him, "Bill, ask Dave to bring us some coffee and toast please?"

Amy sat in front of Anna's desk and placed a clipboard on her knee. She ran her finger down the list. "All the suites are booked for tonight and tomorrow night, but I managed to keep Mrs. Wexford in her suite."

"Good." Anna didn't feel like having a confrontation with Isabelle. Although she had been more compliant lately, Anna was reminded that Isabelle's permanent accommodation still had not been resolved.

"And how many guest rooms are booked for tonight?"

123

Amy counted half under her breath, smiled and looked up at Anna. "Twenty tonight, fifty tomorrow night and fifteen are staying through the weekend and most of the suites are booked until Monday."

"Do you have enough staff? And does Bill know?"

"I called in three of our best regular summer maids. They are pleased to have the work out of season and I don't have to train them. I gave Bill the list a couple of days ago and I have spoken with Mr. Lytton to notify Mr. Smyth. The dining room will need extra waiters."

Anna led Lady Cardish to the Emily Carr Dining Room, where Isabelle was waiting for them. "Lady Cardish, may I introduce my daughter, Mrs. Isabelle Wexford."

"I'm pleased to meet you, milady. We have spoken many times on the phone and it is nice to meet you in person. Please, follow me. I hope the room is decorated to your liking. We still have a few last minute touches to add but I think…"

Lady Cardish interrupted with a gasp. "It is beautiful!"

Anna took a breath and glanced at Isabelle, feeling delighted as she saw the pride in her daughter's face. Pink, red and white floral arrangements, tastefully shaped into hearts, decorated the perimeter of the room, with small matching bouquets set as centrepieces on the tables. White napkins fanned in the shape of hearts contrasted the red tablecloths and at each lady's place setting stood a single red rose in a crystal vase and a mini box of chocolates. The stage where the quartet would play was draped in fine, soft, red and white fabric. The musicians were rehearsing and a pleasant Mozart waltz floated onto the dance floor. Anna closed her eyes for a moment, wishing she could dance. Opening her eyes, she saw Bill standing by the service door, he moved his arms as though he had a dance partner and they both smiled.

"Mrs. Wexford, I am extremely happy with the room. I don't know how you managed in these days of shortages, and the flowers are far beyond my expectations."

"Thank you, ma' lady. I see Chef Bill is waiting to see you." Isabelle beckoned to Bill.

"Ma' lady." Bill bowed slightly. "Do you have any questions about the menu?"

"No, I am looking forward to dinner. If it is as wonderful as the décor, which I'm sure it will be, I'll be delighted. Perhaps you could speak to Lord Cardish about the wine selection."

"I spoke to him a few moments ago." Bill looked towards the door and a tall stiff gentleman came striding towards the group and nodded to Bill.

Unbeknownst to the group, Sarah had crept onto the dance floor and was dancing to the music. Lady Cardish spotted her and clapped her hands. "Bravo, what a talented and delightful little girl." Sarah stopped dancing, glancing at her mother, not quite sure what to do.

"Lady Cardish, please meet my daughter, Sarah." Sarah stepped cautiously towards the lady. Looking at Isabelle she said, "Sorry. The music just started my feet tapping."

Lady Cardish laughed. "Sarah, I am very pleased to meet you. You are adorable and you dance beautifully."

"Thank you, milady." Sarah curtsied, holding her skirt. "I like dancing, especially in such a beautiful room. Don't you think it is pretty? My mummy and Mrs. Peterson made all these things; I helped with the red hearts."

"Sarah mind your manners. Lady Cardish is busy."

"You have a lovely daughter, Mrs. Wexford. And Sarah, the hearts are wonderful."

Lord Cardish drew closer and Sarah backed away in spite of his smile, his voice was deep and loud. "My dear, Brook is waiting for you."

"Robert, isn't this quite delightful?"

"Um." Lord Cardish gave the room a cursory glance. "Yes dear, it's quite lovely, but it's time we dressed. Your maid is waiting."

Lady Cardish smiled. "Thank you. My husband doesn't notice the finer points, but I assure you that if he had not liked the décor, he would have made his opinion known." She waved to Sarah as she took Lord Cardish's arm, exiting the dining room. Sarah waved back.

"Nana, is that lady a queen?"

"No. She is a lady, but actually she does know the Queen. Off you go and see if Dave has a snack for you in the kitchen."

Anna turned to Isabelle. "I think Sarah made an impression on Lady Cardish. As did you, my dear. She was delighted with your décor. Isabelle, I am ecstatic, it's amazing what you have done with this room. How did you manage the flowers and chocolates?"

"I called in a few favours and I found a supplier who has access to European markets. The chocolates are handmade by a lady here in Bexhill and Bill helped me figure out the coupons. I am pleased you like it. Now if you'll excuse me, I still have to finish decorating the stage."

The leader of the quartet, tapped his foot and said, "One, two, three," and lifted his bow. Mozart flowed from their strings.

Bill took Anna's hand and they began dancing. Anna closed her eyes, feelings Bill's warmth. He whispered, "Do you come here often?"

Anna giggled and squeezed his hand. "Every day, to see my lover." They both laughed. An enthusiastic clapping brought them back to reality. Anna blushed and Bill gave her a hug as they parted. Neither had seen Mr. Smyth and three waiters arrive to set up their stations.

Anna, blushed as red as the roses, excused herself and returned to her office. James Lytton gave her a strange look. "It's all right, James. Bill and I embarrassed ourselves with an intimate moment, dancing in front of Mr. Smyth and the waiters."

James chuckled. "Mr. Smyth would not understand such tenderness. I wouldn't be embarrassed. You and Bill have something special few of us ever experience."

"Thank you, James. It was a lovely moment but quite inappropriate."

The Valentine's party was still in full swing when Bill served the buffet of coffee and sweet treats at midnight, and the party showed no sign of subsiding as the dancing continued. The kitchen cleaned up everything except for the buffet and Bill let his staff go. He placed two glasses, a bottle of desert wine and a plate of chocolates on a tray and joined Anna in her office.

"Happy Valentine's!" Bill said. Kicking the door closed, he pulled Anna towards him, throwing her backwards and kissing her with great drama."

Gasping for breath, Anna said, "More please, Gregory Peck."

Laughing, Bill replied, "Shall we dance, Ava Gardener?" A slow waltz filtered into the office and they danced close and silent until the music stopped. Bill gently pushed Anna to arm's length. "Loving you, Anna, has been an adventure, and more wonderful than I could ever have imagined."

Anna put her arms around his neck. "I agree."

"Get out!" Henry's voice yelled from the lobby, breaking the romantic mood. Anna and Bill ran out of the office to find three young men attempting to punch Henry, who was throwing punches with remarkable precision at the intruders.

Isabelle was already on the phone. "Police please? This is The Sackville Hotel and we have three violent intruders."

Hearing Isabelle's request for the police the men ran off. Henry quickly bolted the door and leaned his back against it, breathing heavily and wiping sweat from his forehead.

"How did they get in?"

Taking a deep breath Henry replied, "I had not locked the door, the party guests who are not staying at the hotel needed to get to their cars and taxis."

"Are you all right, Henry? Come and sit down." Anna was pleased she had hired a younger man for the night shift. She thought about Albert, who worked mostly days—he was in his sixties and she realized he would not have been able to fight back.

"I'm fine. I can give pretty much as good as I get." He laughed. "I was quite the scrapper as a kid."

There was a strong knock on the door. Anna clasped a hand over her mouth to muffle a scream, before realizing it was the police. Henry unlocked the door. The constable walked in looking puzzled.

"Someone called a disturbance?"

"Yes, I did." Isabelle answered. "The offenders left when they heard me call the police. They threatened the doorman."

"Constable, would you mind coming into my office?" Anna guided everyone except Bill into her office. "As you can see, we have an event on tonight. Henry, tell the constable what happened."

"What time did this incident occur?"

"About twelve-thirty. The door was not locked because guests were leaving the party. There were three of them. Two looked in their late teens. They look alike, they could be brothers: brown hair, rough, scrawny-looking, clothes were old. They came up to about here." Henry put his hand up to his shoulder. "They looked at the third man for approval and said, 'What you got mister, looking for a fight are ya?' and started punching. I put my hands up to defend myself and they punched me in the stomach. I punched back and then the third one began laughing. He was older, probably in his early twenties, black hair, dark skinned, tall and thin. Well dressed, not rough like the other two. I heard Mrs. Wexford call the police and he must have too because he called, 'Come on lads, we'd better get out of here,' and they ran off towards the Promenade." Henry pointed to his right. "That's about it except for the other night or morning. I am pretty sure it was the same three men."

The constable turned to Anna. "Was this reported?"

"No, they only rang the doorbell and ran off. Although one of my staff said she was threatened on her way in to work that morning."

The constable looked at his notes. "Would that be Mrs. Fulham? We had a complaint earlier tonight from Mr. Sam Fulham to say his wife had been threatened and harassed by a gang of youths on her way home from work. The description of the perpetrators is similar to Henry's."

Anna began to shake her head at the name and then remembered Amy telling her she didn't use her married name at the hotel. Anna asked, "Mrs. Amy Fulham?" She felt cold thinking of poor Amy confronting an attack.

"You know this lady."

"Yes, she is the head housekeeper here but she is known as Amy Peterson. She's worked her a long time and continues to use her maiden name. Is she all right?"

"A little shaken but they only taunted her with names. Two of the boys are known to the police: young scrappers, kids of fourteen or fifteen, poor family. We had a few theft problems last summer and they were sent to Borstal for a few months but they were recently released to their families. I am puzzled as to why they are here in February, it's pretty cold at night." The constable closed his notebook. "I suggest you exercise caution and keep the door locked."

"Henry, you can go back to your post now." Anna walked with Henry to the front door, which Bill was closing and locking behind the constable.

Bill gave a long sigh and put his hand on Anna's shoulder. "I may not be Gregory Peck but our lives have enough stories in them for the movies. Shall we dance?" Anna laughed. "No, we have guests." Anna looked at her watch. "How much longer do you think?"

Isabelle said, "The quartet is booked until one-thirty." Anna peered through the dining room door. "It seems to be thinning out. Ah, listen. They are playing the last waltz."

"Mum, Bill, why don't you call it a night? I don't have anything on tomorrow and can sleep in. I know you two will still be up at five. I'll see the waiters clean up and get the tables set for breakfast."

Anna yawned. "Thank you dear, I'm exhausted. What a night."

Sarah Goes Missing

～◌⚬◌～

After the Valentine's festivities, The New Sackville plunged into quiet with only five or six guests, and even with a few locals for dinner or lunch, the Emily Carr dining room was almost silent. Wild storms raged through to the end of February and March came in like a lion.

Anna stood at her office window watching the dark black clouds gather on the horizon and move towards the shore, stirring the sea into massive waves boiling to white caps that roared onto the beach and leapt into the air. The spray from the last pounding wave reached the Promenade and water dripped down her window. Aware of the dangers of such storms, she went to the reception desk.

"Miss Jenkins, please notify each guest that we have a bad storm approaching and to stay indoors. James, can you check all the doors and windows? We may need to lock the front door. Sometimes the wind blows under the portico. I'm going downstairs. In storms this bad we may have flooding in the service area."

Bill was already directing a throng of maids, waiters and kitchen staff to move stuff off the ground. Woody was outside filling sandbags to put against the door and window.

"Looks like a bad one, Mrs. Blaine," Amy said, handing a set of clean linen to a maid.

Anna sounded breathless. "Amy, just the person I wanted to see. Can you check that the windows are closed in the occupied rooms and suites?"

"I already did it. My Sam told me we were in for a big 'un, when he walked me to work this morning."

Anna gave Amy a worried look. "Are you still nervous walking alone? I thought the police had caught the little thugs?"

"Ye', they were caught and sent back to Borstal. I'm fine, but Sam, he worries, and it's nice having company to and from work. He likes looking after me. Once it gets light in' morning he probably won't bother then."

A blast of cold wet air forced its way down the passage. Woody struggled to close the back door. "It's bad. Woody stacked sandbags by door and windows."

"Thanks, Woody."

"Amy, there isn't much more you and I can do. Can you come to my office and we'll look at the Easter bookings? Isabelle will be away. I'll need you to take up her duties where necessary."

"Mum!" Isabelle called from the top of the service stairs.

"On my way up. What's wrong?"

A windswept, Isabelle her hair dripping wet stood at the top of the stairs. "School called. They let the girls out early because of the storm. I went to pick up Sarah and she wasn't there. The teacher said someone picked them up. She thought it was me or Mrs. Elliot. I just called Lizzy's house and they aren't there." Isabelle burst into tears. "Mrs. Elliot has called the police."

Albert called over the roar of the wind. "Mrs. Blaine, the police are here."

Anna went to shout but the roar had ceased as Albert closed the door and the police constable approached Isabelle.

"Mrs. Wexford, I understand your daughter Sarah Wexford has gone missing with her friend Elizabeth Elliot."

"Yes. You've found them?"

"No, but we have police enquiring where they might be. Mrs. Elliot gave us your address. Could your husband or a friend have picked them up?"

"My husband is in Scotland and there is no one else. I didn't tell anyone.

They were all busy with the storm, so no one knew I had gone to fetch her." Tears ran down Isabelle's face. Anna handed her a lace hanky and took her hand.

The constable opened his notebook. "Can you give us a description of what she was wearing."

"Sarah is tall for her age and she has red curly hair and hazel eyes. She was wearing her school uniform and carried a brown leather satchel, like every other girl in the school."

"Forgive me, but I have to ask. Did something happen at home that would cause Sarah to run away?"

"What? No, she's not nine years old yet. Why would she run away? She's a happy kid."

"I'm sorry. Try not to worry. It is my experience that there is a logical explanation and we'll find her safe and sound. We'll keep you informed." Albert opened the door to another blast of cold wet air and the constable left.

Anna felt a cavern in the pit of her stomach. How could this happen? Sarah missing in one of the worst storms she could remember! Bill joined them and comforted Isabelle. Anna stared out of the window as the storm grew angrier. She felt helpless as the time ticked by in slow motion. Isabelle paced up and down the office. Anna felt her pain and wished she could comfort her, but there was no comfort for any of them. No one said it, but they were all thinking the same thing: *Who had taken Sarah and Lizzy, and why?* Anna held her breath, thinking of the horrors of child abductions she had heard on the news.

"I can't stand here doing nothing. I'm going to see Mrs. Elliot. Perhaps between us we'll figure something out."

"The police said to stay here." Anna insisted. "You won't get far in this storm. Wait until it subsides."

Isabelle burst into tears again. "Sarah is out there in this storm. Do you think she can wait until it subsides?"

Anna's throat hurt from holding back tears, but the thought of losing Sarah forced the warm moisture down her cheeks. She wound her arms around Isabelle, a little awkwardly as Isabelle was considerably taller than Anna. Mother and daughter clung to each other, crying quietly as the hostile, howling wind intruded on their otherwise silent torment.

Bill didn't know what to do or say. He didn't belong. Only a mother could understand. He wrapped his arms around them both and whispered, "I'm here if you need me." He crept out of the office; his leaden legs moving in slow motion as he brushed his eyes.

The storm had reached its peak in mid-afternoon, although it was dark enough to be midnight, when a bolt of lightning lit up the sky, followed by a loud crack and another blast of brilliant light before everything plunged into darkness. Staff came running into the lobby and guests appeared on the stairs, their expressions indicating an expectation of disaster.

Bill raised his arms in the centre of the lobby, the lifeless crystal chandelier above his head. "Don't panic, everyone. It would appear that the storm has knocked out the electricity. Please go back to your rooms and the maids will bring you candles. If you wish to have company, we will have the lobby lit and comfortable for you in about fifteen minutes."

Bill felt someone pulling his sleeve. Woody stood by him with a wide grin. "Mr. Blaine, Woody went outside." He stretched his arms as high as they would go. "A tree fell across the telegraph pole and BOOM! It cut the wires."

"Thank you, Woody." Bill raised his voice. "Our maintenance man has just informed me that an uprooted tree has fallen on the electricity and phone lines. The Sussex Electricity Board will be notified and repairs will begin as soon as possible."

Anna and Isabelle gathered candles from the storage room and Amy distributed them to the maids. Relieved to have something to do, mother and daughter threw their energy into the task of illuminating the lobby with candles, giving guests somewhere to gather. Desperately trying to conceal their anguish, she glanced at Isabelle's tear-stained face and knew she was feeling no better than Anna. James opened the bar and Bill instructed the kitchen staff to make sandwiches. Mr. Smyth and Balaji served afternoon tea in the lobby.

On his way back to the kitchen, Bill squeezed Anna's hand. "How are you holding up?"

She squeezed back. "I'm okay, I wish we had some news." Bill leaned in and kissed her cheek.

"Soon. The storm is subsiding. I need to go to the kitchen and determine the best way to cook dinner. Thank heavens we have gas cookers."

Anna turned to Isabelle and was shocked to see Mr. Smyth whisper something in her ear. Isabelle walked away towards Anna, her face taut, gasping to stifle tears.

"Come, let's go in the office and call the police station and see if there is any news. I don't want guests prying."

"They already know. Mr. Smyth just said he was sorry to hear about Sarah."

"How would he know?"

"Mum, the police were here and we talked to them in the lobby. Someone must have overheard."

Anna shrugged her shoulders. "You're right." She picked up the receiver. "Of course, no phone. The lines are down." Anna closed her eyes and held her breath. For Isabelle's sake she tried to control the muscles in her face as they pulled into misery. She felt so afraid that something terrible had happened to Sarah and now they were cut off, not knowing anything. She smiled unconvincingly. "No news is good news. Right?"

"I can't take it any longer. The storm has eased up. I'm going to talk to Mrs. Elliot."

"I'll come with you. James and Bill can manage here. There's not much we can do until the electricity is back on."

The rain had eased but they had to brace themselves against the wind as they walked to the garage. Isabelle took the wheel and drove around the downed utility pole, steering the car along the back streets to avoid the flooded Promenade. Initially, Anna felt relief just in being outside and then reality hit. Sarah was missing. Isabelle swung Bill's Hillman around fallen trees and other downed utility poles and avoided wayward dustbins rolling in the middle of road. The Elliot's house was a mansion that stood on the cliff overlooking the sea. Almost every window was lit up—definitely electricity there. A gust of wind threw the car door open as Anna tried to get out. Isabelle pressed the doorbell, holding onto her hat and scarf. A maid answered, Mrs. Elliot was standing behind her looking worried and disappointed.

"Mrs. Wexford, do you have news?"

"No. We have no phone or electricity because of the storm. I was hoping you had heard something."

"Come in, please." She motioned to the maid. "Molly, bring us some tea." She glanced at Anna. "You must be Sarah's grandmother. She talks about you all the time. I'm sorry we meet under such difficult circumstances. My husband and I dine frequently at the Emily Carr Restaurant." Anna nodded, wondering how this lady could talk pleasantries when her daughter had been missing for six hours. Fighting back tears, Anna thought her throat might strangle her and Isabelle looked about the same. Mrs. Elliot showed them into the sitting room.

"My phone works but the line is always busy at the police station. I called my husband but he's not in the office. His secretary said she thought he was on his way home. I thought the school had called him to pick Lizzy. I didn't know she was missing until you called this morning. My husband has disappeared too." She took a crumpled handkerchief from her pocket and dabbed her eyes. The maid re-entered with tea and cake. Such a normal thing to do seemed so abnormal in the circumstances.

Mrs. Elliot said, "That will be all." Molly curtsied and scurried from the room. Anna sighed as the warm liquid eased her tense throat. A shrill ring made her jump and spill tea in the saucer.

Mrs. Elliot picked up the phone, the relief on her face quite dramatic. Isabelle smiled and glanced at Anna who took a deep breath and smiled back, trying to follow the one-sided conversation.

"Your secretary said you were on your way home."

She listened, her face turning pale, and then answered, "Lizzy is missing. I thought she was with you." She listened without comment and finally said,

"Goodbye." Dabbing her face with the wet ball of fabric.

Trying to compose, herself she said, "My husband was with a client earlier not, as I had thought, on his way home. Both the school and police had called his office, leaving messages, which he only just received. He has no idea where the girls are."

Isabelle held onto Anna's hand, one as tense as the other. "Mrs. Elliot, please call the police again. If they don't answer we'll drive to the police station."

"I don't even know where my driver is. He has disappeared too."

Anna jumped on this comment. "Was it your driver who picked up the girls? The teacher said it was a big black car."

Mrs. Elliot seemed not to hear, picked up the phone and asked the operator for the police station. This time the line connected. The conversation one sided but good news lit up Mrs. Elliot's face. She replaced the receiver and smiled. "It seems the police have found both my driver and the girls. A constable is on his way to the hotel with Sarah, and Lizzy is on her way home. It was my driver who picked them up from school. The wind blew the car off the road. A good Samaritan took them in, but they too had no electricity or phone and couldn't let anyone know. The police found the car and then the girls. They are safe and unharmed.

Sarah stood under the portico beside Henry as the Hillman came to a stop. Isabelle ran out of the car, leaving the engine running and the door wide open. She grabbed Sarah in her arms. "Are you okay? Are you hurt?"

"No, I'm okay. We were a bit scared." Sarah flung her arms in the air. "The lightening suddenly surrounded the car, the car shook, Lizzy and I screamed and the car stopped. The driver told us to stay in the car, while he looked for help. The rain poured down the windows." Sarah imitated the rain falling. "Then Lizzy screamed again when a face appeared at the car window." Anna's tears of relief turned to a smile as her granddaughter described her ordeal with all the drama of a film star. "Lizzy opened the door and this nice lady held a big umbrella over us and we ran to her house.

Mrs. Watson, that was her name, sat us at the kitchen table and gave us a big slice of cake and some orange cordial."

"Quite an adventure," Isabelle said, hugging Sarah one more time.

"Are you crying, Mummy?"

Isabelle wiped her hand across her cheeks. "A little bit. I am so happy to see you."

Sarah frowned. "I don't cry when I'm happy."

They all laughed and it was Anna's turn to hug Sarah. "You are so precious!"

Anna went to her office, relieved the ordeal was over.

Hillcrest Hall

⸎

T he winter of 1949 had difficulty letting go, made worse by a late-April Easter. The hotel season would be late starting. Anna had anticipated a slow winter—many hotels closed for the winter in Bexhill—but she had not expected the revenue to be so low. Staring at the books and seeing more red then she would like, Anna called James into her office.

"James, what is the occupancy rate for Easter?

Balancing folders on his lap James answered, "About fifty percent for the weekend, and about twenty next week and the week after. And then it drops off dramatically until May and picks up to about twenty percent again in early June."

"I thought as much. I'm a little worried. The winter was harder on us than I expected, although I am grateful for the Valentine's party that gave us a revenue boost. I had thought that pre-Easter bookings would be closer to twenty percent, but I think they are about ten and that is not enough to sustain the business. The conference that Isabelle booked for early April was postponed until September. I can't remember why." Anna picked up the phone. "Miss Jenkins, ask Mrs. Wexford to join me in my office please."

Isabelle knocked on the door. "Hello, what's up?"

"James and I are talking about occupancy rates and I have some concerns. The conference that postponed, what happened?"

"The post-war economy, I think. They said the company was undergoing changes and they would not be ready to make announcements until September."

"The economy is worrisome." Anna paused. "Do you have a gut feeling for future bookings?"

"Mum, gut feelings are your department." Isabelle smiled at Anna. "I prefer concrete bookings and we are doing well. Easter bookings are still coming in. I've some children's activities planned to bring families here. I've asked Bill to make up a children's menu."

Anna frowned. "Too many children disturb our more elite guests and this is not a Butlin's holiday camp."

"I understand, but our elite guests have children, usually well-mannered children who are looked after by nannies. If we offer amenities for children and nannies, we increase our market. Bill suggested we have an early sitting. The children's menu will only be offered at that time. We'll call it Children's Dining Hour. Nannies or parents wishing to dine with their children will have access to the full menu, as will anyone who wants to dine early. But guests who do not want to deal with children during dinner will know not to dine early."

"I like that idea and it might bring in casual diners too." Anna made some notes in her notebook. "Isabelle, have you thought about who will look after the Easter activities while you're away?"

"I have decided to stay until after the Easter Parade on Sunday. Sarah wants to join in and I should be here. I talked to Belle. She's opening the gift shop but wants to get rid of the old stock, so there isn't much I can do during the busy weekend. We decided Sarah and I would go on Monday. Darcy is sending the car to pick us up."

"That's nice. You'll have a lovely time at Hillcrest." Anna's attention went back to bookings. "Bookings between Easter and June are sparse. What can we do to boost numbers?"

"I'll do some promoting for the Emily Carr Restaurant. I was talking to Rolls-Royce in Derby about a company conference in the summer. I'll see if I can tempt them to bring it forward to May. I'm not keen on summer conferences as it interferes with holiday guests. Back in the early 1900s Bexhill was famous for racing cars. Maybe we could feature some of that history. We could involve other Bexhill merchants."

"If you could get Roll Royce to come in May that would be perfect and I like all of those ideas. What do you think, James?"

"Rolls-Royce might also be interested in a racing car weekend. It sure appeals to me. Do you think we have time to plan that?"

Isabelle hesitated for a minute. "Maybe not this year but I could put it in plans for 1950." Isabelle moved to the door. "What about a fashion show in late May or early June? A fashion show would be easy to arrange."

Anna shook her head and smiled at James as Isabelle departed. "Isabelle amazes me with her ideas. It looks as though our problem is solved, so why do I still sense trouble?" *Isabelle is right* Anna thought *I need to waive the intuition and deal with concrete facts.*

"Anna, you have always worked through your instincts and they are rarely wrong, but I think Isabelle is right this time. Her ideas will bring in a good stream of revenue."

"Yes, I agree, James. Can you do the numbers for the Rolls-Royce conference? I'll go and talk to Bill about this children's menu. I'm doubtful it will generate much revenue."

On Easter Sunday morning the sweet fragrance of spring flowers greeted Anna as she walked through the lobby to her office. The bright yellow daffodils seemed to nod 'happy spring' and the tulips burst with colour. Cute, soft toy bunnies and tiny fluffy chicks sat among colourful foil-wrapped Easter eggs that filled every surface.

"Good morning, Henry, and Happy Easter."

"And to you, Mrs. Blaine. It's going to be a lovely day."

Henry was right, Anna thought as she watched the sun rise from her office window. The sea, calm and tranquil, shimmered pink from the rising sun and she welcomed the sense of peace. The trauma of almost losing Sarah preyed on her mind. Being strong for Isabelle, she had forced her fears deep inside. Or was it more than that? Speaking to no one, she said, "Isabelle has moved on as though nothing happened, and I can't shake off the fear."

By nine-thirty the lobby was buzzing as guests gathered for taxis and cars to take them to St. Andrew's Church. There were plenty of nods and smiles of approval for new spring outfits, especially hats and perhaps a giggle or two at some overly-ornate Easter bonnets.

Dressed in a white dress with pink sash and a pink bonnet, Sarah led the children's Easter Parade winding between the luncheon tables, handing chocolates to guests. Anna watched the faces of proud parents and realized Isabelle's judgment had been right. Done properly, featuring children's activities would be an asset.

Monday morning, Harris pulled Lord Thornton's black Rolls-Royce under the portico. Anna kissed Sarah and Isabelle and waved good-bye, secretly wishing it was she and Bill being whisked off to Hillcrest Hall. But she acknowledged that Isabelle had worked hard and deserved a rest. Perhaps she and Bill could go in the autumn when the hotel quieted down after the high season.

Exhausted from excitement, Sarah slept most of the way. Isabelle smiled. *This is the life,* she thought to herself, *being chauffeur driven in a Rolls-Royce.* She was looking forward to spending a week with Belle and Darcy—perhaps they would entertain while she was there. In anticipation of at least one dinner party she had packed her strapless emerald green dress. She doubted they had any friends who didn't have titles or money and some would have both. Ever since she had started serving Britain's elite while working at Drapers in Rugby, she had wanted to be one of them. And yet she had married Sandy, a mere engineer, and she was once again serving the elite. She stroked Sarah's curls and a stab of anxiety hit her chest at the thought of losing her. She never wanted to experience that sense of helplessness again. If she couldn't have a life of luxury, she decided to do everything in her power to give it to Sarah.

Isabelle's mind turned to Sandy. He had called, wanting to see Sarah, and Isabelle had heard the disappointment in his voice when he realized they would be away for Easter. Sandy challenged something decent inside her; affection and warmth she had not felt since Little Gran had died. She smiled, hearing Little Gran's voice warning her to stop flirting with Ralph. Little Gran knew her so well, perhaps even better than Papa, who never had the heart to say no. And the day he died, a vital part of her died too. She never wanted to feel that hurt again, although it had come very close the day Sarah went missing. Tears sprang unexpectedly and rolled down her cheeks, she brushed them aside sharply feeling a sting on her face.

The car leaned to the right and the smooth road turned into crunching gravel. Sarah woke up. "Are we there yet?"

"We just turned into the driveway. Look, there is Hillcrest Hall Estates." Isabelle felt as excited as Sarah at the sight of this grand mansion. People were milling around cars lined up on the lawn, a makeshift parking lot. Isabelle could see a sign over what she thought was once the stable, Belle's Gift Shop and Tea Room. Harris drove the car slowly around the side of the building stopping in front of a small door at the bottom of a huge red brick tower.

"This is the entrance to Lord and Lady Thornton's private apartment. Not very grand, but the main entrance is open to the public." Harris's lips sneered slightly, showing his disapproval at the word 'public.' Sarah jumped out of the car before Harris could open the door. She ran in circles with her arms spread wide. Belle opened the door. "Auntie Belle, I didn't know you lived in a fairy castle. Do you have princesses here?"

Laughing, Belle said, "No princesses, except you Sarah. Welcome to Hillcrest." Belle opened her arms to Isabelle. "It is wonderful to see you. I hope you had a pleasant journey." Belle took Isabelle's arm and Sarah grabbed her other hand. "I am sure you are ready for a cocktail before lunch.

The small entrance opened up into a large oak-paneled hallway and a set of stairs to one side circled up inside the tower. Sarah peered up the tower. Belle led them into a surprisingly modern sitting room with a sleek teak cabinet and upholstered chairs in turquoise and orange stripes, and clean-lined wooden Danish-style tables.

"I see you're surprised at my modern décor? I find the heavy old furnishings beautiful but overwhelming, so this room is my home away from home. Most of the other rooms are traditional. Darcy hates the modern styles, but indulges me here with a little modern Chicago. In the winter time we live in the house with its traditional furnishings and glowering ancestors on the walls."

"I love the modern look. I wish mother would update the hotel."

"I don't think art décor would suit the Sackville."

Harris walked in with a tray of drinks. "Harris, would you open the French doors please?"

"Yes, m' lady. It is maybe too cool to sit outside."

"I know, but the fresh air is pleasant and Sarah might like to explore the garden. Is Master Felix home?"

"Yes m' lady, he'll be joining you for lunch."

After lunch Sarah played in the garden while Belle showed Isabelle the gift shop. Holiday shoppers were milling around the somewhat sparse shelves, eager to buy. Isabelle observed the disappointed expressions, as the visitors picked up cheap trinkets with Hillcrest Hall stamped on them: tatty looking knitted gloves and scarves proudly announcing they were handmade by the local Women's Institute, were picked up and dismissed. A few copies of Beatrix Potter's *Benjamin Bunny* and a selection of seasonal chicks and bunnies sat on a small round table. People weren't spending more than a few shillings at the most.

Isabelle listened to the customers. One couple asked the clerk if they had anything with the family crest on it, another lady asked if the Hillcrest china pattern was Royal Doulton or Minton—she wanted to know where she could buy it. The clerk didn't know and looked over at Belle.

"Lady Thornton is right over there. I am sure Her Ladyship would know the answer." All heads in the store fixed on Belle.

Belle smiled. "Unfortunately, the Hillcrest dinnerware is a private collection and not available in stores. The pattern is called Thornton's Lady Rose, made by Royal Crown Derby. It was originally made in 1812 for Lady Rose's wedding—Lord Thornton's great, great grandmother—and it has been Hillcrest's dinner service pattern ever since." Belle looked at Isabelle. "My friend Mrs. Wexford has suggested we have some made for guests to purchase here at the gift shop. Would that interest any of you?"

Several women put their hands up. "When will it be available?"

"I want to buy some."

"Umm…" Belle had no idea what to say.

"If I may interrupt. Ladies and gentlemen," Isabelle shouted over the hub of questions. "If you would like to leave your name and address with us, Lady Thornton will write to you when she has a list of available dinnerware. However, we ask for your patience. As you know, post-war shortages often affect production. It may take up to six months." A throng of women moved to the cash register. Seeing the look of horror on the clerk's face, Isabelle turned to Belle. "Take these awful chicks and bunnies…sorry," Isabelle giggled, "off that table and get me some paper and a pen."

Belle gathered up all the chicks and bunnies and took them into the back room.

"Ladies, if you could make a queue over here, Lady Thornton and I will take down your names and that will allow the clerk to serve customers."

Belle placed a notebook and pen on the table and Isabelle began writing down names. People swarmed towards Belle wanting to shake her hand and ask questions about what it was like to be a lady and had the queen been to dinner at Hillcrest and was Lord Thornton a good husband? Belle glanced at Isabelle, raising her eyebrows at some of the personal questions. Half an hour later, ladies were still coming in to leave their addresses as news spread of Lady Thornton's offer. Isabelle thought the late stragglers, mostly local people, were more interested in getting a letter from her ladyship than ordering china. The crowd eventually died down enough for the clerk to take over. Belle and Isabelle went into the tearoom to discuss merchandise for the store.

"Look who's here." Belle pointed to a table where Felix and Sarah were sitting, eating strawberry ice cream and sipping lemonade.

"Hello Mother, Aunt Isabelle! I found this young lady wondering in the terrace garden looking very bored and in need of a cheering up and nothing does that better than strawberry ice cream."

"And fizzy lemonade," Sarah added, glancing at Isabelle for approval.

"Is the lemonade good?" Sarah nodded, her mouth full of ice-cream.

"I think I'll have that instead of tea," Isabelle said to the waitress. "Felix, how is school? I used to live in Rugby. My parents owned the Kings Head Inn and many of the parents from Rugby school stayed at the Inn before and after holidays. I was a bit of a snob then and thought it beneath me to live in a pub. I lived with my grandmother in town. Quite a coincidence."

"I know the King's Head, it's a Whitbread house. Nice pub." Felix's cheeks flushed with a sheepish glance towards Belle. "Of course, I've never been in it, I'm not old enough to drink yet. Mum, did you ever stay there?"

"No, I didn't know Isabelle's family back then. I knew Uncle Bill when we lived in Chicago before you were born. We usually drove down to Rugby from the London flat and returned the same day."

The spoon clinked on the empty bowl as Sarah finished her ice cream. "Felix, can we explore some more?" She leaned in to Felix and whispered, "Can we go up the tower?"

"Great idea, I hope you have the energy to climb one hundred and twenty-five steps."

Sarah jumped up and called, "Bye Mum," running to the door with Felix at her heels.

"Those two are getting along well." Isabelle said, waving to Sarah.

"Felix is having trouble growing up. I think he is enjoying being with Sarah, giving him an excuse to be a kid. Darcy wants him to grow up too fast. Felix maybe the heir to Hillcrest but he has a lot of years to learn the business, giving us time to make the estate profitable."

"Um…the lord-of-the-manor days are over. England loved its gentry and still does, as you saw today. Belle, being Lady Thornton makes you mysterious and special, mostly because in days gone by the lady of the manor kept to herself and there was always this big divide. I think your

American roots bring something refreshing to Hillcrest and I suggest you capitalize on it. It will help you and Darcy maintain the estate. What you saw today confirms there is quite an opportunity."

"Isabelle, I don't know what you did in the gift shop but, oh my, I did not expect that kind of response."

"Neither did I." Isabelle laughed. "I thought they might wait until we actually had the china. Can you imagine how much money you could have made today if you had the Thornton china for sale? I just hope we can get it now."

"I think so. The housekeeper orders it all the time if we have breakages."

"I also have another idea. Your guests really want to meet you. I suggest when the china arrives, you give a little talk in the shop about its origin. The ladies loved hearing about Darcy's great, great grandmother."

"It feels strange. Remember, I came to this through marriage. I'm a southern American girl, who has lost most of her southern drawl but is still about as far from British society as you can get. I do enjoy the history of this place, it goes back way beyond the 1700s. The tour guides inside the house tell the guests all that on the tour."

"I haven't taken the tour yet but I'm certain you could talk about the detail and make it more intimate. People want to meet you, Lady Thornton. Maybe you could get Darcy to do something too."

"I don't know. Darcy is busy managing the estate and the tenant farmers. I'll ask him, or *we* can ask him over dinner tonight. Now let me take you on a tour of Hillcrest Hall."

Isabelle nodded appropriately as the guide took them around the house. She noted the colours of the Hillcrest coat of arms and some of the less severe portraits of the Thornton ancestors. She paid particular attention to the detail of the now famous dinnerware. There were a few figurines that she thought might be worth duplicating. The tour ended in the orangery, where much to Isabelle's surprise there were orange trees about to blossom. Their guide moved on to another group of visitors and Belle took over as they toured the gardens.

The estate was closed to the public except for holidays and weekends until

June. The day after the Easter holiday, Belle and Isabelle went to the gift shop to discuss changing the layout and suitable merchandise.

"My suggestion is to start with a few new items and build on it as you see which items sell well. Where do you want to start?"

"Thornton's Lady Rose china, but what do I order?"

"Start with cup and saucer sets, sugar bowls and cream jugs and maybe a few plates. I doubt people will want more than that, but if they do you could always make a special order."

"That is easy. I can probably have those by Whitsun Weekend in May. Shall I tell the local ladies to stop knitting?"

"Definitely, but see if any of them embroider. If so have them embroider the Hillcrest coat of arms in on lace hankies. You need small, nice, but inexpensive items that visitors can buy as a keepsake. Find a photographer to take pictures, inside and outside for postcards and some larger ones for framing." Isabelle thought for a moment. "I think that will be a good start. I'll make a list of other things you can add later."

"I am so grateful, thank you."

"Don't thank me yet. Now comes the hard part, making sure the merchandise sells. A retail business will only survive if you sell what people want to buy at a price they are prepared to pay and still make a profit. Belle, you have to run this as a business."

"I understand and I'm learning fast. Where did you learn all this?"

"Mostly at Drapers in Rugby. I enjoy retail. There's a science behind what people buy and why they buy it. That's why I knew right away the kind of things in your shop were not what your visitors wanted. As we observed yesterday, visitors want to buy something with class. They can buy cheap trinkets at Woolworths. They don't expect to find them here at the home of Lord and Lady Thornton. And they will pay for it, but you need a variety of price points for different levels of income. A word of caution, buyers will dismiss the merchandise for three reasons: one it is too cheap, two it is over-priced and three they see no emotional value."

"It's a balancing act. I'm going to enjoy the retail…" Belle stopped and listened. The crunching sound of gravel meant a car was heading for the gift shop. Belle sighed, "People don't read the sign saying we are closed. I hate turning them away." She opened the door. "Oh my! Isabelle, it's your husband."

"What! What's he doing here?"

Sandy's Unexpected Arrival

B elle opened the shop door as Sandy got out of the car. "Sandy, what a surprise. Welcome to Hillcrest!"

Isabelle stood back, gathering her jumbled thoughts. She was at first irritated that he had intruded on her time with Belle, followed by a burst of pleasure, which took her by surprise and annoyed her even more. She didn't want to feel anything for Sandy. After all, wasn't she planning to divorce him? Tears sprang to her eyes at that thought and then a smile curled her lips, appreciating his thoughtfulness in coming to visit. He'd probably been to Bexhill first and found out they were here.

She heard Sarah call out, "Daddy, Daddy!"

A pleasant sensation filled her body, hearing Sandy's voice. "How's my best girl in the whole world? Where's Mummy?"

Belle answered. "She's in the back of the shop, checking on stock. She'll be out in a minute."

Isabelle took a deep breath, grateful for Belle's cover up. She wanted to hide. She didn't want to deal with Sandy, and why were her emotions in such turmoil? Under her breath she said, "Get a grip Isabelle, be nice for your daughter's sake." She checked her hair in the mirror; she'd inherited her father's red curls that she cursed most of the time, but today it looked smart. Straightening the waistband on her floral skirt, she went to the shop door and put on the best bright smile she felt capable of mustering.

Sarah rushed over to her and took her hand. "Daddy's here. I have to find Felix and tell him." Sarah went running off towards the garden, calling as she ran, "I'll be back in a minute, Daddy. Don't go away."

"Sandy, what brings you here?"

"To see you and Sarah of course," Sandy said with a distinct edge of irritation.

Isabelle found herself rising to his tone but decided to ignore it. "I'm pleased you came. How did you know we were here?"

"I missed you both and decided to drive to Bexhill. I stayed at the hotel last night and had a nice visit with your mother and Bill and they told me you were here."

"You should have called and let us know you were coming."

"Really? I wasn't sure I was welcome." Isabelle didn't answer nor did she look at Sandy, trying to stay neutral resisting any show of emotion. But Sandy's presence alone was disquieting.

"I think it's time for cocktails before lunch," Belle said, attempting to break the tension. "Sandy why don't you drive the car over there? Harris will bring in your suitcase and park the car in the garage. I'll see if I can find Darcy. He's probably in the estate office. If not, he'll be back for lunch."

Sarah came running back, "I can't find Felix. Daddy, where are you going?"

"Over there to the garage. Here," Sandy opened the passenger door, "hop in." Sarah beamed and jumped into the car.

Belle glanced at Isabelle as they began walking towards the house. "How are you doing?"

"I don't know. The last time I saw Sandy I asked for a divorce but today I'm not sure what I feel. I want to be angry, but I don't feel angry. I'm actually happy to see him."

"Perhaps you're still in love with him."

"Maybe. So why am I also irritated that he's here?"

"I can't answer that. I do think this is a great opportunity, away from other influences, for you and Sandy to get to know each other again."

"By other influences, you mean Ralph. You've been talking to Mother and I bet she told you about Sandy and my friend Judy. The Ralph thing is over but I can't speak for Sandy and Judy."

"Yes, I mean all those things: Ralph, Judy, your mother, and everyday hotel life. Be yourself and let Sandy be himself. Be a family, enjoy each other and your daughter."

"And what if we can't get along and it doesn't work?"

"Then you can part amicably, knowing you tried."

Harris greeted them at the door, obviously waiting for instructions. "Harris, Mr. Wexford will be staying with us for a few days. Can you tell cook and would you meet Mr. Wexford at the garage? And we'll have cocktails in the drawing room."

Isabelle wondered how Harris was going to do so many things at once. He bowed saying, "Yes, milady," without moving a muscle and then disappeared towards the out buildings.

Belle led the way into the drawing room, which was more in keeping with a country house. Heavy red velvet curtains hung at the long windows, tied back with long gold tassels to allow light into the room. A fire had been lit to take the dampness out of the air. Isabelle sat by the fire in a pretty chair with floral upholstering and Belle sat in the chair opposite.

"Isabelle, I hate to ask, but I need to tell the housekeeper to make up a room for Sandy. Do I put him in a separate room, in your room or I can move you to the Rose Suite, which has a double bedroom and a large adjoining dressing room? You can pretend you have time travelled back a hundred years, when husbands slept in their dressing room unless invited into their wife's bed."

Isabelle laughed. "The Rose Suite, and Sandy can sleep in the dressing room. Isn't that open to the public?"

"Not always. We don't open it if we have guests. Excuse me, I will inform Mrs. Dickson to move your things and prepare the Rose Suite."

Isabelle stared into the fire, the flames flickered and she felt warm and safe. Belle didn't make judgments and her advice made sense. A voice from the doorway made her jump. "May I come in?"

"Sandy, of course. I was miles away in thought. Belle just went to arrange a room for you."

"Oh, not your room?"

"Adjoining rooms for now. Let's see how things go."

Sandy smiled, moving towards her he said, "Fair enough," and kissed her cheek. Isabelle's face tingled at his touch.

She looked up. "I am happy to see you. If somewhat surprised."

A quiet cough announced Harris entering the room and offering them a glass of sherry. Felix entered with Sarah bouncing at his heels. A frown from Isabelle told Sarah to stop bouncing.

Harris asked, "Master Felix, can I offer you and Miss Sarah lemonade?"

"Yes please," Sarah said before Felix could reply.

A deep voice drove Sarah to her mother's side. "I think you have found your match, Felix. Young Sarah knows her own mind." Everyone laughed and Sarah clung to her mother, her cheeks flushed with embarrassment. Darcy raised his glass. "Cheers, here's to friends. Welcome to Hillcrest."

Sandy had spent the past two days with Darcy on the estate while Isabelle and Belle worked at setting up accounts and ordering product for the gift shop, seeing little of each other until dinner. A big formal dinner had been planned in honour of Isabelle and Sandy's visit. Isabelle was to meet Lady Cardish, and was thrilled to be meeting titled guests on a social footing.

Too excited to sleep, Isabelle was up early the morning of the dinner and surprised to find Sandy already up and eating breakfast. She stopped in the doorway and watched him butter his toast, spreading the butter on and scraping it off, putting the crummy excess back in the butter dish, a habit she had hated and scolded him for but this morning she smiled, embracing the familiarity. She felt her heart stirring with warmth towards this handsome man. He is *handsome* she thought, a few days of fresh air had made his cheeks glow healthily. Suddenly he looked up. "Good morning. You couldn't sleep either? Come and sit with me. Would you like some coffee?"

She smiled. Typical Sandy, always wanting to please. "Thank you."

"It's nice having a little time alone. What can I get you for breakfast? There are some stewed apricots, you used to like those, strawberry jam, and hot buttered toast. I'll ask Harris to make you some fresh toast."

Harris appeared with a silver toast rack and took over from Sandy at serving the fruit. Isabelle sat back, enjoying the attention.

"I was planning on going for a walk around the estate this morning. Darcy is busy and Felix has promised Sarah a trip into town."

"I would like that. Belle is busy getting ready for the dinner tonight, so I don't have anything to do until we meet for our hair appointment this afternoon. I'll get my coat."

At first it felt awkward and Isabelle wondered if this was such a good idea as they walked in silence through the terrace garden. She focused on the daffodils, jonquils and sweet-smelling hyacinths. Walking through the arbour, they giggled as they squeezed together to get through the passage that wasn't quite wide enough for them to walk side by side. On the other side, they gazed at the wide-open space of green acres, Sandy slipped his hand into Isabelle's. She didn't resist.

"I can't believe how quiet it is here. I'm glad I came…" Sandy hesitated and peered at Isabelle for her reaction.

"I'm glad you're here too. I wish I could explain how I feel, but everything is so mixed up."

"I know what I want," Sandy said firmly. "I want us to be a family again. I miss you and Sarah."

"What about Judy?"

"Judy means nothing to me. She's your friend. I'm sorry for taking her out and upsetting you, but there is nothing between us. There's only one person I love and that's you."

"Why does Judy write, telling me what a great time she's having? Although I haven't heard from her in a while."

"She has a crush on me, but I didn't realize it until we had the fight at Christmas. When I returned to Edinburgh I made my position very clear and I haven't seen her since. I'm afraid you may have lost a friend."

"I'm not sure I'd call her a friend if she's making a pass for my husband." Isabelle laughed and leaned against Sandy.

"It's nice to feel you close." Sandy held her in front of him. "I don't want to break this moment but I need to know. Isabelle, I have to ask about that waiter. Your mother told me you were maintaining an employee-employer relationship. But I did see you in an embrace on New Year's Eve. Heck, you were kissing him."

"You have every right to be upset and I made a terrible mistake." Isabelle took Sandy's hands in hers and stared directly into his eyes. "Sandy, I am so very, very sorry. I don't know what got into me. It started with harmless flirting. He took advantage and I didn't care, he made me feel good. When I left Edinburgh you were engrossed in your work. I was bored and I felt worthless. Working at the hotel gave me purpose again. Ralph's attention was wonderful and I knew mother didn't approve, which made it exciting."

"Is it really over with Ralph?"

"Yes, I have no interest in him. He was only interested in me as the boss's daughter. It was Belle who made me see how foolish I was being. She confirmed what Mother had been saying but I wasn't listening." Isabelle frowned, "You know, his attitude towards my mother is strange. He constantly fed into my grumblings and berated her abilities. Mother made no secret of her feelings towards Ralph, she neither liked nor trusted him. I accepted their mutual dislike and I didn't see it at first, but for Ralph it was personal, as though he had a secret vendetta."

"Isabelle, you're changing the subject. What about us?"

"Us? I don't know. Where do we start?"

"I am trying to be patient, but I don't understand your reluctance. I'm your husband and Sarah's father. I love you. Do you love me?"

Isabelle hesitated, her thoughts racing. She did love Sandy but she missed the excitement of Ralph; she wanted Sandy's love and Ralph's excitement. "Sandy, I do love you, but I'm not sure about us. You are very boring. I want some excitement in my life." Seeing the pain in his eyes she immediately regretted her hurtful words. "I didn't mean...that came out wrong."

"What you're saying is you prefer the excitement Ralph gave you. I'm a slow and steady man, the same man you loved and married almost ten years ago. I'm excited at being in the same room as you. I will do anything for you, but it seems that isn't enough. I don't know what excitement you want.

I'm not Ralph." Sandy moved away from her and they were walking side by side with enough room to drive a Mack truck between them.

"I don't want Ralph. I told you. But I am afraid of getting bored and depressed again. Slow and steady is what I love about you, and you temper my impulsive side, but I need more. My reason for being jealous of Judy was because she was so excited about going to the theatre and having dinner with you."

Sandy perked up. "I can take you to exciting places but it's difficult to put excitement in our lives when you're in Bexhill and I'm in Edinburgh. We could sell the house as we originally intended and I'll move to Bexhill." He smiled and lessened the gap between them, pleased that Isabelle didn't move away. "I have something to tell you. My visit to Bexhill was more than a family visit, although I took advantage of the trip and added a week's holiday. I'm glad, otherwise I would have missed this time with you at Hillcrest."

"Tell me, what other reason did you have for being in Bexhill?" Isabelle's tone was skeptical.

"I...um...went for a job interview. Isabelle, I'm tired of being away from you and Sarah and you scared me, flirting with Ralph and asking for a divorce. I want my family back. I don't care that you don't know what you want, because I will fight and I won't give up until we are a family again." Sandy took a deep breath, his face the colour of beetroot. Isabelle took his hand and felt him tremble. "I have never seen you so passionate." Something stirred inside her. "Let's talk."

Suddenly a clap of thunder jolted them into paying attention to their surroundings. The southern sky was black and heavy with rain. A fork of lightening cracked and shot through the sky as the heavens opened, dumping bucketsful of rain on them. They began to run, but there was nowhere to run to, they were too far away from the house. The lightening flashed again. Isabelle was frightened, standing in the open they were vulnerable and in danger from the storm.

"There!" Sandy yelled, pointing to a structure surrounded by bushes partway down the hill. "It will protect us from the lightning, not sure about the rain." Carefully avoiding the trees, they ran towards shelter.

It turned out to be an old wooden hunting blind. Judging by the creaking and scraping as they opened the door, it had not been used in some time. Isabelle screamed as a little creature scurried out. It smelled musty and dried leaves crushed under their feet. The door creaked as Sandy pulled it shut, throwing them into darkness. Two gun slits on each of the three walls let in some light as their eyes became accustomed to the shadows. Chipped, rusty enamel mugs, linked together with cobwebs, sat on a wooden table with benches on each side that stood in the centre of the shack. Something rocked under her shoe and Sandy caught Isabelle as she lost her balance. She bent down and picked up an old empty shell casing.

She put her hands over her ears as a loud cracking noise filled the air, followed by the sound of wood splitting in slow motion and then an enormous thud that shook the ground like an earthquake. Sandy pulled Isabelle close. "What was that?" They peered through one of the slits. Half of a large, dismembered oak tree, the white exterior of its trunk exposed by the fury of the storm stood a few yards away. The other half lay on the ground.

"A lucky escape," Isabelle said, holding onto Sandy.

It felt good to be close. He looked into her eyes and she didn't move, anticipating a kiss. He bent his head and pressed his lips against hers. She felt an explosion inside her that rivaled the storm outside; his hot breath flamed against her neck and her knees weakened. She ran her fingers through his hair and took his face in her hands, kissing him until they were gasping for breath. He pulled his coat off, throwing it on the table before picking her up and laying her down on top of it. The mugs clattered to the floor as he climbed up beside her. "I'll never stop loving you." Kissing her neck, he opened her coat and unbuttoned her dress. She moaned, arching her back and tugging his shirt.

"I love you," she whispered.

Content and happy, they lay in each other arms, listening to the rain pound on the roof and the thunder rumble in the distance as the storm moved on.

Sandy kissed her forehead and said, "Was that exciting enough for you?"

She giggled. "I feel like a naughty schoolgirl and I'd definitely put this experience in the category of exciting." She nuzzled her head into his shoulder. "I want to give us another try. You didn't say whether or not you got the job in Bexhill."

"They said they would let me know, but without sounding conceited, I think the job is mine."

"I'm pleased. Listen, I think it has stopped raining."

"Yes, and I also her a car engine." Sandy looked through the gun slit. "Quick, straighten up. It's Darcy with the Land Rover."

"Hello, anyone there? Sandy...Isabelle!"

Sandy called back, his voice shaking with laughter, "Darcy, we're in here."

Darcy opened the door, almost knocking Sandy over. "Am I glad to see you two. We've been worried sick." Darcy stopped talking and smiled seeing Sandy's coat on the table and Isabelle attempting to straighten her hair. "I see you put the blind to good use."

Isabelle felt her face heat up. Trying to force her smiling lips to be serious she said, "It was a close call—did you see that oak tree?"

"Struck by lightning." Darcy kicked something and bent down to pick up one of the mugs. Removing Sandy's coat, he placed the mug on the table. Chuckling, he handed Sandy his coat and gave him several hard slaps of approval on his back.

"I'll give you two love birds a ride back to the house." Darcy held the Land Rover door for Isabelle. She began to shiver, only now did she realize how wet and cold she felt. Darcy wrapped a blanket around her shoulders.

Belle and Isabelle returned from the hairdressers and ordered tea in Belle's sitting room.

"Well? Are you going to tell me what happened on your walk with Sandy? Ever since you came back you look like the cat that caught the canary."

"Oh, is it that obvious?" Isabelle could feel her cheeks flush. "We walked much further than we intended, as was evident when the storm came. We sorted a lot of things out and we're going to try again. Sandy has been for a job interview in Bexhill. He thinks it looks promising."

"I'm very pleased for you. I think it's the right thing to do."

"We still have a lot of things to work out. The storm interrupted the walk and that's how we finished up in the hunters' blind." Isabelle began to giggle. "I think you've guessed what happened next."

Belle smiled. "Things are going to work out just fine. You and Sandy are made for each other. All marriages have bumps in the road. Now, we must away and get ready for dinner."

Isabelle entered her bedroom and immediately opened the adjoining door to the dressing room. Sandy was with Darcy, who was showing off his wine cellar. She looked around the room: everything neat and tidy, just like Sandy. It used to annoy, her but today she found it endearing. A black dinner jacket hung on the wardrobe door. Harris must have found a spare one, she thought.

Returning to the bedroom she opened the wardrobe and took out the emerald green dress and held it against herself. She wondered if she should have brought a long dress, but short was more fashionable, she hadn't thought to ask Belle. The bodice fit into her waist and the soft fabric fell to just below her knees. Her red curls looked vibrant against the green and brought out the green in her hazel eyes. "If I can seduce him dripping wet in a hunters blind, he won't be able to resist me tonight," she whispered to herself.

"Talking to yourself?" Sandy said as he walked through the door. "I see the adjoining door is open. Is that an invitation?"

She spun around, laid the dress on the bed and wrapped her arms around him. "Perhaps, after the dinner. If you behave yourself," she teased. "Now off you go to your dressing room. I need to get ready."

An hour later, Isabelle tapped on the open door. "How do I look?"

Sandy turned, frowning, the two ends of the bowtie hanging from his fingers dropping as a broad smile pushed away the frown. "You take my breath away. Isabelle, I have never seen you look so beautiful." He gently held her smooth, creamy, bare shoulders; his touch tingled, making her take a sharp breath.

"Here, let me do your tie." She stepped back and said, "You look extremely handsome."

Sandy linked his arm in hers and said, "Mrs. Wexford, let us hobnob with British society."

Isabelle glanced at Sandy as they stood at the top of the great oak staircase. Their heads held high, they began the descent. Her silk dressed rustled as her heart pulsed a million beats a minute. Heads turned as the handsome couple reached the grand hall. A waiter held a silver tray and offered them a glass of sherry. Sandy took one for Isabelle and one for himself. Isabelle was feeling a little uneasy, and her eyes searched the room for Belle when a familiar voice said, "Mrs. Wexford, how nice to see you."

"Lady Cardish, Lord Cardish, it is a pleasure. Allow me to introduce my husband, Sandy Wexford."

Belle appeared from nowhere. "Mr. and Mrs. Wexford are our house guests. Isabelle is helping me set up the gift shop."

"Oh, how lovely." Lady Cardish gave her mouth a brief curl. "It is sad that you have to open your home to the public. Strangers poking around, their dirty feet on the carpets."

"It really isn't that bad," Belle replied. "Most of the guests are well behaved and genuinely interested in the history. I enjoy talking to them. Perhaps my American roots make it easier for me. It's a lot of fun. I enjoy breaking the rules and having fun, Caroline. You should try it."

"Not for me, my dear Belle, but I do love to have fun. We had a wonderful time at the Valentine's party at The Sackville. Mrs. Wexford organized a fabulous evening."

"Isabelle is talented and The New Sackville is the best kept secret this side of London. I told you it would be a great event." Belle smiled.

"Thank you, we do our best." Isabelle glanced at Belle. She hadn't realized that Belle and Lady Cardish were so close. Friends in high society usually meant acquaintances at best but first names meant real friendship.

"I'm pleased you enjoyed it, Lady Cardish."

"How is your adorable daughter, Sarah? I was charmed by her dancing and I see she has your hair and hazel eyes."

"Sarah is in the playroom under the supervision of one of the maids and not too happy about being treated *like a baby* she informed me. Our colouring comes from my father—curly red hair is more appealing on a nine-year-old than for taming into modern adult styles."

"You wear it well. My dear, that dress is exquisite."

"Thank you, Lady Cardish." Isabelle wanted to pinch herself, chatting with Lady Cardish was more than she had expected.

Darcy joined the little group. "Shall we go in for dinner?" He and Belle led their guests into the dining room.

Isabelle was familiar with formal dining, and the Thornton's table was exquisite. The fragrance from the vases of spring flowers filled the room and the tall silver candelabras flickered with lit candles, making the Waterford crystal glasses sparkle and the monogrammed silverware shine. Even Isabelle wasn't sure what all the silver was for. *There must be eight or nine courses,* she thought. And there it was, the Lady Rose Thornton's dinnerware, the exquisite pattern delicate and refined. She had the feeling that her smile from all the events of today was now permanently engraved on her face. She couldn't have been happier.

Isabelle and Sandy

andy held the car door open for Isabelle while Sarah climbed into the back, waving goodbye to Hillcrest. They were leaving a day early so Sandy could drive the family to Bexhill before starting his long journey back to Edinburgh. Isabelle would have preferred the chauffeur driven Rolls-Royce to Sandy's old Ford but their newly-rekindled love compensated for the sacrifice and Sarah was delighted to hear that her father was moving to Bexhill.

"Mummy, did you know that Felix lives at his school? He only comes home on holidays."

"Most young boys go away to school. You have girls that board at your school."

"Yes, but their parents are abroad. I wouldn't like to live at school."

"Did you have fun at Hillcrest?"

"When can we go back? I like playing with Felix." Sarah yawned.

"Summertime maybe." Sandy added, "But Felix is a young man, I'm not sure he will be interested in playing."

"Well by next summer I will be older and I won't want to play either." Sarah gave a yawn and went quiet.

Isabelle glanced at the back seat. "She's asleep. Felix has been very kind to her. She'll be disappointed if Felix has outgrown playing with her by summer."

"That's a long way off. What are we going to do? Shall I take the job in Bexhill?"

"Yes. I want us to start again."

"What about living arrangements? I'll sell the house. Do you want to find a house in Bexhill?" Sandy glanced sideways at Isabelle. "I don't mind living in the hotel for a while but I want us to have our own place."

"I agree, but living in the hotel is a great help with Sarah. Mum, Bill or someone on staff are always there when she comes home from school, school holidays and if I'm busy with an evening event."

"But if I'm home that wouldn't be a problem."

"I hadn't thought of that. You know, Mother offered us half of the fourth floor that we could use as a penthouse."

Sandy squinted. "The fourth floor is staff quarters. How would that work?"

"Mother only uses half of the floor, not many of the staff live in these days. We could have an architect design a penthouse suite, permanently closed off from the staff side by a wall and with its own private entrance."

Sandy thought for a moment. "Who is going to pay for this? Will your mother pay for the conversion?"

"We could use the money from the sale of the house. It would be cheaper than buying a house."

"If I agree to have an architect in for design, will you call an estate agent and look at some houses? We can compare and decide which option is best for us."

"Yes." Isabelle rested her head on the seat and closed her eyes. Sandy turned the volume up on the radio and glanced at Isabelle as Anne Shelton sang *If You Ever Fall in Love Again*.

Anna's instinct told her right away that Sandy and Isabelle had patched things up. Sarah ran from the car to the lobby and clutched at Anna's hand. "Nana, Daddy's coming to live here."

"That is good news. Welcome home." Anna reached out to Isabelle. From the corner of her eye she saw Smyth clearing a tray in the lobby lounge. His expression dark, he threw a napkin onto the tray. Judging by Isabelle's reaction, she too had seen it.

"Sandy is getting the bags. He still can't get used to the fact that we have staff to do that. Mum, we need to talk. Sandy and I are getting back together."

"I am pleased for you. Are you happy?"

"Very!"

"It's almost lunchtime. Shall I see if Bill can join us, or is this something between you and I?"

"Lunch would be nice. We can celebrate together and talk about our plans. I would like to change from these slacks first. I'll see you in half an hour."

Anna took the stairs to the service quarters. The warmth and chatter from the kitchen made her feel good inside. How it had changed. She remembered the yelling and tense atmosphere when Bill worked for Chef Louis, thirty years ago. Now the staff worked just as hard, perhaps even harder, but there was no tension, just busy people doing a good job. Bill was instructing a new prep cook and looked up when he saw Anna.

"Hello, and what have I done to deserve the pleasure of a visit to the kitchen?"

"Isabelle and Sandy are back and they want us to join them for lunch. Can you get away?"

"Of course. We're not busy today. Is this good news?"

Anna nodded. "Sandy is moving to Bexhill. They look like two kids in love. The old spark is back and little Sarah is over the moon."

Bill hugged Anna. "I am so very pleased for you." Kissing her, he whispered, "Love you." Anna gave an embarrassed laugh as the kitchen staff gave a friendly whistle.

"Behave yourself, Chef Bill," she said loudly enough to make everyone laugh. "Isabelle has gone to change. We'll meet in the dining room. Half an hour okay?"

Lunch was one of the most pleasant family meals Anna could remember in a long time. Her daughter's little family was bubbling with enthusiasm for a bright future. Sandy had already called Bent Engineering to say he would take the job. Anna and Bill happily agreed to the help with the renovations for a penthouse. Anna smiled to herself, wishing Sandy good luck with his idea of buying a house. *He doesn't have a cat in hell's chance. She's just humouring him,* Anna thought. *Isabelle wants that penthouse.* Mr. Smyth hovered around the table, serving more than assisting the waiter. His trained congenial smile did not reflect in his face or eyes. Anna caught his cold fleeting glance towards Isabelle and decided that from now on she would insist that Balaji serve them. She couldn't quite remember why Smyth had taken on the unusual task of serving the family table. She wondered if Isabelle's rejection would have consequences.

Sarah was terrified that her father would not return and it was a sad scene the day Sandy left for Scotland. Even Isabelle's promise that he was coming back in a few weeks to start his new job did not comfort Sarah. She finally grasped the magnitude of her selfishness and how it had hurt Sarah, separating her from her father. To cheer her up and help convince her that her father was indeed coming back, Isabelle took Sarah to see some houses—keeping her promise to Sandy but looking forward to meeting the architect about the penthouse the next day. Renovations in a working hotel had to be planned carefully so as not to interfere with the guests' comfort. Isabelle was hoping they could have a liveable portion finished before the summer rush and complete it in the autumn. But if Sandy didn't sell the house, they wouldn't have the money to start. All she needed was a firm deal on the house and she could go to the bank for a loan.

Since her return from Hillcrest, Isabelle had managed to avoid Ralph Smyth. She had thought he might back off, but her attempt to finish the relationship had apparently not been convincing. It was obvious to everyone except Smyth that Isabelle was making a love nest for the Wexfords at the hotel. The day her mother told him that Balaji would be responsible for the family table; Isabelle had noticed his jaw tense. From then on she often caught him staring at her. There was a time his stares had excited her, but sensing his hurt and anger now, she felt a chill. It had never occurred to her that Smyth would fall in love with her. Isabelle was painfully aware that she had made a big mistake flirting with Smyth and regretted ever getting involved, but not ready for her mother's 'I told you so,' she kept her concerns to herself. Today she had to speak to him about the spring fashion show. Holding a clipboard and pen, Isabelle took a deep breath, straightened her grey suit and marched into the dining room.

"Mr. Smyth, we need to discuss the spring fashion show."

"At last you condescend to speak to me...*Mrs.* Wexford."

The sarcasm and emphasis on *Mrs.* she chose to ignore. Although insubordinate, she acknowledged that only a short while ago they were on first name basis. She continued. "The Emily Carr Restaurant has to be rearranged to accommodate a catwalk for the fashion show and as many tables as possible arranged lengthwise around it, but not in a straight line, we don't want it to look institutional and the waiters need to be able to get around serving tea. Chef has planned a special afternoon tea, we'll use pale pink table cloths and napkins..." Isabelle gasped for breath, she was rambling. Taking a quick glance at Ralph she saw his amused look.

"You are always so beautiful when you're rattled." He looked around the empty dining room. "I know this thing with your husband is a sham to please your mother." He touched her hand and the pleasantness of his touch surprised her. "I know you'd rather be with me."

"Ralph, no, it was a mistake. I'm sorry I misled you. Sandy and I are getting back together. We are converting the west wing of the staff quarters into a penthouse."

"Ah, a few quick steps from my room on the fourth floor."

"Ralph, please. Stop. I'm serious, no flirting and certainly no affair. Work is our only relationship. Now back to the fashion show." Isabelle dared not look up from her clipboard. It took great effort to quell her trembling hands.

She closed her eyes thankfully when she heard her mother's voice. "Sorry to interrupt but Madame Clarice just called." Anna frowned.

"Isabelle, is everything all right?"

"Of course, we're just talking about the fashion show. What did Madame Clarice want?"

"She's concerned about the models' changing facilities and they will require a well-lit room for make-up. She's coming down from London on Wednesday."

"Good, there are a few things I'd like to finalize. Mother, will you join us? I need your advice on the set up." Sensing trouble with Mr. Smyth, Anna didn't need to be persuaded to stay.

"How would you arrange the tables, Mr. Smyth?"

It was rare that Ralph Smyth appeared flustered, but Anna's question caught him off guard. Clearing his throat, he stood up and viewed the dining room. "The waiters will have difficulty serving if the tables are moved. I don't think this is a good idea. The dining room is not large enough for an event this big." Surveying the room, he was forced to turn his back on Anna and Isabelle. A smug look of satisfaction spread over his face.

"I asked for your opinion about the table arrangements, not the event. Neither Mrs. Wexford nor I need your approval. Watch yourself, Mr. Smyth."

Isabelle held her breath, hoping there was enough familiarity left between them that without saying a word her stare would tell him, 'Not another word.' His fiery eyes flipped from Isabelle to Anna and for the first time Isabelle saw something truculent in his expression

"Mr. Smyth, return to your duties. Isabelle, we'll continue this in my office."

"I'll order some tea, although you look as though you could do with a brandy, and so could I."

"Tea is fine. The way that man looks at me sometimes…" Anna paused, "And yet I don't see him look at the guests or even the staff in that way. I must be imagining it."

"I don't think so. I saw it too today and now I can understand. I thought you had it in for him because of me. Mum, he has to go."

"You're right and I'm pleased you agree. Now that you and Sandy are back together he's out to get you, and for whatever reason, me too."

"He knows you didn't approve of me flirting with him. Perhaps he blames you for terminating our relationship, which was not a relationship for me, but I did egg him on."

"I need to speak with Bill and James because technically the dining room staff report to James but operate under the executive chef. I'll have James take care of his pay etc. And we need to find another maître d'. Balaji can take over in the meantime."

"We are quiet at the moment," Isabelle hesitated, "but it might be an issue during the fashion show. We'll manage…" A knock on the door stopped Isabelle. She couldn't believe her eyes as Ralph Smyth walked in.

Concentrating on his feet, he put his hands up in submission and said, "Please hear me out." Isabelle took a breath to speak but Anna touched her arm to silence her. "I'm very sorry for the regrettable manner I spoke today and you have every right to fire me. I am not myself. My father is very ill and maybe dying. I can't focus on work and I'm short tempered with my staff. I know the timing is bad with the fashion show coming up, but I think it best if I take some time off."

"Mr. Smyth, your insubordination will be noted in your file." Anna spoke quickly before Isabelle. "I will give you two weeks leave of absence without pay. Upon your return, we will discuss whether or not you have a future at the Sackville."

Smyth lifted his head and Anna saw genuine anxiety fill his face. "I need my job to support my father."

"This is not the first time you've been out of line, but I will explain your circumstances to Mr. Lytton. Do you have far to travel?"

"He lives near Dartmouth in Devon." Anna noticed his body straighten. She thought he might be lying as his subservient act slithered into a slight curl on the corner of his lips. Anna was glad to be rid of him even for a short time.

Fashion and Fury

⚓

Albert opened the rear door of the Bentley and Madame Clarice's signature accessory—a long black cigarette holder—appeared on the end of a shimmering, elegantly-gloved hand held above the car door and a wide-brimmed, cream coloured hat followed. Her face was framed by wisps of black hair as she raised her head. She was older than Isabelle expected. A sable stole wrapped her shoulders and Isabelle noted the mid-calf length pleated black skirt with a cream jacket that nipped into the smallest waist she had ever seen. She glanced at her own hemline that seemed a little too short for today's fashion. She had thought about dropping the hem, but that always left a tell-tale line; slightly shorter than current fashion was preferable.

Isabelle extended her hand and Madame Clarice gave her a warm smile. A loud whistle followed by a chorus of catcalls came from beyond the hotel entrance. Isabelle strained her neck to look past the car and saw four young men swaggering towards the portico. She glanced at Albert, who nodded and sent one of the bellboys to halt the young men.

"Madame Clarice, this way please," Isabelle greeted her guest and ushered her through the large glass doors, feeling a sense of relief as Albert swung them closed as soon as they'd passed, blocking the sounds from outside that were more suitable for a work site than The New Sackville Hotel. "Mrs. Blaine is waiting for us in her office. The girls arrived early this morning and the changing facilities that we discussed at our last meeting are to their satisfaction."

Madame Clarice smiled. "My girls are all good girls—I chose the prettiest for here. I am looking forward to this show. I have deviated from the normal sales format; this will be the first time I've invited the public." She smiled, "A leap of faith. Clothes rationing is finally being lifted and women will be able to choose their wardrobe without the limitation of coupons." Glancing around the crowded lobby, she added, "We have quite a crowd."

"The show is by invitation only except for resident guests, and of course the local Bexhill merchants, who I am sure are thinking along the same lines as they prepare for the summer clientele and…" Isabelle was interrupted by a tap on the shoulder "Belle, Darcy you made it." Turning to Madame Clarice, Isabelle added, "Allow me to introduce my very good friends, Lord and Lady Thornton." Darcy stepped aside and said, "and our friends, Lord and Lady Cardish."

"How wonderful to see you all. Lunch is being served in the lounge bar. We'll chat after the show. Please excuse us as we have a little preparation to do."

As they approached Anna's office, Madame Clarice leaned in to Isabelle and said, "I had no idea you were acquainted with Lady Cardish; she is quite a fashion icon."

"Lady Cardish has also hosted events here at The New Sackville. It's a long story. Lord and Lady Cardish are close friends of the Thorntons who are close friends of my mother and step-father. My mother knew the previous Lady Thornton, Darcy's mother, during her early days at the original Sackville and my stepfather became friendly with Lord Darcy during his years in Chicago. Long before my time, but the friendship has extended to me by association."

The Emily Carr Restaurant exuded elegance and sophistication. The room was brimming with fashionable guests; extra chairs had been lined across the back of the room. The stage, usually crowded with musicians, had been given a backdrop of soft white chiffon, carefully curtained to allow the models to make a grand entrance, walk around the dance floor and along a red carpet through the audience.

Madame Clarice, dressed in a shimmering aqua satin evening gown with bold and intricate embroidery around the skirt—one of her own creations—stood to the side at a podium. Squeezed in at the other side of the stage a trio played softly as she introduced the show, Summer Fashion in Bexhill, and the parade of models began. Crisp summer dresses in bold checks and pretty florals with full swinging skirts and swaying pleats. Emphasizing the seaside motif, there were wrap-around dirndl skirts, which the models flipped off to show neat beach shorts, two-piece bathing suits that showed a little midriff and one-piece strapless suits to allow for tanning. The eveningwear was light, soft chiffons made to flow in a summer breeze.

The final gown—a surprise even to Isabelle—was a Dior wedding dress in off-white satin that flowed from an intricately embroidered bodice into a long train. A communal gasp filled the room as a demure bride entered, the long veil moving slightly with each step and trailing the long satin train. The applause was deafening and everyone rose for a standing ovation. Anna glanced at her daughter with pride and whispered, "I'm so proud of you. You just put The New Sackville on the map."

"Thanks, Mum. It has certainly exceeded my expectations and judging by the look on Madame Clarice's face, she feels the same way."

At a quarter to six the next morning, Anna was startled by a knock on her office door. She looked up expecting to see Bill, but Amy put her head around the door. "Mrs. Blaine, are you busy?"

"I'm never too busy for you, Amy. Come in and take a seat. Would you like a coffee? I have a spare cup. Bill is busy this morning."

"Thanks, I had a cuppa with Sam."

"I imagine the young models have left a mess for you this morning. Do you need something?"

"No, they won't be up until noon, so I have extra staff coming in late today. It's not about the hotel. Remember back in February those young punks were hanging around? Well they's back."

"Really? I did wonder. Yesterday, when Madame Clarice arrived she was greeted with catcalls from a group of youths. I asked Albert to deal with it. Amy, did something happen?"

"No, they just followed me to work this morning. There were more of them than last time—four or maybe five, and a couple of 'em were foreign looking. They aren't the same ones. Why are they following me?" Tears filled Amy's eyes, "It brings back such bad memories."

Anna reached out and touched Amy's arm. "I'm so sorry. I didn't suffer nearly as badly as you did but I know how those memories can trick your mind and they never go away completely. These are kids with nothing better to do. I don't think they will hurt you."

"Why me?" Tears rolled down her cheeks.

"I think this is a matter for the police. In the meantime, would you like to live in until this is resolved? Or if you prefer, I could have Albert come pick you up in the car."

"That's kind but my Sam can walk me like he did last time. They back off when they see Sam." Wiping her cheeks, she laughed. "They don't want to tangle with my Sam, he's a big fella. Now I best get back to work. Thanks, Anna—sorry, Mrs. Blaine—I had to tell someone."

"Anna is fine; in fact, I would prefer it. We've known each other a long time and have much in common. Stay a while Amy, I'll order you some tea."

"No, I got work to do. I feel better now." Amy left the office and closed the door.

Anna stood in her favourite place by the window, watching the clouds glow in the morning sun. She shuddered at the thought of Amy's story. Her own explanation of "They're just kids," hadn't convinced her any more than it had Amy. It was unrealistic, but Smyth kept coming to mind. Was he mixed up with these thugs? She hated it when her intuition invaded her thoughts—the tip of the iceberg, she could not shake the feeling of danger. Filing a police report was futile as no crime had been committed. Slipping on her jacket, she went into the lobby. It was seven o'clock and Henry was opening the front door.

"Good morning, Mrs. Blaine." He frowned. "Going for a stroll?"

171

"Yes, I thought I would get some fresh air before the guests wake up."

Walking along the Promenade she wondered why she didn't do this more often. The air was fresh, if a little cool and she pulled her jacket tighter and crossed the road. She felt at peace listening to the waves swoosh onto the beach, the pebbles making a tinkling sound as the water receded. It reminded her of the first time she walked along the beach. Not much had changed. The white bathing huts on wheels were now permanent fixtures, painted bright colours set against the Promenade wall. She smiled, comparing the cover-all bathing suits of 1913 and the bare midriff, two-piece bathing suits Madame Clarice had shown yesterday. People had changed. Perhaps it was the war, but Bexhill had not changed. Or had it? She spotted rolls of barbed wire on the beach, and a shelled out building. Not many, the council had done a wonderful job of cleaning the beaches and repairing the damage from German bombing. She was grateful she had been in Rugby during those years.

Loud catcalls and whistles shook her from her thoughts. She looked for where the noise came from but saw nothing. Suddenly, from behind one of the bathing huts came first one, then two, and finally five young men swaggering towards her. They had to be the same men that had followed Amy. Two were dark-skinned, Indian-looking Anna thought, and she recognized one of them, but from where? Realizing she had walked further than intended, she quickly crossed the road and picked up her pace, heading back to the hotel. The gang was now behind her, matching her pace and yelling remarks: "Bitch." And other words too bad to even keep in her thoughts.

Terrified they would attack, she began to run. One of the darker men grabbed her arm and knocked her over. As she lay flat on her back on the pavement, he bent forward and leered at her. Anna screamed at the top of her lungs and one of his mates pulled his arm and they ran off laughing. Terror immobilized her limbs. She screamed again as someone took her arm. "It's me, Albert, Mrs. Blaine. Are you hurt?"

"Oh no, just my pride and I'm a little shaken. Albert, where's Henry?"

"He's left for his breakfast. I was just taking over when I heard you scream."

Albert walked her back to the hotel entrance. Her body wouldn't stop shaking. "I think we need to call the police."

The young police officer's thick mop of short mousy hair sprang to life as he removed his helmet and tucked it under his arm; his smooth baby face had seen few razors. She smiled at his nervous fumbling as he tried to retrieve a pencil and note pad from his uniform pocket.

"What seems…" he cleared his throat, trying to lower his voice an octave, "to be the problem, Mrs. Blaine?"

Anna smiled at his innocence. She remembered her mother saying, "When the policemen look too young, it means you're getting old."

"I was taking a stroll along the Promenade this morning and five young men jumped out from the bathing huts. At first they whistled, made catcalls, and then began calling me names, most of which I would rather not repeat. I crossed the road and began running back to the hotel when one grabbed my arm. I stumbled and fell. They ran off when I screamed."

Frantically taking notes, the officer asked, "Did you recognize any of them? Were they known to you?"

"I've never seen them before, except there were two coloured men and one of them looked familiar but I can't place him."

"Has anything like this happened before?"

"Yes, yesterday a gang of youths approached the hotel making catcalls and earlier that morning the same gang followed my head housekeeper to work. She starts work early, so it must have been five or five-thirty. They didn't hurt her, just taunted and jeered at her. And a few weeks ago, she experienced the same kind of thing."

"I would like to speak with her."

"Of course."

Anna called Amy and a full report was made. Gangs were not common in Bexhill, the odd youth shoplifting would be the sum total of this young officer's experience. Anna had the distinct feeling that he didn't know what action to take.

173

"Ladies, leave it with us. No need to worry." Anna smiled at his attempt to ease their concerns. "I suspect this is just a teenage prank. It seems to be an isolated incident and nothing to worry about."

Raising her eyebrows at the last remark, Anna said, "Officer, I have already explained that this has happened before. Whether or not this was a prank, it needs to be stopped. If the police have not had any other reports of this behaviour, then why are these men targeting The New Sackville?" No longer charmed by this officer's inexperience, Anna was irritated at not being taken seriously. "My hotel and most of Bexhill cater to society guests. Even a hint of gang activities, pranks or not, would affect all the businesses in town. I doubt your superiors would agree with your explanation."

"No ma'am." His face was scarlet. "I mean, yes ma'am. I'll report the incident to my sergeant and ask him to contact you."

"Thank you."

The hotel was slow to wake up; fashion models and their chaperones and superiors started their day around noon. Madame Clarice started her day with a martini at the lounge bar while the models began with lunch, if you could call their scanty nibbles lunch. By mid-afternoon the lobby was full of suitcases, bags and gowns draped in cloth sleeves. The frustrated bellboys were trying to follow confusing instructions from the models as they squabbled over which car they would travel in.

Madame Clarice had migrated from the bar to the lobby, where Anna and Isabelle were trying to oversee the chaos.

"Mrs. Blaine and Mrs. Wexford, thank you. This has been the best fashion show I have ever organized." Suddenly, Madame Clarice turned towards the portico, alarm in her voice. "What is that commotion? My girls are out there."

Hearing the familiar catcalls, Anna left Isabelle to calm Madame Clarice. The scene that greeted her was shocking. The gang was swaggering around the girls and pushing the bellboys as they tried to load the car boots.

The dark-skinned man who had seemed familiar to Anna, the same one who had knocked her over, stared at Anna and defiantly swaggered towards her. Suppressing the urge to scream, she called. "Albert please tell Miss Jenkins to dial 999, they will know what this is about. I met with them earlier today."

Anna stared right back at the man. He didn't flinch. She realized he was the ringleader as he yelled, "Time to scarper boys." He glared at Anna. "And don't think we won't be back, whore!"

The chattering models went silent. Anna took a breath, placed her hand on her mouth and closed her stinging eyes. Quickly composing herself, she turned to the girls, smiled trying to make light of the situation. "Ladies, I am sorry. It would seem that Bexhill's youth is not used to seeing beautiful ladies." The models began to giggle and chatter among themselves. Madame Clarice gave a sideways glance towards Anna as she motioned for the models to group around her. Speaking in a low voice, too low for Anna to hear more than the stern tone of her voice, Madame Clarice spent some time coaxing the girls to calm down. She nodded to the drivers, who escorted the girls into waiting vehicles.

Madame Clarice returned to Anna's side. "Perhaps I will reconsider a second visit. Mrs. Blaine, you seem to have a problem with the criminal set."

"Just overzealous teenagers. Bexhill is a quiet seaside resort town. I regret this happened today, but I can assure you it won't happen again." Relieved to hear the police sirens in the distance Anna smiled, pointing to the blue flashing light. "As you can see the police are quick to respond."

Madame Clarice placed her cigarette holder in her mouth and puffed a circle of white smoke in the air, striding with more elegance than Anna thought possible as she moved towards the Bentley."

Isabelle and Anna waved off the entourage and greeted the police. Isabelle had not seen the episode with the gang and asked, "What was that all about?"

"We have a gang of teenagers with nothing better to do than harass innocent people."

"Mum, this is serious. You heard Madame Clarice."

"I know. That's why the police are here." Anna nodded towards the door.

"Mrs. Blaine, my name is Sergeant Patterson. The constable was in the middle of his report about the earlier incident when we received your 999 call. This is very disturbing. I have dispatched some constables to find the culprits based on your earlier descriptions." He shook his head from side to side. "I find it unbelievable that something like this could happen in Bexhill. The inspector will not be pleased." He looked down his head still moving. "Please describe what happened."

Gathering her thoughts about the incident, Anna found herself distracted. She couldn't help wondering why the inspector would be displeased? *Perhaps Bexhill constabulary doesn't have the manpower or expertise to handle the situation,* she thought. *And that's not very comforting.*

"Mrs. Blaine?"

"Oh yes. Shall I begin with the first incident?"

The next morning, James Lytton rushed into Anna's office and placed *The Daily Mirror* on her desk. She looked up. "What's this?"

"Open it to page three." The paper crinkled as she flattened it on her desk and turned the pages. Her heart stopped as she saw the headline "Local Gang Swarms Models at Bexhill's New Sackville Hotel". There was a photo of the Sackville portico, and a picture of Madame Clarice in the Emily Carr Restaurant and another of the models on the catwalk. Anna sighed; she had forgotten the press had been invited to the fashion show.

"James, can you ask Isabelle to come to my office? She needs to speak with Madame Clarice. I was told the reporter was from *Vogue Magazine* not the newspapers."

Isabelle marched into the office, visibly angry. "I've seen it and I've already called Madame Clarice's office. Her assistant confirmed the reporter was from *Vogue* and insisted they had nothing to do with the newspapers."

Only half listening, Anna read the report and studied the photos. "Something is not right with this. The reporter left after the show—he wasn't here when the incident happened. And why show a picture of the portico without cars, models or the gang? The photo of the fashion show is quite flattering, even the report on the show talked positively about the standing ovation. Although the description of a violent gang attacking the models is anything but flattering."

"Mother, listen to me. This is disastrous!"

"Isabelle, calm down. We need to get to the bottom of this. It's not all bad, some publicity is good. James, call the *Daily Mirror* and see if you can find the source of this report. I'll speak to the police and see if they released anything. And Isabelle, speak to Madame Clarice in person."

"I think we need to make a statement first and explain what really happened."

"No, it's better not to respond. It'll just go away. There's nothing substantial in the report and most of our guests don't even read the *Mirror*."

Shortly after lunch, Anna had all the answers she was going to get. The police confirmed that someone from *The Daily Mirror* did enquire about a disturbance at The New Sackville but only minimal information was given. James reported that *The Daily Mirror* had received information about the fashion show in Bexhill, and were surprised by the anonymous tip regarding the disturbance, which was confirmed by Bexhill police. There seemed to be a lot of finger pointing from Madame Clarice's office and Isabelle came to the conclusion that someone, without authority from either the office or *Vogue*, had given away an unauthorized description and taken an unauthorized photo of the fashion show. Anna decided nothing more could be done and the best thing was to carry on. Fortunately, they still had a few weeks before high season.

Communists in Bexhill

T wo weeks had gone by since the *Daily Mirror* report and there had been no cancellations or slowing down of new bookings for the summer. Madame Clarice had expressed concern, but as the publicity had actually generated interest for her fashion designs, she considered it an enhancement to the official *Vogue* pictures and article and she would likely book a show next year.

In spite of the positive outcome, Anna felt uneasy, jumpy and on edge most of the time. The police were investigating the gang element and there was an increased police presence around the hotel. From her office window she could see a bunch of youths fooling around on the beach, far enough away not to cause the police concern but close enough to taunt Anna's paranoid mind. James tapped on the door and she almost jumped off her chair. "Come in."

"Just had a call from Mr. Smyth. His father is much better and he is returning tomorrow. You look as pleased as I am. I don't know what it is about that man—an air of darkness surrounds him."

"My thoughts exactly. You couldn't have put any better. I wish I'd fired him when I had the chance. Balaji does a good job. He's not as experienced but is a quick learner. We agreed to give Smyth another chance. One step out of line and he's gone."

"I nearly forgot. Isabelle asked if you could meet her on the fourth floor."

"Now? She never changes, that daughter of mine." Anna smiled. "I'll go and give her the news that Smyth is back tomorrow."

Anna took the lift to the third floor and walked up the service stairs to what used to be Mrs. Banks bedroom. Isabelle was talking to a tall, neat-looking man about Isabelle's age. Anna said nothing and listened to the plans for a private lift leading into a spacious entrance hall on the far side of the building, knocking walls down to use the full height for living space and changing the roofline for more height. The main bedroom was to have a private bathroom. Anna's mind was ringing like a cash register.

She hated to put a damper on Isabelle's enthusiasm. "A private lift is much too expensive." She looked at the architect. "Couldn't you make a nice staircase off the third floor, where the emergency stairs are? They're only needed for the third floor down. And you are not changing the roofline. I agree the dormer windows are a problem, but if you can't change it internally then perhaps the idea of making a penthouse is not as viable as we thought."

"Mother, you said we could have this as our flat. I'm sure it can be done without being too expensive, and as soon as the house is sold we'll contribute to the refurbishing."

"I'm afraid your mother is right, Mrs. Wexford. Installing a private lift is not only expensive but it requires some structural changes to the roof, as would building out to give more head room. But you could have a private staircase from the third to the fourth floor and I can design a plan to utilize the height for living space without structural changes."

"All right, bring us some plans with costs. Is that okay, Mother?"

Anna nodded her approval as they returned to the main floor.

"Isabelle, I nearly forgot, Smyth is returning tomorrow. His father's health has improved."

"Oh, I can't say I'm looking forward seeing him again."

"I agree, but everyone deserves a second chance. Don't they?" *Or do they?* she thought.

Miss Jenkins interrupted, "Mrs. Blaine, there is a gentleman waiting to see you in your office."

She handed her a business card: "Chief Inspector Durham - Eastbourne and District Police Force," Anna read. "Isabelle, I need to deal with this. Meet me later to talk about the cost and timing of the flat?"

"Chief Inspector Durham, my name is Anna Blaine. My husband and I own The New Sackville. How can I help you?" The inspector stood up and shook hands. Anna sat behind her desk, feeling slightly intimidated by this large, severe policeman.

"Mrs. Blaine, you recently made a complaint regarding some gang activity."

"Yes, I've had cause to call the local police twice. A gang in Bexhill is unusual. I thought I was being paranoid. One of the leaders, a coloured man, perhaps Indian, more man than boy, did push me hard enough that I fell on the pavement." Anna felt the fear of that moment grip her insides, feeling the same fear she had felt so many years earlier, she reprimanded herself. *Anna Blaine, you are being paranoid and letting a bunch of silly kids get to you. So why is a high-ranking police officer asking you questions?* Anna became aware of the chief inspector's stare and awkward silence. She cleared her throat and stared back. "At the time I was more concerned about the hotel's reputation. Sergeant Patterson ordered his constables to keep an eye on the hotel. I couldn't be sure, but I think they are still hanging around at a careful distance. In fact, if you look beyond the Promenade you can see a group of kids fooling around on the beach. It's too far to see details, but I wondered if it was part of the gang."

The chief inspector glanced out of the window. "Maybe? But as you say they look like kids and the gang I'm concerned about includes adult males, not just kids. I'll speak to the inspector at Bexhill police station and have them moved along. The gang I'm concerned about includes two coloured men. One we know nothing about, but the other one is the leader and matches your description of the man who assaulted you. We believe he arrived from India in April 1948. He is a known activist and troublemaker. I'm curious, why would such a person be harassing your hotel?" Durham paused, glaring directly at Anna and making her feel uncomfortable. She thought, *He's accusing me of something.*

"What connection do you have with this man?"

"None! I've never seen him before." As she said the words, she had a vague memory of this man.

"You do have a connection. I see it in your face." Durham sat back with a look of satisfaction.

"No, but he reminds me of someone I saw on the ship coming back from India."

"You were in India?"

"My husband and I spent our honeymoon in India." Seeing a look of confusion, Anna continued, "Mr. Blaine is my second husband. My first husband, Alex Walker, died in 1945. Visiting India was a life-long dream for Bill and I. Perhaps naive on our part, not understanding the magnitude of the religious and political situation at that time. India is a beautiful country and the people are wonderful." Anna stopped as Inspector Durham cleared his throat, obviously not interested in the beauty of India. She continued, "I honestly do not know this man." Anna felt the urge to convince this policeman there was no connection. "I remembered him because I had seen him in Calcutta. We happened on a riot and he was standing on a soapbox yelling at the crowd. A policeman recognized us as tourists and swept us out of danger. He, the policeman, gave us a good talking to for being there and took us to safety. I thought I saw the soapbox man on the ship coming home, but my husband said I was being paranoid. I couldn't be certain."

"You sound certain to me." Durham said with a nod of agreement. "Is there anyone else in the hotel that could have a connection? Anyone from India?"

Relieved to hear the accusatory tone disappear she said, "Our maître d'hôtel, Ralph Smyth, told us he was born in London but he may have been born in India. I understand that Balaji—one of the waiters—came from a rural area outside Calcutta and they knew each other as children. Both have been in the hotel business in London for several years, working at the Dorchester and Savoy before coming here." Anna thought, *Is Smyth connected in some way?*

"We'll take a look into Smyth and Balaji's background. Would it be possible to speak to these men?"

"Balaji is here, but Mr. Smyth is away. His father is ill, but he will be back tomorrow. I'll get Balaji for you." Anna went to the office door. "Mr. Lytton, would you ask Balaji to come to my office."

"James Lytton still works here?"

"Yes. You know him?"

James walked in. "He's on his way." His eyes opened wide and he said, "Detective Durham, how are you?"

"I am well, but it's Chief Inspector now. You didn't move on then?"

"No, Mr. Kendrick made me general manager and I've been here ever since. I even stayed and did my bit during the war with injured soldiers. Mrs. Blaine and her husband bought the hotel from Mr. Kendrick and revitalized it, putting us back on the map."

"I had notice the offices have changed. That big old office has gone."

"We built two smaller offices and what was the old office is now the reception lounge. Removed some bad memories."

"Um…nasty business that. What happened to the little maid?"

"Amy? She still works here, she's the head housekeeper now. We both stuck it out and Miss Jenkins came back after her fiancé was killed. Mrs. Banks retired to Hastings. Of course, you know Mrs. Blaine used to work with me on reception and as Mr. Pickles secretary." James stopped and glanced at Anna. He saw her face change as she realized they were talking about the arrest of Mr. Pickles.

"No, I didn't know Mrs. Blaine worked here, but when she mentioned her first husband the name Walker rang a bell." He turned to Anna. "I believe you had just left for Scotland or Australia."

"Your memory is sharp, Inspector. Alex and I did go to Scotland, intending to go on to Australia, but we couldn't get a passage and ended up going to Canada. We lived there for fifteen years before coming back to England. I didn't find out about Mr. Pickles' arrest until my brother brought us a newspaper clipping, many months later."

"Charlie Neale, a special agent with the Royal Canadian Mounted Police."

Anna felt uncomfortable…Chief Inspector Durham knew a lot about her family. "You know Charlie?"

"By reputation. He was quite a hero during both wars and now the Cold War."

"He still lives in Canada with his wife and daughter. He was always secretive about his work and I knew better than to ask."

"I think you are very adept at keeping secrets, Mrs. Blaine." Durham, stared directly at Anna. "I've always found it strange that we never found the identity of the mystery woman who worked with Dr. Gregory to expose Pickles. She must have known Pickles quite well, judging by the detail in her statement." Anna willed her cheeks not to blush with guilt as she felt her throat and chest tighten. She gave an audible sigh when Balaji opened the door.

"Come in Balaji, this is Chief Inspector Durham. He's investigating the recent gang activity and wants to ask you some questions."

Balaji's eyes darted from Anna to the inspector. "I'm most happy to be here, Mrs. Blaine. I know nothing of gangs."

"We know that but you may know someone…"

Durham interrupted her. "Mrs. Blaine, I'd like to talk to Balaji alone please."

"Of course. James and I will wait in his office next door."

Anna and James sat in silence at first and then they both began to speak at the same time. James nodded to Anna to continue. "What do you think is going on here?

"I'm not sure, but it definitely isn't about teenage kids. Durham is smart and a stickler for detail. I remember when he arrested Pickles, he came back several times asking questions about the smallest thing. In fact, it may have been the detail that finally put Pickles away. I think he's guessed you are the mystery woman."

"I have no doubt about that, but I don't intend to confess. Bill doesn't know about the attempted rape and I don't want him to know. Neither do I want my daughter to know. And reputation in our business is everything. A scandal could ruin us."

"I'll do my best, but Miss Jenkins and Amy both know what happened. If Durham starts questioning them, your identity may be revealed."

"Maybe, but I think there is more to this whole thing. I saw the way Charlie dodged around things to take the focus off what he was really investigating. Durham is doing that with us. He's not interested in gangs. Although, that one Indian guy he's interested in…I think he's looking for spies."

James laughed. "Here in sleepy Bexhill-on-Sea?"

"What better place to hide? Residents don't even lock their doors here. We think the war is over, but it's not. The Germans hate us as we hate them. What's going on in India is our fault. The Russians want the bomb and the Americans are terrified."

"I agree Durham is after more than kids and perhaps there is a conspiracy. There's certainly a lot of mistrust and we are sheltered from it."

"Not as sheltered as we think. I don't think Balaji is involved, he's too transparent. But I reckon Smyth is. A pity he's not here. I'd prefer the chief inspector to surprise him. But no doubt Balaji will tell him when he returns, giving Smyth chance to concoct a story."

James looked at his watch. "It's been half an hour. Let's see what's going on."

Balaji sat at the small conference table, as a white as a sheet. Anna immediately went to his side. "Balaji, what is it?"

"I have asked Balaji to accompany me to the Eastbourne police station." Durham's voice was stern, leaving no invitation to question the decision.

"Are you arresting him?" James asked.

"No, just routine questions."

The little group moved in unison to a waiting, unmarked police car. The chief inspector and Balaji got into the backseat and the car drove off.

"James, tell Albert and Miss Jenkins to keep this quiet and I'll tell the dining room staff that Balaji had a family emergency. I think Durham is grasping at straws. Balaji is no more a criminal or spy than you or I. The good thing is that he probably won't be here when Smyth returns. I'm convinced that Smyth has something to do with the gang. Perhaps he's the spy?"

Everyone, including Bill and Isabelle, accepted that Balaji had been called away on a family matter. Anna brushed off the police visit as reassurance that the teenage pranksters were being dealt with appropriately. And, as if on cue, the gang disappeared.

Ralph Smyth returned on the morning train and immediately asked to speak with Anna.

"Mr. Smyth, I hope your father is feeling better."

"He has a heart condition, but as long as he follows doctor's instructions, eats well and limits his activities, he is expected to make a full recovery. Thank you for asking."

Anna looked up from her desk; Smyth's change in tone surprised her. "You asked to see me. What can I do for you?"

"I wanted to apologize for my behaviour before I left and to assure you it won't happen again."

"It won't happen again, because if it does Mr. Smyth, you will be fired."

"It won't. Mrs. Blaine, I would like to see Woody. I think I owe him an apology for the way I have spoken to him in the past."

"It sounds as though your father has given you some good advice."

Smyth actually smiled slightly, and with genuine positivity he said, "Yes he did. He's a very wise man. Our time together was good for both of us and has sparked a strong father-son relationship."

"Very well. Talk to Woody but please understand he is timid and easily frightened." Anna looked at him as he nodded; she couldn't help being suspicious of this new compliant Smyth. And, she thought it almost sounded as though he didn't know his father until this visit. *Stop being so negative,* she reprimanded herself, *he's learned a lesson.*

"I gave Balaji a couple of days off, so you are short one waiter. But we aren't busy at the moment. I'm sure you can manage."

"That is fine. Will I be serving the family table?" Anna looked for sarcasm but there was none.

"No, assign another waiter until Balaji returns. Mr. Smyth, as maître d' your job is to oversee the waiters and not wait tables unless there is a problem. Now, back to work." Smyth left the office as her phone rang.

Anna's hand hovered over the receiver as she waited for Smyth to close the door, and upon hearing the chief inspector's voice she was glad she had.

"Good morning, Chief Inspector Durham. Do you have news for us?"

"We've finished questioning Balaji and are satisfied that he is not connected to our suspects, but he did give us some valuable information."

"And what would that be?" Anna asked.

"I'm not at liberty to say. This is an ongoing investigation. I can tell you that you will no longer be harassed by teenagers."

"Oh, so the little gang was nothing more than a bunch of kids?"

"I didn't say that, but you are safe and Balaji will be released in an hour. By the way is Mr. Smyth back?"

"Yes, he returned this morning. Will you be questioning him?"

"No. Will someone be collecting Balaji?" *That's odd,* Anna thought, *why would they not want to speak with Smyth?* "Tell Balaji to wait, I'll send a car."

"Goodbye, Mrs. Blaine." A sharp click and Anna was listening to the dial tone. Curious as to what had transpired between Balaji and the inspector, Anna decided she would drive to Eastbourne.

Picking up her handbag and jacket, she told Miss Jenkins that she would be gone for the afternoon and asked Albert to bring the Hillman to the front.

It was a perfect sunny day for a drive. The roads were quiet—come July there would be traffic jams at every corner but today was lovely. She needed time to reflect: when she and Bill had bought the Sackville, it had never occurred to her that some unknown force or person would try to sabotage the hotel's reputation. Was the hotel really being threatened? Durham had implied it was more to do with spies, conspiracy and atom bombs and the Cold War and not anything personal. Anna thought it *was* personal. She glanced in the rear view mirror as she turned onto the road to Eastbourne. A black Ford pulled up behind her. The distance was so precise that she began to wonder if someone was following her. Five miles further on, the car was still there. She swung left into a small village. Relieved that the car had not followed, she pulled back onto the main road. As she approached Eastbourne the traffic had increased and that black Ford was two cars behind her. *Not possible,* she thought, *there are hundreds of black Fords on the road.* But this one was keeping pace. She shook her head, overzealous imagination. Before she turned into the police station, the black Ford turned off into the town centre.

It took Anna's eyes a minute to adjust from the bright sun to the dimness of the police station, which smelled of sweaty men and sour beer from the previous night's drunks—a more seedy side of Eastbourne she didn't often see in Bexhill. A constable stood behind a tall wooden counter, in front of which the linoleum floor was worn to a patch of bare floorboards from anxious scuffing feet.

"Can I help you, ma'am?" Anna looked up, her neck bent backwards to speak with this giant constable.

"I'd like to see Chief Inspector Durham please."

"You would, would you? Well he's not here. If you have a complaint I can take the details. No need to bother the chief inspector."

Anna pursed her lips and stared upwards. "My only complaint is your rudeness. I spoke with Chief Inspector Durham this morning. He is expecting me."

"Sorry ma'am." The constable's cheeks were quite pink. "CI Durham has been called out on a case. May I help you?"

"I am here to collect Mr. Balaji. He was helping the inspector with an incident in Bexhill."

"Oh, the coloured man. Pretty upset he is. I had to take him a cup of tea to calm him down."

"Constable, would you fetch him for me please."

Detecting Anna's impatience, the constable called, "Hey Charlie, can you get the Balgie guy from the back?"

Anna was shocked as Balaji walked towards her. He looked as though he hadn't slept and he tried to smile as he smoothed his wrinkled uniform. "Mrs. Blaine, I'm most sorry my uniform is…" He stared at his feet.

"Balaji, don't worry. We'll get you a clean uniform back at the hotel. Are you all right?"

"Balaji fine, most tired."

"Strange thing to carry about?" The constable said, handing Balaji a corkscrew and glancing at Anna. "The only thing he had in his pocket. Sign here, please."

Anna stared at the ignorant man. "He's a waiter. He opens wine bottles." She rolled her eyes and guided Balaji to the car.

Secrets

I sabelle couldn't concentrate. Her mind was full of disappearing walls and bright windows. She agreed that she could manage without the lift, but the cramped feeling of those dormer windows bothered her. Deciding she could work on the wedding later, she grabbed her clipboard and ran upstairs to the fourth floor, trying to picture what the architect had described. She made sketches and was studying how the light would come through when a familiar voice startled her.

"Isabelle, I see you are starting the plans for your penthouse." Ralph's voice prompted her heart to miss a beat.

"Mr. Smyth, you are back. It is Mrs. Wexford to you. How is your father?"

"He is well on the road to recovery. I have just met with your mother to apologize and I would like to tell you how sorry I am for my behaviour. I was very worried about my father. As I'm sure you worry about your mother."

"Why would I worry about my mother?" She frowned at the strange comment.

"Our parents have ways of keeping secrets, as I have discovered."

"Really? My family is close. There are no secrets."

"Things happen before we are born or were not old enough to understand. But there are secrets all the same."

"I'm pleased you bonded with your father. Now if you'll excuse me, I have work to do and so do you."

Isabelle was annoyed that Ralph had intruded on her penthouse planning. Instead of drawing her plans, she ran back down the stairs. She was relieved that Smyth's remarks had not been about them, but confused by his reference to secrets. Deep in thought, she entered onto the third floor landing and bumped into Anna.

"Hello Isabelle. I just brought Balaji back from Eastbourne and Smyth returned this morning."

"I know, I just saw him. He's quite emotional about his father. The first thing I want the builders to do is build a wall between the staff quarters and my flat."

"Why? Did Smyth upset you?"

"No, in fact he was apologetic and a bit strange, rambling on about parents having secrets. It's not just Smyth. Being so close to the staff quarters, I don't want the staff prying into our lives."

"I know what you mean. It's nice to get away in your own space. I'm going for some quiet time. Do you want to join me?"

"Thanks, but I have to work on a wedding proposal. We already have three this summer and this will make four, although one's not until October."

"I couldn't have done what you have done, and without these events, the hotel would be struggling. Take a break and let's have a chat. There is something I need to tell you."

"All right."

Isabelle stood by the French windows. "I think you have one of the best views in the hotel"

"I know. It was one of the reasons I chose this suite for our home. I remember walking in here the first time: the French doors were open and I saw this view. I was nineteen and absolutely terrified of old Lady Thornton. She had a parrot that kept saying, 'Anna, get out!' Nervous and confused, I didn't see the parrot and thought I was being yelled at."

Isabelle laughed. "A parrot!" Anna nodded and they laughed together, sipping sherry, comfortable with each other's company.

"I drove into Eastbourne this afternoon to collect Balaji from the police station."

"I thought he had a family emergency."

"I made that story up. The chief inspector from Eastbourne came to see me. He was convinced Balaji had a connection to the Indian men in the gang. I didn't want the staff to start rumours about gangs around the hotel, and more importantly I didn't want Mr. Smyth to know."

"Why? Does he have something to do with this?"

"That's where I am confused. The inspector showed interest in Smyth, but when he called to say Balaji was free to go, he asked if Smyth was back but didn't want to talk to him." Anna sipped her sherry, rehearsing in her mind what, if anything, she was going to reveal to Isabelle. "On the way back from Eastbourne I asked Balaji what had happened at the police station. At first, he said little. I think he'd been told not to repeat the interview but finally he broke down. He was very upset by the whole incident. Chief Inspector Durham's interest was in his association with Smyth. We already know that they grew up together in India. He said Smyth was a great friend until his mother died and then he became angry. The family that his mother worked for took him in and sent him here to school. Darcy already told us that. Although he looks white, he's mixed-breed—half-caste. Balaji calls him Ravi, his Indian name. Smyth became an angry young man and obsessed about finding his father. But he was always a kind friend and when Balaji arrived in England Smyth got him a job at The Dorchester. But they lost touch until they met here."

"I'm not getting your point, Mum. What does this have to do with us or the police?"

"Durham drilled Balaji about Smyth and his father. They accused Smyth of being connected to the gang that was harassing us."

"Smyth wasn't even here when that happened."

"Smyth is suspected of plotting against the government and the police told Balaji that unless he helped them, he would be a suspect by association. Poor fellow was beside himself. And then the next morning they thanked him for his help and told him he was free to go."

"Who is this Inspector Durham and what does he have to do with us?"

"He's the chief inspector for Sussex County and..." Anna hesitated wondering if she should tell Isabelle about Durham arresting Pickles in 1920. Just the thought of that man stirred fear in every bone in her body. How could she tell her daughter what he did to her? And if Isabelle knew, would Bill find out?

"Mum! What is it?"

Anna shook herself from her thoughts. "Oh nothing, I was thinking of something that happened a long time ago. What were you saying?"

"I wasn't saying anything. You were talking about the inspector."

"When Durham was a mere detective, back in the early 20s, he was involved in the arrest of ... James' predecessor, fraud or something. It happened after your father and I left."

"Parents with secrets," Isabelle muttered.

Anna frowned, ignoring the comment.

Isabelle added, "Is there something you're not telling me?"

"Another time. Not now. It's time for you to pick up Sarah from school and I have things to do. Let's go down together."

"You are being mysterious, Mother. I'll talk to you later." Isabelle went to fetch Sarah and Anna went into her office.

Anna felt unsettled, even though the harassing had stopped. She couldn't help feeling that something was about to burst. She'd heard Isabelle mutter "parents with secrets" and she had secrets that she'd thought would be buried forever. Was it a coincidence that an unrelated remark made by Smyth would trigger Anna's guilt? And yet she had done nothing wrong. Or had she? Hiding in Canada when she should have been a witness was cowardly, and not telling Bill and Alex the truth was not totally honest. *I always meant to,* she thought. It had surprised her that wounds from long ago were so painful and the memories of Mr. Pickles attacking her had surfaced as though it was just yesterday. She knew why she hadn't told Bill, and the thought of her daughter knowing brought back her shame, both for her family and the hotel. Mr. Kendrick had been right to keep the scandal from the hotel. Was she going to let him down too, by allowing events of the past to blemish the hotel's future?

She wondered how he was doing. She hadn't seen him since the opening and phone calls had been sparse as his health deteriorated. Remembering his birthday was coming up, she picked up the phone, "Miss Jenkins can you make a long distance call to Mr. Kendrick please?"

"Mr. Kendrick's residence. Andrew the butler speaking."

Anna replied, "This is Anna Blaine calling, may I speak with Mr. Kendrick?"

"Mr. Kendrick is not available; can I take a message?"

"Please ask him to call Anna Bla...Anna Neale from The Sackville Hotel." Placing the receiver in its cradle Anna felt a chill and was annoyed that she hadn't insisted. She knew better. Andrew's job was to protect his master—a reflection of times gone by. An unexplained sense of urgency washed over her. Was something wrong? Was Mr. Kendrick ill? Should she wait for him to return her call? Andrew had not indicated there was anything wrong but then he was a butler. "I'll wait."

Fifteen minutes later her phone rang and Miss Jenkins informed her Mr. Kendrick was on the line. She smiled, brushing away her worry until she heard a woman's voice.

"Mrs. Blaine, this is Mr. Kendrick's nurse. He is very ill and weak. But against my advice, he insists on speaking with you. Please keep it brief."

Anna's heart sank as she replied. "Of course."

The line went quiet except for bed sheets rustling.

"Is that you Anna Neale? " Anna pressed the phone tightly to her ear, straining to hear his frail voice.

"Yes it's me, Anna. How are you, Mr. Kendrick?"

"I'm having...trouble with the old...ticker." Anna could hear the effort it took him to speak each word. "How...are...you? How's...The Sackville?" His laboured breathing frightened her.

"We are all fine and the hotel is doing very well. My daughter has planned all kinds of weddings and conferences. Why don't you come and visit us?" Taking a breath of her own she knew how fruitless her invitation was.

"I would like that but…Anna, I'm dying. I'm old and it's time…" he paused, gasping for air. "I wanted to…hear your voice…and thank you."

"Thank me? I should be thanking you."

"It's time to join my wife…it's been a long time…" Anna's ears were assaulted by a hacking, unrelenting cough and then silence.

"Mr. Kendrick!" she yelled at the phone and waited and waited, she didn't know how long but there was no answer—no breathing or coughing, just dial tone.

A steady stream of tears flowed down her face as she placed the receiver in the cradle. She didn't need to be told that Mr. Kendrick had taken his last breath. Her tears took away the worries of her earlier thoughts and sadness took over: sadness for losing such a lovely person and for an era closed. She felt orphaned. They weren't close, but over time he had placed so much faith in her. With Mr. Kendrick gone, she was truly alone at the helm of The New Sackville. It was a comfort to have Bill at her side but his attachment was different. Anna considered it entirely her responsibility to guide the hotel successfully and build a legacy for her daughter and granddaughter. Mr. Kendrick's death forced her to think of her own mortality.

"Mum, what is it? You look as though you've seen a ghost."

"I didn't hear you come in." Anna took a deep breath. "And Sarah. How was school today?"

"We had art today, my favourite subject. I painted a picture for my new house. I know our new home is a penthouse but I like painting gardens." Sara held up a well-proportioned and artfully painted house and garden; a gathering of people with an incredible likeness to each member of the family posed in front of the house. Anna looked at Isabelle. "She is very talented." Anna patted Sarah's shoulder, "Sarah, this is magnificent. I can see you are going to be an artist like Emily Carr."

Sarah frowned. "Who is Emily Carr? I know we have an Emily Carr dining room. Was she a real person?"

"Emily Carr was a Canadian artist that I admire. She painted the pictures in the dining room and I named it after the artist."

Sarah thought for a moment. "I've always liked those pictures. Did you

194

meet the lady when you were in Canada?"

"No but I met a friend of Miss Carr's in a café in Vancouver, which is where I first saw her paintings."

"Nana, you almost met a famous artist. That is cool. I have to tell the girls at school. I might even tell my teacher and see if she can show me how to paint like Emily Carr. I could do that."

Isabelle laughed. "Sarah, don't be silly, you could never paint like that."

Anna shot a disapproving glance at Isabelle. Seeing the hurt in Sarah's eyes, she said, "Of course you can. It just takes practice and judging from this painting, you have made a very good start. Now run along and find Grandpa Bill and something to eat before you start your homework."

"I wish you wouldn't encourage her."

"Isabelle, she's talented. Nurture her talent."

"I don't want to nurture my daughter to be a starving artist. You never answered my question."

"You're changing the subject."

"As are you." Anna glared at Isabelle but chose to drop the subject. "I'm upset because I just spoke with Mr. Kendrick and discovered he is very ill. I actually think he died this afternoon." Anna continued to relate the phone call, trying to hold back tears.

"Oh Mum, I'm sorry. I know you were fond of the old man, but he was in his nineties."

"That's a very cold remark. Mr. Kendrick is the reason you have a job and I have a hotel—one which you will inherit one day. No matter how old he is or was, he is a great loss to us."

"I'm sorry, Mum." Isabelle gave Anna a hug. "That was an insensitive remark and a poor choice of words. I didn't mean to be unkind. "

The official announcement of Mr. Kendrick's death came the following day and the funeral was two days later. Anna, Bill, James and Amy drove to London to attend. Isabelle declined. Darcy and Belle came up to London from the estate to attend, out of respect for Lady Thornton's friendship with the Kendricks. They invited everyone to stay at the flat that night. Darcy took Bill and James to his club, leaving the ladies to a light supper at home.

Amy, more comfortable with the housekeeper, chose to stay downstairs.

Anna pushed the food around her plate. Glancing at Belle, she said, "I'm sorry. It looks lovely but I'm not hungry. It has really shaken me, losing Mr. Kendrick."

"I can see that. I hadn't realized you were that close."

"We weren't, but he believed in me, although in my younger days at The Sackville I wasn't aware of it. But when he sold the hotel to us, I realized how much I meant to him. His death has closed an era and there's a portion of my life that I am glad to see the back of." Anna hesitated, "I have a strange sense that my past is about to revisit me."

"Now that is an odd thing to say."

"I'm being far too morose and I should be grateful the hotel is doing so well. So, how is the estate doing? Was Isabelle able to help you?"

"Hillcrest is doing well and the gift shop sales have tripled. Isabelle did a great job. I'm pleased that she and Sandy are getting back together. And Sarah is such a sweet kid. Felix entertained her for the whole two weeks. Even Felix has buckled down at last. He's been accepted at Oxford starting in September."

"Excellent. You must be proud of him." Anna yawned. "Excuse me, it has been a long day. Would you mind if I turned in?"

"Not at all. I'm not waiting for up for Darcy. Can you find your way?"

Anna nodded. "Goodnight."

Talking to Belle after the funeral had lifted Anna's spirits and she returned home with new determination, even excitement. Belle's success with the gift shop had made Anna appreciate her daughter's talent. She had also realized that she had subconsciously resisted Isabelle's ideas.

James pulled the Hillman up to the entrance, allowing Anna to get out of the car. Bill and Amy waited to be dropped off by the garage near the service entrance.

She needed some quiet time and took the lift to the third floor. She glanced up as she heard noise from the floor above. Had Isabelle started the renovations already? *Not possible,* she thought. *I've only been away a day.* Then she heard voices, the architect perhaps—but the voices were loud. Then Isabelle's voice, "No, leave me alone."

As Anna ran up the stairs, she heard a loud thud. Reaching the landing, she was terrified by the scene unfolding before her. Ralph Smyth was pushing Isabelle up against the wall.

She screamed, "Stop it!" Smyth glanced at Anna and she recoiled, seeing the loathing and lust. She snapped. It was Pickles all over again: her mind heard the books falling off the bookcase and felt his body thrusting at her. She grabbed at the only thing at hand, the water jug on the washstand, and with all the force she could muster she slammed it down on Smyth's head. Once, twice...he fell to the floor, blood pouring from a cut on his forehead. Anna kept hitting and hitting; tears streaming down her face. Isabelle jumped forward and grabbed her arm; Anna clung on to the handle, the rest of the jug in smithereens on the floor. Realizing what she had done, Anna stared at the body on the floor; suddenly recognizing Smyth's lifeless body, not Pickles, curled in the fetal position with his blood spattered hands clasping his head.

Isabelle stared at Anna. "Mum, what are you doing?"

"He was attacking you! I heard you scream. I thought it was…" The scene came back to her. *Oh my God, what did I do?*

"I screamed because Ralph startled me. He was making unwanted advances but he wasn't hurting me." Isabelle looked worried. "Mum, are you all right?"

Anna glowered at Smyth's still body. "Is he dead?"

Bill's voice came from the doorway, "Is who dead? What happened?"

Anna's eyes widened as she glared at the jug handle still in her hand and threw it to the ground. Not knowing what had happened but Anna's face told him she had suffered a crisis, he took her hand and whispered, "It's all right. Look at me, Anna." Anna looked at Bill, and the trance-like feeling lifted, leaving a sense of alarm at what had just happened. Bill waited for an explanation but she couldn't form the words. He looked to Isabelle.

"Mum thought Ralph was attacking me and she hit him with the jug."

Isabelle glanced at the body.

"Well I don't think he's dead, just dazed," Bill said as Smyth moved his legs and groaned.

Smyth sat up, bleeding and with a massive bruise forming over his almost-closed eye. Still holding his head, he stood up. "I'll report you for this." He threw his head back, winced in pain and then cackled, sending quivers through Anna. Unsteady on his feet, he turned his back and walked slowly towards his quarters, ignoring the scene behind him. He gave a wry smile, whispering, "I'll get you for this."

Anna felt violated and shaken. She was convinced that Smyth had intended to hurt Isabelle and yet the person she had seen as clear as day, was not Smyth but Mr. Pickles.

Placing his arm around Anna's shoulders, Bill guided her away from the scene. "Come, let's go to our suite and you can explain what happened."

The three sat in the sitting room. Anna started the conversation. "I heard Isabelle scream and when I went upstairs Smyth was pushing her against the wall and I don't remember much more."

Isabelle patted her mother's arm. "Mum, what you saw just now was the end of events that happened while you were in London. Ralph was not attacking me aggressively but flirting." Isabelle drew a deep breath, feeling guilty. *And,* she thought, *the flirting was my fault for starting it in the first place.* "Ralph proclaimed his love for me and wanted me to leave Sandy. I told him I loved Sandy. At first he said he didn't believe me, that I was only going back to Sandy to please you, Mum. Then he accused me of misleading him. Today he followed me around like a puppy. It was creepy." Isabelle paused.

"So he wasn't aggressive. He didn't try to hurt you?" Bill asked.

Isabelle hesitated, his playful flirting had been more intense. *Was that aggression?* she wondered, but answered, "Not really, but he did say some strange things. 'I'll ruin you. Sandy won't want you when he learns the truth, and the hotel is ruined,' and the most bizarre comment, 'Your mother has dirty secrets she's afraid to tell you.'" Isabelle looked at Anna, "Do you know what he's talking about?"

"I don't. At least nothing he would know about." Anna struggled to stay calm. She kept wondering if the comments about secrets had anything to do with her early years at The Sackville, or was it just her mind that was putting them together? Her mind was definitely playing tricks on her today.

Bill's eyes were riveted on Anna, soft and tender, but there was also puzzlement. "Anna, is there something you are not telling us?" She broke the gaze and knew she had to tell them.

"I should have told you years ago, but there never seemed to be a right time and I just wanted to forget. My old boss here at the Sackville, Mr. Pickles, attempted to rape me twice. The first time, I was only nineteen and new at my job."

Bill interrupted. "I knew the bastard had touched you, but you kept saying you were all right. That was when you refused to marry me. And if I recall it was called *Anna's desk incident.*"

"I know. I'm sorry, Bill. I couldn't bear anyone to touch me and I was so ashamed and afraid to tell you." She gave Bill a knowing look. "And I really messed things up. You went off with Sophie and I married Alex."

"Yes you did. I should have known. And the second time?"

"It was during the first war. Alex was in France and you were at sea. That was much worse—I was injured. Mrs. Banks called Dr. Gregory and I told him the whole story, which he documented and it was in fact the evidence that put him away. I am the mystery woman. I was afraid Alex would kill Pickles. My intention was to tell Alex after we left England, but I never found the right opportunity."

"Oh, and I have no doubt that Alex would have hurt him very badly. You were wise. Did Alex ever find out?"

"No."

"This happened so long ago, what made you tell us now?"

"It never goes away; the trauma stays with you forever. I buried it for a while, but silly things trigger it. I must have seen something in Smyth because he provoked some memories. Then Chief Inspector Durham recognized James and talked about Mr. Pickles' arrest, more memories stirred, and guilt because I think the inspector figured out I was the mystery woman. And finally, seeing Smyth attack you, Isabelle, my mind took me back to Pickles' office thirty years ago."

"Mum, I'm sorry you went through that. Mind you, I'm not sure I'll get the image of you bashing him on the head out of my mind anytime soon." Isabelle smiled.

Anna glanced from Bill to Isabelle, "You're not ashamed of me?"

"Of course not," Bill said. "I wish you'd told me sooner. I think it's time to get those memories out in the open and deal with them, so you can finally leave them behind. Now, what do we do about Ralph Smyth?"

"Fire him! I want him out of here." Isabelle said.

"He's a troublemaker and I don't trust him, but I can't see how he can ruin anything." Anna's words sounded convincing to everyone else, but suspicion lurked in her thoughts. *Smyth is involved in something. Was that why I attacked him? No, I saw Pickles, not Smyth. Why does Smyth remind me of Pickles?* She wanted to fire him but was afraid of the consequences. *What consequences?*

"I think we should notify Durham." Bill hesitated, "We know Durham has suspicions about Smyth, but admittedly we don't know about what. So let's fuel the fire a little. Or, he may even quit of his own accord. I doubt he'll show up for work for a few days with that bump on his head."

Anna sighed. "You seem to be forgetting I hit him hard enough to knock him out cold, and by all accounts without provocation. What if he goes to the police and accuses me of assault?"

"I doubt he will do that. And even if he does, you thought he was attacking your daughter. Who are the police going to believe?"

"You have a point." Anna didn't feel well and every ounce of her energy had gone.

"I think you should rest, you look pale and exhausted. I'll send room service up with some tea." Anna didn't object. She wanted to be alone. She gave Bill a peck on the cheek and went into the bedroom. Flipping off her shoes, she lay on the bed and stared at the ceiling. What a day she thought, wondering what Mr. Kendrick would say about the afternoon's events. He was aware of the importance of reputation for a hotel serving the rich. Scandals could be their undoing. She felt her eyes close. Too tired to think, she fell asleep.

James, who was standing at the reception desk, beckoned to Bill as he came down the stairs. "A funny thing just happened. I saw Mr. Smyth, looking as though he'd been in a fight. He went into Anna's office briefly. I asked if I could help him and he brushed by me without saying a word, walked through the lobby and got in a taxi."

"James, I don't have time to explain now but we might have seen the last of Mr. Smyth."

James raised an eyebrow. "Really? I am intrigued."

Smyth goes to Devon

$\sim$ ✧✧✧ $\sim$

The taxi pulled under the portico and Henry opened the car door before realizing the passenger was not a guest but Ralph Smyth. He opened his mouth, intending to send him to the service entrance, but upon seeing his swollen face he said nothing.

Smyth threw his bag on the backseat and glared at Albert, anger simmering below the surface. He yelled to the driver, "Bexhill Station and fast!" and slammed the cab door, wishing he hadn't as his head throbbed and the cut over his eye kept bleeding. He thought it might need stitches, but if he stopped now, he'd miss the train. If it was still bleeding when he got to Plymouth, he'd find a doctor.

The train's whistle blew as the taxi stopped. Smyth shoved some coins into the driver's hand and ran on to the platform. The guard held the carriage door open for Smyth to jump in and the train began to move. His head felt like a child's spinning top and he wobbled along the corridor, afraid that he might pass out, and quickly found an empty compartment. Blood trickled onto his eyelid and his stomach churned. He thought he might be sick and pulled the strap to open the window. A rush of air hit his face as the train gathered speed and the sickness passed. Leaving the window open, he leaned back in the seat and closed his eyes. Too angry to sleep, his eyes sprang open again. He wanted to punch something; he kicked the seat in front of him and lashed out with his fists. Blood dripped onto his shirt and the punching and tenseness hurt his head. He opened his bag, rummaged inside and found a handkerchief and dabbed his bloody forehead. Trying to calm down, he pressed the handkerchief on the cut. "Bitch, bloody bitch!" he yelled through the window. "And you, Isabelle, made me fall in love. That was not my plan." He laughed, "Like father like son, like mother like daughter. I should have known, you're just like your mother. I hate all of …" He turned his head as the compartment door opened.

The conductor stood in the doorway, holding the sliding door open and tentatively said, "Tickets please." He leaned forward, allowing the door to close and stared at Smyth. "Mister, are you okay?"

Smyth quickly pulled himself together. "Yes." He laughed, pulling his wallet from his trousers pocket. "You should see the other bloke. I need a ticket to Plymouth."

The conductor relaxed and approached Smyth, opening his leather satchel. He took Smyth's money and placed it in the bag, punched the ticket and handed it to him. "Change at Paddington. You need to get that looked at," he said, gesturing towards the cut.

"I know, but it'll have to wait until I get to Plymouth."

"I've got a first aid kit in the guards' van. It's got iodine and plasters in it. As soon as I've finished collecting the tickets, I'll bring it down."

"Thanks." Smyth was relieved; perhaps a plaster would stop the bleeding. He took several deep breaths to quell the rage inside him. The only other time he'd felt this out of control was when his mother died, and he'd been angry ever since. He thought of his beautiful mother and wished he could feel her gentle touch and soothing words. He was just a kid, the only time he remembered being happy and loved until he met Isabelle. His body tightened.

The conductor returned, carrying a large white tin box. He opened it up and took out some cotton wool and a small bottle of iodine. He dabbed some of the brown liquid on the cotton wool. "This will sting, but it'll clean the wound." Smyth flinched each time the cotton touched the cut. The conductor took a butterfly plaster and closed the wound. "There, the bleeding has stopped. I'll just put a plaster over it."

"Where did you learn to do that?"

"St John's Ambulance, first aid course. It's come in handy a few times on the train. I would get some rest; you've got a long journey ahead."

"Thanks."

Smyth closed his eyes and this time they stayed closed. He thought about his father and he began to rehearse what he would tell him. Apprehension and fear replaced the anger. His father would be disappointed and upset—not working at the Sackville would make their plan difficult to execute. But, he thought, I didn't quit, although he had no intention of going back. Quite pleased with himself, he recited the letter he had left for Anna Blaine: *Due to the injury sustained at your hand, Mrs. Blaine, I require some time off. I have not reported the incident to the police, but should you decide to report me to the police I will tell all, and that will include the newspapers, I know far more than you think and without a doubt I could ruin you, your daughter and the hotel.* He opened his eyes and began laughing and said aloud, "I've got you where I want you, prim and proper Anna Blaine. And my darling Isabelle, as much as I love you, nobody betrays me like you did and you will pay for it." Content with his threat, he decided that his father would approve and concluded that if his father insisted he go back to the Sackville to finish the job, he could do that.

After a long wait at Paddington Station in London and an even longer wait in Plymouth, he finally arrived in Yelverton. Most of the alighting passengers were service men heading to Harrowbeer RAF station: happy, smart, young men laughing and talking. He sat on the station bench watching them, hating them; hating their youthful bravado in their smug uniforms. Of course, he thought, he'd had the chance to sign up himself, but he was too afraid. He looked down the tracks and could see a hint of light on the horizon. He sat there until the sun came up and the smell of frying bacon drifted towards him. He looked at his watch: three hours before the train to Princeton. Realizing how hungry he was, he followed the smell to a café opposite the train station. A bell rang as the door opened and a cheery voice called, "Take a seat and help yourself to tea, waitress will be here any minute. She's late this morning."

Smyth yelled, "Thanks, make mine two eggs, bacon, sausage and fried bread, toast and marmalade, please. Take your time, I'm in no hurry." He picked up the big aluminum teapot and poured black tea into a thick cup, the smell of the tea strong and fresh. A young paper boy threw a stack of newspapers onto the nearest table and yelled, "Mornin' papers!" Smyth took a *Daily Mirror* and sat at a chipped Formica table by the window. He watched a pretty young woman pass the window and enter the café.

"Sorry I'm late, Dad. The baby kept us up half the night." She gave Smyth a nod and disappeared in the back.

Smyth listened to the hum of their voices, father and daughter. *A family*, he thought, and wondered what it felt like to have a nice family and work together. He'd thought he and Isabelle could have that. He felt the anger bubbling up and stifled it quickly.

"Good morning," the young woman said, tying a white apron around her waist. "You're early. Dad's frying your eggs; they'll be another minute or two. More tea?" Looking up from her apron, she added, "Oh my, that looks like a nasty cut."

Smyth smiled pushing his half empty cup towards her. "Warm it up, please. Yes, it's better than it was, stopped bleeding finally."

"Just off the Plymouth train are y'u. I don't know why they make you wait so long for the Princeton train, but that's British Rail for you."

He didn't like her assumption. "What makes you think I'm going to Princeton?" he retorted.

She smiled. "Except for the train you just got off that goes to Tavistock, the Princeton train is the only one that stops here."

"Oh," he said, not wanting to confirm her assumptions. She seemed to understand and changed the subject. "Here, you've got some blood on your shirt. I can get that off if you like?"

He'd forgotten about the blood. "Can you? I'd be grateful. I have another shirt." He suddenly felt awkward. "I could go into the men's room and change."

The men's room smelled of disinfectant, barely masking the odour of urine. He pulled his shirt over his head and looked in the mirror to smooth down his hair and was shocked. One eye was turning black and his forehead was swollen near the cut. There was no sign of blood, so it had stopped bleeding. He splashed water on his face, careful not to get the plaster wet. The cool water felt good and he grabbed his toothbrush from his bag. He felt better.

When he returned, his breakfast was on the table and he handed his carefully-folded shirt to the waitress. "You're a neat one," she said, looking at the shirt. "I'll see what I can do. Now eat your breakfast while it's hot."

He smiled, her kindness warmed him and he ate and read the paper. A steady stream of railway workers and RAF men came in for breakfast and the café hummed with several conversations going on at once. Suddenly she stood next to him, teapot in hand. "More tea? It'll be awhile before your shirt's dry, but I got the stains out."

"Thanks. I'm in no hurry. The train isn't due until nine." He smiled. "But then you know that."

He thought about his father and wondered what it was like being old and living in a cramped communal space. They'd taken good care of him in the infirmary when he'd had his heart attack, but he would be back in his old place now, as grumpy and sarcastic as ever. He couldn't imagine what his mother had seen in him all those years ago. He wished he'd known him when he was a boy; perhaps he was different then. It was that woman that changed him, ruined his life; he lifted the cup, his tea rippled from his rising anger. He quickly looked around the café and was surprised to see it almost empty; he'd lost track of time and hadn't noticed people leave. The waitress came over, holding his folded shirt. "It's still a little damp, but it's clean."

"You have been very kind." He placed the shirt carefully in his bag and picked up the bill placing a ten-shilling note on the table. "Buy your baby something nice." He walked out of the café feeling good. He'd forgotten how kindness felt. He thought of his mother as he walked back to the station for the train to Princeton.

Smyth's heart pounded in his ears as he walked through the enormous stone archway, aware of hidden, watchful eyes. He approached the reception window.

A gruff voice said, "Who are you here to see?"

Smyth coughed and swallowed hard. "Ebenezer Pickles," he said staring at the sign overhead— HM Dartmouth Prison—avoiding making eye contact with the guard.

"A relative? What's your name?"

"Son, Ravi Pickles."

The next part was humiliating as his bag was searched and taken away from him and then he was searched, clothes and body. He was sure the guards enjoyed making the visitors uncomfortable. Finally, to the sound of clanging keys and slamming heavy doors and gates he was escorted into the interview room and told to sit at a table. The place smelled of anguish, sweat and violence. He couldn't place the smells, but those were the images it evoked in him. He shivered at the damp seeping through the stone walls. The single light bulbs hanging high in the ceiling did nothing to relieve the gloom of the windowless room.

Hollow footsteps approached and stopped, a steel door clanged shut, the footsteps came closer followed by a loud metallic bang, the sound of keys turning and the prisoners' door to the interview room opened. Chains rattled as Pickles' feet shuffled with small steps to accommodate his manacled ankles. The guard held his arm and shoved him into the chair opposite Smyth.

"Hello, Dad." Smyth tried to smile but he was shocked at his father's deterioration in only the few days since he'd left the infirmary. He looked even more than his seventy-nine years and the grey pallor was back. Prison colour, Smyth thought.

"I see you lost a fight." Pickles curled the edge of his mouth. "I thought you were tougher than that. Anyway, why are you back so soon?"

"Because we have to change plans. The bitch attacked me."

Pickles started laughing. "She did that to you?" The chain attaching the handcuffs to his feet rose snake-like as Pickles pointed to the plaster on

Smyth's head, his laugh turning into raspy breaths. Smyth squirmed in the metal chair, hurt stung the back of his eyes. He wanted his father's sympathy—he wanted what the waitress and her father had, not more humiliation.

"It wasn't my fault. Isabelle came on to me. She wanted me. I know she did. I kissed her and her mother caught us and slammed something on my head. She nearly killed me."

"Have you fallen for Isabelle? That wasn't in our plan. You are supposed to hurt her. I want them to suffer." The latter words spit out of his mouth and red blotches appeared on his neck and face, contrasting against his grey complexion, and his tiny sunken eyes looked comically sinister.

"I know what you want, but I can't hurt her. I love her. Her mother persuaded her to go back to her husband. I know she doesn't love him, she told me as much. They separated and she was going to get a divorce. But while I was here last time, something happened and now he's moving into the Sackville."

"Stop your whining. Women are tramps, whores. Useful for only one thing, believe me, I know. They lead you on and then cry foul. Your own mother almost got me killed; her brother tried to kill her because she was pregnant. They disowned her and decided to kill me instead and they would have, if I'd returned to India. Ruined me as a sea captain, lost my ship because I was afraid for my life and refused to sail to India. Like I say, all whores. If the husband is back, you don't stand a chance—forget about her."

Smyth didn't know if he could forget Isabelle, but his father didn't need to know that and their plans had to change. He watched his father's calculating eyes and waited for the solution.

"Reputation! The hotel's reputation, we have to ruin it. That will destroy them all, even old Kendrick. It'll kill him if we hurt his precious Anna."

"Sorry Dad, Kendrick died last month."

"Even better. She has no support; it'll be easier."

"What do you want to do? Last time it didn't work. I had Dhar arrange for the gang to harass that French fashion woman and reported it to the *Daily Mirror*. They published it but it had no impact on the hotel. I arranged for them to harass Amy and Mrs. Blaine while I was with you at the infirmary, but when the police got involved, the gang backed off."

"Police?"

"Nothing happened. They questioned my friend Balaji and then dropped the whole thing."

Pickles stared at Smyth, the chains clinking as agitation stilted his movements. He leaned across the table. "You're useless, pathetic!" Pickles slammed his fist on the table, Smyth gasped and leaned back in his chair. The guard came over, placing a hand on Pickles' shoulder.

"It's okay." Pickles looked up at the guard, who stepped back to the door.

"Do you still have a job or did you get fired?" Pickles' piercing stare unnerved Smyth. He couldn't say a word. Pickles yelled, "It's a simple question."

Smyth thought of the letter he had left and felt his confidence rise—his father would approve. "I'm not stupid. I left Mrs. Blaine a note threatening to go to the police and report the assault. I said I knew more and would go to the newspapers. I didn't quit, nor was I fired."

"You surprise me, I'm impressed. Now what do you suggest we do?"

Smyth went quiet, his brief spell of confidence disappeared. He didn't know what to do next.

"Scandal!" Pickles dropped his voice, making sure the guard couldn't hear him. "A murder, a brawl, prostitutes using the hotel." Pickles gave his sinister cackle. "A rape, now that would be sweet revenge."

"I want no part of murder. I don't want to finish up in here. You ask too much."

"*You*, don't have to do anything. Use your Hindu friend Dhar from Calcutta, he knows how to make a disturbance and make sure the newspapers hear about it."

"Time's up!" the guard shouted.

Pickles leaned across the table and whispered, "Carry out your threats and get back to work." Taking shallow breaths, he added, "Don't come back here until she's ruined." Hatred poured out of his glazed eyes. "Son, do this one thing for me. Make me proud," he said over his shoulder as the guard yanked him to the prisoners' door.

Smyth couldn't move. He wasn't sure if his father's hatred was for Anna Blaine or him. But he couldn't help smiling. His father had never called him son before, and he did want to make him proud. He went to the gate and waited for the guard to unlock it and return his belongings. He blinked at the bright sunshine and the fresh country air of Dartmoor. Taking several deep breaths he began walking towards the village of Princeton. He remembered seeing a pub near the train station. He needed a drink to wash away the taste of that awful place and to think.

He ordered a pint and took it over to a corner table. The pub had just opened for the evening, so it was quiet. The publican was used to visitors from the prison and asked no questions. Smyth thought about his father's words and wondered if he was capable of murder. Could he kill Sandy Wexford, make it look like an accident? And comfort the grieving widow. After a respectable amount of time he could run off with her and have the family he'd always wanted. Knowing his luck, he would get caught and he definitely did not want to join his father in Dartmouth. Downing the last gulp, he went back to the bar for another.

"Same again. Do you have anything to eat?"

The barman pulled another pint and pushed the glass across the bar. "Ham sandwiches, cheese and pickles and shepherd's pie if you want something hot. But I doubt you have time. The Yelverton train is due in fifteen minutes, and the next one's not 'til mornin'."

Smyth took a gulp. He didn't want to go back just yet, although he thought it might be nice to stop at the café and see the waitress again, but it would be closed by the time the train got in. "Do you have rooms to rent or is there a hotel nearby?"

"We do bed and breakfast—five bob a night."

"I'll take it. Can I go to the room now? I'd like to clean up before I eat."

"Been up *there* have you?" The publican nodded his head in the direction of the prison. "I don't blame you wanting to get that stink off you."

Smyth wasn't sure how to reply so he nodded.

"I'll have the wife show you up."

Smyth stayed two nights before heading back to Bexhill. He made plan after plan, trying to decide which one his father would approve of most. He needed help, and the best choice was his friend and activist Dhar. Not exactly a criminal, as far as he knew, but he knew how to hurt people to get what he wanted. He decided to take the train to Eastbourne and meet with Dhar before returning to the Sackville.

Back at the Sackville

~~~ ❧❦❧ ~~~

Anna woke early, and felt the pit of her stomach clench even before she opened her eyes. The image of Smyth attacking Isabelle, whether real or imagined, terrified her and she could feel Pickles' groping fingers fiddling with her blouse. It was as vivid as if it had happened yesterday. She felt the force in her arms. She had wanted to kill him, the thought horrified her as she thought of the consequences if Isabelle hadn't stopped her. *Was she capable of murder?*

Bill rolled over and kissed her cheek. "Stop worrying, he deserved it."

"Reading my mind? Seriously, I could have killed him."

"I know you, and you could never kill anyone. So stop thinking about what could have happened."

"I was so angry. I saw Pickles, not Smyth, and I wanted to smash his head in."

"I have to admit that I have never seen you so angry. How do you feel this morning?"

Anna took a breath and thought for a moment. "You know I feel good. Worried that I was out of control, but not in least bit remorseful."

Bill chuckled. "I know it isn't funny but the sight of Smyth curled up on the floor, surrounded by fragments of china and you standing over him with the jug handle was quite comical. I saw Isabelle grab your arm. You were in control; you had stopped hitting him."

"I guess it would look funny. I remember looking at the jug handle in my hand and throwing it to the ground. Do you think he'll come back?"

"Will we take him back? We keep talking about firing him and then it doesn't happen."

"Let's wait and see. Time to get up. I could do with a coffee this morning and I'm hungry. I don't remember having dinner last night."

"I'll make coffee and how about an omelette?"

"Sounds good."

They walked down together; Anna went to her office and Bill to the kitchen. She stood at the window, watching the sea. It was already light, the water a mirror reflecting the flushed morning sky. In spite of her fear of losing control, a heavy burden had lifted from her shoulders, her attack on Smyth had been liberating. She hoped she was rid of him.

Bill arrived with a tray of coffee and two omelettes with toast and placed it on the table. Anna poured the coffee and tucked into her omelette. Swallowing the last morsel of toast, she said, "That was good. I feel much better." She glanced at her desk. "I need to get some work done. I left my desk in a mess last night. What's that?" Anna pointed to the envelope. Bill got up and handed it to her.

She lifted the flap of the unsealed the envelope, and pulled out the letter. "It's from Smyth."

Bill leaned forward. "What does it say?"

"Here read it. I think he's threatening us. He's accusing me of assaulting him."

Bill scanned the letter. "What could possibly be newsworthy enough to report to the newspapers? What does he want? Anna, these are idle threats. He has nothing to gain by making a scandal of who knows what."

"Do you think he intends to come back?"

"Perhaps. I say good riddance. Forget about him, promote Balaji and let's get on with running the hotel."

"You're right." Anna said with little conviction.

Bill picked up the tray. "I must get back to the kitchen." He kissed Anna on the head. "See you a little later."

Two days later the architect arrived with some preliminary plans for the penthouse. Isabelle excitedly ushered him into Anna's office, where he rolled out the thick design paper and described the drawings. "As per your instruction, Mrs. Wexford, we will build the wall on the left, that will be a straight wall no windows but it will have a door that can only, be opened from inside the flat. You must have a second exit for safety. The main bedroom will have a private bathroom. I thought you might like a small den or office so I added one here."

"I like that idea; I could work from here." Isabelle pointed to a large expanse of space. "Is this the lounge area?"

"Yes, and the areas that have low ceiling under the eaves I have made them into a feature with window seats and screens. And there is a dining area that has an archway to the kitchen."

"That's amazing. The kitchen looks small, but I don't need a big kitchen since we eat in the hotel dining room most of the time. I like the entrance leading to the stairs, nice and big."

"Mum, what do you think?"

Anna had watched in silence. "It looks nice, but how much is this going to cost?"

Mr. Grant, the architect, pulled out another sheet of paper from his briefcase. "It all depends on the materials used and the kind of finishes you want and what is available. I quoted the basic renovations, knocking down walls, building walls, plumbing for the bathrooms and kitchen and finishing the entrance stairs. Once that is underway we can talk about the finishings: carpet, paint and wallpaper, kitchen appliances, etcetera."

Isabelle looked at her mother. "As soon as the house is sold we can pay for this, but can you pay for us to get started? I'd like to have the basics done before Sandy starts his new job."

"When do you think you can start? I know it is difficult to find contractors these days. I remember the problems we had renovating the hotel."

"Things have improved in the last year. I have a group of workers who are just finishing up a job in Hastings. I can pull a couple of the workers off early and start here, possibly tomorrow or the day after."

214

"That would be terrific, the sooner the better for me."

"I will need you to sign a contract and pay fifty percent up front."

"Mr. Grant, we will need time to go over your contract, and if it is suitable I am prepared to pay you a down payment, but not fifty percent." Anna's tone was adamant. "I would prefer to pay in increments as you do the work, starting with ten percent. A previous bad experience cost the hotel a lot of money. If you agree to my terms and I am satisfied with your contract, we have a deal."

"Mrs. Blaine, I understand your concern but we need a considerable amount of cash to get the work started. You probably wouldn't realize that fifty percent is normal today."

Isabelle panicked. "Mother, we need him to start now. I'm sure we can trust Mr. Grant."

"If I'm paying the bill, those are my terms. Mr. Grant, please do not treat me or my daughter as though we don't know what we're talking about. I have been in business all my adult life and have experienced my fair share of placating men. Your reputation precedes you. You are a highly respected architect and your company has done well and you have plenty of resources. My first payment will be enough for you to start the job. Take it or leave it."

Mr. Grant smiled. "I see I have met my match. Your terms are accepted."

"Thank you, the family will discuss this tonight and you will have our answer in the morning. Mrs. Wexford will show you out."

The work began as planned. Anna signed the contract and made the first payment, making it clear that the remaining renovations would be paid from the proceeds of the house sale. Anna desperately wanted Isabelle and Sandy to be a family again for Sarah's sake and pushed her doubts to one side. Isabelle was like her father, impulsive and rarely thought her actions through. Her flirting with Mr. Smyth was a perfect example, and thank heavens she had learned her lesson. Anna was aware that the fancy penthouse flat was possibly as important or even more important to Isabelle than reuniting with Sandy, but she thought if it's a means to an end, mission accomplished.

The cost worried her, Isabelle had expensive taste and resources were low. If Sandy didn't sell the house soon, she would have to dip into their reserves. The hotel business was fickle at the best of times, and it didn't take much to tip the scales one way or the other: another competing hotel offering unique or better services, disgruntled guests, uncomfortable stays. The noisy renovations sprang to mind as she heard the muffled banging from the fourth floor.

Scandal, true or not, might be her biggest enemy. On the bright side, she thought, the right kind of scandal could bring guests in, but perhaps not the kind of guests they were used too. Smyth's use of the word "newspapers" sent a shiver down her spine. She wasn't as convinced as Bill that the threats were idle. Smyth knew something, *but what, and was it newspaper worthy?*

Bill interrupted her thoughts. "Guess what? Smyth is back."

"I can't say I'm surprised. What did he say?"

"I didn't see him. Dave was having a smoke in the back. Smyth said hello to Dave and went inside and up the service stairs. To collect his things and his wages no doubt."

"No, he's back. I had a feeling he'd come back. What shall we do? We can fire him but that note scares me."

"Anna, you are not seriously thinking of giving him another chance." Bill stared right at Anna. "Are you?"

She dropped her gaze. She hated it when Bill stared at her like that. And he was right, she was thinking of letting Smyth come back. *Why am I so afraid that he might retaliate? Over what? I've done nothing wrong.*

"You aren't being rational. Talk to me?" Bill's voice had an edge of panic to it.

"I don't think you understand. Men like Smyth don't care and are brazen enough to continue as if nothing happened. He will appear in the dining room for his dinner shift. I suggest we speak to him before his shift. Then I'll make a decision."

Bill stared. "*I'll* make a decision. Anna, we own this hotel together. Don't forget that. I have as much to say in the staffing as you. I want Smyth gone. But if having a meeting makes you feel better, let me know what time and

I'll be there. Now, I have to get back to work." Bill stormed out of the office bumping into Isabelle who announced, "Smyth is back." Bill walked right passed her and replied, "I know. Talk to your mother."

"Mother, what is going on? I've never seen Bill so upset."

"Smyth is the problem. What else is new? Bill wants him gone and I'm afraid he'll start a scandal. I did hit him pretty hard and he's made threats." Anna gave Isabelle the note.

Isabelle read the note. "Idle threats. If he accuses you of assault, you can accuse him of attacking me. I can say his advances were not welcome or something. Ignore it. I agree with Bill; I want him gone too. Mum, you've let him get under your skin. Don't forget, I know the man. He manipulates. Let him go. Say it's for the best for all of us. He'll find another position and forget us."

"You make it sound so simple."

"Because it is."

"You don't think he'll retaliate?"

"Mum, what is it with you? You did nothing wrong. Giving this man a second chance is ridiculous. Believe me, the man has no backbone. If he thinks that cut on his head is insurance to keep his job, he is mistaken. And he doesn't have the guts to go to the police or newspapers."

"Maybe you're right. Bill said the same."

"I know I am right. There's nothing more to discuss on the subject. I have more exciting news. The workers have already got the wall up between my flat and the staff quarters. And Sandy called to say there's a buyer for the house. They still have to confirm their finances, but he says it looks good."

"That is good news." Anna smiled, glad of some happy news. What she perceived as the consequences of what she had finally decided to do was filling her with dread. "Ask James to come in. I want him to make up Smyth's final wages. Give me an hour and then ask Bill to join me. You can have the pleasure of telling him that I changed my mind and Smyth is gone."

Bill knocked on Anna's door and stepped in quietly. Anna was staring out of the window. A wind had got up, urgently pushing the waves onto the beach and the grey sky hung heavy with rain. She wasn't sure if a storm was brewing or just a rainy day. She felt the same. Was she looking at a few dark hours or a full-blown storm?

Bill put his arms around her. "It'll be okay. You'll see how much better we are without the man."

"He will be angry. I think it all depends on how angry." Anna turned to Bill. "But you are right. It has to be done."

James came in and handed Anna an envelope. "Here are Mr. Smyth's wages."

"James, please ask Mr. Smyth to come to the office."

Minutes later, Ralph Smyth walked into the office and glanced at both Anna and Bill and then at the envelope on the table. He pursed his lips. "What's this all about? I took time off to heal my injured head." He glared at Anna. "I meant what I said in my note."

Bill spoke first. "Mr. Smyth, Mrs. Blaine and I have given you one chance after another and we have decided it would be better for everyone if you found employment elsewhere. If you feel you have to go to the authorities, go ahead."

Smyth's jaw tensed. "Are you firing me? I'd never get another job without references. I have commitments to my father. I need to work." Anna watched him closely and saw a dark shadow when he mentioned his father. And she realized something to do with his father was his driving force.

"You will have to use your references from London. I can't recommend you to another hotel."

Ignoring Anna, he continued, "I swear I'll go to the newspapers." He laughed. "Remember the scandal in the *Daily Mirror?* Well, that was me. So don't think I wouldn't do it."

Anna took a deep breath. *So, Smyth was the leak.* It hadn't worked, but it proved he was capable. She felt a wave of panic and tried to catch Bill's eye. *Perhaps we're not doing the right thing.*

Bill handed Smyth the envelope. "Here are your wages plus an extra week. As far as your threats are concerned, listen carefully: neither Mrs. Blaine nor I will be held to ransom and if you try, Chief Inspector Durham will be informed and he already has his eye on you. Now gather your things and leave."

Bill opened the door. "James, will you take Mr. Smyth to his quarters to pack his things and escort him off the premises."

"You'll be sorry for this!" The words spat from tongue like a hissing snake. Anna almost cried out. She'd seen it before. He turned and stopped at the door. "I'll ruin you, like you ruined my father."

James pushed him as Bill jumped out of his chair and yelled. "Out! Get out!"

Anna turned pale. She couldn't breathe. Pickles' face appeared in front of her. That was it! Ralph Smyth's father was Ebenezer Pickles. Alone, Smyth was not capable of carrying out the vengeance he had just displayed, but as a puppet to Pickles there was no saying what he might be capable of. Pickles had waited thirty years and managed to reach from his prison cell to reap his revenge.

"Well, I'm glad that's over." Bill's expression changed to puzzlement. "Why so worried? It's over. Believe me, he won't be back. His sort just move on."

"What if he had someone pushing him? He keeps talking about his father." Anna swallowed hard. "I think his father is Ebenezer Pickles."

"Pickles! Where did you get that? He's in jail serving a life sentence. If I recall, Pickles had no children. It's not possible. We already know that Smyth was born in India." Bill took her by the shoulders and gently moved a grey curl from her forehead. "Anna, you worry too much. This whole business with Smyth has stirred some bad memories. I think you need a break. Why don't we pack up and go visit Darcy and Belle for a few days?"

"We have responsibilities. I would love to do that, but with the renovations on the fourth floor, I don't trust Isabelle. I'm afraid we'll finish up with a massive bill. Perhaps when Sandy arrives."

"By then we'll be into high season. Let's plan a visit in September."

"Definitely. I'll call Belle. But I would like to get out of here. A walk along the Promenade?"

Bill looked at the dark clouds and steady rain running down the window.

"It's a bit wet for walking. How about a drive to Eastbourne for dinner?"

Anna laughed. "There was a time when we were young and foolish and walking in the rain was fun."

"Never, just more sensible." They laughed. "I'll go and change out of my whites and tell Dave he's on his own tonight. Have Albert bring the Hillman around."

Anna and Bill at Hillcrest

ummer had passed quickly at The New Sackville with an overall occupancy rate of ninety percent and, during late July and August, there wasn't a room to spare. Isabelle's new children's program had been a big hit. Although spoiled and somewhat demanding, children of society were well mannered, and polite. The key to success was to keep the children entertained and their minds busy and acquire parent's approval all at the same time. Bexhill's history of smugglers had romanced society for years. Organized trips to what was once Galley Hill, now eroded into the sea, and the Coast Guard's lookout tower, Martello Tower was ripe for stories and mystery. The result was longer stays with extended family members and more revenue for the hotel, which accounted for the capacity bookings. By September, the children were back in school and the hotel accommodated a more sedate and mature crowd. It was perhaps Isabelle's ability to change and cater to different segments of hotel clientele that made the hotel so successful.

Isabelle had corporate conferences booked to start in October. Anna wondered where she got all her energy from; she was always on the go. In contrast, Anna was feeling tired and not well. She couldn't relax; she constantly checked over her shoulder, expecting Ralph Smyth to appear. It didn't seem to bother anyone else. Bill never mentioned it again. Isabelle was happy in her new flat and Anna was happy for Sarah, who in turn was ecstatic to have her father home. The major renovations had been completed and paid for from the proceeds of the house in Scotland but it had not covered some of Isabelle's fancy ideas about furnishings and décor. Anna was thankful to pass this on to Sandy, who attempted to curb Isabelle's spending.

Now at the end of October, Bill had persuaded Anna to take a few days off and they were heading to Hillcrest Estates. She gave her last list of instructions to James, which was not necessary. He smiled. "Anna, go have a good rest. We can manage."

"I know I can trust you, but my daughter, I'm not sure about."

"I'll keep an eye on things. Now, off you go. Bill is waiting in the car."

"We're finally on our way. I'm looking forward to seeing Darcy and Belle again," Bill said.

"Me too, and to relax. I'm so tired." Anna yawned and closed her eyes. Bill glanced across the seat and smiled towards his sleeping wife.

Anna woke as the tyres crunched on the gravel driveway. She rubbed her eyes and there in the distance stood Hillcrest Hall. Large, regal and old, she sensed she was entering a world more familiar to Jane Austen's imagination than reality. She wondered how the once petulant young Anna had risen from middle class Rugby to hotel owner hobnobbing with the Lords and Ladies of England.

"Have a nice sleep?" Bill smiled, "You missed the lovely countryside."

"We're here already?" she said, opening her handbag and taking out her lipstick she pulled down the sun visor and checked herself in the mirror, touched up her lipstick and patted her hair. "There, will I do?"

"You look ravishing."

Darcy and Belle were waiting for them at the main door. Harris took their bags and they went into the big sitting room. Anna was in awe of the furnishings. Portraits and antiques were everywhere, and yet Darcy and Belle made them feel so comfortable in such formidable and formal surroundings.

Darcy poured them sherry. "How are things at the Sackville?"

"We had a busy summer. I think people are trying to put the war behind them. The reinstating of petrol rationing affected us last year but doesn't seem to have had an effect this summer. People just want to get away," Bill said.

"We found the same here. People just want to get their lives back. The number of visitors far outgrew our expectations. I think we had more coach tours, which can be a nightmare when thirty people get off a bus at once, but we managed. And thanks to Isabelle's help, the gift shop brought us a tidy profit. How are Isabelle and Sarah?" Belle asked.

"The penthouse is almost finished. Sandy started his new job in June and the family is together again. I think, thanks to your wise words, Belle." Anna smiled, "My daughter is strong-willed and impulsive. She takes after her father. But she has seen the error of her ways and is really happy. She's doing an amazing job at the hotel."

"What happened to that Smyth fellow?"

"We fired him after a really bad incident. I was afraid he would retaliate, but Bill and Isabelle insisted he go and they were right." Anna suddenly wanted to tell Belle how afraid she was in spite of nothing happening in the last six months. "Someone from Eastbourne called for a reference, so we assume he's working there."

"Why do I get the feeling there is more to this story?" Belle said directly to Anna.

Bill answered. "Smyth made some idle threats that upset Anna, but he won't do anything. It's been months since he left."

Anna laughed. "My imagination." She leaned over to Belle. "We'll talk later."

Belle cocked her head to one side and said, "I'm intrigued."

Harris entered and waited for a lull in the conversation. "Luncheon is served, your Lordship."

Darcy stood up and said, "Shall we? I'm hungry and you two must be too after your long drive."

"The drive wasn't that long but I am hungry," Anna said, realizing that she had been worrying so much that she had not been eating and it felt good to be hungry.

Bill laughed. "The journey was short because you slept all the way."

"That is true."

After lunch, Darcy took Bill on a tour of the estate. Belle and Anna went to the gift store. Anna looked up at the old-style sign hanging over the door, "Ye Olde Gift Shoppe," she read aloud. "I like the sign. It reminds me of the one over the King's Head Inn."

"I wanted to keep the older antique look." Belle unlocked the door and a bell tinkled. "The shelves are a bit bare. We sold out of so much and I didn't want to re-order until the new season. We've decided to open up for Christmas, so I'm bringing in some Christmas stock. Not sure if it will work, but it's worth a try."

"I think that is a really good idea. I like the layout and is that the Thornton china?"

"Yes, that was your daughter's idea and I'm having difficulty keeping it in stock, especially the cup and saucer set. It is astonishing how much money can be made from these trinkets. The overhead is low, staff mainly, and the profit averages fifty to seventy-five percent."

Anna picked up a set of lace hankies with the Hillcrest Hall crest hand-embroidered in the corner. "These are lovely. The hotel has an impressive crest. I wonder if our guests would be interested in this kind of thing?"

"A gift shop in the hotel? Brilliant idea. I'm surprised Isabelle hasn't thought of that."

"She is so busy with so many new programs. The children's program has been a great success. I was not convinced that children would mix with our clientele, but Isabelle arranged separate dining for families, and planned programs that kept them busy and out of the public lounges. Um…gifts and maybe a few books and toys. You've given me a great idea, Belle. Guests often ask us for books and we keep a few they can borrow, but selling them would be better."

Belle led the way into the café, which looked sad with the tables and chairs stacked in the corner, making the room sound hollow and bare. "We serve sandwiches, cold drinks and tea all day. Ice cream if we can get it. Even with rationing, we sell out quickly. During holiday weekends, when we make most of our money, the queue for afternoon tea can be twenty or more and people get fed up and often leave. I'm planning a Christmas fair in December and hoping to raise enough funds to pay to expand the café by using some of the adjoining stables that haven't been used in decades. I'm not looking forward to renovations, workmen are hard to come by and expensive."

"The architect who did the Sackville renovations agreed to do the penthouse and he managed the whole project. My problem was not the workers, but Isabelle's expensive taste. But now she's Sandy's responsibility. She's amazing in business but, personally, she's still a spoiled little girl. I have Alex to thank for that."

"I never met Alex, except in the dining room during my brief stay at The Sackville. Darcy's mother didn't like me."

"She made that very apparent. I was in awe of you: this modern lady. I still remember you wearing a cravat and thought it very chic and even tried it myself when Alex came back on leave. Look at us now."

"Times have changed. We're getting old, Anna."

"No, not us." They both laughed.

"Let's go back to the house, it's chilly in here. I'll show you my little sitting room and we'll have tea. We use it in the summer when the house is open to the public."

Belle led the way to the side door and into her sitting room. Anna was taken aback with the modern style, but she liked it.

"I escape here when the old stuffy antiques get to me. Darcy hates it. She rang the service bell and Harris appeared. "Tea and cake please, Harris."

"When are you going to fill me in with what happened to Smyth?"

"I'm not sure where to start. It actually goes back many years to my young days as secretary to Mr. Pickles at the hotel. Do you know about his arrest and incarceration?"

"A little bit. I think Bill might have said something and we saw the newspaper report but that was a long time ago.

Anna briefly described Pickles' arrest and her part in it. She was surprised at how easily she talked about it and how much she trusted Belle.

"I've never discussed this with anyone except Dr. Gregory. I was so ashamed and these things stick with you. Anyway, all that to say, I was the mystery woman the press talked about. I only recently told Bill and Isabelle and didn't give all the details. I'm relying on your discretion."

"Of course. I'm a good listener. You know, my friend Julia went through hell with her husband Luigi. I can't imagine what it's like, and, like you, she was not able to tell anyone. I'm so lucky to have Darcy."

"I was lucky to have Alex and now Bill. He told me about Luigi."

"Anna, I'm honored to have you as a friend."

"I'm a bit overwhelmed at times."

"You get used to it. Darcy has never been conventional unless he has to be. And for me, being an American raised on a cotton plantation, where money was plentiful and we had servants, the protocol of British society is still a mystery to me. I struggled with this privileged title and perceived wealth. Unfortunately, many of our peers are in great financial difficulty and still try to uphold a lifestyle they can't afford."

Harris came in with tea and the conversation stopped while he poured. Anna looked at his white gloves and immaculate dress and what appeared to be a neutral expression, but she sensed he enjoyed his work.

"Curiosity is getting the better of me." Belle looked at Harris. "That will be all." He bowed and backed out of the room. "I'm really curious as to how this fits in with Isabelle and Smyth?"

"I believe Ralph Smyth is Mr. Pickles' son."

"How can that be possible?"

"I don't know. Bill thinks I'm crazy."

Belle looked skeptical. "When Darcy spoke with the waiter, I thought they discovered Smyth was born in India. It seems far-fetched that his father would be Pickles...and isn't Pickles in jail?"

"There is a connection, albeit very small. My uncle used to travel to India frequently and he met Pickles there. He was a sea captain at the time. Uncle Bertie was a lady's man, and we know Pickles had an appetite for woman. Is it so far-fetched that he fathered a child in India?"

"It's possible." Belle frowned. "He really upset you?"

226

"I'm afraid of Smyth. He has that same deep-seeded hatred and lust for vengeance that Pickles had. He's out for his father's revenge and I think he'll be back. When you hear the full story, I think you'll see my point."

While consuming several cups of tea, Anna revealed the entire saga. Belle listened carefully and replied thoughtfully. "I can see why you would think Smyth had an ulterior motive, and I believe he does. But a connection with Pickles? That seems implausible. How can we delve further into his background? Did you report the attack on Isabelle to the police?"

"No. I had assaulted Smyth. Smyth had a cut and a black eye. I worried I might have been charged."

Belle grinned. "You hit him that hard?"

"Yes, I was very angry. And it felt as though I was hitting Pickles," Anna responded with a cheeky grin. "It felt good."

"What about the Inspector from Eastbourne. Was he investigating Smyth?"

"He accused Balaji at first, and asked questions about Smyth and a communist group. He wanted to speak with Smyth, who was away looking after his father. When I told Durham he was back, he dropped the whole thing. It was strange. So, do you think I'm crazy too?"

"No, I don't. I think there is merit in your suspicions. We need more evidence to prove or disprove a relationship between Smyth and Pickles. But I do agree with Bill that if Smyth hasn't retaliated in six months, I doubt he will now."

"You're probably right. I need to put it into perspective."

"Gosh, look at the time. I need to freshen up before dinner. Don't look worried, we have relaxed protocol somewhat and, unless we are entertaining, we don't change for dinner. You look fine as you are."

"I only brought one cocktail dress."

"Save that for tomorrow. We've arranged a dinner party; the rest of the time is casual."

A Tragic Death

⚜

Anna and Bill reluctantly departed Hillcrest. Waving goodbye and promising to visit again soon, they began an uneventful journey home. Arriving in Bexhill, Bill turned the car onto the Promenade, a view Anna treasured. She smiled and said, "The sun glistening on the sea never ceases to amaze me. I feel the same excitement as I did the first time, when Carter pulled the horse and cart around this corner." She laughed. "That was a long time ago. I can't believe how far we've come since then."

"Life has certainly been interesting." Bill turned his head slightly. There was no need for physical touch, a cocoon of warmth surrounded them. She wondered what she had done to deserve such happiness and contentment. Contentment, she thought, an unfamiliar feeling for Anna who was always on guard, and even now a shadow lurked in the corner of her mind. The towers of The New Sackville drew closer and the shadow grew darker. She sighed, sensing the euphoria was to be short lived.

Bill drove the Hillman under the portico. "It's quiet. Where's Albert?"

"Too quiet." Worry lines creased Anna's forehead.

Bill touched her hand. "You worry too much. It's November. We have three guests staying. Remember, that's why we decided to go away. I bet he went for a cup of tea."

Climbing the steps to the entrance, Bill's expression changed. "What the heck...?" He stopped and held the door open, surveying the chaos: chairs were on their sides, the coffee tables upside down with broken legs, the carpet wet from overturned flower vases and lamps missing shades.

"The place has been ransacked."

Anna, now close on his heels, rushed through the door. "Albert!" Albert was slumped in his chair not moving. She gently lifted his head; a large lump stuck out from his forehead. She felt his warm breath on her face and took his hand, shocked to see blood on his white gloves. She scanned the lobby, her eyes moving to the lounge and reception area. Where was everyone? James should be at reception. She could hear her own short, anxious breath above the silence. Not even muffled voices from behind the baize door. Darkness entered each cell of her body, slowly torturing her senses; her ears filled with her own heartbeat. She closed her eyes and her body swayed. Bill's strong arms supported her, the fog swirled in her head as an image of Isabelle appeared. She opened her eyes to chaos.

Holding Anna, Bill tried to get his balance. "Oh dear God, what is happening."

She felt his heart pounding against her chest and calmed her own breath. "Where's Isabelle?"

"I don't know." Bill released her and they sat on the sofa. "I don't know what happened here but we need the police and Albert needs medical care." He frowned. "I'm sure Isabelle is fine." He tapped Anna's hand. "Stay here, I'll phone."

He leaned over the reception counter to grab the phone, the receiver hung off the cradle behind the reception counter. "Oh my God, Isabelle!" He leaped over the counter. Isabelle lay twisted awkwardly on the floor. Her face was a pallid grey, making her red curls seem brighter where they fell on her face and black where her head rested in a pool of dark red blood. The telephone receiver swung gently on its cord brushing the tips of her fingers.

Anna flew off the sofa screaming, "Call the ambulance!" Sobbing, she held her daughter's bloody head, rocking and whispering, "Hold on, please hold on."

Isabelle's lips moved and husky words came on each breath. "Mum... look after... Sarah."

"Yes, but you're going to be okay, the ambulance is on its way." Even as the words left Anna's lips, it was too late.

Quiet tears ran down Anna's cheeks, the grief and sadness as intense as when Alex had died. *How can I bear this?* she thought, *And why?* She was beginning to understand Isabelle; she wanted her back to explore the things they could enjoy together. She thought of Alex. He would be so angry that she had not protected his daughter. A pang of jealousy crept in and she shook it off, disgusted with her thoughts. Her head tilted to one side as she stared down at Isabelle and rocked to and fro, as though she was cradling an infant. "Be with your father, my darling Isabelle."

Sirens and noise jolted her from her thoughts. An arm tried to lift her from the floor but she resisted. Closing her eyes, she willed Isabelle to be alive when she opened them. Her heart missed a beat as she saw wet tears on Isabelle's face. She brushed them away feeling the lifeless cold against the warmth of her own falling teardrops. She kissed Isabelle's cheek. "Goodbye."

An ambulance attendant lifted her gently to her feet, his words kindly, "Ma'am, let me tend to your daughter."

Anna felt Bill's hand slip into hers and a police constable guided them to a sofa. She stared at the broken coffee table. She felt violated—attacking her space had been personal. Attacking her daughter was unforgivable. Shivers trembled through her. *He had dared to retaliate.* Bill pulled her closer and she could feel his chest heave with silent sobs, her throat too tight to speak. No matter how many tears spilled, there was no relief. She clung to Bill as though her life depended on him, and at that moment, it did.

Voices invaded her thoughts, "Ma'am...Ma'am." The voice coughed. "Ma'am...Sir."

Bill looked up. "Yes."

A policeman stood in front of them. He hesitated, rubbing his hands. "I'm sorry to disturb you. My name is Detective Sergeant Green. I have to ask you not to leave the hotel. Chief Inspector Durham is on his way. He will want to interview you and the staff."

Staff, Anna thought, where were the staff? "Detective, the only person here when we arrived was Albert." She looked over to his chair. "And now he's gone."

"He's been taken to the hospital, ma'am."

Anna felt tears spring to her eyes again. She thought of poor Albert. Her brain was jumping from thought to thought. She couldn't concentrate and suddenly she felt panic. "The staff should be working." She glanced at Bill.

Bill released his arms from Anna and frowned. "Detective," he croaked, clearing his throat and brushing the back of his hand across wet eyes, before continuing, "This is a quiet time at the hotel so we actually only have a skeleton staff. Miss Jenkins, the front desk clerk is on holiday, but James Lytton should have been at the reception desk, where Isabelle…whatever happened here, the noise must have alerted the staff downstairs. Where are they?" Bill started to walk towards the baize door. The constable placed his hand firmly on his shoulder. "Sir, remain here please."

"We need to find these people. They may be hurt."

"Officers are searching downstairs and the staff are not there." Bill turned towards James' office. "At least let me see if James is in his office."

"Sorry sir, my orders are not to touch anything, secure the crime scene and stay with you until the inspector gets here."

"What?" For the first time Bill realized that police officers were standing on guard at various points around the lobby. "Are we under suspicion?"

"Following orders, sir."

Hearing scuffling and a loud moan coming from her office, Anna jumped up, a police officer grabbed her but not before she reached James leaning on the door frame. His face swollen, his lip cut and bleeding he tried to speak, "Smy…" He yelped with excruciating pain when Anna tried to take his arm. She jumped back in shock and James fell to the floor.

"Medics, over here!" A constable called.

Anna was led back to the sofa as James was lifted into a stretcher.

"Is he…?" Anna could hardly speak through tears.

"No ma'am, he passed out. It looks as if he has some broken bones."

231

A pounding on the locked front doors brought the police constables to attention. DS Green opened the door for Chief Inspector Durham as the medics carried the stretcher to the ambulance. Anna watched the procession, realizing the ambulance had been there for Isabelle, but was no longer needed as they waited for the coroner.

Anna leaned on Bill, grateful for his warmth. She closed her eyes and Isabelle's bloody face appeared, her mouth opened and closed in silence and Anna heard Sarah's name. She sat up straight and said, "Sarah, what are we going to tell Sarah? I can't believe I forgot about Sarah! Bill, what time is it? She'll be waiting for Isabelle to collect her from school."

"It's only two o'clock. School doesn't finish until four."

Anna couldn't believe so much had happened since they arrived home. Her mind was racing. She couldn't bring Sarah here, to all this chaos.

"We have to tell Sandy."

Chief Inspector Durham interrupted, "Who is Sandy?"

"Isabelle's husband. They live here in the penthouse. Inspector, we have to tell him. He's at work in Eastbourne and Sarah is in school…" She couldn't hold back, her words drowned in tears.

The inspector looked at Bill. "I'll send an officer to fetch him. How old is the child?"

"Sarah just turned ten. How do you tell a ten-year-old her mother has…" Anna's sobs concealed her words.

"Is there anyone close who can pick Sarah up from school and take care of her for a while?"

Bill shook his head. Anna took a deep breath to calm her sobs and said, "Her best friend, Judy Elliot. Isabelle was friendly with her mother and they often helped each other out picking up the girls. I don't know how to reach her. I think they live up on the hill."

"We'll find her and ask Mrs. Elliot to take care of Sarah as there has been a family crisis. No further details will be given."

"I should speak to Mrs. Elliot," Anna said.

"I'm sorry, Mrs. Blaine, but I cannot allow you or Mr. Blaine to have contact with anyone until you've been formally questioned."

"Are you saying we are suspects?" Bill's voice sounded shrill.

"Yes," the inspector said and moved away, glancing towards Bill and Anna as he spoke to DS Green.

Anna felt like a naughty schoolgirl: her feet firmly planted on the ground, her knees together and her hands cupped on her lap, waiting to see the headmistress. She knew the inspector was talking about them, it fed into her own guilt of not protecting her daughter and she couldn't help thinking she was being punished for being a bad mother. She reflected, *I haven't been the best of mothers. Isabelle was difficult from birth.* She hated herself for thinking that way. *But once Isabelle came into my world, I loved her in way that I never thought possible.* Anna leaned her head against the back of the sofa, she was so tired. She closed her eyes but Isabelle's bloody head had settled in the darkness behind her closed eyes. She opened them quickly, choking back the image and relieved to see Bill's face looking at her.

"What is it?"

Anna shook her head and whispered, "Nothing."

Time had disappeared into an abyss. DS Green had posted a constable at their side, not moving, not talking for an hour or more. Suddenly, his body tightened and he retrieved a pencil and notebook from his chest pocket. Anna idly mused at how incredibly small the notebook appeared in his large hands. He moved to one side to allow Chief Inspector Durham to sit across from Anna and Bill. The questions began—a grueling interrogation.

Another hour went by. The inspector's words were not making sense, the scratching of the constable's pencil was irritating. Anna was having difficulty keeping it together. She glanced at Bill as calm and composed as ever. *Dear sweet Bill,* she thought.

Anna physically jumped in her seat when the inspector asked, "Mrs. Blaine, did you and your daughter get along? Have you had any arguments recently?"

"Hum…we had our differences like most mothers and daughters, but we didn't argue. She was happy. She loved her work and she and Sandy had just completed the penthouse for their new home."

"Excuse me, sir!" A young policeman flushed as he spoke, "There's something you need to see."

The inspector frowned and Anna suspected he was about to reprimand the young man for interrupting but changed his mind and said, "This had better be important." He nodded and led the way through the baize door. Anna heard voices as the door swung shut. Almost immediately the inspector reappeared. "Mrs. Blaine, come with me please."

Anna felt panic rising like bile from her stomach. *Was she about to see another scene of death?* She walked in slow motion towards the inspector, he held the door open and she could hear someone crying in the otherwise quiet staff quarters.

"In there." Durham pointed to the staff dining room. "We found him in a cupboard hiding."

Woody sat on the floor his knees under his chin, rocking to and fro, crying. A constable was trying to make him stand up.

Anna yelled, "Leave him alone. He's harmless and frightened. He doesn't understand what's happening." She pushed the constable to one side and sat on the floor next to Woody.

"It's okay, Woody. Nobody is going to hurt you. Can you tell me what happened?"

Woody nodded.

"Woody, can you come and sit at the table with us?"

Woody briefly lifted his head and shook it towards the constable.

"Inspector, Woody is afraid of the constable…could you ask him to leave?"

The inspector sat down and motioned to the constable to wait outside. Anna guided Woody to the table and sat next to him.

"Woody, this is Chief Inspector Durham. He's a nice policeman who is going to help us find out what happened here today. Can you answer some questions?"

"Mrs. Blaine, Woody is sorry I was too scared to stop them."

"Stop who?"

"Men in black jumpers and things on their faces. They tried to hit me with a bat." Woody smiled. "Woody strong and twisted his arm." He mimicked the movement and then looked at his feet. "I think I hurt him."

Anna touched his arm. "That's okay, Woody. They are bad men. Do you know where the others are? Amy, Dave, Balaji and the maids?"

"Bad men took them, down there." He pointed down the passageway to a door and then turned, pointing to a large storage cupboard. "Woody hide in there."

The inspector nodded. "That's where we found him."

Anna looked puzzled. "Inspector, he's pointing to the cellar door. There's no way out. They must be locked in the cellar."

Now the inspector looked puzzled. "The cellars were not locked and they have been searched, no one is hiding down there."

Woody had settled enough to answer the inspector's questions, although there were no clues as to where the staff had gone. But the description of the assailants was a clue as to their identity.

Grief

～⚬ᘐᘗ⚬～

Thé inspector's demeanour changed. Anna noticed his tense, bland expression relax and his cheeks lift, not quite into a smile. He was investigating, not accusing as they alighted the service stairs.

"I'm no longer a suspect?" she asked.

"No, there were intruders. I had to be sure. You and your husband are no longer suspects. However, please don't leave the premises until I say. And, Mrs. Blaine, I am very sorry for your loss. I'll find who did this." His eyes were genuine with sadness and understanding.

What a difficult job he has, she thought. *Underneath the harsh exterior is a kind man.* She smiled to replace the words that would not come. During the episode with Woody, she had briefly forgotten her daughter. How easy it had been to forget. *No! I must never forget,* screamed inside her and grief burst into her head as tears gushed down her face. Concentrating on each word, she said, "I need some time." She sat on the stairs and the inspector acknowledged her wishes and returned to the lobby.

Her blouse, wet with tears, felt cool against her skin. She no longer wanted the tears to cease, the freedom felt comforting. Her throat relaxed, her breath flowed and the pain released from her insides, carried away by her tears. How long she sat there, she didn't know, but the tears stopped, leaving a pain of sadness deep inside. This she could cope with. She knew this pain. It nestled in her heart, where she carried the pain of Alex's death.

She moved to the staff room and sat in the old rocking chair, which creaked from old age and many repairs. To and fro she rocked. Her head cleared and her thoughts untangled into something intelligent and uncomplicated. She would leave the law to Chief Inspector Durham. He was a good detective and had done a good job all those years ago putting Pickles behind bars. Again, the thought of Pickles prompted her to wonder what part he had played in this brutal attack. Her thoughts turned to taking care of Sarah. From now on, Sarah would be her priority and the hotel second.

She went into the kitchen to make tea. It was eerie, as if time had stopped: food was on the chopping boards half chopped. The oven was on but nothing was inside, a roast of beef sat on the counter. The tap was running in the sink, vegetables lay in the prep area unpeeled, bread dough had risen over the bowl and collapsed leaving strings of doughy cobwebs on the bowl and table. Uncooked eggs had been cracked into a frying pan, now gelatinous and slimy, and bacon sat crispy and brown on a server. Anna picked up the big kettle and filled it. *It must have happened around breakfast time* she thought as she placed the kettle on the burner. *But what did happen?*

"Here you are," Bill said, "I don't know what to say, Anna. I feel as though we're in a nightmare." He hesitated, "And you're making tea?"

"There's nothing to say. It *is* a nightmare and my heart is breaking." Anna's voice was hoarse as her throat tightened again. "I cannot cry anymore. We need to be strong for Sarah. Making tea keeps me busy and helps me think."

"It happened during the morning prep." Bill said surveying the various workstations. "It doesn't make sense. Staff doesn't just disappear."

Bill carried a large tray of tea up to the lounge, Anna followed. The scene had changed. What Anna assumed was the forensic team had arrived and there seemed to be a throng of drones walking around, frowning and putting things in bags. They returned to the sofa and watched. Anna wondered how Albert was doing and if James was as badly hurt as he'd looked. Injuries to the face often looked worse than they were, but his screams of pain indicated something more serious.

"I know we only had a few guests registered but where are they?" Bill asked Anna.

"I was thinking the same thing. If I recall, there were three bookings. Two were checking out either yesterday or today but there was a Mr. and Mrs. Diggen. Not our usual type of guest, a bit rough around the edges, but they had lots of money. I thought they were booked until the end of the week."

"I noticed only one breakfast order when we were in the kitchen, bacon and eggs for table three, so someone was in the dining room when this happened. Who was at table three, the Diggens? And where are they?" Bill paused. "We need to tell the inspector."

Anna turned when she heard Sandy's voice talking to the inspector. She wondered how to tell him and then saw his white face drawn in deep lines—he'd been told. He looked over to Anna. No words, none needed. The constable had his notebook out and DS Green and the inspector began questioning Sandy, the interrogation shorter than Anna and Bill's—Sandy had been at work when this happened.

Finished with the inspector, Sandy sat in silence with Anna and Bill. She felt more tears burn her eyes, tears for Sandy. He had loved Isabelle without question throughout all their troubles.

"I have asked if I can go to the hospital...the morgue... to say goodbye." Sandy's voice trembled. "The inspector tells me Sarah is with Judy, and Mrs. Elliot has agreed to keep Sarah for as long as we need. She doesn't know yet. I don't know how to tell her." He gave a loud sob and his shoulders shook but he continued, "When I left this morning... she was so happy, she had come up with a new idea for the hotel...I didn't listen...I was annoyed because I was running late and she asked me to drop Sarah off at school." He stared into space. "The inspector advised we talk to Sarah before they release any information to the press." Sandy stood up and walking towards the door. "I need to see Isabelle."

"The press!" Anna said louder than she intended. Imagining reporters swarming the lobby, firing all kinds of questions about Isabelle about their lives and headlines in the *all the papers*, she thought, not just a cursory mention from dubious sources.

The inspector sat down in the chair Sandy had vacated. "My men have searched all the guest rooms and with two exceptions, the rooms are clean and tidy. Suite 204, the guests have left but the room has not been cleaned yet. Do you know who was in that room?"

"I don't remember their names, the information will be in the ledger. I believe they were checking out early this morning."

"We're checking the register now. And the other room was Suite 209. Now that room was a mess and they may have left in a hurry. There was a jacket forgotten in the wardrobe, a jar of cream in the bathroom and a book on the night table but no suitcases. Do you know these guests? I'd like to question them."

"Mr. and Mrs. Diggen. Not our usual type of guest and they arrived the day we left for Hillcrest and were booked in until the end of this week. I remember them as it is unusual to have guests stay two weeks in the off-season. The ledger will have their address." Anna paused. "We noticed in the kitchen there was an unfilled breakfast order for table three, so they were in the hotel this morning."

The inspector glanced from Anna to Bill. "Is there anything else you can tell us?" They both shook their heads. "I have put a missing persons bulletin out for the missing staff. The forensic people will be finished soon. I would appreciate it if you would be available for another hour or so. Do you have any guests checking in today?"

Anna shook her head. "Not as far as I know. There are some bookings for the weekend and there is a conference coming next week and then we're quiet until Christmas. Why do you ask?"

"I was going to advise you to cancel bookings, but we'll be finished before the weekend, then you can get back to normal. I would suggest you close for a couple of days."

Normal, Anna thought. *It would never be normal again.* Her thoughts drifted to Sarah: was Sandy going to fetch her and tell her? Should they bring her home? How could she cope with a conference without Isabelle? Should she cancel? She heard the inspector's voice droning in the background. She should listen, but her head wouldn't focus. Bill held her hand. She looked up and he was talking to the inspector. It was strange she couldn't hear the words. Bill stood up and with the help of a constable began straightening the furniture. Anna just stared into nothing, grief riveting her to the seat.

"Anna…Anna!" Bill shook her shoulder gently. "Anna."

She took a deep breath coming back into the scene. "Yes," she said.

"We can straighten up, they've finished." Bill said, giving her a quizzical look.

"I'll go fetch Woody to help and call the maids…oh, we have no staff."

Anna went downstairs. Woody was still in the staff dining room. "Woody, will you go upstairs and help Mr. Blaine? And there is some furniture that needs repair. Bring it down here." Woody ran up the stairs, obviously relieved to have something to do.

Anna had felt grief before but nothing like this, every cell, every part of her was weeping. The only relief was to keep her body and mind moving. She wandered around looking for clues to where the staff had gone. She opened the cellar door, peering into the dark. Flipping the light switch, she ventured down the stairs. She thought she heard something in the wine cellar. The wine racks were off centre…the wine bottles were facing the wrong way. Something white had caught in a rack— a handkerchief with 'A' embroidered in the corner. She recognized it as one she had given Amy last Christmas. She heard a noise, a rustle and then a voice in the distance. She began pulling the bottles off the rack. She screamed as a mouse scurried past her feet. Her heart pounding, she rested against the wall, not sure why she was removing the bottles. She heard the voice again and for a brief second she heard Isabelle call out and then silence and more tears. She sat on the damp earth floor, her ears straining to hear a voice she would never hear again.

"Anna!" Bill called, thudding down the stairs. "What are you doing down here?" Bill bent down and pulled her to her feet.

"I thought I heard…something. I have to keep moving. Look at this, the wine racks, they are wrong."

"You're right, the cabernet has gone, someone stole it, this rack shouldn't be empty, and it's been pulled away from the wall and those bottles have been turned the wrong way, the corks will dry out." Bill squeezed behind the rack. "There's nothing here."

"Is there a way out of the cellar?"

"There's nothing back there and I think the police searched. Maybe they moved the wine."

"Listen." Anna pressed her finger to her lips. "I thought I heard voices."

"No doubt from upstairs." Bill raised an eyebrow. "You've had a stressful day."

"Don't placate me Bill, I heard something. What if there are passageways under the hotel?"

"I'm sorry." Bill slid his arm around her shoulders. "Come, there's nothing down here, let's go to our suite and get some rest."

Anna shrugged him off, screaming "Rest!" She lashed out with her arms, punching the air. "I can't. I have to keep busy, thinking of other things so I don't think of Isabelle and what I could have done to protect her, of all the things she's done for the hotel that I didn't appreciate. There's a way out of here and I'm staying here until I find it."

"You're not making sense." Bill brushed tears from her cheeks. "Back in the old days I worked down here with Alex setting up the wine cellar for Chef Louis. The walls are solid, there are no doors. Alex loved telling stories of smugglers rolling barrels of wine along the beach." Bill smiled. "Alex was always convinced there were smugglers' passages under the hotel, but we never found any."

Anna's outburst seemed to have calmed her and she smiled at the memory of Alex's stories of smugglers. "Even more reason to search. Please humour me and help me look, and if we find nothing I'll stop."

Bill sighed. She wasn't sure if it was love, pity or resignation that reflected in his eyes, but it didn't matter when he agreed to help. She pecked his cheek, her eyes glassy with tears.

"Let's start here where the wine racks have been moved, this is where I found Amy's hankie." She pulled the lace-trimmed fabric from her pocket.

One by one they took the wine off the racks. Fortunately, because of war shortages the racks were not full, and as Bill had pointed out, several bottles were missing. Bill wondered if Smyth had stolen the wine, he was the maître d' and had full access to the wine cellar and was just the sort of thing he would do. He was worried about Anna. A lump the size of a rock stuck in his throat, hard and unforgiving. He struggled to hold back tears. He needed to be strong for Anna. Isabelle was like a daughter to him and, at times, he had understood her better than Anna did. He couldn't imagine not seeing her smiling face or her curls bouncing with her determined walk, so much like Alex. He remembered how alone he was when Alex died, how he buried the pain so deep he lost himself. He couldn't do that again. Losing Isabelle had uncovered the pain and he couldn't bury it. He had lost the two people he loved the most in the world with the exception of Anna. His love for Anna was different and he shuddered at the thought of ever losing her. Not realizing he was shaking, he heard Anna say, "Are you cold?"

"A bit," Bill replied. "Wine cellars are cold and damp for the wine but not too good for humans."

The bottles were lined up in the centre of the room. They slowly moved the racks away from the wall. Anna placed her palms on the walls, pressing and moving up and down the wall. She leaned her face sideways on the damp stone, it had a metallic smell to it while the earthy scent of the dirt floor gave her a sense of confinement. A vision of imprisonment crossed her mind. She was even more convinced that Amy and Dave were somewhere behind these walls. She pressed her ear hard against the stone, hearing echoes of the sea, like the sound from hollow seashells. She listened and felt every inch of the wall. Now side by side with Bill, he shook his head. She crouched on the floor leaning on the wall; suddenly she straightened and placed her hand on the stone.

"Bill, feel here, tell me what you feel?"

"Cold stone, no wait a minute. I feel air."

"Shush!" Anna's head pressed tight against the wall. "I hear the sea, it's not a seashell sound. I hear the waves. It is hollow behind here."

"I'm not sure that means anything. The hotel is on the beach or close enough."

Anna jumped knocking over a bottle of wine as a voice boomed into the cellar. "What are you doing down here?" The inspector appeared from around the wine racks. "We searched the cellars."

Handing him Amy's handkerchief, she said, "That was on the wine rack, and it belongs to the head housekeeper, Amy Peterson." She pointed to the wall. "It is hollow behind there, I can hear the waves." She wrinkled her nose as the red wine soaked into the earth giving off an unpleasant odour.

"Maybe you can hear the waves, maybe you hear voices. I don't know, Mrs. Blaine. But I deal in facts and no one can get out of this cellar except by the door up there." His face contorted with frustration and he shook his head in disbelief, staring directly at Anna.

Seeing Anna's lips purse tightly, holding her temper, Bill intervened. "Inspector, I think it might be worth taking a look...and listen. I had my doubts too." Bill quickly glanced at Anna with a "don't say a word" look. "Not only is it hollow behind here, but I can hear faint voices."

The inspector walked over to Bill. "Not you too! But I'll listen and put a stop to this." He waved his hand slowly over the wall and he stopped, crouching on his haunches he leaned his face close to the stone.

"Hum...Yes, it's hollow behind there and I admit I could hear voices." He lifted himself from the crouch. "I'll look outside. I suspect the voices are from the Promenade. It's probably a ventilation shaft or something. I don't think it's kidnapped staff. There is no way out of here. But to appease you, Mrs. Blaine I will send a team down here."

"Thank you. I know you will find something."

"I thought you would like to know that Albert is resting in hospital. An officer is interviewing him right now and Mr. Lytton has been released and is upstairs. That was why I was looking for you."

Conspiracy Unfolds

⬦⬦⬦

Anna ran all the way up the stairs to find James' face looking like Sugar Ray Robinson after a fight. His arm was in a plaster cast and wrapped in a large sling. It took him a long time to stand up, his face grimaced at every move, and once up, he leaned heavily on his cane.

"James, how are you? Should you be out of hospital?"

"I couldn't stay away. My arm is broken and my shoulder dislocated, but they patched me up." He smiled. "Sorry I screamed at you, it was the shoulder. My face is a mess but that will heal and the old war wound took a beating." He stopped, visibly shaken, and anguish filled his eyes. His voice was uncertain. "Anna, I don't know what to say…I tried to stop them. There were four, maybe five men. Smyth was one of them, some waving truncheons—here to fight. Isabelle tried to talk to Smyth but the ringleader, a dark-skinned man they called Dhar pushed him away. Smyth argued with him, told him to leave her alone.

When I approached, Smyth grabbed me and pulled a gun, forcing me into your office. Dhar was mad and began shoving Isabelle against the reception counter. She slapped his face and punched him in the gut. As I turned to go into your office, I saw Dhar lift his truncheon. Smyth must have seen too because he yelled for Dhar to stop. Then he twisted my arm out of its socket and pushed the gun into my back. He demanded the keys to your desk and cabinet. He was yelling, 'My father will be exonerated; he is innocent. The whore put him behind bars.' He wasn't making sense and when I wouldn't give him the keys, his rage escalated. He yanked my arm and I screamed and…" James put his hand up to a white bandage on his head. "He brought the butt of the gun down onto my temple. He seemed afraid to shoot, thank God. I felt a massive blow to my head and don't remember any more." He stopped, gulping back emotion. "I didn't know about Isabelle. I am so, so sorry."

Anna swayed, holding the back of the sofa for support. She swallowed bile that had risen in her throat. Feeling such revulsion that she retched, she held her breath to stop the vomit. She knew who had done this. She slid to the floor and howled, "No! *He* finally reaped his revenge."

Bill sat beside her. "Who reaped their revenge?"

"Pickles!" She screamed and tightening her arms around her legs, she buried her head in her knees, convulsing in violent sobs.

Bill wanted to ask her how she knew, but there was no point. He gently rubbed her back and let her cry—there was nothing else he could do.

Shadows lurked in the corners of the lobby. Bill felt chilled and realized that it was dark outside. He had no idea what time it was, but it must be late evening. Anna had calmed but she would not move from her position on the floor. He got up to turn on more lights. The inspector appeared from the baize door. DS Green spoke to Durham in whispers and the inspector stepped back. James walked painfully towards them. Bill returned to Anna, grateful for the intervention. The last thing Anna needed was more interrogation. The conversation seemed intense. He wondered if there was more evidence or maybe a passage had been found. He crouched down and sat beside Anna and she relaxed a little, enough for Bill to pull her close to him. He rested his cheek on her curls. He couldn't remember how many times he had done this and he smiled inside, aware that the once golden brown wayward curls were almost white, but still as soft and unruly as the day he met her, and he kissed the top of her head. He felt her pain and wanted to make it go away, but nothing would bring Isabelle back. He wasn't sure Anna would recover and if Pickles was behind this conspiracy he had truly won. Bill felt his heart snap, the pain physical, he felt the dampness of her hair against his face—the tears were his, unbidden and unstoppable.

Totally unaware of his surroundings or time, Bill realized the lobby was quiet. *Had he fallen asleep?* Anna slept, resting on his shoulder. He tried to move his stiff back and legs without disturbing Anna. He glanced around the quiet lobby, James was lying on the sofa and DS Green was sitting in Albert's chair by the door.

"Where is everyone?"

James answered, "The inspector left a while ago. He'll be back with his crew tomorrow. DS Green is staying the night and there's another officer downstairs. If you don't mind, I will stay here rather than go home."

"Why don't you take a guest room? You'll be more comfortable."

"Thanks, but it's too hard to move. I'll stay here."

Anna stirred, rubbing her swollen eyes. "I'm so tired." Her lifeless voice gave Bill chills. He took her hand and walked to the stairs, he thought climbing the stairs to their suite might separate them from the horrors of the ground floor.

Anna woke and snuggled towards Bill putting her arm around him like she did every morning, and for a brief second life was normal. And then the horrors of yesterday gripped her mind and body. She lay still, waiting for Bill to stir, hoping he would tell her she had dreamed it all—just a nightmare. But it was all too real. She was living the nightmare. Her daughter was dead, the hotel a mess and Pickles had reached from his jail cell and destroyed everything she loved. She felt Bill's warmth and thought, *No, not everything. I still have Bill.*

"How are you this morning?" Bill said, sitting up.

She swung her legs out of bed. "I don't know. Numb perhaps. I can't feel anything. I must get up. There are things to be done."

"I'll make some coffee and bring it to your office. There's a lot of cleaning up to do in the kitchen." His eyes moistened as he glanced at Anna. *How can*

I be so matter fact? For Anna's sake.

"No, not my office. The lounge would be better," Anna said as she flung her clothes along the railing of the wardrobe. "I need black, but black is too dull. Isabelle would hate that." Her throat tightened. "Simple is best," she said, holding up a plain navy dress with a slightly flared skirt. "Perfect," she said with a hint of determination. Satisfied the dress looked appropriate, she sat at her dressing table, shocked at the haggard face in the mirror. She brushed her hair and applied lipstick and scrubbed it off—the colour was too bright. Searching the drawer for a paler shade, her fingers caught the smooth lapis crystal of her blue pendant. She lifted its silver chain tears spilling down her cheeks she pressed the pendant to her heart, breaking into sobs.

"I promised this to Isabelle and now she'll never have it. I always thought it was an omen when the velvet ribbon broke."

Bill stood behind her, his hands on her shoulders. He leaned down to kiss her. They each stared into their bonded reflection. "No, darling no omen. The pendant is important, not the ribbon or chain. You can pass it on to Sarah."

"You're right. I'll wear it today." She handed it to Bill and he fastened it around her neck. She touched it, thinking of Uncle Bertie. "When Uncle Bertie gave this to me he said 'follow your dreams' and I did but never imagined it would lead to owning a hotel. Isabelle had the same dream, and I imagined my dream passing on to my daughter and she would pass it to her daughter."

"I know. We can still pass it on to Sarah." Bill wrapped his arms around her and his gentleness dried up the tears. She patted his arm and he stood, watching her dab her eyes, powder her face and add a pink lipstick.

Bill moved to the door. "I'll bring the coffee to the lounge."

"Bill, wait. Let's go down together. I can't face it alone." She took his hand as they headed down the stairs.

It seemed odd. The lobby looked the way it always did: the chairs and sofas set around coffee tables in conversation groups, the lamps on the side tables giving off a welcoming glow. The only thing missing was the vases and flowers as most vases had been broken and the flowers destroyed. Anna glanced towards the reception counter that too looked the way it always did, except for the "Caution - Wet Floor" cones. Her knees buckled, someone had cleaned up Isabelle's blood. Bill caught her, she took a deep breath and blinked. *Pull yourself together,* she thought. She turned her gaze to the lobby lounge where James was stretched out on the sofa where they had left him.

"How are you this morning, James?" Bill asked.

"Stiff and sore and lacking sleep."

"Perhaps some fresh coffee will help." Bill disappeared through the baize door.

"Is it very painful?" Anna asked.

"It's okay as long as I don't move. It was the racket and moaning from Woody that kept me awake."

"Woody?"

"He spent all night putting the furniture back and cleaning up. Judging by the glue smell, he even mended the table leg."

"I thought I smelled something off."

"Probably the pine smell from cleaning, where…"

"Yes, he must have washed the blood…" Unable to finish the sentence Anna's eyes stared at the reception area.

"He's very upset, Anna. I tried talking to him but all he could say was 'Mrs. Wexford' and 'bad men, bad men' and some other stuff he mumbled under his breath. I'm not sure where he went, but he left about an hour or so ago."

"Where's DS Green? Did he leave?"

"No, he went outside for a smoke. He said he needed some fresh air to stay awake. Poor man has been on duty for twenty-four hours."

"What did you see when the place was attacked? Where are the staff? Dave, Amy and Balaji and maids…I'm not sure how many were on duty."

"I think there were five men, two stayed up here, the dark-skinned man called Dhar attacked Isabelle. When Amy came up to see what all the noise was about, Dhar ordered them to get Amy back downstairs and round up any other staff. That was when Smyth forced me into your office. I don't understand how Amy and the others could have disappeared. There are

248

some caves and passageways under the hotel. One of the local historians who studied the Bexhill smugglers found the passageway during the war and we used it as an air-raid shelter. The only access is from outside the hotel under the Promenade. However, if you don't know which caves are safe you can get cut off by the tide. The council blocked it off a couple of years ago because two kids got lost inside and one drowned. It's a rock garden now. There is no way of getting access."

"Does the chief inspector know about this?"

"Yes, I told him last night."

Bill arrived with a tray. "The pastries are a couple of days old, but we need to eat something. Woody has cleaned up the kitchen. He looks exhausted, so I sent him to his room to sleep. Has anyone seen Sandy?"

DS Green's voice boomed from the door. "He came in late last night and went to his flat."

CI Durham entered, followed by two workmen with ropes and pick-axes. They headed for the baize door.

"Good morning. I have brought some experts to search the cellar. If we don't find anyone, we will change tactics and assume an abduction or worse." Without waiting for an answer, the inspector and the two men disappeared into the service area.

Tension filled the room once again. The inspector had given them a warning: finding the missing staff might not be so simple and the consequences could be more heartbreak.

Anna thought of Amy and her family. Someone should go and see them and she appealed to Bill, "Can you call on Amy's husband, Sam Fulham? He may not know anything. Amy often stayed overnight if she finished too late to go home. I'm going to talk to Sandy and decide what to do about Sarah—she has to know and she can't stay at Judy's forever." Anna surprised herself with her matter of fact attitude, recognizing that paying attention to practicalities made it easier to cope. "James, are you well enough to call any reserved guests and dinner bookings? We'll close until the weekend. Um…tell them we are decorating or something and re-book them for next week. By then we will have the staff back." Anna paused, taking a sharp breath. "Or we may have to recall the seasonal staff. Isabelle had booked a conference for next week, please check the details and we'll discuss it later."

James eased himself up off the sofa, grimaced as he moved and put his hand up to stop Anna helping him. "I'm all right, just a little stiff. I can get to my office and do as you ask. Better to keep busy. Shall I call Miss Jenkins back from holiday? I don't think she went away."

"Good idea. She needs to know what happened."

Anna knocked on Isabelle's door, she corrected herself and thought, Sandy's door. Sandy's voice called, "It's open."

Still dressed in the clothes he'd worn yesterday, Sandy sat in the lounge with his shirt open, the sleeves half-rolled untidily and his tie pulled halfway down his chest, his trousers crumpled and hair uncombed, red rings around his eyes. "What am I going do? I called to see Sarah last night and told her we were busy and she was to stay with Mrs. Elliot and Judy. Do you know what she said? 'Thank you Daddy and tell Mummy I love her.' It was as though she knew. I looked at Mrs. Elliot and shook my head, I couldn't tell her. Mrs. Elliot said she would tell the girls there was no school today and I could fetch her when I was ready."

"We'll go fetch her together and bring her home to tell her."

"Thank you. I look around here and it's all Isabelle, everything is a cruel reminder. We were so happy at last." Sandy looked at Anna guiltily. "We went through a bad patch but since I started the job in Eastbourne, we were happy. Like the old days when we were first married."

"I know. Isabelle was not an easy person but she had changed. I'm sorry, Sandy. I know you are hurting. So am I, but we need to be strong for Sarah. She will need you more than ever."

"Will it ever stop hurting? Do you remember what it was like when Alex died?"

"No, it never stops hurting, but it does get easier and eventually life goes on. I was lucky. I had Bill but even with Bill at my side there was a corner of my heart that died with Alex. As time goes by, the happy memories surface and you will realize Isabelle is always with you."

"And Sarah?"

"She will grieve in her own way. Tell her the truth and be there for her. Never let her mother's memory slip away."

"I'll clean up and we'll go and fetch Sarah."

"When you are ready, I'll be in my office."

Anna tentatively stepped into her office and said aloud, "It's time to get back to work." Expecting it to be disturbing, she looked around, but it looked the same as always except for a stack of papers on her desk. "Woody must have cleaned in here too." She sat at her desk, staring at the sea. The sun had risen from the horizon and there was a warm rosy glow on the mottled cloud formation, a view that usually inspired her. Today it was a comfort to know some things don't change. Losing Isabelle was like losing part of herself. She had a million regrets, especially harsh words said in anger and frustration. Isabelle challenged her daily, and even loving her was difficult at times. She wished she had understood her better. One thing she did understand was Isabelle's ability to sell the hotel features and services and she had made The New Sackville into a classy destination. "The success of this hotel is your legacy, Isabelle, and you will never be forgotten."

"Talking to yourself?" Bill said. "And I agree, we have Isabelle to thank for what it is today and we will find a way to keep her memory alive."

Anna fought back tears and said, "No more tears, we have work to do. Did you talk to Amy's husband?"

"Yes, he is here helping with the search. I came to tell you the inspector has some news."

Anna followed Bill into the lobby.

"We found a passageway, well hidden in the floor, of all places. The men are searching now, but there are many passageways and caves down there. It has to be organized so they don't get lost. It could be awhile but I thought you would like to know." Hesitating, the inspector added, "And voices have been heard. Mrs. Blaine, it looks hopeful.

A young constable burst into the hallway. "We found them."

Consequences

Dirty and tired but unharmed, the abducted group filed into the staff dining room. Balaji was taken to one side, and the inspector ordered him to be taken to the police station. *Poor Balaji*, Anna thought, *the colour of his skin and his association with Smyth makes him unfairly suspicious.* Sous-chef Dave tried to brush dirt from his white coat and the two young maids talked excitedly. It appeared to be an adventure to them. It took the constables more than an hour to take statements from the captives.

CI Durham announced to the group, "If you have finished giving your statement and contact information you may go home." Durham looked directly at Amy. "Mrs. Peterson, I would like to talk to you separately. When the others have left." Amy clung to her husband; fear and anxiety creasing her pale face. Durham smiled. "Don't be afraid, I'm not accusing you of anything."

Dave was the last to leave and Anna sat in his chair. She wasn't asking the inspector if she could stay, she just made it obvious she wasn't moving. The inspector took his position across from Amy, a constable stood at his shoulder with notebook and pencil.

"Please tell me what happened yesterday."

Amy cleared her throat. "I was working in the laundry with Alice, sorting linen that needed repair. I could hear loud voices, and thought we must have an irate guest. I thought it might be Mr. and Mrs. Diggen as they had been obnoxious for most of their stay. The noise escalated to banging and I went upstairs to see what was happening. I saw the Diggens disappear through the front door. A group of men in black were kicking the furniture. I yelled at them to stop. Mrs. Wexford was standing by the reception counter. The leader yelled, 'Get her out of here,' meaning me. They pushed me down the stairs. There were three of them and one stayed with me and the others grabbed Chef Dave and Alice and we were pushed into the cellar. A few minutes later Balaji and Daisy were pushed down the cellar stairs. The men swung truncheons at us and one pulled a gun." Amy looked directly at the inspector. "Balaji was a prisoner the same as us. He was not part of it." She took a deep breath. "The only person on duty who was missing was Woody. We were herded into the wine cellar and shoved into a hole in the floor and into another cellar. I heard a bolt thud shut, and we were locked in until you arrived."

"Did you recognize any of the men?"

"Yes, they were the same group of men that attacked me on the street. The ringleader was the man who yelled upstairs. His name is Dhar, he's known in the area for spouting about communism."

"We know, he is on our watch list," the inspector said.

"Is everyone okay?" Amy asked Anna.

Anna realized that Amy didn't know about Isabelle, nor did the other staff that had been abducted. "I'll answer that, Inspector. Woody is safe and James and Albert are hurt but will be okay." Anna hesitated, mustering the courage to say the words. Her eyes filled with tears and her voice trembled, "I'm sorry to say that Isabelle was hurt badly...she...she died from a blow to her head."

Amy closed her eyes and her hand clasped around her mouth to muffle a cry. Anna felt the finality of her statement and the room fell silent. Minutes later, although it seemed like hours, the inspector cleared his throat and said, "There is nothing further Mrs. Peterson. You may go home if you wish."

Amy nodded and turned to Anna. Brushing away persistent tears, she uttered, "I am so sorry, Anna."

Sam took Amy by the arm and led her out of the room.

"How much longer will you be here, Inspector?" Anna asked, seeing Sandy exit the lift. She didn't want the police around when they brought Sarah home.

"We're finished up here, but my men will be working in the cellar for some time. It's difficult to say how long."

"Sandy and I are going to bring Sarah home and I'd rather not have policemen milling around."

"Understood. I'll tell forensics to use the service entrance."

Anna looked into Sarah's hazel eyes, so much like her mother's. She saw the confusion and even sadness, and thought, Sarah knows something terrible has happened. She took her father's hand and they drove to the hotel in silence.

"Sarah, Daddy and I have something to tell you. Would you like to come to Nana's suite or... the penthouse?"

Sensing the gravity of Anna's words, Sarah looked from one to the other, her confusion obvious. Sandy spoke up, "I think Nana's suite. If that's okay?" He glanced at Anna. "Too many reminders," he said leading the way.

Sarah had been quiet since they had left the Elliot's. Her questions took Anna by surprise. "Where's Mummy? Has something happened to her?"

"Would you like some biscuits or a drink?" Anna was stalling.

Sarah stamped her feet. "No, I want to know where Mummy is." Anna heard the fear in her voice.

Sandy's face grimaced in agony. He opened his mouth but no words came out. Sarah ran to Anna. Putting her arms around her granddaughter, she realized it was up to her to break the news.

"Sarah, some bad men broke into the hotel yesterday and some people were hurt. Mummy tried to stop them and there was a terrible accident." Anna gently rocked Sarah. "And Mummy was badly hurt, so badly hurt that we couldn't make her better. Sarah, I'm so sorry, but Mummy died."

The only noise in the room came from Sandy's raspy breaths, his hands covering his face. Sarah clung to Anna, not saying a word and then she felt her chest heave in quiet sobs. Anna rocked her and stroked her hair, kissing her forehead, desperately trying to hold back her own tears. Sarah gave Anna a big hug and said, "I have to go."

She jumped off the sofa and took Sandy's hands, staring at his wet tear stained face she climbed onto his knee. "Daddy, please don't cry. Mummy wouldn't like that."

Anna watched them embrace, a private sadness between father and daughter. She tip-toed out of the suite, leaving them to grieve.

It shouldn't be this normal, she thought. Then the quiet hit her; it was two in the afternoon, but you could hear a pin drop. The lounge, the bar and the dining room were empty, James had gone home for some rest, and Miss Jenkins stood alone at the reception counter with no guests to serve. All the staff had been sent home or, for those who lived in, to their rooms. The front door was locked and no doorman was in his chair. She felt uneasy. *Was this the beginning of the end? Had Pickles won? But how? How could he reach out from his jail cell?*

The phone broke the silence and Anna almost jumped off her chair. Taking a deep breath, she answered, "Hello, Mrs. Blaine speaking." She listened carefully and a chill rippled through her as the caller asked for Mrs. Wexford. She couldn't speak. Miss Jenkins appeared at her side with a large folder in her hand, which she placed on the desk in front of Anna. She heard her voice answering the caller, "Mrs. Wexford is not available, how can I help you?" She opened the file and Miss Jenkins pointed to the relevant pages and Anna answered the questions. The receiver wobbled in her shaking hand as she replaced it in the cradle.

"That was hard. Thank you." Anna pointed to the chair. "Take a seat, Miss Jenkins." She paused. "Dorothy, we've known each other for a long time. I remember back in the old days when I was a young and petulant assistant and how relieved I was on the weekends when you took over the telephone exchange." She smiled, before adding, "and how you discreetly supported me over *the desk incident* and your help when Mr. Pickles attacked me."

"I had experienced his advances. If it wasn't for my Frank, he would have attacked me."

"You must miss Frank."

"Well the war took a lot of them and Frank was one; at the Somme he was. I could never look at another man. He was the only one for me. The Sackville became my purpose in life."

"I was lucky. Alex came home from the Somme but the illness that killed him was a result of the war. But at least I had twenty-five years."

Anna looked down at the file marked, London Insurance - Conference. "Dorothy, you worked with Isabelle on these conferences? How familiar are you with the clients and procedures?"

"I did all the paperwork and discussed each client and their needs, ordered the food, booked the guests and, if necessary, I talked to the clients, but Mrs. Wexford usually liked to speak to them herself."

"You did a lot and I know very little. I always left this up to Isabelle. It wouldn't make sense for me to take over when you already know the job. Can you take over London Insurance until we get things sorted out?"

Dorothy Jenkins grinned from ear to ear. Anna realized how much she had been taken for granted and it was about time her skills were recognized.

The smile gone, Dorothy replied, "It doesn't feel right so soon after…"

"I know, but the job has to be done," Anna paused. The effect of being matter of fact was breaking her heart. "I think Isabelle would approve and you know the client. You won't be alone. I'll be here to guide you if you need me."

"All right, I'll give it a try."

"I'll ask Mr. Lytton to look after your reception duties and I'll do my own secretarial work until we get busy. You look after the London conference. The next few days will be difficult.

"What shall I say to Mr. Barr, from London Insurance?"

"Nothing for now. We have a week before the conference starts. Can you continue with the arrangements?" Anna looked at Dorothy's too long skirt, hand knitted cardigan, and heavy brogue shoes. Her attire was neat and clean and okay for behind a desk and Anna didn't want to offend her, but she had to ask her to change her wardrobe. "I was wondering if you had a business style suit you could wear during the conference." Anna felt awful pointing this out. Dorothy was a lovely person and everyone in the hotel accepted her spinster-like looks.

"I understand and I will dress appropriately. Mrs. Wexford was a good example." She paused. "Mrs. Blaine, don't worry. Honestly, I am not offended."

"Thank you, I seem to be thanking you a lot today. I am grateful."

"If there's nothing else, I would like to get home."

Anna looked at her watch. "Almost six o'clock, of course, I had no idea it was so late. Time seems irrelevant." Anna slipped into her own thoughts as Miss Jenkins closed the office door.

HM Dartmouth Prison

❦

Dhar generally incited people into action from his soapbox at public meetings. It was easy to make people think they were not getting fair wages when their bosses were scooping up all the profits of their labour. He could stand on his soapbox and preach equality for all through communism. But attacking the Sackville was different. His plan was flawed and the attack had gone horribly wrong. They were supposed to take hostages and hide them in the smuggler's caves under the hotel. He smiled. Who knew there were caves under there? *Not important,* he thought. The task was to take hostages and mess up the hotel, break some furniture, distract the staff while Ravi searched the office for some kind of evidence of wrongdoing to his father. And then leak the attack to the police with false information about communist gangs. Bad publicity would scare the hotel guests away. It seemed to be a bit flimsy, but he'd wanted a good fight and hotel owners were part of the establishment—serving society guests. The goal was to ruin the hotel's reputation. He realized his choice of men had been poor and people had been badly hurt, which wasn't in his plan. He called off the raid and everyone scattered.

Running to the car, Smyth grabbed Dhar's arm. Gasping for breath, Smyth said, "Isabelle was hurt. That wasn't supposed to happen."

"Sorry mate, these things happen. But the press will have a field day. Mission accomplished. You can tell your dad that we ruined the hotel. Isn't that what you wanted?"

"Yes, but nobody was to get hurt. If anything happens to Isabelle, you'll pay for it."

"She's fine, a knock on the head," Dhar said but his thoughts were not so confident. "Let's get out of here. We'll need to lay low for a while."

"Okay, but I'm going to Dartmouth to report our success to the old man as soon as the coast is clear."

The police were watching both the Bexhill and Eastbourne train stations; he and Dhar spent the night in an abandoned farm. Using little used country roads, Dhar drove Smyth to an obscure train station in Kent where he boarded a milk train to Plymouth. The journey was agonizingly slow, but he arrived just in time for the train to Yelverton. He was looking forward to breakfast at the little café. He imagined the waitress's kind words and concern for him. He wondered if she was married and then remembered she had a baby, so of course she was married.

The waitress greeted him with a big smile as he sat in a booth. "Same as last time?" she asked, walking towards him with a mug in one hand and the oversized aluminum teapot in the other.

"Yes, please. You remembered?"

"I remember all my special customers." She beamed. "I see your head has healed."

He nodded, wishing he could take her in his arms. She made him feel warm and he wanted to hold on to that warmth forever, to escape from the ugliness of his father in prison. But at last, his father would be proud of him. The hotel would be ruined. He wondered if it was worth it. His mind switched to Isabelle and he shuddered, remembering the thump as she fell to the floor.

"Penny for 'um," the waitress said, smiling.

"Nothing." He gave a weak smile sipping on the hot tea. "Good tea."

He ate his breakfast but not as heartily as the last time. He didn't have much of an appetite. As much as he'd looked forward to the café, suddenly he didn't want to talk. She reminded him of his mother. He hardly remembered her, but he didn't feel worthy; instinctively, he knew she wouldn't approve of his actions towards the hotel. He thought there might be a decent person inside him who might be feeling guilty, but he dismissed the thought—he wanted his father's approval more. He strolled across to the station and sat on a bench waiting for the nine o'clock train to Princeton. He bought a newspaper but didn't open it. The headline read "Murder or Accident?" He had enough to think about without reading about someone else's bad news. The train came barreling into the station and its noise and size filled him with dread. He kept telling himself his father would be proud of him and he thought, *Isn't that what you wanted?*

He marched through the great stone archway of HM Dartmouth Prison. The guard only gave him a cursory search and took his bag and the newspaper. He sensed the guard had ushered him into the interview room very quickly. It must be tea break he thought. He felt a disturbing shiver go down his spine as the metal door clanged shut and the keys rattled turning the lock, almost simultaneously the prisoner's door clanged and rattled opening wide to allow Pickles to enter the room.

Smyth involuntarily recoiled as Pickles approached, a nasty smirk on his face he looked down his pointed nose at Smyth. "You did well son. Looks as though you ruined her." Pickles leaned over and whispered, "Killed the wrong one, but she will suffer anyway."

"What are you talking about?" Panic spread through his body like a swollen river, he thought he was drowning. "How do *you* know what happened?"

"Prison walls have ears. It looks as though you'll be joining me, son."

"Stop talking to me in riddles. I came here to tell you The New Sackville Hotel is close to ruins. I was there," Smyth lowered his voice, "but there was no killing. I told you I wanted no part of murder. I don't want to end up here."

Pickles threw his head back and cackled like the wicked witch of Oz. "Too late, son. I guess you didn't know Dhar's older brother is my cellmate. He murdered someone during one of his communist rallies. His brother Dhar escaped. You don't think it was an accident that you two met." Pickles was laughing so hard he began gasping for breath. "You are...more stupid than...I thought. But I have to say, I never thought you had it in you to attack the hotel and get rid of one of the bitches, albeit the wrong one. Maybe some of me did rub off after all."

Smyth's face drained, a hammer was pounding in his head, his ears filled with static noise, fading his father's voice into oblivion. He held on to the table to stay upright. There were only two women his father could be referring to, and Isabelle was the only one there at the time. Something snapped. He hated this man who had taken the only two people he had loved and destroyed them. He stared at the twisted, perverted monster sitting in front of him. At that moment he understood the stories of rape and violence were true. He was serving the sentence he deserved. Smyth leaned across the table and grabbed Pickles' prison suit, his fists pushing Pickles chin into his mouth. His face inches away, he spat at him, "I will see you pay for this." He let go, shoving Pickles with such force his chair wobbled backwards and the guard caught it before it toppled over.

"Hey! *You*, enough of that," the guard said wagging his finger.

Smyth ignored him sneering at his father. "You disgust me! Guard, we're done here, let me out." Smyth stood up and waited for the clang of the keys to unleash him from the pugnacious misery that seeped through the prison walls. He sensed Pickles' piercing stare on his back and heard his witch's cackle as he walked away. He collected his bag and newspaper and hiked to the Railway Inn.

It would be another hour before the bar opened, but he decided to take a room for the night, he needed time to think. Following the publican's wife down the hall she said apologetically over her shoulder, "This room's not as nice as the other. There's another gentleman staying, he's a regular."

Smyth wondered what she meant by regular, a commercial traveller or a regular at the prison, but said nothing, bobbing his head up and down to acknowledge her constant chatter.

"Here we are. Bathroom's down the hall. Sixpence in the meter for hot water. If you want a bath, it's a shilling," she said, handing him the key. "Will you be wanting dinner?"

Realizing he had not eaten since the morning, he suddenly felt hungry. "Yes please."

"Shepherd's pie, treacle pudding and custard. Five sharp or it'll be cold."

"Thank you," Smyth said as he ushered her out of the door. He wanted some peace and he needed a hot bath to get the stench of Dartmouth off his skin.

He put his newspaper on the dresser and threw his bag on the bed, taking out a clean shirt and his toilet bag. He made sure he had some coins in his pocket and wrapping the towel around his neck he headed for the bathroom. One shilling gave him two inches of water, barely enough to cover his legs, but it was hot. He scrubbed until his skin was raw and then lay back and relaxed. He dared not think of Isabelle, afraid he would break down. He thought of his father and immediately tensed with anger. The hate he felt was homicidal; perhaps he did have murder in him after all. He lay there, shivering in the now cold water. He frowned at the door vibrating. *Was he shivering that hard?* he thought, and sat up. Someone was pounding on the door.

"What you doing in there, mate? Other people need to take a leak."

"I'll be out in a minute." Smyth listened to the familiar voice. "Dhar, is that you?"

"Who's asking?"

"Smyth, I mean Ravi. What are you doing here?"

"Get the hell out of the john."

"I'll be out in a sec. Hey, you didn't tell me your brother was in Dartmouth."

"Not something I'm proud of." Dhar kicked the door. "Will you get out of there?"

Smyth dried himself off, but when he opened the door, Dhar had disappeared. He looked down the empty hallway, shrugged and returned to his room. The draft from the door lifted the newspaper on the dresser and Smyth physically leaned back as if to dodge the words as they leaped out at him. MURDER OR ACCIDENT? He didn't want to acknowledge that people had been hurt in the raid. Dhar had beaten James Lytton pretty badly and Albert hadn't looked too good slumped in his chair. Isabelle, he thought, had just fallen. Tripped on something he assumed, or had she been pushed? He regretted not staying to check on her. He read on, "Mrs. Isabelle Wexford the victim of a brutal attack by a communist gang in the quiet upscale seaside town of Bexhill. The police are being cautious and have not yet ruled out murder. A family member told *The Daily Telegraph* that Mrs. Wexford suffered a head injury from a fall." Tears dripped, leaving grey spots on the newsprint. His eyes glazed with moisture—he could read no more.

Dhar's voice yelled through his door. "Ravi! Are you coming down for dinner?"

His breath caught in his throat and he gulped air to fuel his voice. "Go ahead, I'll be down." He pulled his fingers hard across his face, determined not to show his grief, he allowed his anger to percolate. First, towards his father and then Dhar until it consumed all other thoughts. Blocking his grief enabled him to walk down the stairs.

The lounge portion of the bar smelled of stale beer and cigarette smoke, the table still sticky from the noon pints. The landlady slapped a plate of Shepherd's pie in front of him, the thick, gelatinous gravy spilling onto the table. Dhar was already eating, shoving great mounds of food into his mouth and talking at the same time. Smyth couldn't take his eyes off the meat and mash potatoes circling in Dhar's open mouth like a cow's cud. Smyth debated whether or not to eat. His stomach was rebelling, but he couldn't tell if it was from hunger or revulsion. He had to eat.

Keeping his eyes on his own plate of food and avoiding Dhar's mastication, he ate the surprisingly tasty dinner. The landlady appeared with two steaming dishes of treacle pudding. He poured thick creamy custard over it and both men sighed with satiety as they finished the meal.

"Why didn't you tell me about your brother? We could have driven down together."

"Did you forget the cops are looking for us? We had to split up."

"I guess so. It seems your brother has quite a lot of influence at Dartmouth."

"Y'er, he's an organizer. Knows the right people, inside and out. Doesn't think much of your old man."

"Neither do I. He told me he was innocent, that he'd been tricked by Anna and was defending himself from an attack. Now I discover he's as guilty as sin. He hurt my mother and, because of him, she died when I was only eleven. He abandoned me and left me with the Brits, who hated me, but raised me any way. At least sent me to fancy boarding school to get rid of me."

"I remember your ma, she was kind and gentle. Life was good on the estate. Then the fancy Brits destroyed my parents after you left. Don't trust any of them, and don't grieve the loss of Isabelle. She was one of them."

"No she wasn't. She was different. Her mother might be, and now because of my dad, Isabelle is dead." Smyth had difficulty controlling his temper. He wanted to hurt Dhar, hurt him badly. But he needed Dhar and his brother. He gritted his teeth and directed his anger to his father. "I want him hurt and dead."

"I can arrange that."

"Yer, right!" Smyth lifted his beer mug to the publican. "Two pints over here."

"I mean it. Things didn't go as expected, let me make it up to you. I'll see your old man suffers and I can arrange a nasty accident. It happens all the time in prison." Dhar's eyes narrowed.

"Revenge. That's what the old man wanted. Turn the tables," Smyth laughed. "I like the idea."

"I'll pass the word during my visit tomorrow morning. Meet me here at noon and then we need to go our separate ways. I doubt the police have connected us with Dartmouth yet, but they will."

Smyth hardly slept. He cried like a baby, his face smothered in his pillow to drown his sobs. He wanted to feel Isabelle's arms around him and her soft lips kissing him. Although most of their trysting had been in his dreams, it felt real and he really needed her. Sensing her warmth he slept for a while until his body broke into a sweat. He thrashed around the bed, consumed with anger and guilt. How could he have been so stupid? First being sucked in by his father and then by Dhar. He wanted them both dead. If Dhar managed to dispose of his father, he had to figure out how to get rid of Dhar. He checked his watch and was surprised to see it was already eight. He dressed, threw his things into his bag and sat on the bed. He was hungry but didn't want to encounter Dhar at the breakfast table. Hearing a car engine, he pulled the curtains and saw the back of Dhar's car disappear on to Dartmoor. He paid his bill and ate breakfast. The landlord handed him the *Daily Mirror* and gave him a strange look. Smyth took the paper but was afraid to open it and idly sipped on his tea. What if the police had posted photos? Dhar was right they would be looking for them. He glanced at the landlord again but he was occupied with beer taps.

He finished his tea and walked to the station to check out train times. Perhaps he wouldn't wait for Dhar to return. He'd missed the train to Tavistock and he couldn't go back to Eastbourne or Bexhill. He ran his finger down the timetable. "There isn't much choice," he said aloud, wondering if he could hitch a ride with Dhar. That wasn't perhaps wise, they probably shouldn't be seen together. He looked up, sensing someone staring. He nodded to the stationmaster and walked back to the pub and sat on the bench outside.

Dhar arrived, all smiles, and ushered Smyth into the pub whispering, "All done, my big brother will make it happen. Now buy me a beer."

Smyth carried two frothy pints to the nearest table. Dhar suddenly looked terrified, staring at the door he said, "We'd better get out of here."

Smyth felt a strong hand on his shoulders and a stern voice say, "Put the beer down and raise your hands where I can see them." He dared not turn around. He kept his eyes on Dhar, watching as a police constable pulled Dhar up by his collar and handcuff him.

"Am I being arrested?" Smyth asked as he felt the cold metal of handcuffs.

"You're needed in Eastbourne. Persons of interest. Don't know anymore. Now shut up." The officer held Smyth's arm and guided him to a van.

Smyth sat in the interview room at the Eastbourne police station waiting for Chief Inspector Durham. It was late and he was tired and scared. They had taken Dhar into a separate room and he didn't trust him, or what he might say. He reprimanded himself for getting mixed up with Dhar. It had seemed like good idea at the time, but then a lot of things seemed to be a good idea. He hadn't thought any of it through beyond fulfilling his father's wishes of revenge, and that turned out to be the worst idea of them all.

The door swung open and the inspector threw a writing pad on the table. "We meet again, Ralph Smyth. Or should I call you Ravi Pickles?"

"Ravi Smyth is my name. After my mother died, my guardians, if you could call them that, gave me their name." Smyth felt his anger erupt. "I want nothing to do with the name Pickles. He's a monster and not my father. I regret the day I decided to find him."

The inspector said nothing, carefully weighing up this complex man.

"Why am I here? I've done nothing worthy of police detention."

"No need to be belligerent. We know you were involved with the attack on the hotel and you are an associate of Dhar Bindu. Are you a member of the communist party?"

"What! No, Dhar and I grew up in India. We lived in the same town. After my mother died, I was sent to school in England. I hadn't seen Dhar for nearly ten years then I bumped into him at a rally."

"So you admit it. You are a member?"

"No, it's just coincidence. I'm not sure how that happened." Smyth frowned. Now he thought about it, it was odd how they met.

"And how does Balaji fit into this?"

"Our mothers worked at the same plantation. We grew up together in India. We've been friends for a long time. I helped Balaji when he came to England and we worked in the same hotels. He has nothing to do with any of this. He's a decent bloke, works hard at the hotel."

"We know. I just wondered if you had anything to add." Durham waited for a reply and then continued, "Mr. Smyth, what were you doing at the hotel on the morning of November 4th?"

"I went to see Mrs. Wexford. There had been a misunderstanding and I wanted to put the record straight."

The inspector raised his eyebrows and looked puzzled. "You realize you are giving me a motive for murder."

"It was Dhar who pushed her. I didn't know she was ... I would never have left her had I know she was badly hurt. Dhar is the activist, not me. I have no interest in communism or politics. I'm sorry I got involved."

"Sorry doesn't cut it, Mr. Smyth. This is murder. You are facing a charge of murder and a plethora of other charges. I'm inclined to believe that you did not intend to hurt Mrs. Wexford, but she died as a result of her injuries during the raid on the hotel that you were part of." Durham smiled. "I can't promise, but if you can give me some legitimate information, about Dhar Bindu and his brother..." He paused, "I can speak to the crown to reduce the charges. But I need the truth, no stories."

Smyth didn't like what he was hearing. Didn't this man understand he loved Isabelle and would never hurt her?

"Where would you like me to start, Inspector?"

"What do you know of his communist activities?"

"Not a great deal here, but his older brother was well known in India, riots against the British. I was only a kid but I remember Dhar idolized his brother."

"That doesn't help me much. I need recent stuff."

"Give me a couple of days and I'll get what you need."

"And how do you plan on doing that?"

"I'll get Dhar to confess and tell the truth about what happened."

"You already know what happened. You and Dhar are going to jail, the only question here is which one of you is charged with murder and who has the lesser charge of manslaughter or bodily harm. I think there is a strong possibility that, with the right evidence, you could have the lesser charge."

A Grieving Hotel

~~~~~~~~~~~~~~~~~

The hotel had a quiet sadness about it. The staff spoke in whispers and either avoided eye contact with Anna or gave her a pitiful smile. Sarah followed her around, but said little. Anna thought she worried about her father as much as losing her mother. The funeral had been sad enough. She had hoped that after the funeral they could get back to normal. The hotel had re-opened but they had no guests and at this time of year they relied on local people for dinner reservations, but the locals weren't quite sure how to act around such sadness and were avoiding the Sackville.

Isabelle's death had been ruled murder. Any form of discretion was impossible; the investigation was breaking news. How much it would affect the hotel was difficult to judge. Miss Jenkins had taken over the London Insurance Brokers Conference and done an excellent job of assuring the organizers that everything was under control.

James was doing his best at the reception counter, but his plaster cast arm and painful dislocated shoulder made it difficult and Dorothy Jenkins was doing it all. She never complained but Anna was aware that she was expecting far too much of both of them.

Anna had placed an advertisement in the local paper and this afternoon she was interviewing the few women who had applied for the secretary position. The only suitable candidate that Anna liked was Mrs. Robertson, a widowed lady supporting three children. She had worked as a telephone operator at the town hall, and perhaps because of Anna's own issues with the telephone exchange, she felt comfortable hiring her, although her shorthand was a rusty and her typing a little slow. Anna figured she could learn, and her biggest asset was that she could start immediately.

Anna was feeling much better. James had told her some local dinner guests had booked for Saturday night. He thought that they were possibly curious, but Anna didn't care, she needed paying customers. Miss Jenkins had taken the afternoon off, which was unusual, but knowing how hard she had been working, Anna didn't object and the conference people were not due until the following afternoon.

Struggling to get into a routine, Anna asked Bill to bring them coffee and pastries to her office that morning. Albert was back and Anna went to greet him and make sure he was fully recovered.

"I'm feeling quite well, Mrs. Blaine. I wanted to be here at the hotel." He pulled the door handle and the massive door swung open to allow a handsome woman to enter. She smiled and Anna looked at her neat French roll, pearl earrings and delicate make up that softened the harsh hairline. There was something familiar about her. Her navy suit fitted her trim figure, and high heels showed off shapely calves. Henry bowed, "Good morning, Miss Jenkins."

"Dorothy!" Anna said, "You look wonderful, I hardly recognized you."

"Thank you. I'm pleased you approve."

"Very much so." Anna was amazed at the slim figure Dorothy had been hiding under her loose baggy clothing, then she remembered a fashionable young woman operating the telephone exchange and realized it had all changed after her fiancé died in the war. "Can you come into my office for a minute?"

Anna sat at her desk and motioned to Dorothy to take a seat. "Yesterday I hired a secretary. Mrs. Robertson starts in the morning. She is well qualified to operate the telephone, but her shorthand and typing skills are rusty. She will not only be taking over my secretarial needs but yours as well. I know you have a lot of extra duties but could you help her improve those skills?"

"Of course."

Anna could not get rid of the sadness that permeated the hotel. The conference delegates crept around the hotel and the staff spoke in hushed voices. She had to do something before Christmas or they would never make it to the summer season.

"James, I want to call a meeting with you, Miss Jenkins, Bill, Amy and Balaji. Please ask everyone to come to my office and order some refreshments," Anna paused, "In ten minutes, finish what they are doing first.

"Is something wrong?"

"I'm worried about the atmosphere. The sadness is affecting the guests."

One by one the chosen few entered Anna's office and sat around the table.

"Good morning, everyone. It goes without saying that we are all sad and miss Isabelle and it will take us a long time to get over this tragedy. However, this is our tragedy and not the guests'. Guests come here to relax and enjoy themselves, or in the case of a conference, to work. The reason I have asked you to come today is to try and find a way to lift the spirits in the hotel, for you and your staff. Life goes on, and Isabelle would not want it any other way. She worked hard to bring in conferences and guests and the children's program. Glum faces and whispering voices would not go down well, so please let's honour her memory with hard work and welcoming smiles. If you do it, your staff will follow suit." Anna smiled and looked around the table. "Do you think you can do that?" Heads nodded and a communal yes came from the group.

"I spoke with the inspector earlier this morning. You will be pleased to know that all the perpetrators have been caught and are currently in jail awaiting trial for a variety of offences including murder, abduction and conspiracy. And, yes, Mr. Smyth is among the accused. It is unlikely that the police will release any more information at this time. I would appreciate it if you would not discuss this with the guests. If asked, answer politely that the hotel is cooperating with the crown and the police and we are not at liberty to comment. If necessary, refer persistent guests to either Bill or myself and should we not be available, ask James. Is everyone clear on that?" Another round of nods came from the table. "Are there any questions?"

Amy put her hand up. "I wonder if it would help if we had a meeting with all the staff? Anna, I think it would help the junior staff if you spoke to them and showed them that you are okay. I think they worry that they are being disrespectful by continuing as normal."

"That is a very good idea. Thank you, Amy. Can everyone round up their staff to meet in the staff dining room at three this afternoon? Unless there are any questions, I'd like to see smiles as you return to your duties and we'll see you all at three. Thank you, everyone." Anna realized that the sadness was in fact for her and Amy had been right, all everyone needed to know was that the family was okay. She felt the atmosphere lift immediately and smiles returned.

When Anna returned to her office after the three o'clock meeting, CI Durham sat in the lobby waiting to see her.

"Chief Inspector, I'm sorry to keep you waiting but I wasn't expecting you. Do you have some news for me?"

"I wanted to bring you up to date. We have been watching Dhar Bindu for some time. He was well known for getting people all riled up in India and he is a known member of the communist party. His brother, Jay Bindu, is in prison for murder as a result of a riot that went wrong. What you might not know is that Ravi Smyth's father, Ebenezer Pickles, is Bindu's cell mate."

Anna closed her eyes. Would this never end? She was right, Pickles was Smyth's father. "I didn't take Smyth for an overtly violent man; he was being driven and you confirmed who was driving him and that explains a lot."

"Smyth's testimony is helping us gather evidence about Dhar, who is a slippery character and deserves to be behind bars. I actually feel mildly sorry for Smyth. His father used him to get at you, and he thought he'd found a long lost father, only to discover a cruel and evil man. The betrayal he felt tipped him over the edge, which worked in our favour. There's not much you can add to a life sentence, but Smyth's rants about his father gave us some pretty damning evidence against Dhar, and his brother. I think the evidence will stick this time. We've been trying to get Dhar behind bars for a long time."

"I hope you are not asking me to sympathize with Smyth."

"No. I thought it might help to know that he didn't intend to hurt Isabelle and he wants revenge for her death. Which brings me to the reason for my visit. Ebenezer Pickles is dead."

"Dead! How? A heart attack? Smyth said he had a bad heart."

"He did, but that's not what killed him. No one is saying why but the thugs, the most violent inmates, decided to attack Pickles in the shower…" Durham blushed, hesitating. "What happens in prison showers…" Durham stared at his feet avoiding Anna's eyes, "…it would be uncouth to repeat to a lady. It appears the guards had been bribed to look the other way. Not unusual I'm afraid. Pickles was half dead and pleading for mercy before the guards intervened and took him to the infirmary."

Anna shuddered at the extreme violence. She expected to feel vindicated, knowing Pickles had felt rape, but her feelings were mixed and tears burned her eyes. She stared at Durham, not able to speak.

"That's not all." Durham waited.

Anna moistened her dry lips. "How did he die?"

"He was stabbed multiple times that same night, in the prison infirmary. His death was one of the most violent Dartmouth has experienced. Deaths and murder are common in prison, mostly as a result of short tempers, bullying and control. The warden identified Pickles' death as a murder of extreme passion and hatred that even he had not witnessed in Dartmouth. How it happened and who is responsible we probably will never know; no witnesses and no one is talking."

"Was it Smyth? The rage he felt for his father would make him want to destroy him."

"You may be right but I have no proof and both Smyth and Dhar were in the county jail when this happened. I suppose he could have arranged it." Durham hesitated.

"Inspector, is there something you are not telling me?" *Who killed Pickles is of no importance to me,* Anna thought. She hated to admit it even to herself that the killer had done her a favour. Durham knew that, so why was he being evasive?

"I am sure you have heard the expression, honour among thieves. Well, there is an unwritten, unsaid rule in prison that prisoners protect each other, most of the time. But there are certain crimes where even criminals draw the line. We suspect, but will never be able to prove, that Jay Bindu stabbed and killed Pickles. His motive was not the obvious one, although connected."

"Inspector, you are talking in riddles. Please get to the point."

"Bindu became an activist because he maintained his father was killed by the British in India. However, his mother was already deceased during the uprising. His father and uncle killed his mother. An honour killing for bringing disgrace to the family because she had been raped by Pickles."

Anna gasped, her mind trying to fathom the horror of such circumstances and reluctantly understanding the hatred the Bindu brothers had for Pickles.

"I had no idea of the far-reaching consequences of Pickles' actions."

"Part of my job is to determine the possibility of getting a conviction. Much of that depends on witnesses and evidence. In the original Pickles case we had evidence but a missing witness." He glanced at Anna.

"We have a lot of history, Mrs. Blaine. I was a young detective when Dr. Gregory approached me to arrest Pickles. I knew he was bad news and at first I couldn't prove it. You were the missing witness, weren't you?"

"I was, and I regret not being around. I couldn't face it and escaped to Canada with my first husband, Alex Walker. I felt awful when I realized he could not be charged the first time because I had not come forward. It was months afterwards that my brother came to visit us in Canada and brought us a copy of the newspaper report of Pickles' second trial."

"Thankfully, based on your evidence and Amy Peterson's testimony, we did eventually get Pickles. I have brought this up because getting guilty verdicts can be difficult. We rely on witnesses, evidence and a multitude of factors. We don't always get the verdict that is deserved. However, I think we have a good solid case against the Bindu brothers and Smyth."

"I hope you are not trying to tell me they will get off scot-free?"

"No, nothing like that. Dhar has been officially charged with second degree murder, conspiracy, abduction and several related charges and several lesser charges against property. Bindu is charged with conspiracy to commit murder, aiding and abetting. Although we know his role in this was significant, it will be hard to prove in court. Smyth has cooperated with my men, supplying evidence that will be key in getting a conviction. He has been charged with the lesser charge of grievous bodily harm and some minor charges of damaging property. According to witnesses, your staff in particular, Smyth was a reluctant participant during the abduction. James Lytton confirms it was Smyth and another man who attacked him in your office, but Smyth did not attack Mrs. Wexford."

"What you're saying is the crown doesn't believe they can get a jury verdict of manslaughter for Smyth. But they are confident that Dhar will be convicted, right?"

"Exactly, and remember juries are fickle and solicitors are clever. Nothing is certain until the jury gives their decision."

"I understand. I do want to hear a guilty verdict, an eye for an eye. I appreciate your honesty."

"One last thing. I should warn you there will be some publicity during both trials and it may or may not be newsworthy. But you and your staff will be called as witnesses and the hotel will be at the centre of the trials."

"What if they connect Pickles as a past manager of the Sackville?"

"It's hard to say, but I doubt that something that happened thirty years ago would be of interest. I wouldn't worry about it. Just be forewarned."

Hotel Returns to Normal

orothy Jenkins worked hard to make London Insurance delegates feel comfortable and she was a master at deflecting questions away from the tragedy. Anna kept wondering who this smart woman was, as she dealt with clients as though she'd been doing it all her life. She questioned how much Dorothy had learned from Isabelle, or perhaps Dorothy was the driving force behind Isabelle. Either way the results were excellent and the lack of drama was refreshing. Guilt flooded Anna's mind for even thinking that way, triggering an urge to weep. She couldn't deny how much she missed her daughter. It was a struggle to maintain a brave face. Her talk to the staff was as much for her as them. She was aware that her need for normalcy was naïve and futile. Things would never be normal again. She had lost a daughter, Sandy a wife and Sarah a mother. She thought how sad Sarah had looked at the funeral. A ten-year-old should not have to grow up without a mother. And Sandy, as much as he adored his daughter, couldn't cope. She was not sure he ever would cope without Isabelle. There was a man who loved unconditionally and easily forgave, but his grief had made him fearful of love, and she worried that might include Sarah. She questioned the wisdom of leaving them to grieve together. She needed to intervene.

Anna took the lift to the third floor and climbed the stairs to the penthouse. It was time Sarah went back to school and Sandy to returned to work. She knocked on the door and Sarah answered, a big smile on her face. "Nana!" She hugged Anna tightly and was reluctant to let go.

"Nana," Sarah whispered, "Can I come and live with you?" Anna was taken aback.

"Well, we do live together."

"No, I mean in your suite. I want to live in your spare room."

"We'll see."

"Please!"

Anna walked into the sitting room and almost gasped at the mess. Sandy was lying on the sofa, his arm across his face. Judging by the beginnings of a beard and crumpled clothes, he hadn't bathed in days. He sat up when he heard Anna. "Come in, sorry about the mess." His eyes were swollen to pinholes, and his colour as grey as a November sky.

"I need to talk to you, Sandy. We need to make plans for Sarah and try and get some normalcy back into our lives. Sarah should go back to school and set a daily routine. Do you think it would help if you went back to work?"

Sandy looked at her with horror and stuttered, "I can't. I can't live without her, and things were going so well. Everything in the flat reminds me of her. I can't." Tears began flowing. "I can't," he repeated.

Anna felt Sarah stiffen. She wasn't sure if it was sadness for her mother or for her father's grief. Whichever it was, Anna knew she had to remove Sarah from the penthouse.

"Sandy, I will take care of Sarah. She can stay in our suite until you can cope. I'll send a maid up to clean. I want you to take a bath and put clean clothes on. Why don't you join us for dinner tonight?"

He looked down at his crumpled suit. "I guess I do need to change. I can't face dinner."

"All right, I'll send Bill up with a light meal for you. You have to eat." He opened his mouth to object, thought better of it, and nodded.

"Sarah, go fetch your nightdress and school uniform and any books you might need. You can always come back to check on your dad and pick things up as you need them."

Sarah flung her arms around Sandy. "I love you, Daddy. Now do as Nana says. Mummy wouldn't like to see you looking all crumpled. I am at Nana's if you need me."

Anna smiled at Sarah's maturity, a reversal of the father and child role. Perhaps she was seeing a side of him that Isabelle saw. She had often complained that he was a wimp. Anna hadn't believed her but maybe there was some truth in it.

Bill was in the sitting room when Anna and Sarah arrived. "It is very quiet, so I thought I'd take some time off. I went to your office but you weren't there."

"I went to see Sarah and Sandy. Sarah is going to stay with us for a while." She looked at Bill. "Sandy is in a bad way. He needs some time to come to terms… Sarah asked if she could stay with us."

"I think that is a good idea. I'll go and check on Sandy later. Here, let me take those for you." Bill leaned over and took Sarah's bag. "Let's get you settled in your room. I'll enjoy having you here. I used to love it when your mother kept me company when she was a little girl." He looked at Sarah's sad face. "It's okay to talk about your mum and it's okay to be sad." He squeezed Sarah's shoulders. "And your dad will be all right. He just needs time. You and I, we'll keep an eye on him. How does that sound?" Sarah smiled as she skipped back into the sitting room and sat beside Anna. Bill joined them.

"How do you feel about going to school tomorrow?"

"I miss school but will the other kids want to talk about my mother?"

"They might. How do you think you will answer?"

"I don't know. I don't want to talk about it."

"Could you just say you miss your mum but you are glad you have Dad, Nana and Grandpa Bill? You could say you don't want to talk about it."

Sarah brightened as she thought about the suggestions. "Yes, I can do that. I would like to go to school tomorrow. I miss Lizzy."

The next morning, Anna took Sarah to school and, after leaving her with her friend Lizzy, she spoke with the headmistress. Anna was right, going back to school, settling into a routine and being with her friend Lizzy helped Sarah adjust.

Bill managed to talk Sandy into going back to work, but it didn't last long. The company suggested he needed time to adjust to his wife's death. Sandy interpreted this as being fired and began drinking heavily. Neither Anna nor Bill could talk sense into him. It wasn't unusual for him to bang about in the penthouse in a drunken stupor so the night he packed up and left, no one noticed.

Amy discovered his absence when one of the maids complained he wouldn't answer the door. Expecting to find him passed out drunk, Amy used her master key to check on him. The place was tidy, dishes were washed and put away, the lounge was neat and the bedroom quite empty. Amy opened the wardrobe door where empty hangers rocked on the rail. She remembered Isabelle's clothes had been cleared out some time ago and noticed a forgotten silk scarf lying on the wardrobe floor. But Sandy's shirts and suits were gone too. She opened the chest of drawers—empty. Nothing had been disturbed in Sarah's room, most of her things had been moved to Suite 305 and Sarah refused to go near the penthouse, leaving what she didn't need untouched. Amy went back to the kitchen and walked over to the sink, the smell of stale alcohol floated up to her nose and the dustbin overflowed with empty whisky bottles. *Turned over a new leaf,* she thought. An envelope sat on the counter addressed to Anna and Sarah.

Amy returned to the lobby and knocked on Anna's office door. "I just came from the penthouse. I think Mr. Wexford has left."

"Left! What do you mean?"

Amy described the scene and handed over the envelope.

Anna's mind raced with terrible thoughts. She opened the letter slowly, afraid of what it might say.

Dear Anna,

First, I must apologize for my drunken behaviour, no excuses but I had to numb the pain. A poor choice. I can't live without Isabelle but don't worry I don't plan on taking my own life, at least, not yet. However, I need to move on and away from everything that reminds me of Isabelle and yes I'm sorry to say that means Sarah too. Please don't hate me, but every time I look at my little girl, who I love more than anything, I see Isabelle. I am sure it will pass and I will come back for her one day but right now the kindest and most loving thing I can do for Sarah is leave her with you and Bill.

I have cleaned up the penthouse. Do with it whatever you see fit. I will never live there again.

Please do not try to find me. I will return when I'm ready. Give Sarah a big hug and tell her I love her and in a strange way I'm doing this for her. This she will not understand, but I think you will. I am grateful to you for all the love and care you gave me over the years. I couldn't have wished for a better mother-in-law and I know my little girl will be well looked after and you will keep her mother's memory alive.

With much love
Sandy

"I'm not surprised," Anna said. "Isabelle complained of his passiveness and without her he's lost. I'm pleased he quit drinking. Perhaps in time he'll come to terms with his grief and come back to Bexhill." She shook her head as she said the words.

"Poor Sarah," Amy said.

"What time is it? I must tell Bill before Sarah comes home from school. It would be best if we told her together. Amy, wait until tomorrow and then tell the staff that Sandy was called away on business. I'm going to find Bill." Before Anna could open the office door, Bill appeared. "Did I hear my name?"

Anna passed Bill the letter. "I'm not surprised. How do you think Sarah will take it?"

"I think we are about to find out." Anna nodded towards Sarah, in her school uniform walking towards the office. The three headed up to Suite 305.

Sarah sat on the sofa in the lounge of what was now her permanent home. Bill put his arm around her and gave her a squeeze. "Nana has something to tell you."

"I have some bad news. I'm so very sorry, my dear Sarah, but your father has decided to go away for a while." Anna paused, waiting for a reaction from Sarah, who said nothing. "He wrote a letter, addressed to you and me. He misses your mother so much he needs to go away, but he loves you very much and has asked Grandpa Bill and I to look after you."

"Dad won't come back. He misses Mum too much. I remind him of her. I love him but I'm better off with you and Mum would want it this way." Anna's mouth dropped open at Sarah's words. Without a tear, Sarah accepted her father's parting as if she expected it.

Bill hugged her tightly. "My brave little Sarah. Nana and I will take good care of you."

"I know. Can I ask Lizzy to come for dinner?"

The New Sackville was exceptionally quiet, even for early December. If it hadn't been for two regulars, the hotel would be empty. Anna was trying to convince herself that the low occupancy was normal, which it was, but she felt uneasy. She called James into the office. "Can you bring the Christmas bookings and schedule into the office?"

"Of course." James placed a folder on her desk. "It looks good. We have six families booked in the suites. Regular rooms are about forty percent booked. You are worried. I can tell by the lines on your forehead. Why?"

"It's never a good idea to tell a woman she has lines on her forehead." Anna laughed. "But you are right and I know it is not rational but I keep waiting for a big headline in the newspapers.

"People are interested in celebrating Christmas. I think this time it is your own thoughts, not intuition, that are worrying you. Miss Jenkins is doing a fabulous job with the children's program, she has reached out and reassured families. What can possibly go wrong? Christmas bookings are as good if not better than last year."

"I understand, but James, please do not let your guard down."

Mrs. Robertson tapped on the door, leaning her head into the office. "Mrs. Blaine, Chief Inspector Durham to see you. He doesn't have an appointment. What time shall I tell him?"

Anna glanced at James before asking, "Did he say what it was about?"

"No. He said if you weren't busy."

Anna looked at her watch. "Invite him for lunch and show him to the family table in the dining room. James and I will join him when we have finished here.

"Very well." Mrs. Robertson closed the door.

James raised his eyebrows, "Do you have more to discuss?"

"I don't believe policemen just drop by. What do you think he wants?"

"Anna, this is not a detective novel. I suspect he was hoping for a free lunch."

"Possibly."

Lunch with the inspector turned out to be pleasant. He happened to be in Bexhill on an unrelated case and had called at the Sackville as a courtesy. There were no new developments in the Smyth/Bindu case; the trial was due to begin after Christmas. Durham reassured Anna that there were no issues that he was aware of that would cause negative publicity for the hotel.

A Toast of Acceptance

S arah had been chosen to be the Virgin Mary in the school nativity play and rehearsals kept her occupied until the day of the performance. Suddenly Sarah refused to go to the morning rehearsal and told her teacher she couldn't go on stage. It didn't take long to figure out she missed her parents and Anna was called to the school.

Between intermittent sobs and copious tears, a difficult conversation ensued about parents in the audience, but not hers. Anna had tried to find Sandy to invite him but he was nowhere to be found. The headmistress finally suggested that Bill and Anna sit in the front, where Sarah could see them—satisfied with Nana and Grandpa in the front row, the play went on according to plan.

The nativity play was a great success. Sarah was showing incredible talent and Anna wondered if they had a budding actress in the family. She had been aware for some time that Sarah was creative; her artwork and essays were far beyond her years. Isabelle had encouraged her academics and it seemed Sarah was accomplished in both art and academics. In spite of the turbulent events in little Sarah's life, her end of term report was excellent.

The walk from the school was pleasant. Anna enjoyed having Bill on one arm and holding Sarah's hand with the other. The wind was cool off the sea but the sun was warm in spite of the season. She wondered if they would have snow for Christmas. It always changed the atmosphere but she worried about people on icy roads. As they walked up the steps, Albert opened the door. "How was the nativity Miss Sarah?"

Sarah beamed. "I did very well, thank you. We had a standing ovation."

"Sarah was brilliant. We are very proud of her. Now take your satchel to your room and get changed." Anna watched her run up the stairs. Sarah stopped and called, "The Christmas tree looks lovely from here." For a second Anna saw and heard Isabelle and smiled.

Anna gazed around the festive lobby. She had discarded her worries about bad publicity. Occasionally her subconscious would remind her not to be complacent, but mostly the merriment of Christmas dominated her thoughts. The tree was taller than ever, the decorations more luxurious and twice as many coloured lights strung around it and colourful parcels were piled under it.

Dorothy had suggested the staff should have their own tree in the staff dining room to boost morale—the last thing the hotel needed was sad, long faces moping around. Anna wrapped presents for all the staff. It was a challenge. Although some rationing had eased, there were still shortages, but she managed to purchase an appropriate present for everyone. She missed Isabelle, as did Bill, but no one need know. Keeping busy helped until the night the tree was officially lit while the local choir sang carols. Anna stood next to Bill, his fingers threaded into hers, and hers threaded into Sarah's, not daring to see each other's tears.

Like her mother and grandfather, Sarah was a social butterfly and the guests loved her as she flitted from one to the other, never outstaying her welcome. She often joined Albert at the door greeting guests, a task she enjoyed and the guests appreciated. Seeing Bentleys and Rolls-Royces pull up under the portico was not unusual, but Sarah screamed with glee when she saw Harris stop the Thornton's Rolls-Royce in front of Albert. Felix jumped out first. She considered Felix to be her best friend, although he was eighteen and had just started at Oxford and she was only ten.

"Sarah, how you have grown since the spring," Belle said, hugging her tightly.

Sarah stood at the side of Felix, looking up at his six feet and feeling a little shy. "I want to be as tall as Felix."

"I don't think you want to be as tall as a man," Belle said.

Hearing Belle's voice, Anna rushed to the entrance. "What a surprise! I am very happy to see you."

"We thought you could do with some company. We picked Felix up from Oxford and here we are."

"I am very happy to see you. I'll see if Bill can join us. Stuck in the kitchen of course. He has trained a good sous-chef but you know Bill, always hands on."

Sarah felt very grown up, showing Felix around her hotel. She knew where all the hiding places were, including the cellar leading to passages and caves the smugglers used years ago. It was also where the staff had been held hostage. Suddenly she stopped chattering and ran out, remembering what happened that day. Felix took her hand. "Sarah, I am so sorry for what happened."

"It's okay, I'm getting used to it. Nana takes care of me, but I wish Dad would come back. Nana says he's very, very sad and will come back when he's ready. I don't think he will ever come back. It's hard sometimes at school when everyone talks about their parents, then they go quiet and look at me, which makes it worse. They are trying to be kind, but I guess I'm odd having grandparents rather than parents. Lizzy doesn't mind, and her parents are kind to me; she's my best friend after you. Are you hungry?"

"Starving. Shall we go to the dining room?"

Felix sat next to his father and was immediately bombarded with questions about his progress at Oxford, which he wasn't really enjoying, but as the heir, his father had insisted he study business, equipping him with the knowledge needed to manage a large estate. Anna came to his rescue and asked what his dorm was like and had he made friends and did he have a girlfriend. Felix blushed at the last question saying he'd had a few dates but there was not much time after studies. He eyed his father as he made the last comment.

New Year's Eve was always special and this year Sarah had been allowed to stay up and join the family toast. Sarah was tall for her age and dressed in a full-length royal blue velvet gown with her hair swept up in curls and wispy ringlets around her face, she looked much older than her ten years. Anna had loaned her the blue pendant, it looked lovely on the royal blue dress—she wished it hadn't had to miss a generation. She watched Sarah flit around the room talking to guests like the perfect hostess. *She's growing up much too fast,* Anna thought as Felix took her arm and bowed and they began dancing a tango. *Where did she learn to dance like that?*

Bill moved to her side. "She's grown up in the last few months."

"I was just thinking that, and look at her dance. Anna leaned towards Bill, grateful for his warm touch.

Bill kissed her cheek and glanced at his watch—five minutes to midnight.

Anna waited for the dance to finish and the band stop playing. She beckoned to Sarah and nodded to the band as she stepped onto the bandstand. This year it was three of them preparing to announce the Alex ritual as glasses of scotch whiskey and champagne were handed out to the guests.

Anna cleared her throat and took Sarah's hand and said, "It is with pleasure that I introduce my granddaughter, Sarah. This is her first New Year's toast to Alex, my father, Sarah's grandfather but a legacy I hope she will continue. It is with great sadness…" Unexpected tears overwhelmed Anna and Bill took over. "As some of you may know, Isabelle, Sarah's mother, died tragically a few months ago. Tonight's toast will be to father and daughter—Alex and Isabelle.

The clock chimed twelve; Anna, Bill and Sarah raised their glasses. "To Alex and Isabelle! And Happy New Year everyone, health and prosperity for 1951."

Tears spilled quietly on her cheeks and Anna clung to Bill and wrapped her arm around Sarah. There was something final in that toast, as though she had handed Isabelle over to Alex and it felt good. A kind of closure and acceptance she had not expected.

Sadly this brings Anna's Legacy - Book 2 of The Sackville Hotel Trilogy to its conclusion. Read on to the third and final book - Sarah's Choice
https://geni.us/VNlg

Epilogue

The New Sackville Hotel survived the scandals of the Bindu/Smyth trials and thrived. Chief Inspector Durham's summary of charges and possible convictions was correct. Ravi Smyth served eighteen months in a minimum-security prison. Dhar was found guilty of second-degree murder and sentenced to 15 years in Dartmouth, alongside his brother who had another five years added to his sentence. Miss Jenkins continued Isabelle's work with conferences and children's programs. Anna raised the hotel's reputation as a holiday destination for the wealthy. British aristocracy declined further as society changed during the fifties and The New Sackville's privileged guests diminished. Lord and Lady Thornton remained close friends and frequented the hotel when business allowed. Hillcrest Hall Estates became one of the top historical country estates for domestic and foreign visitors. Felix graduated from Oxford and joined his father on the estate and they too survived and thrived. In spite of the age difference, Felix and Sarah nurtured a tight friendship, seconded only by Sarah's friendship with Lizzy, which continued into adulthood.

Wealth drained from the privileged through death duties and taxes. Intuitively, Anna knew that without change The New Sackville was doomed and her tenacity and need to pass her legacy on to her granddaughter pushed her to find the solution in a new sector of rich people, the nouveau riche. Once frowned upon and certainly treated with disdain by the aristocracy, the nouveau riche were supporting the economy; some who had made their fortunes during the war and others through business and commerce as the economy grew. Anna saw the opportunity and, through conferences and services, she catered to this new group of people.

Sarah, a clever and artistic child, finished school at the top of her class and grew into a beautiful and smart young woman. She continued to study the arts. She had always known that Anna wanted her to study business to take over the hotel, a promise Sarah once made but was not sure she could keep.

Sandy Wexford disappeared completely. Sarah missed her father, but would never admit it to Anna or Bill and secretly vowed to search for her lost father.

As the story continues in the final book of the trilogy, you will discover Sarah's struggle to commit to her first love, execute her childhood promise to return her mother and grandfather to Canada and strive to fulfill the promise she made to her grandmother and The New Sackville Hotel.

Read on to the third and final book - Sarah's Choice
https://geni.us/VNlg

Acknowledgements

Writing is a solitary occupation, one that I enjoy. My solitude is broken by characters who become my friends as I write and get to know them. This is Anna's second novel, so I know her pretty well and I am always a little sad when I hit the final period. The sadness is tempered slightly in knowing there is a third book coming.

My journey has not been totally solitary and there are many people to thank for making not just this book, but the whole trilogy, possible.

My sincere thanks to my friend Myriam McCormick who patiently listened to my various scenarios of plot and character while we walked Sammy, Myriam's black and white terrier, and for reading and commenting on the final story for content, blunders and picking up the homonyms, which, she tells me are far too frequent and quite amusing at times and for her keen eye proofing the galley.

A million thanks to editor Mark McGahey who worked on the first edition of this book and to my current editor Meghan Negrijn who edited the second edition.

I am grateful for the encouragement and support of my wonderful friends and fans. I especially want to thank Mary Rothschild and Angela Sutcliffe for reading the final manuscript.

Many thanks to Team Tellwell, Erin and Jordan, for their hard work, patience and tolerance with the design, formatting and publishing on the first edition published in 2016.

In 2021 I decided The Sackville Hotel Trilogy needed a face lift. The second edition has a new cover and thanks to my current editor Meghan Negrijn, we have made a few corrections and changes.

About the Author

Susan A. Jennings was born in Britain of a Canadian mother and British father. Both her Canadian and British heritages are often featured in her stories. She lives in Ottawa, Canada with her little five year old puppy, Miss Penny, her constant companion and author assistant. Susan writes, historical fiction, women's fiction and contemporary later in life romance, always with a love story. She has published numerous short stories and contributed to several anthologies.

You can connect with me on:

🌐 https://susanajennings.com

📘 https://facebook.com/authorsusanajennings

Subscribe to my newsletter:

✉ https://geni.us/NewsfromSusan

Also by Susan A Jennings

The Sackville Hotel Trilogy - Books 1,2, & 3

The Blue Pendant - Book 1
   If you like the elegance of Edwardian society, bold characters, and decades-spanning adventures, then you'll love this historical fiction

Anna's Legacy - Book 2
   Secrets and hidden agendas plague Anna but none are as dark as her own secrets. Might they be the deadliest?

Sarah's Choice - Book 3
   Sarah, Anna's granddaughter has to make hard decisions in this final and exciting trilogy novel. Lives and livelihoods depend on Sarah's choices.
   Her dream of fame through art or Anna's dream of a prestigious hotel?

Sophie Series - Novels of the Great War
   Prelude to Sophie's War
   Heart of Sophie's War
   In the Wake of Sophie's War
   Ruins in Silk - The prequel Prelude to Sophie's War
   Sophie's young life.

The Lavender Cottage Books - Love and suspense at Katie's B &B
   When Love Ends Romance Begins
   Christmas at Lavender Cottage
   Believing Her Lies
   Second Chances

Nonfiction

Save Some For Me...and what about you?

Is a heartrending story of one woman's struggle to survive spousal abuse and, consequently, single parenthood.

Printed in France by Amazon
Brétigny-sur-Orge, FR

13171331R10176